"An audacious con job, scintillating future technology,
and meditations on the nature of fractured humanity."
Yoon Ha Lee

"Künsken has a wonderfully ingenious imagination."
Adam Roberts, *Locus*

"Technology changes us—even our bodies—in fundamental
ways, and Kunsken handles this wonderfully."
Cixin Liu

"I have no problems raving about this book. A truly wild
backdrop of space-opera with wormholes, big space-fleet
conflict and empires.... What could go wrong?"
Brad K. Horner

"This brainy sci-fi heist novel uses mathematics like magic to
pull you through a caper worthy of Jean-Pierre Melville."
The B&N SciFi and Fantasy Blog

"*The Quantum Magician* is the type of book
you go back to the beginning and read again once you
know how everything pans out and have those
'why didn't I see that the first time?' moments."
Strange Alliances

"A delightfully engaging heist story."
Caroline Mersey, *Science Fiction Book Club*

"*The Quantum Magician* is a space adventure built on the scaffolding of a classic con job movie (think *The Italian Job* or *Ocean's Eleven*). It hits all the right beats at the right time, and part of the fun in reading it is wondering: what will go wrong? Who will betray who? What will be the reversals? When done well, as in the case of *The Quantum Magician*, it's a delight to read."
The Ottawa Review of Books

"*The Quantum Magician* feels like what would happen if Locke Lamora landed in Bank's Culture, and if Locke had a lot to say about depraved humans. And I do love me a con artist story! Also? The writing is brilliant, the pacing is damn near perfect, the dialog is fun and snarky, the characters are great, I couldn't put this book down!"
The Little Red Reviewer

"Con games and heists are always hard to write – one like this, which comes out pitch perfect, wrapped in a nuanced and striking sci-fi narrative is, to say the least, a rarity."
SF and F Reviews

"*The Quantum Magician* is a fabulous debut, it would make the most fantastic movie. It has everything and more, it seriously needs to be read by way more people. Highly, highly recommended."
The Curious SFF Reader

THE QUANTUM
WAR

DEREK KÜNSKEN

SOLARIS

First published 2021 by Solaris
an imprint of Rebellion Publishing Ltd,
Riverside House, Osney Mead,
Oxford, OX2 0ES, UK

www.solarisbooks.com

ISBN: 978 1 78108 924 8

A CIP catalogue record for this book is available
from the British Library.

Designed & typeset by Rebellion Publishing

Printed in the UK

THE QUANTUM
WAR

I would like to dedicate this novel to Brandon Crilly, Evan May, Nicole Lavigne, Tyler Goodier, Jay Odjick, Matt Moore and Marie Bilodeau, great friends who patiently re-introduced me to role playing games which taught me new things about character.

CHAPTER ONE

April, 2515

THE SULFURIC ACID clouds of Venus floated beyond the window, their ochre puffs and hollows and shadows expanding and contracting as winds pulled them. The Scarecrow hadn't spoken for long moments, which wasn't strange for these AIs and their secretive human souls, but this one hummed tunelessly. Lieutenant-Colonel Bareilles had never heard one hum and didn't know what to think. The Scarecrow might not even know it was doing it; the humming had overlapped with a lengthy assessment of Bareilles' career. A swivelling lens eye zoomed audibly on Bareilles. The Scarecrows were designed to unsettle observers, but the humming hinted that the Scarecrow might not be entirely stable, as if a parallel track of information processed in the artificial intelligence without its knowledge, as if the AI were haunted.

"You performed quite satisfactorily in Epsilon Indi for the last four years," the Scarecrow said.

Her gravelly, feminine voice sounded distant, reaching from the other side of a death. The impression of femininity might be genuine although Scarecrows carried little of their identity past the death of the spies they'd once been.

"Thank you," she said.

This Scarecrow's lines of logic seemed to follow more indirect paths than the one she'd worked with in Epsilon Indi. That vanished one had been pragmatic, focused, dogged and rarely mysterious. This one reasoned in elliptical arcs, following multi-layered, musical logic.

The winds outside became ghostly sounds to those in the mid-levels of the Ministry of Intelligence. The globe building followed the winds at various altitudes, its location at any time a state secret. The Scarecrow lumbered to the window, sounding of flexing piezoceramic musculature and carbon steel joints. Floppy gloved fingers adjusted a button on the plain carbon-weave shirt.

"I appreciated your espionage findings on the Puppets," the Scarecrow said. Her tone was sweet and ghastly, and her accent an antique French from last century. "Your post-graduate work in biotechnology made you uniquely insightful in the field."

"I could be out there again," Bareilles said. "I didn't apply for this promotion and I haven't been to staff college. And I like field work."

She hadn't found her rhythm in this new role in the last three weeks either. It felt like an ill-fitting tunic. And even if she could go back, Epsilon Indi was different now.

"The disappearance of the Scarecrow is unfortunate," the spectral voice continued. Her statement didn't surprise Bareilles. The emotion-reading software in the interrogation suites was powerful, and they read facial expressions constantly, especially their own people. One became accustomed to feeling exposed.

"I should be continuing his work," Bareilles said.

"That would be a waste," she said with a flat, definitive tone that belied the winsome and flighty feel in the humming. "Your three years under the Epsilon Indi Scarecrow were testing."

"What kind of testing?"

"The kind of testing that never relents."

That was a euphemism about the living Venus, the kind of things grandmothers say as they tuck children into bed during bucking winds.

"Your new posting," the Scarecrow finally said, "it is good?"

Upon her transfer back to Venus, Bareilles had been installed at the head of a new division in the Future Threats Branch of the Analysis Sector.

"It feels like a desk job."

The second lens whirred and zoomed onto Bareilles. The mouth on the metal cloth had been painted uneven and expressionless, but the humming and the higher register of the voice gave it some illusory implied motion. Another Scarecrow trick of psychology.

"You've been given policy influence here, and the ability to task units in the field," the Scarecrow said. The humming tune, on some other channel, slipped its way under the AI's answer, lonely, lost. "We know we want you, but our wanting only goes so far. At some point, you need to want it."

"What do you hope I'll want?"

"A broader canvas for your talents."

"What does that mean?"

"Sometimes meanings have to come when they're ready," the gravelly voice said. "Learn more and we'll talk again."

Despite the dismissal, Bareilles didn't salute. Scarecrows existed outside formal chains of command, like political officers, commissars and *les petits saints*. Bareilles walked back through the gray and white carbon corridors of the Ministry of Intelligence. She had guesses of what her test was, but she didn't know what she was testing for, which was very Venusian. Venus taught her children many subtle and easily misunderstood lessons. Sometimes she taught the questions after the answers.

The strangely unfulfilling feeling suddenly gave her an awkward idea. Maybe she was mourning. She missed the Epsilon Indi Scarecrow, the half-machine, half-petrified person, the inhuman thing of performative gears and vengeful thoughts. But that was hard to credit. How could a person miss an intelligent weapon? What did that say about her?

Lieutenant Rivard, one of her deputies, waited outside her office. Rivard was dark haired and blue-eyed, twenty-six years old, a bit plain and academic in his demeanor, but a good analyst who knew how to make junior analysts work hard. He saluted and followed her in. The window looked out onto the hazy, coiling mists of the middle cloud decks of Venus from another angle, a subtly different canvas upon which meaning could write itself before being blown away. The door closed and the security seal went green.

"I analyzed the reports you wanted, *madame*," he said. "It's not promising."

She indicated one of the chairs. He sat, unrolled his data scroll and turned it to face her.

"There are three mentions of time travel," he said with a professional wince. "The captured *Homo quantus* say that Arjona and Mejía told them that they had a time travel device and that they'd come from a few weeks into the future. All tell the same story, but they're simply reporting what they heard someone else say, someone they didn't believe."

Her stomach tingled, like the start of an elevator descent. Beyond the window, gaseous striations of brown and yellow, textured in indistinctness, were edging downward. They'd entered a pressure cell big enough to lift even a building as big as the Ministry of Intelligence.

"We don't know exactly what capabilities the *Homo quantus* have," Rivard said. "The Banks might not even know. Arjona may have laid down this story to misdirect us and the other *Homo quantus* from guessing his full abilities."

"So you're saying Arjona and Mejía guessed that *Les Rapides de Lachine* would be deployed to the Garret and told their own people that they knew because of time travel?" Bareilles said.

"No one has measured the full mathematical modelling abilities of the *Homo quantus*. The ones in detention aren't fully functional. They might have calculated a prediction. The other possibility is that Arjona or the Banks, with years of preparation, placed some intelligence assets on *Les Rapides de Lachine* or at Epsilon Indi command."

"It's more plausible than time travel."

"The second piece of intelligence on this is from informants in the Union Cabinet," Rivard said. "There are several allusions, over about six months, of a time travel device associated with the Sixth Expeditionary Force. At first, these reports were euphemistic and oblique. After the break-out from the Puppet Axis, the references become less cautious and take the tone of a resource they no longer have. Something to do with Major-General Iekanjika."

Rivard advanced his presentation to a tiled display of faces and names. The Union Major-General hovered at the center of these, among a series of officers about whom the Congregate knew almost nothing. They came from nowhere. They'd not graduated from the military academy at Harare. Congregate political commissars hadn't interviewed and vetted them. It wasn't even known how much French they spoke. It lent credence to the otherwise implausible story that the Sixth Expeditionary Force had somehow endured forty years without resupply, adapting their ships with new technology no one had ever seen or imagined.

"The last lines of intel are from captured Union personnel. No one below major ever mentions this time travel thing," he said, his tone adding quotation marks. "In three cases, older captured officers, Colonel Alweendo, age sixty-four, Lieutenant-Colonel Aschenborn, age sixty-six, and Brigadier-General Hamaambo, age sixty, referred to a time travel device, something that the Sixth Expeditionary Force had found a long time ago."

"None of them had ever seen it," he added, "nor could they confirm that anyone else had seen it. But two of these officers, and another prisoner of war, Sergeant Witbooi, age sixty-six, also reported that the Sixth Expeditionary Force had found a small permanent wormhole of the Axis Mundi network, something small enough that they could carry it in the hold of their warships."

"If this is counter-intelligence," she said, "it's very long game."

Rivard's finger advanced the presentation to a wall of scientific facts.

"Agreed. Our best scientists have covered the ground on time travel before, as have experimental teams from the Ministry of Defense. Time travel is not theoretically impossible, but in practice, even if the engineering challenges were overcome, what scientists would call a success would underwhelm, like moving a particle or an atom back a minute or something."

"Your conclusion?"

"We know of no way time travel could happen. These reports might all be counter-intelligence, begun with some select Union officers as their targets, possibly as a test of loyalty, and continued now by Arjona on us. Misdirection."

"Hard time travel, meaning more than just moving an atom back in time," she said, "might explain how the Sixth

Expeditionary Force got into the Puppet Axis without being seen on the Port Stubbs side. Maybe they entered two centuries ago and while in the Axis, shifted into the present."

"We haven't captured anyone who'd been a navigator during the break-out," he said, "but our best information places the Sixth Expeditionary Force above Hinkley in the hours before the breakout. The time travel story could be a counter-intel cover for the miniature wormhole. Maybe they discovered some way to make it interact with the Puppet Axis, making a third opening for them. Maybe it wasn't stable. Or maybe the process used up or destroyed the small wormhole. That might explain why they didn't use a similar tactic on the Freya Axis and why the Union Cabinet seems to be upset with Iekanjika."

"Do you have any scientific thinking to back this up?"

"Science teams are thinking it through, but it's at least less implausible than a time travel device."

"Keep working on the time travel angle."

"I... but the... There's no scientific backing to this, *madame*. Arjona's a con man."

"They took me out of the field to worry about the future. And him. Your team will keep working these other angles too. The wormhole idea. The possibility that this is all counter-intel. But keep working on the time travel. The chance that it's true is tiny, but if it is, it's a catastrophe for whoever doesn't have it."

Rivard's expression went through phases of protest, reluctance and resignation. He stood, gave a *"Oui, madame,"* and then went off to chase the flimsy possibility. But many impossible things were dangerous. The Union had caught them off-guard and that couldn't happen again.

Barielles watched a cloud slowly bulge upward, lifted on an upwelling of warmer air, mushrooming outward, spreading yellow-white and uneven across the view outside the window.

She might watch for hours as variable winds distorted and thinned it. While she thought. The Scarecrow meant for Bareilles to have time to think, but hadn't told her what to think about. The immediate tactical and strategic situation wasn't it, but she wasn't in the mood for puzzles. She headed towards the labs. The Ministry of Intelligence building was the size of a large town, with three thousand analysts, executives, technocrats, and security staff, and of course the hundred and fifty-five *Homo quantus* detainees.

Doctor Gagné met her at the security door. He was portly with slick dark hair and deceptively sleepy eyes. They exchanged pleasantries and proceeded inward, entering a wide, white-walled research area ringed with computers and scientists along a mezzanine around a work pit overlooked by marine guards. In the pit, white-gowned research staff interrogated, probed, sampled and analyzed different *Homo quantus*. The Bank project records suggested that only about ten to fifteen percent of the genetically-engineered people actually functioned. The rest were duds. She had a hundred and fifty-five duds.

"Are we getting any closer to reverse engineering the *Homo quantus*?" she said.

"We captured decades of research notes and we have living samples."

They took a glass-walled elevator to the pit. In a cubicle two doctors examined readings from a subject. Holograms detailed his neurology, lines and filaments showing the highways of the nanotube system and colored clouds showing ion gradients and magnetic micro-fields.

"Edmer Vizcarra," Gagné said "is the best of the lot."

After an extensive analysis of the best genetic baseline for beginning the *Homo quantus* project a century ago, the Banks had chosen recruits from an Afro-Colombian region of Bank territories on Earth. Vizcarra was dark-skinned, clean-limbed, with a shy posture and a distant expression.

"He's in savant?" she said.

Gagné gestured to the attendants and they set a plastic and wire cap on Vizcarra's head.

"He's capable of savant, but not the fugue," the doctor said. "Once we knew that savant was induced by micro-currents to the cortex, it wasn't hard to construct an external magnetic field system to snap them out of it when we want."

The attendants turned on the cap. Vizcarra winced and was suddenly... present. The holographic displays shifted color patterns.

"All his anatomical parts work," Gagné said. Vizcarra watched them in growing alarm. "Electroplaques. Electrical nanotube wiring. New anatomical brain structures. Anti-pyretic systems. He says he can't get into the fugue because of fine control of the electrical signals."

"Is that true?" Bareilles asked Viczarra.

"I... my microcurrents are leaky," he said in *français* 8.2. "Silicon atoms contaminated my carbon nanotubes during embryological development. Their electrical resistance is too high. They waste too much heat so I can't sustain quantum coherence." He looked at both of them pleadingly. "Can I go home now?"

She supplemented her education with nightly dives into the documentation of the *Homo quantus* project. She didn't doubt what Vizcarra was saying. Given the heat and molecular jostling in the human brain, she was surprised quantum coherence could happen at all. The Banks had done it in just eight generations of engineering. It was almost admirable what they could do with all their money. The Congregate had a different kind of wealth and a different kind of appreciation for human dignity. But falling behind wasn't an option.

"We'll need him and all the data on him," she said to Gagné. "And the next ten closest to achieving the fugue."

"We're not done studying them."

"This one is going to lead me to the others."

Gagné had trouble finding his words. "When can I have him back?"

"What I'm considering falls into the category of destructive testing."

"There are only a hundred and fifty-five of them."

"We won't be safe until we net all four thousand."

The Scarecrow had given this mess to her and there was little Gagné could do to gainsay her. So assistants and doctors began to prepare Vizcarra and nine others to move to a different lab. Rivard met her outside the research area.

"They said I can task field ops," she said. "There's someone I want brought here," she said. "A geneticist."

CHAPTER TWO

August, 2515

MAJOR-GENERAL AYEN Iekanjika moved hand over hand through the transport tubes of the *Mutapa* towards the ventral landing bay. Two bodyguards preceded her. Like Iekanjika herself, the flagship of the Sub-Saharan Union had taken some hits, but had given better than she'd got. Technicians were cutting away damaged frame sections and sparks expanded outward like tactile light in the zero-g. The *Mutapa* was patched and refitted, constantly resupplied with ammunition, armour, fighter craft and pilots. She led the fight against the Congregate navy, always just one step ahead of the overwhelming forces looking to crush the Union's war of independence.

The leading bodyguard peeked around an awkward angle in the transport tube, which sometimes curved counter-intuitively, following the lines of a drive system not made for the architecture of the ship. During their decades in the wilderness beyond civilization, the Sixth Expeditionary Force had worked with what they'd had, making things fit, making things work.

The *Mutapa* was her command now. Only a year ago, Iekanjika had been a major. Every day, she wished she'd been promoted the intervening four ranks because she'd accumulated years of experience and gotten the right grades in staff college. But the *Mutapa* was one of five warships of the original dozen to have survived this far into the rebellion. They'd lost experienced crew and officers, even as new warships and fighters rolled off factory asteroids. At forty years old, Iekanjika had clocked in twenty-five years of military experience and would have been a logical candidate for warship command. Taking command of the whole fleet was less intuitive, but with General Rudo's ascension as the Minister of Defense and their middle husband's promotion to Minister of War Supply, Rudo had wanted a fleet commander she could trust. So, terrifyingly, the fleet was hers.

The Puppet ship in the landing bay was ugly and inelegant, its design lines reflecting the use of drive systems from a century ago. Crusty lines of snow along the outside of the cockpit seals indicated leaks. Its miniature passengers disembarked. Their space suits added thirty or forty centimetres to their height, but even at that, the peaks of the helmets of even the bigger ones would only come up to her breastbone.

Instead of clean space suit surfaces that could be inspected and patched, stupid religious symbols and early Anglo-Spanish names she didn't know seemed to have been finger-painted onto the material. The decorations on the priests were more careful, applied with brush, suggesting the folds of robes and the peaks of headdress she'd seen in the Puppet Free City.

The three clerics floated close enough for the military police to scan them. This was a diplomatic meeting, but one MP used x-rays and millimeter wave scans, while a second detached all the batteries from the Puppet suits and plugged them into a sequestered ship battery equipped with cautious fuses. A different set of marines had already done this to the Puppet ship before letting it enter the bay. Iekanjika came out of the airlock and into the bay. Her bodyguards each kept a shoulder between her and the three priests. It wasn't the bishop in the center who spoke first, but a blond Puppet to his left.

"It's good to see you again, major-general," he said.

He'd shaved his beard and cut his blond hair bristle-short. Manfred Gates-15. The traitor who'd almost cost them the Sixth Expeditionary Force. They'd discovered his betrayal early enough to build it into their plan. Pity he hadn't been blown up when the Sixth Expeditionary Force had burst out of the Puppet Axis.

"What do you want?" she said.

"We have information," Gates-15 said. "We're looking for help. And offering help. This is Bishop Arnold Grassie-6, one of the leaders of the Episcopal Conclave."

The little Puppet bishop held out his hand hopefully. Iekanjika didn't move. He smiled tightly.

"It's a blessing to meet you, major-general," he said. "I also brought Rosalie Johns-10, a priestess and a friend of Belisarius Arjona. Is there somewhere we can speak privately?"

"Speak here," Iekanjika said.

"I'm coming with military intelligence, major-general."

Iekanjika waited out heartbeats. Three. Four. Five. She signalled her aide. Lieutenant Coulibaly squeezed between the bodyguards and held out a small device with two spools of insulated wire. She unwound one and handed the end to Iekanjika. She did the same and handed it to Bishop Grassie-6. He looked at it strangely and then pressed it to his face plate as she had.

"Turn off your radio and talk," Iekanjika said. "The vacuum can't carry your voice and the wiring is insulated."

The bishop's pale face looked side to side to his companions, but then he smiled reassuringly at Iekanjika.

"The Union and the Theocracy haven't always been... aligned." His voice vibrated in her face plate, sounding distant. "Many in the Conclave are resistant to dialogue with those who... betrayed our hospitality."

"Betrayed?" Iekanjika said. "You tried to hold us captive and steal our ships."

"Our demands were part of a negotiation," Grassie-6 said. "The misunderstandings were cross-cultural in nature. We come in a renewed spirit of negotiation."

"I have sixty seconds left."

Grassie-6 raised his chin, then tapped his chest meaningfully. "I'm the good boy," he said emphatically, "minding the divinities. And the enemy of my enemy is my friend."

"Forty seconds."

"The Congregate stole something from us," Grassie-6 said with a rigid calm. "We want it back. Enough that we are ready to commit troops to your cause and form an alliance with you."

"You have no tactical or strategic value."

"We'll join your assault on Venus."

"We're not attacking Venus," she said derisively.

"How will you end your war?"

"Time's up."

"Wait!" he said, reaching a hand out. A guard slapped it aside. "They stole Del Casal from us! He was helping our Numen. They ripped away the one man who could help stabilize the health of our divinities."

"I don't care about Puppets or the Numen or Del Casal."

"Major-General! This is bigger than you or I. Such is the nature of divinity! We can—"

She released the wire and signalled for the Puppets to be loaded back into their creaky ship.

CHAPTER THREE

April, 2515

PUPPET ENDOCRINOLOGISTS STOOD on tip-toes, tugging at Del Casal's lab coat, craning her neck. He yanked the coat from small fingers and turned away from the screen. The histological sections there were an artscape of tiny cells rendered in soft mauves and purples, revealing not only the microstructure of an apocrine sweat gland, but the many types of bacteria colonizing it.

"*That's* the right microbiome pattern?" Doctor Rockfort-8 said dubiously. She was a pretty Puppet with brown hair and a doubtful expression.

"It's not *the* right pattern," Del Casal said. "It's one of many patterns that will work, and may be more stable."

Doctor Teller-5 leaned close, squinting, pushing Rockfort-8 aside. The other Puppet woman shoved back. Neither were real doctors. The Federation of Puppet Theocracies didn't have universities or medical schools, only automated teaching modules that barely supported their genetic research. Grassie-6, the green-robed Puppet bishop, inclined his mitred head to Del Casal.

"One of many patterns, rather than *the* pattern," he said musingly in his antique Anglo-Spanish patois. A young priest wrote that down on a pad of paper with the stub of a tooth-marked pencil. "Your work asserts the existence of multiple routes to divinity. That has fascinating, hopeful ontological implications."

Del Casal did not enjoy the theological puzzling of the Puppets.

He could have been living luxuriously at the Lanoix Casino designing biological art, or at his lab complex at Shackleton City on Earth's moon, or he might have taken another board position with a corporation. But those were mountains already conquered, accolades already earned. Instead he was in the rogue state, mastering a genetic problem no one else could defeat.

The Puppet divinities, the genetically-engineered Numen, were going extinct. Every generation, fewer and fewer Numen children expressed the unique pheromonal traits the Puppets perceived as divine. The Puppets had been trying to slow the decline for eighty years, but they hadn't the skill. The secrets to making the Numen had died with their engineers. But he could recreate and surpass their accomplishments.

He found the Puppets religious nonsense slightly nauseating, but in one respect, they shared a need for immortality. They found an imminence and permanence in the world. Accomplishments could last forever. Writing. Vast feats of engineering. Leaving the Earth. Creating new life. Del Casal was on his way to a kind of immortality as well, through feats of intellect.

"We'd considered the creation of the Numen to be a singular cosmic event," Grassie-6 said, "but you've proven that multiple creation events are possible. We'd thought that a singular biochemical state defined the Numen, but now, if you're right, we have to explore and comprehend multiple states of divinity."

Johns-10, the young priest, wrote as quickly as possible, flipping the tiny page and transcribing the bishop's words. Grassie-6 caught Del Casal's eye and smiled with a kind of knowing self-deprecation. The Puppets were accustomed to all of civilization looking down on them, considering them insane slavers. Del Casal had been with the Puppets for two months, beneath the ice of Oler, in a medical complex adjacent to the Forbidden City where most of the Numen were held in captivity. He'd asked for nine million Congregate francs to teach them how to make more Numen.

It was delivishly complex. The original creators of the Puppets had wanted an unhackable control over their slaves. They'd succeeded in building that system in a language of pheromones produced by hundreds of species of bacteria in the sweat glands. The genetic changes in the Numen chromosomes were relatively well understood, but no one had succeeded in replicating the exact mix of microbiome populations in their glands. Those bacteria had been engineered by those immoral geniuses, and until now, no one had cracked that code.

Speakers near the ceiling funnelled sounds of confused terror into the lab. "Get away! Get down!" Beyond a transparent wall, Gonzalo Cornell, one of Del Casal's first Numen creations, an ex-Anglo-Spanish shareholder, faced Puppet doctors and priests. A hundred days ago Cornell had been in a debtor's prison on Nueva Granada, with no practical skills with which to earn oxygen and food for the rest of his life sentence. The Puppets had bought out some of Cornell's debt sentence, as well as three dozen other similarly destitute lifers. The subcontracting agreements only stipulated that the Puppets had to keep the debtors alive.

Beyond the transparent wall, Puppets with television cameras and boom microphones filmed Cornell, recording every word he might say for their ongoing and forever-growing Puppet Bible. The doctors and theologians tested Cornell and the other newly-made Numen, trying to detect any difference between him and their naturally born Numen. They trotted in Puppet workers, Puppets with medical conditions, Puppets who'd donated organs to Numen, Puppet ascetics and dazed, sated Puppets who'd just seen true, traditional Numen. None of them reacted to Cornell any differently from the Numen in captivity. Del Casal's genius had done this.

It didn't surprise him that they'd failed to make any Numen of their own. The Puppets had learned to faultlessly follow the instructions of the first genetic engineers, fastidiously constructing the Numen microbiomes of their early Edenic period. But they'd not realized that the Puppets and the Numen had been drifting genetically. The lock and key had drifted in synchrony because the Puppets applied a strong selective force on it, executing anyone who couldn't produce the pheromones or smell them. Del Casal had succeeded in building Numen because he hadn't tried replicating the key for the lock of the Edenic period, which didn't exist anymore. The microbiomes in the pheromonal sensors of the Puppets were far different now and he'd built a key for today's lock on Puppet behavior.

Del Casal's bodyguards pushed a few staring priests out of the way. The Puppet attention on him was tedious; he couldn't imagine what it would be like for those debtors who'd become divinities. He supposed here was still better for them than gradually suffocating in a debtor's prison during one of the periodic cost-saving, 'accidental' pressure leaks.

"Did you know that Rosalie Johns-10 here is highly intelligent?" the bishop said. The young priest blushed and looked away. "Belisarius Arjona used to debate theology with her. That's how smart she is."

"That doesn't sound like Arjona," Del Casal mused.

"Johns-10 is one of our leading thinkers. She's pursuing a new theory about you."

"How interesting," Del Casal said without interest.

Grassie-6 nudged the young priest. She looked at Del Casal, averted her eyes and made a kind of curtsy with her green vestments, a symbol of Puppet submissiveness designed to lift the hem of robe and sleeves to show manacles at wrist and ankle.

"I'm exploring the possibility that you represent a new theological domain, sir," she said in her old Anglo patois.

Del Casal began walking away.

Grassie-6 hustled Johns-10 along behind Del Casal.

"We've always understood there to be three domains to the cosmos," Grassie-6 said. "The divine Numen, the Puppets who can perceive their divinity, and the non-divine, who can have no real effect on divinity."

Del Casal and his little bodyguards had squeezed through to a wide hallway, relatively warm for the icy crust of Oler from which they'd carved the Free City. Small trees grew here among cold, pathetic gardens that fronted decaying mansions from before the Puppet Rebellion. Del Casal had chosen one of the finest villas, about a kilometer away.

"You're not divine, but you have profound effects on divinity," Johns-10 said, her short legs flapping her sacral robes as she puffed to keep up with him. "You may be a kind of generative force that we could never directly study. The humans who made the first Numen and Puppets must have had some spark of divinity, but they were long dead before Puppet theologians could study their ontological truths."

"Imagine the feelings when humanity discovered the archaea," Grassie-6 said. "For decades they thought these things in their microscopes and samples were bacteria, and then poof! They found a whole domain of life right in front of them."

"You may be a discovery like that," Johns-10 said, her enthusiasm rising as Del Casal lengthened his paces. "Through you, we might be able to study the vital impetus, the spontaneous morphogenesis of the universe, whatever it was that caused divinity to be born."

"Geneticists caused it a hundred and fifty years ago," Del Casal said. "And a geneticist is now. It isn't spontaneous if I do it."

"On first glance, of course!" Grassie-6 said. "You're part of the material world, which is only a cold, unreactive substrate. Yet here you are, entirely material, yet generative."

Del Casal stopped and a bodyguard face bounced off his buttocks. Del Casal leaned down a little to emphasize his point.

"You hired me," he said. "Your money is the generative force. And I'm teaching your people how to make more Numen. Think about me all you want when I'm not around. But maybe your more important question is what all your craziness means when you addicts can create your own drug. If I were you, I would worry less about the theological implications, and more about the pure game theory of it all. At some point you'll remake a superior Numen class. You don't know what they'll want now, but they won't want to be held captive."

Grassie-6 smiled tightly. Puppets didn't like when people framed the Numen-Puppet relationship as an addiction.

"We and our divinities face extinction, doctor," Grassie-6 said. "It's a time for bold ideas. Those problems will still be waiting for us when the risk of extinction is controlled."

"Six more months should bring you out of that," Del Casal

said. "You'll still be ringed by enemies, but the evolutionary clock shouldn't be ticking against you."

Both the bishop and his little sacral prodigy seemed overwhelmed by the words and Johns-10 began jotting them down. Del Casal moved towards his villa. They didn't follow this time.

The mansion had short towers of stone and mortar and a complex plastic roof under a vaulted cavern ceiling, dug out of the naked dirty ice of Oler's crust. They'd offered him larger villas, ones formerly occupied by the legendary families like Blackmore, Gold, Stubbs and Malone. He'd chosen this one for its defensibility should matters go awry with the Puppets. The Puppets were feckless, mercurial, and insane; this villa had its own access into the warren of tubes and caves leading to his yacht at a private landing pad on the surface.

The sergeant of the guard saluted him from the base of the double row of curving stairs leading up to the expansive entrance of the villa. Her expression was one of vague happiness. She brushed at a bit of blond hair that had escaped her helmet.

"The villa is secure, sir," she said.

While his guard entered the villa by a small side door for servants, he proceeded up the main stairs, made for human dimensions. The glass doorway opened with a light pull. Danny, one of the house servants, waited in the lobby with a tray of bite-sized vegetable pastries. He looked up expectantly, a tiny bit of excitement twitching at his lips. Many Puppets didn't know what to make of Del Casal. He wasn't divine, but they understood that he could make more gods. It made some of them love him, hope for him, while others became star-struck and anxious.

"What is this, Danny?"

"Hors d'oeuvres," he said breathlessly. "The chef just made them."

The Puppets were deaf to irony. Few enough of them could cook appetizing meals. The pastry looked crisp and shiny though. This might be one of their best trial-and-error results. He took a bite. Not bad.

"Turn up the heat again," Del Casal said. "I'll be using the pool at seven and eating at nine. In the meantime, I'll be in the office and don't want to be disturbed."

Danny curtsied awkwardly with one hand holding the tray. It ended up looking like he'd ineptly aped a ballet *plié*. He had an excited look on his face. Del Casal leaned down and took the tray.

"What wrong with you?"

"Nothing!"

Over the months, Del Casal had mastered the cues of Puppet behavior. Danny had seen a Numen, off-schedule. They were always squirming and hustling into seeing Numen when it wasn't their turn, like junkies looking for a hit.

"Did you get to go to communion?" Del Casal asked.

Danny beamed a smile and shook his head vigorously.

"Were you scheduled?"

Danny shook his head harder, his smile widening. Danny would be both more and less useful for the rest of the day, maybe for a few days. Their hit of divinity induced many physiological changes and the full implications of the awe effect was still incompletely understood.

"Heat," Del Casal said. "Pool at seven. Supper at nine. Repeat."

"Heat," Danny said, counting on his fingers. "Pool at seven. Supper at nine."

"Go."

Danny scampered away. Del Casal backed into his office and ate another of the pastries. The office had once been a court or throne room, with a large chair on a plinth before the wide glass doors to the balcony. It was difficult to know for sure from the architecture or the grandiose and exaggerated Puppet records of the pre-rebellion era, littered with nonsense. Del Casal had added a large desk with holographic displays and a bank of networked servers for large genomic and metabolome analyses.

The displays lit as he sat in the throne which, despite Puppet fretting, had become his office chair. The Puppets were exhausting. Yes, they treated him like a figure possessing religious meaning, but itched when he sat in the old chair of one of their dead gods. The vents hummed as the heat came on. He pinched the bridge of his nose and then rested his forehead on his palms. He was more tired than he thought. He rested that way, losing track of time until the door opened.

"Sir?" Danny said.

"What did I tell you, Danny?" he asked without opening his eyes.

"Heat. Pool. Supper."

"I told you I didn't want to be disturbed."

"Oh," Danny said. The door didn't close. Feet shuffled. "You didn't say it twice."

Del Casal rose angrily and stopped when he saw it wasn't just Danny. The whole staff had appeared: six Puppets in the villa's livery, including one of his bodyguards. They flushed with excitement and held rubber clubs, fanning into a semi-circle. Del Casal drew a small flechette gun from his jacket. It had only four darts.

"What are you doing, Danny?" he asked, pointing the gun at Sally, the closest. She flinched and backed away, but the others inched forward.

"Our job," Danny said with nervous exhileration. "We got a quest!"

Del Casal shot Hank, a single dart to the center of mass, probably not the heart, but he went down flailing. The rest charged him. He got off another dart, a glancing shot that made Wendy curl over in pain. Someone grabbed the flechette gun. They swung their rubber clubs at his head. One grabbed his leg and clung tight, biting. He fell.

"You idiots! What are you doing? I'm here to help you!" he managed to say as a set of teeth bit the hand holding the gun, trying to crunch the bone. The gun came away. The clubbing to the head dazed him, but there was something more. His arms were heavy. His whole body numbed even as they jumped on him. They'd drugged him. Or were drugging him now. The food. Or the vents. Sedating him. After a time, they realized he wasn't moving anymore and their blows had become desultory, performative. He groaned as they sat around him, panting.

"We should gag him," Wendy said, "like Princess Esmeralda." She was holding her side, but wasn't bleeding badly.

"Did anyone bring a gag?" Danny said.

They made disappointed sounds. Hank was still alive and he'd brought rope, which they congratulated him on while he bled to death. The drug still held Del Casal in its bone-numbing grip but he began to hope. The longer these idiots couldn't get their act together, the more likely it was that his other guards would rescue him.

"No!" Wendy said. "Tie his hands behind his back!"

"In the movie, they tied Esmeralda's hands in front."

"In the play, it was in back," Hank groaned from the floor, blood painting his lips.

"It doesn't matter!" Danny said. "Behind is better. We're on our own mission."

Del Casal's fuzzy vision didn't give him a good sense of what was happening to his numb body but for a time he was suffocating and maybe blacked out. A hard knock on his forehead and bone-chilling cold brought him around some time later. The bony shoulders of three Puppets held him up. The icy ceiling was just above his nose and when the Puppets ran too fast in the weak gravity, their feet left the floor and rammed his head into the ceiling. These were the private tunnels. He could tell from the low air pressure caused by leaks the Puppets never seemed to fix. He'd explored some of these with his guard, just in case he'd need an escape.

The ceiling rose as they emerged into one of the old engineering tunnels built before the Edenic period, when the people who would become the Numen had still done their own work. The Puppets held up his limp body.

"Look!" Danny said. "We got him."

Danny spoke with breathless excitement, a bit distant from his words, like he was seeing or feeling something else more important. The awe effect. The Puppets were smelling a Numen, inhaling divinity. Del Casal lifted his head and saw a pale-skinned man in black clothes, his breath clouding around his smile. Two black-clothed people in vacuum suits stood to either side of him. They had rifles at the ready.

"Good boys," the man said. Danny groaned in a kind of deep satisfaction, as did the others.

The man wrapped his fingers in Del Casal's shirt and handled his weight with just one arm in the faint gravity, holding him like luggage.

"Your actions hallow you," the man said. Not just a man. This was a Numen. Not one of the captive ones. Where had he come from? What the hell was happening? "Missions hallow you. Quests prove to me who you are."

Wendy trembled in religious ecstasy.

"Show me the good listening boy," the man said.

The four Puppets sat on the icy floor, cross-legged, hands folded politely before them. They looked with expectant joy at the Numen. Then gunshots pierced their bodies, spattering blood onto the ice behind them as they fell backward, surprised expressions not quite overcoming their distant state of grace.

CHAPTER FOUR

August, 2515

By the time Iekanjika reached the biolabs for her second meeting, the bridge confirmed that the Puppet shuttle was off the *Mutupa*. The surgical chief saluted while the others came to attention. Iekanjika had grown up with the other scientists in the room. She returned the salute. Strapped to the table under plastic were three corpses recovered from the debris of Congregate fighter craft, bloody, torn by battle, and riddled with wires. The chips inside them had been removed for study. A monitor on the wall showed a dark image, where every so often a monstrous fish-like face came in and out of sight in the gloom. Iekanjika hooked her feet under a metal bar on the floor.

"You're sure of the gravities they were pulling, Stills?" Iekanjika asked.

The fish aspect came into focus in the monitor.

"Normal ships wouldna cost us many mongrels," the toneless machine voice replied. "They were hard as fuck to shoot down, and if it's hard for me, they sure as shit are pulling gees that ain't normal."

"How fast?" she said.

"I was pullin' fifty. Once I saw that didn't cut it, I tapped above sixty a few times. They were blowing reaction mass like crazy, and I thought the Congregate were catching up with the tech, but that wasn't the difference, although that's shitty enough for you."

Congregate fighters maneuvering at fifty gravities wasn't good news at all; at those accelerations, the enemy fighters would be as hard to hit as missiles, like the mongrel themselves. But how? Stills' people were engineered to survive the pressures at the bottom of an ocean, which meant that at sixty or more gravities of acceleration, no lungs collapsed, no bones broke.

"It was like the fuckers knew what we were gonna do," Stills continued.

"They outfought you?" Iekanjika said.

"Nobody outfights us, darlin'," he said. An edge of testiness crept into the flat machine tones of his translator. Stills normally used coarser language, but he'd become increasingly cautious with her as the war had progressed. Stills wasn't responding to her rank; he'd bad-mouthed other Union generals and colonels, including Rudo, since she'd known him. But he didn't swear at *her*.

"They can figure out your tactics?"

A barking sound emerged from the speakers, the sound associated with mongrel laughter.

"Even the dogs don't know where we're gonna move from one minute to the next," he said. "I seen a mongrel pilot weave off a perfect attack path at the last second to make it harder. We're showing *cajones*. Combat AIs can't figure us out."

Iekanjika had seen recordings of mongrel fighters harrying Congregate warships and defending Union ones. She'd stopped trying to control or shape the mongrel chaos. She'd detached the mongrels from the normal chain of command and let them find their own way through a fight. They were most frightening when simply loosed into a hot battle like a swarm of wasps. Until these new Congregate pilots entered the scene.

"How did these pilots stay in the fight, doctor?" Iekanjika said.

"They were in acceleration gel," the surgical chief said, approaching the bodies. "Soft prosthetic plastics reinforced their organs. These weren't small surgical modifications and would be difficult to reverse."

"Even harder to reverse now that we blew their asses off," Stills said.

"What are the wires?" Iekanjika asked.

"We've heard of similar artificial neurology in some augmented Bank pilots, although we don't have any samples to compare."

"Second Bushido," Still said flatly.

The name didn't mean anything to Iekanjika. The Banks of the Anglo-Spanish Plutocracy guarded their technological secrets, as the Union guarded the mysteries of their inflation drives, but in the end, someone was always shot down and reverse engineering became another race in any conflict.

"So the Congregate captured or killed augmented Bank pilots... Second Bushidos, in some skirmish and reverse engineered something to throw at the mongrels flying for the Union?" Iekanjika said.

"Their chips contain AIs like we think augmented Bank pilots do, ma'am," a major from the encryption team said. "We can't decrypt any of their code."

"AIs wouldn't explain it," Stills said. "I ain't flown against the Banks' best, but other mongrels have and these fuckers here don't fly like anything I heard of the Second Bushido types.

37

There's something wacked going on."

"Can you explain, doctor?" Iekanjika said.

"There's been extensive DNA rewriting, most of it all the way to the germ line, but we think there are some recent somatic changes too, but I don't know what any of these modifications are for."

"So the genetic modifications were twenty years old or more" Iekanjika said. "What kind of modifications would these pilots need be able to keep up with the mongrels? Faster reflexes? Faster cognition?"

"Good looks," Stills said.

"From everything I've heard, Congregate laws are restrictive," the surgical chief said. "And AI-human mergers run contrary to their mores."

"Yet here are these pilots, damaging the mongrel squadrons," she said. "How many were there, Stills?"

"Do I look like an accountant?" the mongrel said. "In the middle of a fight, fighters engage and disengage. I sure as fuck don't know which ones are modified and which ones are cannon fodder."

"Dig into this, doctor," she said. "Stills, I'd like the mongrels to give me some recommendations for the next encounter."

"Half the dogs are probably higher than piss right now," Still said. "And we ain't general staffers. Don't you have majors and lieutenants to think for you?"

"You're better," she said. Then, she left.

CHAPTER FIVE

April, 2515

ORBITAL SECURITY WAS too tight around Venus for Marie Phocas to meet with her aunt's lawyer nearby. Defensive sub-AIs tracked and catalogued every satellite, bit of cargo, passenger traffic and piece of debris over thirty centimeters. The lawyer could have used a laser to communicate, but Marie had too much at stake to risk a Ministry of Defense microsat happening to be at the wrong place at the wrong time.

So Marie met the lawyer at 163693 Atira, an asteroid between the orbits of Earth and Venus. The small station of three hundred people was not very exciting. It was very corporate and industrial. They did solar research and supervised robots that mined iron, silicon and magnesium to make raw metal ingots for the outer solar system and solar panels for the inner. Boring. But 163693 Atira was actually two bodies. Merwin was a lumpy rock five kilometers at its widest and they'd built the habitat there. Greer was about a kilometer wide, orbitting Merwin at six kilometers. There was an observation deck right under Greer, so that the huge rock looked like it could come crashing down at any moment. Cute. Maybe asteroiders didn't feel it, but she grew up in gravity and knew very well how falling worked.

Marie drummed her hard nails into the cafe tabletop again and then stopped. People were looking at her. Annoyed. She could be really annoying if she tried, but her heart wasn't in it, hadn't been for months. She'd been stealth Marie, keeping a low profile while all the world was looking for her. Not even one fight. She was exhausted of laying low and she was tired of holding back and she was done with waiting for this stupid lawyer in a cafe set on an anvil.

"Miss Sine?" a woman said. That was Marie's cover name today. Elizabeth Sine. A dumb Anglo name.

Marie turned in her straps. A sturdy woman in a business suit floated towards her. She was nordic pale with brown hair and elegant, looping acid burns on one cheek forming an artistic motif that had been popular on Venus twenty years ago.

"Yeah," Marie said.

The woman took hold of the other chair, pulled herself in and fastened the straps. They made blah-blah conversation while the table delivered new drinks in plastic bulbs. Marie spotted the very small camera tucked above the lawyer's ear, the kind people used when they had AIs hooked up to tell when people lied. The woman pulled out a multi-spectrum white noise generator and attached it to the table. Its whine was low, but Marie's hearing had always been sharp, so it was one more piece of irritation. She was going to get a headache at this rate.

"I'm Michèle Ouellet," she said in *français* 8.1, "from the firm Gagnon, Pinardon et Pinault."

"Were you the guys that got my sentence reduced for beating up that officer?"

Now Ouellet looked irritated too. What? It was just a question. Who were they to judge?

"Madame Hudon has other law firms to handle things like that," Ouellet said. "Gagnon, Pinardon et Pinault deals with more complex files. We offer more services. We solve problems."

The way Ouellet said it didn't make Marie feel better, not that she'd been optimistic these last couple of months. She'd been paying too much to criminals to stay hidden and too much to smugglers to move her around Venus' solar system.

"Why don't you go to one of the provinces?" Ouellet said. "Or better yet, leave the Congregate? Make some new home in the Ummah or the Middle Kingdom?"

"I thought you were coming here to help me."

"I am helping."

"Venus is my home," Marie said. "I grew up in the clouds. This is where my family is."

"You're too much of a liability, even for your family," Ouellet said, "and if they found out you were this close to Venus, they have the full resources of the state to make this embarrassment disappear in any way they want."

Marie's insides clenched like she'd eaten bad shrimp again.

"Tante Marielle wants me," Marie said quietly.

"Madame Hudon hasn't made her decision yet. She's empowered me to assess the risk to her. The price on your head is enormous and there's an interstellar war. Bonds of family are important, but at some point, they can't bear more weight."

"Tante Marielle was always kind to me though."

"Too kind," Ouellet said. "What was your part in this mess? Are you a real terrorist? Were you an unwitting accomplice? Were you the getaway driver or minor hired muscle?"

"Nothing like that. I had two jobs. I was hired to set explosives to distract the Puppet constabulary. And I flew one of the ships that was our payment. I never fired at any Congregate asset. I never told anything to terrorists. I don't even know anything anyone would want to know."

Ouellet pursed her lips, like Marie telling the truth was an annoyance.

"People don't get two million franc bounties for bombing embargoed Puppets or flying a getaway vehicle," the lawyer said.

"It's probably a big fake. I'm probably a person of interest," Marie said, adding air quotes. "I probably saw stuff they want to ask me about. They may want to ask me about the other people who have bounties on them. But I didn't do anything. Except blow up some stuff. Not Congregate stuff."

"This was all to help the Sub-Saharan Union rebel against the Congregate?" Ouellet asked.

"Well... Yeah. I guess."

"An ongoing rebellion that has not yet been put down, that has caused thousands of Congregate deaths, hundreds of lost military ships and the loss of the Freya Axis?"

"It sounds bad when you say it like that. How could I know that the Congregate would fumble everything that badly? Did you ever think anyone could do that?"

"That's not a very persuasive argument," Ouellet said.

"I'm looking for a little understanding here."

"Miss Sine, your aunt is an important figure in Venusian society," Ouellet said. "She's respected. She already pulled in a few favours a few years ago when she got your assault charges downgraded. And then you did a jail break. Right now you're one step from being labelled a traitor or a terrorist. I'm authorized to give you money if you leave Congregate space for good."

"Venus is my home," Marie said. "I know the hot winds. I know the bite of acid. I know what it feels like to be enveloped by a world, squeezed by it. I speak French, real French, not like the provinces, not like listening through a translator. I just want to come home and Tante Marielle is my only chance."

Ouellet began unsnapping her straps.

"You're not going to help me?" Marie said.

"I'm going to tell your aunt that this is very dangerous for her," the lawyer said. "If she wants our firm to make quiet inquiries with the security apparatus to find out if there's some sort of deal that can be made if you turned yourself in willingly, we'll do that. If she wants us to ease your way into the provinces in some way, we'll do that."

"I want to come home."

"You didn't come to this point at random, Miss Sine. You made a series of choices. It may be that coming home in anything other than handcuffs is impossible."

CHAPTER SIX

August, 2515

IEKANJIKA'S THIRD MEETING was delayed to the following day, by which time she'd received additional inconclusive reports from the surgical chief, the analyses of the flight recordings by her intelligence teams and nothing from Stills. She played the recordings five times slower to make sense of them. The confusion of battle seemed to be the environment where the mongrel pilots came into their own, a place too fast for human eyes to keep up. Unfortunately, these new Congregate fighters seemed adapted to live there too; they flew like nothing she'd ever seen. They weren't the swarming chaos of the mongrels; they were like a web of chess pieces blunting the speed, ferocity and unpredictability of the mongrels. And they scored hits on the mongrel pilots, losses she couldn't afford. Who were these pilots?

It had been a week since the last major Congregate assault on the Union positions around the Freya Axis. The mongrel fighter squadrons, backed by some risky counter-attacks from the Union warships, had barely repelled them. Telescopic observations also showed a massing of Congregate warships, supply ships and fighters collecting in the *Epsilon Indi* system. The Congregate had many strengths and it looked like the next attack would deploy overwhelming numbers. And yet that wasn't the worst of it.

In the months they'd been holding back the Congregate from the Freya Axis, small signs of Congregate ships had been elusively appearing in the Bachwezi system, mostly faint and hard-to-verify magnetic anomalies deep in the system's Kuiper Belt. If Iekanjika's worst fears came true, they would soon face a Congregate strike force assembling at the extreme edge of the Union solar system. They'd not arrived through a convenient axis, but through short jumps of one light-years through induced wormholes.

All this swam in her thoughts as she floated into the dorsal stateroom to meet her guests. She came across the ceiling hand over hand and strapped herself into the seat at the head of the table. The surgical chief sat down table, beside one of General Rudo's staff, and behind the representatives for three of the six Banks that ruled the Anglo-Spanish Plutocracy.

Admiral Thomas Gillbard, a member of the Plutocracy's Joint Chiefs of Staff, was supposedly the highest-ranking envoy and leader of the delegation. Tall, brown-skinned and gray-haired, he wore the naval fatigues of the Bank of Pallas Navy. A silvery half-dome of metal bulged from his right temple, an external AI companion called the outer eye. It was surely capable of no end of passive and active sensing, so the stateroom and hallway to it had been Faraday caged to protect the architectural secrets of the *Mutapa*. Spies suggested that the inside of Gillbard's cranium would also be layered with processing chips running an AI more intimately connected to the admiral's thoughts, augmenting memory and information processing; the theorized inner eye. His was a remarkably dangerous mind.

Luisa Pacheco was introduced as a special technical advisor from the Lunar Bank, supposedly a senior military stock analyst, about the same rank as an assistant branch manager, but that would have made her out of her depth in this meeting. More likely, she was a military or diplomatic staff officer, directly advising a Bank territorial head or a regional vice-president. Pacheco was of an age with her, and Iekanjika could see herself distorted in the silvery bulbous surface of the augment at Pacheco's temple, although her outer eye was smaller than Gillbard's.

The third delegate, Juliana Teixiera, was a senior officer reporting to the Risk Management Committee of the Bank of Ceres. She was very tall and slim, with close shaved dark hair and beautiful red tattoos incorporating the blotchy pigmentation characteristic of those genetically engineered to endure the radiation at Ceres. She had no outer eye, but that didn't mean that she hadn't the same capabilities as her two companions. Teixiera might be the risk analyst she said she was, but the Bank of Ceres had no investments in Epsilon Indi and lacked the Bank of Pallas' longstanding enmity with the Congregate. So she was most likely more than she appeared.

"Apologies for my delay in meeting you, general, technical advisor and senior officer," Iekanjika said.

"It's to be expected," Gillbard said. "You're running a war."

"A war among patron nations expands to occupy the space it needs," Teixiera said, her hands moving with the slow liquidity of those raised in microgravity.

Iekanjika inclined her head appreciatively. Four of the major Banks had recognized the Sub-Saharan Union as a free and independent patron nation soon after the Union had captured the Freya Axis. The Banks had their selfish reasons for this, not least to destabilize their long-time rival the Congregate.

Patron nations controlled some of the permanent wormholes of the Axis Mundi left behind by an ancient, unknown forerunner civilization. The exclusive group had five members: the Venusian Congregate, the Anglo-Spanish Plutocracy, the Ummah, the Middle Kingdom, and now, the Sub-Saharan Union. Despite their single permanent wormhole, no one considered the Puppets anything more than a failed state.

"How goes the war, major-general?" Gillbard said.

Iekanjika's patience for verbal games, never particularly large, evaporated a bit more.

"I'm sure that I have nothing to add to the conclusions drawn by your own analysts," she said.

"Massing of Congregate naval forces on the Epsilon Indi side of Freya?" he said. "A larger complement of smart nuclear missiles, enough to overwhelm even your mongrel fighters. And our intelligence suggests they're bringing anti-matter. Luckily you haven't fortifications to defend. You're mobile. Almost a guerrilla navy. That will blunt some of what those missiles and ships can do, and you maintain a propulsion advantage."

Iekanjika's commanders had seen small quantities of anti-matter being test-fired. Anti-matter was a strategic asset of such power that the patron nations would hold it in reserve in case they ever needed to use it against one another. That the Congregate was mainlining anti-matter weapons against the Union was perhaps the surest measure of how impatient they were to obliterate the rebellion.

"And the Congregate forces massing on the edge of the Bachwezi system," Gillbard continued. "Grim."

"You're in Bachwezi too?" Iekanjika asked.

Teixiera shrugged with an insouciant carelessness.

"Investors need analysts to measure risk," Teixiera said. "We recently discovered that we needed to have listening devices in Bachwezi. Moving them through the Freya Axis while it was being... contested, would be a distraction for everyone involved. The Bank of Ceres is happy to pay the appropriate fines for not having secured visas and permits prior to setting up a listening satellite in Bachwezi's Kuiper Belt."

"I'll ask the Foreign Office to assist in the regularization of your visa situation," Iekanjika said cautiously. "You'll need to send me the listening satellite's coordinates and orbit so that it doesn't get mistaken for a combatant."

"Of course," Teixiera said. She handed a small data wafer to Iekanjika's aide.

"We're maybe missing something important," Admiral Gillbard said, "but your military situation isn't promising. Maybe your *Homo quantus* allies will be able to turn the tide?"

"Your intelligence may be faulty," Iekanjika said. "We have no alliance with the *Homo quantus*. We don't know where they are and you probably know more about them than we do. You made them."

"Yes and no," Gillbard said. "The First Bank funded them, but since the beginning of your rebellion, all the Banks of the Plutocracy have bought significant stock in the *Homo quantus* project."

"They bought stock in a fractured asteroid with no *Homo quantus* on it?" Iekanjika said.

"The First Bank naturally had all the experimental records and data, held many patents, and even storehoused extensive DNA samples," he said.

"So you can build more," Iekanjika said.

"We're restarting from fertilized eggs," Pacheco said. "We won't get to where the *Homo quantus* project left off for perhaps twenty years, and quite obviously something happened to them, some unrecorded change that transformed them from a bit of an R&D joke into a very dangerous military asset. That missing information is very valuable to us, worth enough that it would be very profitable for the Union to have a role in helping us answer those questions."

"The *Homo quantus* turned down my request for an alliance," Iekanjika said. "They want nothing to do with the war or any of the patron nations."

"The destruction of the Garret in March must have been shocking for them," Pacheco said. "Nothing in our risk analyses suggested they would ever become a target. If we'd guessed that the *Homo quantus* technology was going to advance so suddenly, we would have moved them to a secure location. We're still offering that."

"I would be happy to have them on my side," Iekanjika said. "I would be happy to receive weapons and supplies from the Banks as payment for facilitating a meeting, but they've vanished. They're using every capability you built into them to disappear."

"That's unfortunate," Gillbard said. "For all of us. The *Homo quantus* are dangerous and it might be that the only ones who have adults are the Congregate."

"What?" Iekanjika said.

"These are deep military secrets," he said, "but our intelligence analysts have proof that some *Homo quantus* are fighting on the Congregate side. At the very least, they have some pilots."

Gillbard measured her silence with his dark eyes.

"I see you know what I'm talking about," he said. "We have reconnaissance fighters, listening vessels and warships in Epsilon Indi. We've observed your battles. Your mongrel pilots and their inflaton engine fighter craft are extraordinary. But the new Congregate small fighters are something else."

"We sent reconnaissance probes into the wreckage of your battles. We analyzed your propulsion technology of course, and mongrel physiology, but also those new Congregate pilots. Imagine our surprise when DNA analysis revealed proprietary Bank genetic IP in them. Maybe the *Homo quantus* didn't go as far away as you thought."

"They're *Homo quantus?*" Iekanjika said.

"It would be good for both the Union and the Plutocracy to speak with the *Homo quantus*. If the Congregate holds a two-decade advantage on this military technology, it won't go well for you or us."

"Give me the DNA sequences you have on the *Homo quantus*," Iekanjika said.

"The sequences are obviously proprietary military secrets, much like your inflaton drives," Pacheco said.

"I can't take anyone's word at face value. We'll do our own analyses. If they really are *Homo quantus* I'll inform General Rudo immediately."

Gillbard, Pacheco and Teixiera exchanged looks. Pacheco touched a data sliver to the small silver dome at her temple, and passed it to Iekanjika.

"These aren't the complete genome, of course," Pacheo said, "but this contains a few hundred novel gene fragments that exist only in the *Homo quantus*."

"We'll check," Iekanjika said.

"It might be a good idea for us to meet General Rudo as well," Gillbard said. "Perhaps we should consider a joint venture with the Sub-Saharan Union."

"An alliance?" Iekanjika said, keeping the incredulity from her voice. The idea was laughable. The Plutocracy rivalled the Congregate in political and military power. The Sub-Saharan Union was an embryonic state struggling to survive the year.

"There are many kinds of partnership in the Plutocracy," Gillbard said. "Investment agreements. Licences and leases, the sharing of technology and patents. Security and military accords. The Congregate has acquired stolen Bank IP, not just technology from the *Homo quantus* project. These new pilots are also carrying proprietary military AIs."

"Your Second Bushido AIs."

"If the Congregate is able to capitalize on the *Homo quantus* and Second Bushido technology," the admiral said, "and have your inflaton technology too, we may all be speaking French in a decade."

Iekanjika couldn't dispute the statement. But neither could she imagine emerging whole and uncorrupted from a partnership with the Banks.

"We could supply you with weapons," Gillbard said. "Ammunition. Explosives. Radioactives. Shielding. Control systems. If you wanted more of your warships, we could come to some agreement and our shipyards could begin turning out your inflaton ships."

"Proprietary information," Iekanjika said.

"For a while," Gillbard said. "Right now it's worth a lot. We were part of the consortium that bought the little inflaton ship of yours after the breakout from the Puppet Free City. We're reverse engineering it, as well as fragments from your destroyed ships and fighters."

"Just like vultures," Iekanjika said.

"Just like the Congregate," Gillbard said. "The further along we are at reverse engineering, the less you have to trade when you finally decide you do need an ally."

"You have a track record of hostile take-overs."

"Contracts can be written in a lot of ways," Gillbard said. "Alliances can be structured to forbid certain outcomes. And the people signing them, like you and Rudo, always get rich."

"I'm not getting rich," Iekanjika said coldly. "I'm freeing a nation."

"Who says you can't do both?" Teixiera said languidly.

"You need missiles, ammunition and armor," Gillbard said, "and if you won't accept help in the form of ships, you could really use anti-matter. A gram or two, in the right weapons, could turn some battles."

The offer was astonishing. Anti-matter, like the wormholes of the Axis Mundi was very much a patron-only asset.

"Our modelling shows that the Congregate navy has been adapting to your inflaton weaponry," Teixiera said. "They seem to have found the edges of its effective range, the recharge time, its area of effect. Their tactical changes are cutting into your strategic advantage."

"We can't afford anti-matter," Iekanjika said. "Not a gram. Not a milligram."

"Partnerships are not about money," Gillbard said. "We have money; you don't. You have inflaton technology; we don't yet. You have... Axes?"

"Axis, not Axes."

Gillbard smiled self-deprecatingly. Iekanjika found herself in the distorted reflection of the silvered dome on his temple, foreshortened to a tiny image.

"I don't want to fence, major-general," he said. "Our intelligence assets claim you've found not one, but the other four Axes Mundi in the Bachwezi system. This is of course, scarcely credible. You wouldn't have been able to hide the discovery of even one from the Congregate political commissars and listening stations while they were here, and since you wiped them out of Bachwezi, you haven't had the time to search using brute force searches. Anyone can stumble upon an Axis by accident, but four? You have a method of finding them. That's worth more than money. That's worth a partnership with the Sub-Saharan Union."

"You overestimate us," Iekanjika said.

"Do we?" Gillbard said.

"I won't comment on the quality of your intelligence, but we have no magical Axis detector."

"You have some magic," Teixiera said. "You vanished for forty years, and returned with fabulous technology decades or even a century beyond anything else in civilization. You mysteriously emerged from the Free City side of the Puppet Axis, without anyone having witnessed you entering it from the Stubbs side. And now we have serious reports that you found four mouths of the Axis Mundi in a handful of weeks."

"If Banks want to believe in magic, it's none of my business," Iekanjika said.

"Teixiera's statistical modelling is like a crystal ball," Gillbard said. "I don't like what she sees. I don't think you will either."

Teixiera's long fingers folded over themselves under her chin as she fixed Iekanjika with an intense, wanting stare. Her lips suggested a smile waiting to emerge, but a predatory one.

"All the modelling methods say that in no more than six months, the Union will fall. The Congregate will recapture the Freya Axis and most of the Union databases. The Congregate will then not only have some apparently functional *Homo quantus* pilots, but they'll have your schematics and probably even your shipyard for your inflaton vessels and fighters. The outcomes don't change even if you scuttle everything before they overrun you. There will be enough captives and existing wreckage to accelerate the reverse engineering of everything you've invented. If you have four other Axes, this will be a further tool of Congregate expansion. If you have a way of finding other mouths of the Axis Mundi and they get that too, well... that's sort of the end for all of us, isn't it?"

"So do something about it," Iekanjika said.

"Your Union parliament can just decide to enter a war," Gillbard said. "In the Plutocracy, shareholders vote on contracts and commercial and economic strategies. War is just another economic strategy and each Bank's articles of incorporation require some formal steps. Contracts. Licensing agreements. IP and patent-sharing accords. Cost and burden sharing understandings. No investor will dash into a war without knowing what their partners are willing to bring to the arrangement, without knowing how long they're willing to fight, under what conditions they should stop, or invest more."

"We may be at an impasse," Iekanjika said.

"Not really," Gillbard said. "The Plutocracy has interests in this conflict, enough to consider action up to and including an alliance. The Bank of Ceres has drawn up a model accord, to show you what sorts of elements would be part of an alliance." Teixeira's thin fingers handed Iekanjika another data wafer. "This is a discussion document, something to open negotiations, but it does show our corporate interests and the investments we would envision bringing to an alliance."

"I'll show it to General Rudo," Iekanjika said.

"Please make sure she understands that she shouldn't say no too quickly," Gillbard said. "It's rare that Banks confront real dangers. The risks to the Plutocracy over the coming months and years are significant. If a Plutocracy-Union alliance can't be struck to keep Union technology out of the Congregate's hands, the next logical step for the Banks would be to simply raid the Union ourselves, to get the technology before the Congregate does. It's a costly option filled with different risks, so it's not one we wish to entertain as more than a back-up plan."

Iekanjika didn't appreciate threats, but liked clarity. MPs escorted the three guests out of the stateroom and back to their shuttle. Iekanjika handed the first data sliver to the surgeon.

"Assume this is hostile software," she said to her aide. "When you've safed it, compare the gene sequences here against the blood samples we took last year from Belisarius Arjona. I want to know how much the Banks are telling the truth. Then test those Congregate pilots against Arjona's gene sequences and against these. Do it fast and do it quietly."

The surgeon left and Lieutenant Coulibaly made to leave to her duties, but Iekanjika put a hand on her shoulder.

"Ground Stills," she said. "I need him for something."

CHAPTER SEVEN

August, 2515

HAVING BEEN BRED and genetically-engineered for prodigious feats of intellect, Belisarius possessed one of the most sophisticated brains in civilization, even compared to other *Homo quantus*. His neuronal networks had been optimized for speed, connectivity and an ability to think multiple thoughts at the same time. Webs of carbon nanotubes infiltrated his brain, layering in additional electrical signals, augmenting speed, information storage and capacity to visualize geometric structures in four, five and six dimensions. His instincts had also been altered, to delight in learning and knowing, his curiosity amplified into a need. And the crowning achievement of generations of engineering and R&D investment was his capacity to shut his consciousness off, to extinguish the self. In the absence of the subjective self the *Homo quantus* brain, that most personal and intimate of spaces, could be occupied by an impersonal intellect capable of perceiving the probability, entanglements and mutually exclusive superpositions of the quantum world.

Belisarius understood, subjectively and objectively, the power of his brain, in the way an athlete understood their body, even from within his dreams. *Homo quantus* dreams were potent, growing from a prodigious intellectual substrate, taking full advantage of parallel thinking, hyper-dimensional imagination and perfect recall. The *Homo quantus* learned as children to shape their dreams, to interrupt them, but those tools depended on calmness and balance.

Dreams had haunted him for weeks. Parts of his mind, the portions processing in parallel to those parts that dreamed, analyzed his hallucinatory experiences like uncaring bystanders, or worse, curious ones, who regarded his discomfort as an interesting source of data.

Disembodied, he often dreamed of the *Hortus quantus,* stiff and slow in the minus a hundred degree chill of their planetoid, beneath a smouldering, unnamed brown dwarf. He dreamed in microscopic detail of the faint infrared of the brown dwarf warming oily black skin and the ice beneath. Even in dreams, his brain calculated energy budgets, ferreting for the secrets of how such a life form could survive in so hostile an environment. He saw the scents emerging from the taut chest of one *Hortus quantus,* travelling in a straight line to others; their energy-efficient language of smells. And he perceived, through the quantum intellect and his punishing, unforgiving memory, the vast rivers of entangled particles that connected them, not just to the individuals in the herd around the time gates, but through the mouths of the time gates to other times, to *Hortus quantus* both unborn and long dead, binding oceans and bays and eddies of superimposed probability that Belisarius had observed and accidentally destroyed.

But in the manner of dreams, what had happened had not happened, and in the manner of *Homo quantus* dreams, they had happened and had not happened. He carried the human horror of his unintentional genocide beside the insatiable curiosity that observed the entanglement as a physical thing, divorced from consequences, the pure pursuit of knowledge. He measured frigid temperatures, the hardness of the fragile ices that were the bones on which the intelligent plant forms lived and thought, finding it so very alien, a gulf unknowable and uncrossable.

Belisarius' dream changed shape, shifted perspective, like a rotation through state space. He became one of the *Hortus quantus*. Flesh and blood, muscle and magnetosomes, brain and blood became tough, oily hydrocarbon skin stretched over a hard skeleton of ice. The cold didn't bite. The brown dwarf's diffuse infrared glow warmed. Belisarius felt fragments of ice melt to droplets and move with peristaltic slowness, collecting and refreezing in new branch points. He grew in observable time. He moved.

The stiff frame of ice moved with a kind of breathless quickness, not the stilted halting he might have observed as a warm outsider. They experienced time so slowly that the faint gravity held them tight, pulled them fast enough that Belisarius felt the nimble agility of his frozen body. Through their eyes, the gasping, near-vanishing wind became a breeze, smelling of future promise. The excruciatingly slow and invisible sublimation of ice to vapor that Belisarius could only have detected with sensitive instruments became a misty fog through the eyes of the *Hortus quantus*. He dreamed their perceptions in sensual detail, and not just as one of them.

He wasn't just one of them.

He was two, three, five, many. He was many of the *Hortus quantus* because they were many. Their thoughts and feeling smixed together and separated again, like water seeping through a wetland delta, droplets and microscopic streams sometimes squeezing between sandy fill, sometimes flowing through fast channels. The threads of entanglement knit the *Hortus quantus* together, faint bits of indeterminacy carried on microscopic bits of pollen travelling on invisible winds into the past. He was the *Hortus quantus,* experiencing their world.

And they'd stopped experiencing the world because he had ended them.

He was weeping.

"Mister Arjona," Saint Matthew said. "Mister Arjona."

Belisarius opened his eyes. That didn't stop the nightmares. His brain's perfect memory and capacity to process multiple lines of thought kept the dream running, driven by the amplified engineered curiosity, supported by the rules of the dream that his brain might have adopted. *Homo quantus* escaped from their dreams rather than ended them.

The lights glowed to half-brightness. The simple box of a room had two sleep sacks strapped to one wall. Even at four in the morning, Cassie's was empty. As mayor, Cassie would be on a shift to do a call with one of the other habitats. They'd comforted one another as teenagers, but their pains had grown beyond hushed consolations in the dark.

"I could get you help," Saint Matthew said.

Belisarius finished exorcising the dream, shutting it down, although that only changed mental geography. No longer actively dreaming, the nightmare itself lived with crystal clarity in his memory. He rubbed at scratchy eyes and stared ahead for three point six seconds, an eternity.

From the dark, the disembodied voice accompanied by the softest of glows became the stiff holographic head of the AI who thought himself the reincarnation of a saint. Saint Matthew still occupied the Congregate service band he'd made his home since leaving *Saguenay* Station. But where the band had once projected a hologram of Saint Matthew as painted by

Caravaggio, a less human hologram now hovered above the AI. The head appeared to be a stone sculpture of Saint Matthew, chiselled in the Neo-Mayan style of the early 22nd century. The ornate face mixed the highly stylized pre-Colombian sculptural motifs with the symbology of the last Catholic cultists. The effect was, to a twenty-sixth century observer, utterly alien.

"You should let the *Homo quantus* psychologists and neurologists help you," Saint Matthew said. "I don't feel like being probed and analyzed," Belisarius said. "Everything about me is an engineering problem to them. Nightmares aren't a pathology."

"Do you want to tell me about your nightmares?" the AI asked.

"No."

"Is it about bringing them back?" the AI said.

More than Saint Matthew's appearance had changed. Since his return from the past with Belarius and Colonel Iekanjika, he'd become more distant, and yet more empathetic and knowing too.

"I broke the web of quantum entanglement connecting the *Hortus quantus*," Belisarius said. "I don't know how to reconstruct it. I'd set my brain to keep thinking about it while I slept, but I dreamt of the *Hortus quantus* instead. This time I was one of them, perceiving the world the way they did. It felt real."

"Your brain is capable of feats of extrapolation and thinking," the saint said. "What did it feel like to be them?"

The images, the scents, the feeling of warm life were diamond memories, clear, unbreakable, unforgettable, but out of his dream, knowing that this is what the *Hortus quantus* had lost, what he'd destroyed, the memories cut like sharp glass. He breathed unevenly.

"Their sense of time was different," he said. "What was cold to me was warm to them. They felt gravity more than we did because the world moved so fast for them. They lived slow enough that the brown dwarf was bright. And... and they were all connected. They weren't just individuals. They'd been something more, something special."

He felt a coolness on his cheeks and found tears clinging there and on his lashes, trembling in the zero-g.

"This wasn't your fault, Mister Arjona. You're doing everything you can to find a way to bring them back. You're a good person."

"It doesn't matter to the *Hortus quantus* if I meant to or not."

"The world can become a set of circumstances we don't control," the saint said, "something we suffer through, enduring until we can come to terms with the world. We can't change the world."

"I can," Belisarius said. Saint Matthew left the silence between them. "I've been trying to manipulate probability," Belisarius said finally.

"Are you chasing miracles?" the AI said.

"Maybe."

"What would this miracle look like?"

Belisarius felt shy all of a sudden.

"Waves and particles, and especially entanglement all follow distributions of probability," Belisarius said. "We don't know what any one particle or wave will do, but we understand their probabilities of doing a range of things. All the microscopic pollen at freezing temperatures going backwards in time, year after year, for hundreds of millennia knitted the *Hortus quantus* together. Links of entanglement connected them through space and time, and these became like neurons, I think, ways the *Hortus quantus* thought together. I saw what all those interacting waves and particles looked like in sum. If I could thread all those countless waves back together, I could remake the *Hortus quantus*."

"You don't control what those waves and particles do," Saint Matthew said doubtfully.

"I think I can."

"You can alter the probabilities by making magnetic fields and such for individual particles? People have been doing that for centuries."

"I think I can alter the probability itself. Directly."

"That's... quite a claim."

"Affecting probability was one of the long-shot, fringe goals of the *Homo quantus* project."

"They didn't reach it in the Garret. Why now? Why you? You're not even the latest generation anymore."

"I don't know. My brain isn't configured the way the project intended anymore."

"You've suffered neural damage and you've suffered through traumatic experiences," Saint Matthew said, "and you've often complained of your people's propensity to see false positives. Do you have evidence?"

Belisarius deflated. It wasn't particularly painful that Saint Matthew didn't believe him; in the big picture, not being believed was a small thing. It was more disturbing that the AI could give voice to each of the doubts Belisarius had tried to smother.

"Soon, I hope."

CHAPTER EIGHT

August, 2515

CASSANDRA SAT VERY quietly, with the not-so-quiet *Homo quantus* children in front of the big window looking onto the dark of the solar system. The children weren't talking or fidgeting or giggling, but because they were still growing into control of their electroplaques, their bodies crackled with tiny incontinent micro-discharges that robbed the observation lounge of peace. The children hadn't finished processing the loss of their old home, any more than the adults, but the elegant mathematical silence of their neighbors charmed and distracted them. They pondered the rows and rows of orbital data, the boxed and highlighted points representing the skates and chasers on their parabolic graphs.

No one knew if the skates were alive or if they were self-replicating machines having slipped their programming, displaying emergent, nonsensical behaviors in the process. They'd examined some closely. They were made of ceramics and silicates, flat and triangular, hence their name. Their interiors were filled with wiring and what appeared to be semi-conducting circuits. If they were alive, they certainly weren't carbon-based and weren't intelligent in any way they could detect. If they were machines, they weren't made by humans. They were only found associated with the wormholes of the Axis Mundi network. Maybe they were artifacts or machines persisting long after the builders of the Axis Mundi migrated away or went extinct.

The skates absorbed the pulsar's microwaves, as did the chasers that seemed to hunt them. Every so often, one of the chasers would catch a skate and grind it to pieces. At other times, the skates circled the pulsar a few times, recharging, before vanishing through one of the five permanent wormholes of the Axis Mundi network in this system. Shades of red and blue showed the time-warping of their relativistic velocities when they flew close to the pulsar. The *Homo quantus* children loved the skates and could puzzle over them for hours, making up theories of how they functioned, imagining their time dilations, calculating their energy budgets. Cassandra often found herself here with them, absorbing some of that youthful *élan*.

She unstrapped herself and floated back down the hallway of containers housing families who didn't have spaces yet in the half-built habitats. They hadn't decided yet if they would remake a new Garret where the three thousand seven hundred and thirty *Homo quantus* could live, or if they would split up into smaller villages of about eight hundred each. The Congregate had tried to exterminate the *Homo quantus* so Cassandra preferred becoming small, distributed targets, with redundant knowledge. Thinking of her people in statistical and actuarial terms was unpleasant, but might keep her people alive.

Cassandra floated down the spine of the cigar-shaped cargo hold, to Bel's lab. He'd become reclusive, which wasn't so strange among a community of introverts, but it was different for *him*. She opened the pressure door to the steel-gray room.

She didn't see him, which meant he'd retreated to his Faraday cage.

The Faraday cage was a three meter cube with netting that, when electrified, blocked all the EM humming of the freighter and the solar system at large. It was a silent room for a people who liked silence. Inside, Belisarius floated perfectly still, toes and head colinear to the long axis of the freighter. A finger twitched, guiding the magnetic field he was producing. His chest rose and fell slowly, but without the perfect rhythms of savant state or the fugue.

He went into the fugue more often than before. He could enter and retreat from it more easily since he'd become something new, since his brain had partitioned itself into Bel the subjective person, and Bel's brain, the objective quantum computational entity. Neurologists and physicists still examined him several times a day to try to understand what unintended, but maybe fortuitous result had come from an accident amid all their directed evolution. Bel was a step, or a half-step, to becoming more, to engaging with the universe in a different way, with other senses and other understandings. The genetic engineers of the *Homo quantus* wanted to try to replicate it, once they understood what had caused the changes. They wouldn't try to replicate the other unintended consequences.

The first unintended consequence, the destruction of the Garret by the Congregate had nearly killed them all. Their "success" was that they'd escaped as refugees. The *Homo quantus* had fled far enough that the Congregate shouldn't be able to find them. And as mayor, Cassandra intended to keep on going. They might need a year or two to make better ships, better habitats, but the *Homo quantus* could now navigate the network of wormholes left by the forerunners.

She and Bel hoped to reverse the second unintended

consequence, somehow, even if she thought it was impossible. In Bel's new state, part quantum perception, part subjective being, he had observed the overlapping, entangled probabilities of a vacuum-dwelling intelligent species of plant. They didn't know if this was humanity's first real contact with another intelligence, but in observing the overlapping probabilities, Bel had collapsed them, destroying all the quantum interactions that had been the substrate of their intelligence. The directed evolution of the *Homo quantus* had inadvertently made Bel capable of causing the extinction of a species that had incorporated quantum phenomena into the very structure of its thought. It wasn't his fault. He couldn't have known that looking at something would destroy it. But the guilt led him to this Faraday cage, day after day.

She knocked on the window. Bel moved like a lizard waking after warming itself. She shut off the electrical field, wheeled open the door and floated in. Bel had the same haunted expression he'd had for weeks. He gave her a timid smile.

"Look at this," he said in a low voice.

Bel gestured to a low-emission smart pad on the wall that showed tables and graphs. She leaned closer, reading legends and scales. It was a decay plot, measuring the amount of radiation emitted by a sample of radium-226. Bel indicated the corner of the cage, where a small lead cube with radiation labels was affixed to the wall.

"These are off," she said. "Is the sample tainted? That's two sigma faster than it should be."

"Saint Matthew's robots purified the sample."

The AI's robots mined radioisotopes from the asteroids to power the growing habitats and industrial facilities. If pure, the radium-226 should decay in a very well-understood way. Its mass would halve every 1,600 years like clockwork.

This sample was decaying faster.

"What's wrong with your sensors?" she said.

"I did it," he said, with a kind of wary elation he hadn't shown in some time.

"What?"

"I influenced the probability. I entangled my fugue state with the probability of the radium nuclei decaying. And I made it more likely for individual nuclei to decay."

"Bel! That's..." she faltered.

What was it? It was more than they'd ever hoped. The *Homo quantus* project had been working for a century on getting to the point that they might be able to try influencing probability. Their original funders had wanted to create beings who might be able to see technological, economic and military futures. They'd never gotten any return on the investment. Cassandra reread the data.

"You did this?" she said again.

He nodded with a reluctant elation.

She grabbed his shoulders, not knowing what to do with herself. She smiled, and she pulled him close and kissed him, holding his neck in both hands as they rotated in micro-gravity. She pulled back.

"Is this real, Bel? What are your methods. Can you teach me?" she said. "Or anyone else? We have to try to replicate your data, and maybe see about engineering it into generation fourteen or--"

"No!" he said, pushing away. They caught themselves on opposite walls. "No replicating it! I didn't do this for the project. I did this to see if maybe this could help bring back the *Hortus quantus*."

"We can do both, Bel. We need to replicate your experimental results. We want this anyway. For us."

"We don't want this because of us, Cassie. Our builders made us want this."

"It doesn't matter where it comes from. We want to know. We want to understand. And this will help. What they made us want isn't bad!"

"We should get to decide what we want."

The argument hadn't changed in twelve years. She wanted to reach for him, to float across the small space, to try to make a physical bridge where a philosophical one wouldn't hold. But her wrist band buzzed and lit red. They froze. Cassandra only got red notifications when human engineered ships came through the wormholes.

The *Homo quantus* were nearly useless at fighting or defending themselves, so Saint Matthew had designed and distributed a network of small, passive robots to watch for any movement through the five wormholes in this system. She spun the lock and they both raced, arm over arm, to the bridge.

"What is it?" she said to Saint Matthew.

"Single fighter craft," the AI said, stylized gray eyes expressionless. "Sub-Saharan Union, inflaton drive, armed, transmitting on the channel we specified."

"Stills," Bel said.

The fighter had turned to solar north, rising out of the ecliptic towards one of the sensor pods Saint Matthew had set in orbit near the axis. The pod inspected the craft and lines of data grew in the displays.

"It looks like Stills," Saint Matthew said. "The pass codes match. He says he has a message from Major-General Iekanjika."

CHAPTER NINE

August, 2515

BELISARIUS WATCHED CASSIE pilot *The Calculated Risk* to a factory Saint Matthew's robots had built inside a potato-shaped iron-nickel asteroid. The factory produced construction and mining robots, as well as steel sheeting and beams, which rail guns shot to whatever orbit they were needed in the solar system.

Stills was their last remaining contact with the wide world and his ship co-orbited with the asteroid. Cassie landed *The Calculated Risk* at the only habitable part of the factory, a small windowless supply and communications house amid the fields of perovskite antennae that harvested electricity from the pulsar's x-rays. Stills' craft followed them down.

"Stills?" Belisarius asked by tight laser. "How've you been?"

"Don't waste our time, *patron*," the monotonal response came back. "I fuckin' hate playing diplomat an' I got a message."

"What is it?" Bel said.

"Did you guys lose some of your big brains?" Stills said.

"What?" Cassandra asked.

"Ah, the princess is here," Stills said. "I said if you lost some of your sheep, the Congregate's got 'em. Word is that they're

71

experimenting on them, trying to reverse engineer you guys. In other words, fuck me."

Belisarius felt cold, dizzy. The precise, detailed memory of the *Homo quantus* who'd refused to join their escape presented itself to his mind. He'd thought they'd died. How many had the Congregate captured? And when? He'd seen them fire on the Garret. If it was all hundred and fifty-five... He didn't know how to finish the thought.

"What do they want?" Belisarius said.

"Who? The Venusians?" Stills said. "Shit if I know. They probably want a whole army of big brains. You gave the Congregate a black eye and now they're in a war. They changed the names of their houses to wartime names and everything. That ain't been done in my lifetime. They don't do war half-assed to start with and now they got themselves some of you."

"That... won't help them," Belisarius said. "We're not useful in traditional conceptions of war."

"I don't give half a shit about your traditions and the Congregate don't either. They been loading your people into fighter ships and they been giving the dogs a rough ride."

"*Homo quantus* pilots?" Cassandra whispered in confusion. "Against mongrels?"

"Surprised the shit outta me too, princess. Iekanjika's people had some of your DNA from when you guys were on their ships. They checked. It's your guys. She gave me tissue samples of the three I blew to shit. You can do your own tests on it."

"The *Homo quantus* would be inept fighter pilots," Belisarius said, feeling like he was drowning.

"These guys were fuckin' ept enough," Stills said. "Iekanjika showed me the autopsies. They were wired up somethin' fierce inside. I don't know how much metal you guys carry around. I didn't think it was much."

"None," Belisarius said. "Our wiring is all carbon nanotube."

"Well then, these saps were wired from ass to brain, and chipped too. You know what Second Bushido fighters are?"

"No," Belisarius said.

"You guys aren't the Banks' only try to make better fighters," Stills said.

"We're not fighters," Cassie said.

"Yeah, yeah," Stills said. "As near as I been told, they make Second Bushido guys by bonding Lunar Bank AI tech into human brains. Looks like the Congregate thought it'd be a good idea to try that with you guys."

"We're not built for that," Belisarius said.

"It don't much matter how you're built," Stills said, "as long as you can be built into something useful."

"We don't work that way," Belisarius said.

"Maybe Del Casal will fix 'em," Stills said.

"What?" Belisarius said.

"Iekanjika got some intel that the Congregate got their hands on Del Casal. I knew I shoulda killed that fucker."

"What's Iekanjika going to do?"

"I don't know. I'm not in her head. But that ain't the question, is it? I guess that after you helped the Union break through the Puppet Axis no one's really excited that the Congregate has their own *Homo quantus*. The question ain't what's Iekanjika gonna do, but what are you going to do?"

CHAPTER TEN

April, 2515

BAREILLES' TEAMS COLLECTED everything known about Belisarius Arjona. The captured *Homo quantus* at first appeared to be a trove of factual knowledge about Arjona, but for some major caveats. First, their interests were quite technical: physiology, biochemistry, genetics and performance, to the exclusion of almost all else. Second, by normal human standards, the *Homo quantus* were barely social; they lived deep and rich private intellectual lives, and communicated with each other through scientific papers, data sets and theories. They made shallow connections amongst themselves and few of the captives had ever spoken with Arjona. Third, what knowledge they had of Arjona began at birth and ended when he left the Garret at sixteen years old.

Her operatives had to fill in the intervening twelve years the hard way. Spies and security officials in Congregate and Anglo-Spanish territories interrogated everyone who had ever interacted with Arjona: casino staff, bartenders, petty bribable officials, convicts who had worked as his crews, marks who'd been fleeced by him, even neighbors. Not a one professed any loyalty or allegiance to him, but she'd expected that given the rigorousness of the interrogations. Neither did any of them corroborate anything said in the other interrogations, other than basic physical information. Arjona kept so many different names, that sometimes even members of the same crew knew him by different aliases. Bareilles found additional hidden identities like Diego Arcadio, Camilo Ortíz, Roberto Quintero, Nicolás Rojás and Juan Cáceres. Her teams unearthed dozens of others, and deeper searches found fully fleshed out lives for each of them, school transcripts, tax filing histories, medical records, even birthday and anniversary photos. And not a one of them was real. Not a single detail.

If it had been anyone else, Bareilles might have thought Arjona a compulsive liar. As a spy she appreciated the craft of compartmentalizing information to protect the mission from exposure, but Arjona had done far more than that. He'd deployed the immense cognitive powers of the *Homo quantus* to building enough false lives to people a village. Her psychologists couldn't build a personality profile from anything her teams learned. There might be some truths hidden in there, but no way to tell fact from fiction. Taken in sum, Arjona's identities formed a blurry, frustrating statistical distribution.

Doctor Antonio Del Casal would know more. He knew Arjona more personally, relevantly and recently than the captured *Homo quantus*. Their intelligence file on the geneticist was extensive. He was born to an affluent family of mid-level managers of the Martian Investment Bank. He'd been educated in molecular biology and medicine at the Hellas Genetics Institute, receiving numerous scholarships, industrial grants and corporate offers. The file contained videos of a younger Del Casal, receiving awards, giving speeches on biotechnology policy on Mars, lecturing at the Lunar Bank, partying on Earth, accompanied by articles pulled from the R&D, financial and celebrity sections of news services.

He'd travelled extensively through the Ummah and Middle Kingdom worlds as a research consultant and had been granted a number of business and academic visas to Congregate territories, most recently to Saguenay Station. The recordings of the Lanoix Casino security AIs were voluminous, showing an elegant middle-aged man with a passion for cards, women and fine liquors. And then a few months ago, he'd ducked below the radar. Del Casal had briefly met Bareilles and the Epsilon Indi Scarecrow on Oler, and then had vanished again until Congregate informants reported him in the Puppet Free City, engineering Numen out of Anglo-Spanish debtors. The AIs and Rivard's analysts had assembled the psychological profile describing a deservedly arrogant genius acquainted with the adulation of admirers, but not beholden to it, a *bon vivant* who enjoyed delicacies, an intellectual who did not often find peers, and possibly a sociopath with few moral boundaries.

During his transport to Venus, Del Casal had been interrogated. Despite his having spoken extensively with Arjona, interrogators concluded that Arjona hadn't trusted the doctor with much truthful information. Del Casal's answers fit within the curve of all the other lies associated with Arjona. Bareilles hadn't really expected more, but that wasn't why she'd brought him.

A intelligence officer shoved Del Casal roughly into a small meeting room overlooking the clouds where Bareilles sat at a table. He looked harried, his salt-and-pepper hair disarrayed, deprived of his rich finery and wearing detainee orange. He controlled his reaction well enough when he saw the clouds behind her. He would be intelligent enough to know that over Venus, he was no one.

"Sit down," Bareilles said.

The geneticist put on a brave face and sat opposite her, feigning a curiosity in the clouds.

"How was the Puppet Free City?" she said.

"The last time we talked, you had a Scarecrow around. Is he on Venus too?" His French was a careful and educated version of 8.3, with good pronunciation.

"You were arrested for violation of embargo statute one hundred and twelve," she said, "aiding and abetting enemy forces."

"I was providing medical consultation to the *Homo pupa*, not your enemies. It was a humanitarian mission and I was kidnapped extra-territorially and illegally by Congregate officials."

"Humanitarian?" She smiled. "Did your patients ask for your help? Did they consent? I know all about Puppet medicine."

He maintained his composure.

"I know quite a lot about the Puppets in general," she said. "I spent thirty months on and around Oler, directing covert intelligence networks in the Free City. Before that, I worked with the descendants of Numen who escaped the Puppet Rebellion. We've even tested their deployment in the field as operatives to interrogate and manipulate Puppets, as you may have noticed. The Federation of Puppet Theocracies is designated under the Convention on Crimes Against Humanity as a state where responsible actors can pursue law enforcement activities."

"I want a Plutocracy lawyer and I want to see a consular official from the Lunar Bank immediately," he said.

"I don't think so. The Congregate invoked the Wartime Measures Act. Even if that weren't so, the Ministry of Intelligence operates under a different set of laws."

He stared at her with eyes on the edge of watering with frustration and terror.

"If convicted of breaking the embargo and aiding enemy forces, you could face thirty years of hard labour."

His shoulders remained rigid. "Get me my lawyer."

She reached casually across the table, slowly sliding her fingers into his hair. Then, she rammed his face into the table. Once, twice. Blood spilled.

"If you ever get a lawyer, have him object to that," she said sweetly. "You're not the first recruit who didn't want to work with me, nor the first who misunderstood who's holding what cards. My teams have photographic and video evidence of you engineering human convicts against their will."

He cowered, his hands hovering above his pooling blood, as if wanting to protect his face but no doubt understanding that resistance would make it worse.

"Trust me when I say that you would not enjoy hard labour on Venus. The injury rate is high and you're not on some insurance plan here, provided with every prosthetic you might want. I'm willing to take the hard labour of your brain instead your hands. My problem is that I get impatient. So it's in your best interest to give me the impression I'm getting your hardest effort."

"*Bueno*," he said in Anglo-Spanish, then, as if remembering where he was, repeated in French "*D'accord*."

She released his hair. Gingerly, he pulled away from the table and sat not so straight anymore. He huddled with rounded shoulders, and didn't look at her. His nose dripped blood that he didn't wipe. She woke the smart screen on her side of the table and changed the window to display mode. Several schematics of *Homo quantus* neurology appeared, masking the clouds.

"You know these," she said.

"I'm no expert on the *Homo quantus*. Do you have some of the project engineers?"

"The *Homo quantus* are mostly their own project engineers now. Those who can't enter the fugue become the engineers, the biological designers, the doctors. They're extremely intelligent."

He regarded her sullenly, and then seemed to think better of it and made as if he were reading the neurological charts. He slid a desultory finger across one icon, expanding it.

"Your perspective on genetic modifications is broader than theirs," she said. "You bring creativities from different efforts and your moral compass is interestingly... flexible."

"What do you want?"

"I have a hundred and fifty *Homo quantus*," she said. "None of them can reach the fugue like Arjona and Mejía."

"Arjona couldn't reach the fugue," he said.

"He lied."

He chewed on that, looked absently for something to wipe his face and finally wiped his sleeve across his lips and nose.

"I wish I'd never met him."

"A lot of people say that."

"You want me to fix your *Homo quantus*? If it could be done, wouldn't the Banks have done it?"

"They're not here," she said. "And I can't drop them into clouds of sulfuric acid if they don't give me functioning *Homo quantus*."

CHAPTER ELEVEN

August, 2515

Belisarius and Cassandra preceded Stills into the freighter that served as headquarters and town hall. They hadn't named it yet. They usually let the children name things, but they'd mostly advanced impractical suggestions, like elegant geometric concepts whose names in Anglo-Spanish were too cumbersome. Robots withdrew Still's pressure chamber from his fighter. Saint Matthew flickered as a new hologram in the comms system.

"Mister Stills, I'm afraid that we don't have anywhere suitable for you to get out of your chamber and swim. If you're staying for a few days, I could have the construction crews build something."

"If these air-suckers make some choices quick I won't be stayin' long," said the monotone electrical speaker on Stills' chamber. The hologram of sculpted stone looked pensive.

"They don't decide anything quickly," the AI said to Stills. "I'll start the crews."

Belisarius and Cassie crossed into the habitable sections. Cassie's back was straight and her lips pressed tight. In the medical clinic, one of Saint Matthew's experimental AIs waited to help. It rode, like many others, in a spidery robotic body. It had adopted a holographic avatar in Saint Matthew's style: a 22nd century neo-Mayan interpretation of a medieval monkish head, tonsured, apparently sculpted in stone. Saint Matthew called it Pedro. Pedro careful opened the box of samples Stills had brought, revealing vials of blood.

The idea that the blood had once been in some quiet, peaceful *Homo quantus* felt obscene. Belisarius imagined their terror, their loneliness, in the power of a wide world they didn't and couldn't understand. At sixteen, fleeing his *Homo quantus* heritage, Belisarius had felt it, but at least he hadn't been hunted. He'd hidden among Puppets and criminals, while his people were under the microscopes of Congregate military officials. Their blood stained his hands.

"It might have been better if I'd never come back," he said finally. "To the Garret."

"Maybe," she said.

"Or if the Union had never made contact with me." Cassie looked away. At the best of times, *Homo quantus* had a hard time dealing with emotions and people. But he knew her needs and his; they'd been built on the same biochemical templates, with the same urges and needs.

"We wanted the time gates," he said. "We wanted the knowledge. We didn't know the price, but we were willing to be billed later."

"Is it worth it to you?" she said.

They locked eyes across the mean little industrial room. There were two answers for each of them, each of those answers wanting to be real, and whichever answer was true would be defining and indelible. And he didn't know what would happen if they didn't get the same answer.

"We changed the first bill," she said. "We said it was too much and we changed the cost."

They had. They'd watched the nuclear detonation of the Garret and then they'd gone back in time, and pulled most of the *Homo quantus* out of danger. Most. That was his problem. Despite all the data he'd collected, despite the thrill of learning some of the nature of the universe, his perfect memory couldn't forget the hundred and fifty-five faces of the *Homo quantus* who hadn't believed him, who'd chosen to stay. He thought they'd died, but the idea of their captivity horrified him more. But worse, it might still be worth it. His instincts, engineered by corporate interests had led him to this, made him feel the cost was acceptable because he'd gotten data.

"If it's true that the *Homo quantus* who stayed behind are prisoners of the Congregate, I don't know what we can do."

"It doesn't make sense," she said, as if persuading. "Can you imagine me as a fighter pilot? Or a soldier? Or as an officer?"

She'd meant it to sound ludicrous. And it sort of was. The *Homo quantus* were impractical, distractable, unevenly absent-minded, more likely to be swept up in the geometries of explosions rather than the passion of battle. Belisarius had been handed the heist of a dozen lifetimes and had focused almost entirely on stealing a time travel device from his employers. But Cassie and Stills had told him what had happened in the hyperspace within that time travel device, while she and Stills had been surprised by a Scarecrow.

In Cassie's mind, she'd directed Stills to run, and to keep running. It was the most logical and militarily useless thing she could imagine. But Stills saw it differently: she'd given him time. She'd kept them alive until Stills could understand enough of the hyper-spacial battlefield to fight back. On their own, as staff officers, as military and economic strategists and tacticians, the *Homo quantus* were like strange artificial intelligences. But sometimes, when paired with someone more focused, someone more *invested* in the world, the odd talents of the *Homo quantus* saw things no one else saw.

The time travel device had shown Belisarius how two wormholes could interact, and so he'd gotten the Union into the Puppet Axis without travelling through one of the mouths. Cassie had understood the twenty-two dimensional hyperspace within the time travel device, in a way only a *Homo quantus* could, and she'd navigated a temporary escape for her and Stills. What could the Congregate do with captured *Homo quantus*?

Pedro approached. Above his little holographic faux head, another set of holograms showed the DNA analyses. The three samples belonged to Martín Revilla, Ana Teresa Trujillo, and Edmer Vizcarra. The DNA samples matched, but with some odd genetic signals. The vast majority of genes, including those separating *Homo quantus* from *Homo sapiens,* were identical, but there were other genes too, in odd, suggestive amounts.

"They are *Homo quantus*," Belisarius said. "The Congregate really has them."

"Somebody modified their genomes," Cassie said.

A scientific problem instead of an emotional one was easier. He slipped his hand into Cassie's and she held his hand back. The names went with faces. Martín, a short, handsome man with black hair, had been worried when Belisarius had last seen him, conflicted, panicked at the Garret splitting up. Ana Teresa had been tall, only just having become an adult, with her hair bound into tight dark curls, her hands moving nervously, her lips set with the anger of betrayal. Edmer an older man, a generation before Belisarius and Cassie, but healthy, one of the administrators of the town, had shown an expression of confusion. Belisarius couldn't forget the faces as he'd last seen them, and couldn't ignore them now as they were, blood samples in vials, taken from bodies blown to pieces by Stills' mongrels, brought to that cross-roads by Belisarius' meddling in the affairs of the wide world.

"They aren't dead. It wasn't revenge," she said, as if processing the politics, the calculations of power that must have been behind the Congregate's actions. It wouldn't be a natural way of thinking for her. It hadn't been for him. When he'd first left the Garret as a teenager, he'd relied on game theory as an early first approximation of human behavior, until he learned the morality and amorality of people living in the wide world.

"The Congregate must have arrived before we ever saw them," she went on. "They'd seen what we could do. They want their own *Homo quantus*. They destroyed the Garret only after they'd taken all the data and knowledge they could."

She and he could understand the value of data and knowledge. It was worth risking lives for.

"Where are the captives?" she said.

"The *Homo quantus* are... military secrets," he said, "like a new propulsion system or a new weapon. A power like the Congregate would bring them somewhere safe, to figure out how we were built, so they could make their own."

"But they aren't making their own!" she said. "They put them into fighter ships and made them fight the mongrels. Why would they fight? We're not made like that."

He couldn't imagine anything that could make a *Homo quantus* fight. Designed to quietly perceive a world entangled and probabilistic and non-local, they were calm, curious, intellectual and mathematical. It was harder to be further from natural soldiers.

"Can we save them?" Cassie said.

He thought of the Congregate, a vast political power spanning the planets and asteroids around thirty or more permanent wormholes of the Axis Mundi, always justifiably wary of the Anglo-Spanish Banks, so armed and fortified to protect their sovereignty that they'd ironically projected power and culture over other nations, forcing the Banks into military build up. The *Homo quantus* prisoners might be in the hands of the Ministry of Defense if considered military technology, or hidden with the Ministry of Intelligence if judged as an espionage or insurgency threat.

"I don't know."

CHAPTER TWELVE

IEKANJIKA CAME TO Rudo's quarters on Manafwa Station at four o'clock. The Bank representatives were in their guest quarters and the Puppet bishop co-orbited with the station at about a hundred kilometers. The *Homo quantus* would arrive within hours. Rudo's quarters were large compared to the suite they'd shared on the *Mutapa*, but as Defence Minister, Rudo needed work space near her living space, including servers for AIs, stations for analysts and aides, and shielding and armor.

Iekanjika and Rudo strapped into seats in a meeting nook for four with various holographic projectors ringing the space. The printed foam cushions felt almost decadent compared to the hardness of the *Mutapa*. A steward brought akara, a fried bean cake, and bulbs of wine, neither of which Iekanjika had tasted before reaching home. She hadn't acclimatized to all the tastes and smells of a cuisine that had been impossible during her life in the Expeditionary Force. Efo riro and fish, roasted plantain, jollof rice, coconut flour pancakes and pounded yams. All her life, she'd eaten whatever the food reactors on the fleet had been able to produce, yeasty and unspiced, never knowing the tastes she'd missed.

Rudo looked tired. Iekanjika probably looked tired herself.

Iekanjika carried the weight of the navy, but Rudo carried the whole nation, struggling with Cabinet, budget negotiations, the press, civilian complaints and fears, and the recession. War had gradations of victories and defeats, but from what Iekanjika saw of Rudo, politics had only gradations of loss: loss of trust, loss of credibility, loss of resolve. Iekanjika knew how to bear the martial pressure of the fleet, but didn't know how Rudo could shoulder the weight of civilian loss.

A technician established a secure laser-line to the government house at Bachwezi and drew curtains further around the meeting nook. Soon, a milky holographic image of a heavy-set Prime Minister Zuma stuttered into view over one of the unoccupied chairs. His expressive eyes and ponderous gestures emphasized the conflicted moods of a prime minister in his second term, on the cusp of history, but feeling his legacy draining away as war losses piled high. He smiled transactionally.

"General," he said in French. "Generals. It is good to see you."

"Likewise, Prime Minister," Rudo said, also in French. Rudo's Shona had gotten quite good, but for sensitive discussions, almost everyone still fell back on French.

"I received your latest intelligence report," Zuma said. "It was... thin."

"I did not include all the details, prime minister."

An undercurrent of frustration showed just beneath Zuma's expression. Rudo just looked patient.

"I appreciate that you've managed to arrest all the political commissars, but I still don't feel we know who and who hasn't been otherwise compromised by Congregate spies. We know the Congregate has no intelligence assets among the Expeditionary Force, so we've been able to keep the details and capabilities and vulnerabilities of the ships away from the Congregate. But

I have no way of knowing who in the Bachwezi Intelligence Service might have been compromised by Congregate agents over the years. So I'm still holding back intelligence."

"Your paranoia is becoming old, General," he said.

"So is your insistence that your government has no spies, prime minister. We've avoided disaster so far."

"Yes! Yes we have! And we'll keep avoiding disaster."

Rudo gave little hint that Prime Minister Zuma's words moved her and the silence became uncomfortable.

"I did not share your pessimism on strategic matters either, General," he finally said.

"Optimistic plans are not good plans," Rudo said.

"Our strategic situation is quite good," the Prime Minister said. "Our forces hold both sides of the Freya Axis and continue to repel Congregate assaults. Without the axis, they cannot attack Bachwezi, nor any industrial facilities."

"I disagree, prime minister," Rudo said. "Without the Freya Axis, the Congregate's next nearest axis is thirty-six light years away. That's quite far for a series of induced wormholes, but not beyond their resources."

"Supplies lines thirty-six light years long?" Zuma scoffed.

"Supply lines are about investing in the logistics," Rudo said. "It depends on how badly the Congregate wants the axis. And us."

"You hold a high view of yourself, general. Bachwezi was never a profitable part of the network for them. Its loss stings, but sober thinking will result in some armistice and eventually peace."

"I think they're embarrassed by the loss of the axis, prime minister," Rudo said, "and insulted by the loss of their warships. They need to make an example of us, no matter what the cost, not just to make sure their other client nations remain obedient, but to make a statement to the other patron nations who might now find them weak. I think the Congregate is going to retake the Freya Axis in a matter of months."

"Your defeatism is not welcome, general," Zuma said. "The Cabinet ordered you to hold the axis."

"The Cabinet can order what it wants," Rudo said. "Some realities won't change. The Government has to reach some sort of new peace with the Congregate before we lose the axis."

"There are ways to hold it," Zuma said.

"I can hold it for three to six months," Rudo said. "It depends on how quickly we can disrupt the long supply lines the Congregate will be building. We'll need guerrilla tactics. We need the Government to accelerate the munitions production. But even more, we need some sort of negotiated peace with the Congregate."

"What negotiated peace?" Zuma demanded. "Our own Minister of Defence doesn't believe we can win. What sort of negotiating hand does that give us?"

"They may be open to some face-saving gesture sooner than three to six months, prime minister. We don't know what kind of political pressure they're facing on Venus."

"Do you honestly think they'll negotiate?" he demanded.

Rudo shook her head. "Not really, but if there's a chance, it could save lives and strategic positioning. The Congregate won't be kind to either of us if they win by force."

"What about the mongrels?"

"Another two hundred will join us soon."

"That's a fraction of the pilots we need," Zuma said. "You gave them an entire axis! They should have come running by the thousands. The Foreign Office has the negotiating skills needed for recruitment and is ready to free up your staff to focus on the war."

"The mongrels have been bleeding in our rebellion for

months," Rudo said. "More will come. We get a dozen each week because of Major-General Iekanjika, not because of me. They certainly won't come at the request of civilians."

"The mercenaries will come because we've overpaid." "Persuading the mongrels to join a losing cause bought us time. We still have twenty more axes, nineteen when we lose Freya."

"Again with your defeatism!" The grainy image of the prime minister seemed to turn to Iekanjika now. "Could you hold the Freya Axis, Major-General?"

"No, Prime Minister," Iekanjika said. "I recommended using stealth ships to transport civilians through the Bukavu Axis."

That was the first of the twenty axes they'd named. They hadn't had time for more. And they might not have the chance to name the others if every bet didn't break their way.

"Evacuate an entire world?" the prime minister said caustically. "This was not what the Government had in mind when the Sixth Expeditionary Force first made contact."

"We took this gamble together, Prime Minister," Rudo said.

"A gamble you seem to think is already lost."

"Not at all. This war of independence will be longer than a single campaign or the ownership of a single axis. If we prepare for the loss of the Freya Axis by moving civilians and strategic resources out of harm's way, we'll be ready for the next phases of the war," Rudo said. "If we ignore military realities, we lose everything."

"What about the *Homo quantus*?" he said. "The Foreign Office is ready to send embassies to them. They owe us for what they stole from your ships."

"We're trying to persuade them," Rudo said.

"You're no diplomat, general."

"They barely talk to us," Rudo said, "and only because they know us."

"How convenient for you. I thought you had a war to run."

Neither woman rose to this bait. Zuma's eyes narrowed.

"If you fail to persuade them soon, the only answer is to force them. Everyone saw that their military value is incalculable."

"An ally who needs to be forced is no ally," Rudo said. "We're teaching that lesson to the Congregate. The *Homo quantus* are arriving shortly. We're working on an alliance."

Zuma's face was stormy and hard.

"In the meantime," Rudo said, "I've delivered my military assessment to the cabinet. I'm prepared to discuss what we do with the assessment, but I won't alter facts or bend logic to soothe anyone. As a contingency measure, we should ship important political figures and industry across the Bukavu Axis."

"Cabinet will meet shortly on all of this, General," Zuma said, "and no part of this conversation will be off limits. In the meantime, the foreign minister is on his way to Manafwa and should be arriving within the hour."

"Cabinet authorized me to lead these talks," Rudo said.

"Lead them," Zuma said. "Minister Yamguen will observe and assist."

Iekanjika's fingers had tightened on the arms of her seat, but Rudo appeared to be completely in control of herself.

"I'll instruct him as to my strategy as soon as he arrives then," Rudo said.

The prime minister's hologram vanished. Iekanjika loosened her grip on the seat.

"The idiot acts like he can tell us what to do," Iekanjika said.

Rudo looked thoughtful. "The whole cabinet can. They can slow down our supply lines, or stop them. They can stop paying the soldiers. They can pass any laws they want. And they control the press. Or the Congregate might still."

"Trimming supply lines is going to kill them and us together."

"That doesn't mean they won't do it if they think we're not fighting hard enough."

"We're the ones risking everything!" Iekanjika said. "We're the ones dying."

Iekanjika floated to the ceiling and then across a grip bar to a refreshment station, but she didn't open the fridge door. She didn't know what to do with her frustration. It wasn't that she was an unlikely or unwilling revolutionary. She was a particular flavor of revolutionary, suited to pointing guns at the enemy and shooting. Convincing people to fight for their own freedom drained her, exhausted her morale, optimism, and perhaps her ability to inspire her officers and crew. And she didn't know how to stop that feeling.

CHAPTER THIRTEEN

CASSANDRA PILOTED *THE Calculated Risk* from within the acceleration chamber. She hated the oxygenated shock gel packing her ears, filling her mouth and lungs, squirming under her eyelids. She hated the weird electrical wire connecting to the jack in the base of her skull that let her talk to the fast little ship. But they needed all of this; they had no idea what kinds of maneuvers might be needed if Congregate patrols or pickets noticed them. Even in shock gel, she and Bel couldn't pull more than twenty gravities of acceleration to escape pursuit. They'd added a bit more armament to *The Calculated Risk*, but nothing that would make it a real fighter.

Cassandra followed Stills through the secret wormholes of the Axis Mundi network that led back to the Epsilon Indi system across many hundreds of lightyears. Each node in the network seemed to have up to five permanent wormholes, each one connecting to a single wormhole at some other node far away. Cassandra and Bel had mapped out some of the nearby nodes, but other than the Freya Axis, they hadn't found a combination of nodes that would connect them to Bachwezi without passing through Epsilon Indi.

The throat of the last wormhole to Epsilon Indi luminesced

indistinctly, like all of the others, very cold in the infrared but speckled with x-rays. She felt safe in this naked galactic artery, hidden within a tube of twisted space-time she would have studied if she hadn't been piloting. Ahead of them, Stills vanished through the mouth, into normal space. She followed quickly. If they needed to run, the decision would be in the first moments.

Stars appeared. Stills ran dark a few kilometers ahead, signalling with a small stern laser. Both ships activated cold jets and then raced away on inflaton drives, squeezing themselves with an uncomfortable twenty-one gravities. Stills changed directions a few times as they neared the mouth of the Freya Axis. Invisible at this distance, hot thermal signatures still orbited with it: weapons platforms, missile throwers, Union warships and mobile fueling stations.

Congregate naval units, hotter in the infrared, showed up on the telescopes, more distant, but still closer to the axis than Cassandra would have liked. The Union held a perimeter, but not a big one. Cassandra had studied the capabilities of the Congregate navy; their lasers and even fast missiles could, with luck, reach all the way to *The Calculated Risk*. Their best defense was looking like one more small and unremarkable Union craft.

Stills was sending passcodes and authentications to Union pickets, and the closer they came to the mouth of the Freya Axis, the more he accelerated. A flight of mongrel fighters formed up around them. Cassandra matched Stills' sudden and unsafe deceleration profile at the Freya Axis. Then they all cut their drives and slipped into the gray throat of the Freya Axis.

Bel hadn't spoken the whole trip. They'd absorbed Stills' news differently, processed pain and guilt differently. Bel took blame onto himself. She... wasn't ready to do that. Or only some. She hadn't created these situations. She hadn't pulled the triggers. She hadn't refused to escape when given the chance. But something in that line of reasoning sounded facile.

She didn't like these thoughts. She would have rather been studying the interior of the Freya Axis with quantum senses, like Bel. Every wormhole differed in the qualities of its quantum entanglements and in quantities like charge and mass and spin, and maybe even which dimensions of space time they uncurled. That gave each wormhole a unique physical identity. Bel got to explore the cosmos while she played pilot.

"Apologies, Miss Mejía," Saint Matthew's voice came into her head through the wire jacked into her skull. "Your thinking and... frustration was leaking out. I wanted to apologize for not piloting. But you're a better pilot."

She wasn't a natural -- hadn't known how to fly anything a few months ago. She'd flown with Stills though, navigating for him when they'd gone into the hyperspace of the time gates. In there, under pressure, running from the Scarecrow, they'd melded her mind and his flying, writing an orbit across a twenty-two dimensional space. She would never be a fighter, but in idle moments, parts of her brain modeled the path, the accelerations, the reversal of charge and parity and time. Those mental visualization and retracings had turned into algorithms, experience, even intuition. She hadn't intended to learn to pilot and didn't particularly enjoy it, but she was now better than Saint Matthew.

She hoped that Bel was enjoying his data.

Stills vanished from the interior of the Freya Axis and moments later, she was in a new system, stars white and hard against the black, in patterns her mind eagerly sorted and mapped. Bachwezi, the home of the Sub-Saharan Union. New orbital fortifications were under construction around the Axis mouth. Stills angled his fighter, signalled a thrusting countdown to her by laser, and then set off at a more comfortable fifteen gravities, towards a blue gas giant six AU away. She settled in for more boredom.

IEKANJIKA, IN THE patched discolored plastic of the warship corridor, seemed smaller. Of course Cassandra could measure quite well with her eyes. Iekanjika hadn't lost any of her hundred and eighty-one centimeters, but Cassandra had an impression of seeing a boulder being worn down. This was why she didn't trust her impressions and feelings. The amplified pattern recognition in the *Homo quantus* made strange false positives out of qualitative information.

"It's good to see you, despite the circumstances," Iekanjika said warily. Cassandra wondered if it were a lie. Their small talk soon faltered and the three of them, trailing a pair of guards, traveled into the *Mutapa*.

The sign above the door read *pekurapwa*. Bel had suggested she learn Shona and Cassandra had absorbed the language on the way. The word meant 'medical space.' Iekanjika floated with her hand on a grip bar beside the door.

"If you're unaccustomed to death, you may wish to take a moment," Iekanjika said. "War does unpleasant things."

A sudden feeling of realness, of observable, measurable reality struck her then and she snaked her fingers into Bel's. He didn't make eye contact. His guilt was like a mathematical transform, changing everything about him in a very precise way, leaving nothing where it had been before. She sent tiny electrical micro-pulses in her fingers, a faint coded speech.

Can you do this? she signalled. *I have to see this, as mayor. I owe them that.*

Me too, he signalled back. This signalling had neither inflection nor tones, but she imagined the anguish in his voice as if he'd sounded it out. Sometimes her imagination was too strong. The door slid open, releasing the smell of antiseptics.

"The surgeon will answer any questions you have," she said. "We can speak later. I have additional guests who need tending."

Cassandra and Bel floated into the medical bay. Doctors and nurses staffed computer banks and medical screens, dressed in gray and white uniforms with the Bachwezi flag on their shoulders. Three gurneys displayed three corpses. The rightward one was complete, long and slender, dark skin broken in places to show fascia turning gray. She recognized the slack face: Ana Teresa Trujillo. Her skull was open, exposing a brain shiny with anomalous wiring.

A sturdier torso was strapped to the middle gurney. Some trauma had removed an arm and the head, but a fuzz of shiny wiring sprouted from the edges of the torn flesh of Martín Revilla's body. The Union had opened the skin and muscles of his arms and legs to reveal the pathways of wiring into the extremities.

The leftmost corpse, Edmer Vizcarra, was complete but perforated, as if struck by shrapnel from behind. Smooth dark skin ran into puckered volcanic landscapes of torn flesh with muscle and fascia erupting through sixty-five or sixty-six exit wounds. Her brain counted.

She hadn't known these dead *Homo quantus* well. They'd shared no confidences or discoveries, yet she knew their personalities, the calm equanimity engineered into them. She knew their love of quiet, the way they would have retired from many human interactions, the way others could itch at their thoughts, the way geometric patterns could elicit their delight, and most of all, she knew their curiosity, the powerful ache to *know*, to understand the workings of the cosmos. And all that was gone, lost now, and she didn't know how to deal with the ache she had.

Some kind of neurological override would have been needed to put these retiring and frightened people into the cockpits of small tactical fighters to face the mongrels in battle. Had they been terrified? She would have been. She had been, when she and Stills had faced the Scarecrow.

Cassandra alighted beside Edmer. From this angle, she could see all three of them, smell the pungent preservatives, trace the metallic wiring violating their bodies. One of the medical staff approached them hand over hand on the ceiling rungs. He was in his forties, temples speckled with gray. A name strip on his uniform read Binqose beside a caduceus. He handed her a data pad from its case on his belt.

"Major-General Iekanjika told me to share our findings," he said.

Cassandra flipped through the charts, the serological and genetic analyses, the anatomic sections, the penetrating radiation scans. The Union doctors had found obvious signs of immuno-suppression. The Union's relatively modest data processing tools didn't make conclusions apparent.

"Show us the raw data," she said.

The doctor regarded her doubtfully, but guided her to wall-mounted screens. She reconfigured them to display data at a density appropriate to her. Within a minute, arrays of raw MRI and x-ray measurements began flashing across the screens for the two *Homo quantus*. Axon-thin metal wiring had been laid along neural pathways without damaging any of the surrounding tissues. Fine, root-like metal fibers had heavily infiltrated the left temporal lobe, where language and social nuance were often processed. She and Bel suppressed those areas with polarized micro-currents of electricity to enter the savant state. But the nano-scale wiring wasn't connected to the electroplaques in the three corpses. Instead, they reached tiny nano-capacitors that had been inserted into the bodies. It looked like the Congregate had wired these three so that savant could be induced artificially. What had the Congregate been trying to do? The images also showed tiny computational devices in the crania, silver-shiny bulbous things.

She turned to the genomic analysis. The Union software could subtract out most of the three billion base pairs and thirty thousand genes that the *Homo quantus* shared with baseline humans. That left the *Homo quantus*-specific genes. She knew many of them; depending on the generation, there were only about a thousand additional genes to memorize. She asked Saint Matthew to communicate with the Union computer to subtract out the known *Homo quantus* genes. Everything looked normal. There were no mutations or additions to their genomes.

But that wasn't all that made the *Homo quantus* what they were. Bacterial microbiomes made up several kilos of every human's mass, living in many tissues. They varied by colony, planet, even continent, and the Union didn't know what bacterial genomes normally lived in the *Homo quantus*. Belisarius and Cassandra had to subtract out the *Homo quantus* microbiome genes from memory, checking one after the other. After all that subtraction, she had hundreds of genes she didn't recognize, all bacterial. Someone had also been modifying the neural microbiomes of the three *Homo quantus*.

"Del Casal could have done somatic cell modifications, but it would have taken time," Bel said. "He's an expert on microbiomes though. Maybe he thought that was faster."

"They wired electrical devices to the left temporal lobe. Were they inducing savant? Maybe they were counting on *Homo quantus* geometric thinking to give them an edge?"

"Or making them easier to control?" he said.

Cassandra floated to the displays where some of the chips taken from the three *Homo quantus* had been x-rayed. They were remarkably complex, too complex to easily understand. Brain-chip connections weren't a well-understood technology.

Does the Congregate have robotic fighters? she said in tiny electrical micro-pulses, her fingertips to Bel's palm.

Drone fighters, he answered in the same way. *But AI pilots aren't as good as human pilots in many ways though.*

Martin, Ana and Edmer had wires connecting to their sensory processing areas, she said. Naming them made something inside her twinge, made the corpses more like the living people who'd cried and argued with them and refused to flee the Garret. *But not higher perception or cognition. Why?*

For long seconds, Bel floated beside her as they absorbed scrolling and flipping data.

What could those chips do, Bel?

Doctor Binqose looked uncomfortable as Bel picked up one of the chips and examined it with fingers and eyes. She felt the faint shift in magnetic field around his hand; the millions of magnetosomes in the muscle cells of Bel's fingers probed at the chip magnetically.

A chip like this would have been dense and complex enough to carry an AI. Saint Matthew is platformed on something smaller and less sophisticated than this.

Why connect a Homo quantus to an AI?

She took the chip from him, feeling at it magnetically too. It was experientially rich; the micro-magnetic fields she made with her fingers felt layers of resistance that altered and pushed back at the gentle force she applied. But she didn't know what it did.

If we suppose the Banks and the Congregate continued to develop their AIs since Saint Matthew, she mused electronically, *where would they be now? They could have made fighter pilots good enough to beat the mongrels.*

If they had that, Stills' people wouldn't be chewing through Congregate squadrons.

They're not anymore, she signalled. *Stills' people are having a hard time and the difference is that the Congregate put our people into the cockpits. But not as we are. At all. Emotionally, temperamentally and intellectually we're completely unsuitable. We don't like loud noises. We don't like sudden movements. We don't like a lot of stimulus. We're exactly the wrong people to be pilots.*

Then it wasn't the people who made the difference, he signalled back. Her breath clouded around her as she processed all the possible meanings in his message before coming to a single one.

If you take away our personalities, our subjectivity, she returned, *what you have left is a massive processor, capable of analyzing and modelling multiple lines of data with classical or quantum logic.*

"And we come with a switch to turn us off," he said bitterly.

We've been built for generations to be capable of extinguishing our subjectivity, he continued in their electrical code through their fingers, *to stop being anyone. Our designers hoped our brains could be taken over by some impersonal intellect built out of our own thinking.*

So the Congregate wired them so that AIs could turn off their subjectivity and then use the brains as external processors, she signalled, *to make the AI even faster.*

They made them into pieces of a computer, Bel signalled. *And then they reinforced bone and organs and muscles, and then put them into fighter craft.*

Parasitism. That was all she could think to call it. She could think fast, very fast, but this was hard to process. She imagined an AI, like Saint Matthew, but a mean one, thinking independently, and using a biological brain for computational support. The bodies and brains of the *Homo quantus* had been objectified, turned into tools. It horrified her. She hoped that whatever the Congregate had done, it shut off the consciousness of the *Homo quantus* pilots. What if Martín could have felt it all? What if Ana Teresa could have seen everything, but had been trapped as a bystander at the end of her life? Cassandra tried to say something comforting to Bel or to herself, but the cruelty of it, the utter inhumanity of the people who had done this was hard to process.

This wasn't their fault, he signalled. *They should have come with us. They would have been safe. They might have been sad, but they wouldn't have had their bodies and minds violated like this. The hundred and fifty-five of them made a bad choice, but part of that mistake was built into them.*

Like your mistake, Bel, she answered, her eyes catching his before he could look away. She squeezed his hand and then took the other as well. *If they chose, even partly, because of how they'd been built, it's not all their fault Bel, or nor is what happened to the Hortus quantus.*

He pulled his hands free and drifted slowly away from her.

"They didn't know this would happen, Bel," she said.

The doctor looked on in confusion.

"The captives certainly regret what they chose," she said, pushing off to float nearer.

He drew his hands close to his chest, but she reached and took them in her own. Out of their joined momentum, they began to rotate slowly, unevenly, but together.

"Can you forgive, Bel?"

CHAPTER FOURTEEN

April, 2515

"As far as I can tell, these *Homo quantus* have the same intellectual abilities as Arjona and Mejía," Del Casal said.

They were in the main labs of the Ministry of Intelligence building. The geneticist still wore detention orange, but was groomed, speaking with guarded confidence, and no small measure of his natural arrogance. Rivard's team read every note, measurement, consultation and medical reference Del Casal made. He was focused on the *Homo quantus,* but he'd also been cross-referencing all known information in the Congregate libraries on the *Homo eridanus,* the Numen, the Puppets and some bio-engineering dead-ends within the Ummah. Despite the generalized restrictions on the genetic engineering of humanity, the Congregate knew many things that were new to Del Casal. AIs estimated his actual useful work as ten to twelve hours a day, before he took to pretending to work, like digging into Congregate research files. Bareilles guessed he was learning their bioengineering secrets or researching some way to escape.

"They can process all the same inputs, whether in classical

bits or qubits," Del Casal continued. He walked through a vast hologram as he spoke, a representation of the *Homo quantus* brain. "Their electroplaques and the wiring in their neural systems mostly work, enough to send data to their brains. But the *Homo quantus* access to quantum probabilities and senses doesn't exist in your subjects."

"You're not telling me you can fix them," Bareilles said.

"They've been engineered to a complexity that's difficult to follow, using sciences I've not mastered. If you want them to go into the fugue, you need to add some physicists to the team, maybe a lot of them."

Even with most of the notes and records from the *Homo quantus* project, the best Congregate engineers couldn't figure out the magical new interactions that had led from common humanity to Arjona and Mejía.

"You want them for war," Del Casal said. "They aren't suited for it. In the Garret they were protected and sheltered and allowed to think abstract thoughts on someone else's budget. Arjona only became a useful criminal because he spent time in the real world, alone, unprotected. You can't replicate environment."

"I want these *Homo quantus* in combat," she said. "I need them to be better than the mongrels."

"What?"

"The Union has recruited *Homo eridanus* pilots. We offered more money, but they've gone to the Union to fly the inflaton fighters. They're doing damage."

"So why aren't you making your own inflaton fighters, so you can offer those to the mongrels?"

"It's being worked on," she said, leaning forward, "but we can do two things at once and I want my *Homo quantus* to be militarily useful."

"It's temperament. In getting these intellectual abilities, the *Homo quantus* lost something, normal tolerances for stresses."

"So change their temperament."

His face betrayed his frustration again. She didn't need a personality profile to tell her he was used to being smarter than everyone else, that it galled him to take orders from an intellectual inferior.

"What do you know of the Second Bushido?" she said.

He frowned, perhaps weighing his answer.

"Not as much as I would like," he said.

"Tell."

The poker-faced gambler wasn't trying to hide any of his loathing.

"Prosthetic AIs," he said, "grown and doing their machine learning while wired to human brains. Sounds like more trouble than they're worth. They might as well build machines if that's what they wanted."

"The Second Bushido fighters are the elite special forces pilots of the Anglo-Spanish Plutocracy. That's what I want."

"Then you require a mechanic."

"The problem of the Second Bushido is not mechanical. Neither is the problem of the *Homo quantus*."

He crossed his arms.

"The Second Bushido fighters solve a very narrow optimization problem," he said. "The AIs have speed, processing power and pattern recognition, but lack the creativity and judgment of human pilots. For the most part, human brains are too slow to handle the fastest AIs; and their neurologies don't adapt to the new pathways required of the partnership with AIs. Only pre-adult brains have the kind of plasticity required. So the Banks grew AIs and humans together in a way that would meet the problem halfway. They succeeded, but could only do so within the conceptual framework of some weird warrior philosophy – the neo-Bushido code. The fighters work, but man and machine exist in some semi-fantastical perceptual world."

"Have you examined Second Bushido fighters?"

"I've seen schematics. Blueprints. Neurological training substrate patterns."

"Their fanciful thinking is a bit exaggerated. The only way to weld human and AI neurology in this case was to run human thinking along different patterns. But they work. We've captured some and reverse-engineered them."

"So make yourselves some."

"We don't engineer Congregate citizens," she said. "There are lines of human dignity we don't cross."

His arms seemed to tighten over his chest. He surely had thoughts about Congregate views on human dignity.

"Even if we wanted to," she said, "they're grown from birth. It takes fifteen to twenty years to grow a Second Bushido fighter pilot. My needs are more pressing."

"Then capture some more *Homo quantus*," he said in frustration. "These are good for nothing. The neurological structures needed to enter the fugue are also grown from birth. Biology is slow nanotech."

"What if you wired some parts of the *Homo quantus* brain electronically? Your work at the Lanoix Casino was very subtle molecular-level inorganic engineering. You could find a way to run supplementary neural wiring in *Homo quantus* brains."

Del Casal nodded, but her emotion-reading AIs detected the resentment and resistance in his facial muscles.

"Try," she said. At the door, she paused. "And don't fail."

The Scarecrow waited in the hallway. She heard the faint humming first, the weird tune that continued uninterrupted as she began to speak with her deathly voice. "Del Casal is a difficult tool."

"In the right hands, all tools do their job," Bareilles said.

The mechanical feet began their thumping walk, arms swung with whirring, hinge and machine sounds for her benefit. Scarecrow anatomy was so sophisticated that except for weaponry, their hulking movements could be unsettlingly quiet. They put on a show; they made themselves heard for the effect it had on their audiences. Bareilles didn't know why this Scarecrow performed for her; she'd worked too long with Scarecrows to be affected.

"You've not worked with the little saints before?" the Scarecrow said. When she said *petits saints*, there was an undertone of endearment.

Bareilles followed. "Not worked, no."

"But you know them?" the Scarecrow pressed.

"Obviously. I met some in school. *Un petit saint* was born to my family."

"A blessing."

The Epsilon Indi Scarecrow had not approached topics with such elliptical tediousness.

"Am I to work with a *petit saint* now?" Bareilles asked finally.

"Your work is straying into interestingly new ethical areas," the Scarecrow said. "A conversation, or several, are warranted."

The Scarecrow led them through polished corridors to a solarium in the upper levels with a wide view of rippling, ochre clouds above them. Many tables had been set with white linen and fine silverware, but only two people sat here. A short man leaned on the back of a chair, looking out the window. Another, in uniform, stood near him. The Scarecrow stopped. Her camera lenses looked down at Bareilles.

"This is your conversation, colonel."

Her test more like it. She walked to the window and the small man.

"*Bonjour, petit saint,*" she said softly.

He turned. His eyes were slanted, across a flattened nasal bridge over the small chin and mouth associated with Downs syndrome. He wore a fine suit and maroon tie with an elaborate bow typical of this year's high-house Venusian fashion. He regarded her without recognition, but she knew him. Damn the Scarecrow and her games.

"Are you Luc," she said, "of the House of Ghosts?" She smiled, to not frighten him. She knew she could be intimidating.

"*Le manoir des esprits,*" he said, the peacetime name of the house.

"I'm from the House of Spirits too," she said. "I think you're my cousin. I'm Thélise à Jean à Simon."

He began to smile.

"I'm Luc à Floriane à Simon!" he said, naming his geneology to their grandfather.

"I'm very pleased to meet you, *cousin,*" she said, offering a hand. He closed the distance and hugged her. She held him, resting her chin on the top of his head. When he let go, she said "I think I saw you once, when I was just a child and you were a teenager. Some party at *grand-père's* palace. You played with me. With your sister, Denise."

"I don't remember," he said, but it didn't seem to bother him. He looked briefly at the man in the civil service uniform beside him, his assistant, but didn't seem to be expecting an answer.

"And now you have a big job," she said.

He did. In adulthood, many of the Downs syndrome children occupied the posts of counsellors, partly ceremonial, but mostly quite real. Downs syndrome children weren't born anywhere else in civilization, as far as Bareilles knew. The Ummah, the Middle Kingdom and the Plutocracy aborted fetuses with any abnormalities. In the Congregate, Downs syndrome children were born at their natural rate, perhaps one in a thousand. For the last two hundred and fifty years, they'd been given places of honor in society because they were so central to the soul of the Congregate.

The Congregate might never have found the first permanent wormhole of the Axis Mundi network, might never have been born, if not for a single family's choice to keep their Downs syndrome child. That child had revealed the soul of the *colonistes* before they'd become the Congregate, and it hadn't been a pretty sight. He'd eventually become the brother of the first *présidente* of the Congregate at its birth. Every Downs syndrome child reminded the Congregate that their own lack of kindness had almost aborted their own empire.

The Congregate understood that fate or chance had given them knowledge of a disaster averted. They kept all their Downs syndrome children, finding places of importance in their society as *les petits saints*, as the conscience of empire, as reminders of empathy. They could be approached for clemency or assistance by any citizen of the Congregate. Several *petits saints* sat on the Praesidium, and within the civil and military services, they were consulted on policies. Matters became more complex with foreigners and matters of security or war, where the values of kindness and survival did not always mix well.

"I used to fly all over Venus," he said in his tumbling, slightly slurred French, "but now I just visit with the Ministry of Intelligence."

"How long have you been with the ministry?"

Luc turned to his assistant, who said "About three months, *monsieur.*"

The same amount of time she'd been back at Venus, the same amount of time the *Homo quantus* had been under study. It wasn't a coincidence that a *petit saint* had been attached to this project, nor that of all the ones they might have assigned, it turned out to be her cousin. The Scarecrow engineered the circumstances of her test.

"Let's sit, Luc," she said.

Her cousin's assistant brought them fresh juices. They talked about family, about what they could remember of their grandparents, of uncles and aunts. At a certain point, she signalled for the assistant to recede. He wandered to the other side of the solarium.

"I'm glad you're here, Luc," she said, moving her chair closer.

"Me too."

"My job has been a lot of time among foreigners, among enemies."

Luc's smile faded. "War isn't good."

"In war we have to hit our enemies, to make them want to stop fighting."

He nodded soberly.

"It isn't just big warships in space," she said. "That's not the kind of war I do. That's the kind of war *oncle* Gérard does, or my sister Héliade."

"I know *oncle* Gérard."

"I'll introduce you to my sister someday," she said and Luc smiled. "My kind of war is sneaking in to hurt the enemy and stopping people from sneaking in to hurt us."

"Do you ever hurt people who aren't the enemy?" he asked.

"I don't think I have," she said. "But I'm struggling with something new. Our enemies aren't just making weapons out of metal anymore. They've started making weapons out of their children."

The look on Luc's face became one of horror. "What do you mean?"

"Our enemies changed their children, making them different, so that they would fight better, or fight differently," she said. "The mongrels are an example."

"The fish people don't look anything like us anymore."

"The mongrels stopped being human like us so that they could live underwater. But they're very good pilots and we use them to fight."

"We give them money and they fight," Luc said. "That's not bad."

"We didn't change them," Bareilles said. "But some of the Banks changed other children, trying to make them smarter, so they outsmart our defenses. That's what started this war. One of their human weapons got through our defenses because he'd been built and designed to fight us, from the time he was just a fertilized egg. They have different childhoods and they want different things. Sometimes they're peaceful, but the Banks and others can use them as weapons."

"Can you save them?" Luc asked.

"I don't know. They're grown up weapons now, even when they're just sitting quietly. We don't know when they'll do something to hurt the Congregate.

"What are you going to do?" Luc asked.

"I don't know. We're studying them right now. You know how a robot or computer can be reprogrammed? I want to find a way to do that to these people. I want to take the programming the Banks put in these people and turn it so that the weapons go back to hit the Banks."

"What do they want?" Luc said.

"I don't know," she said. "They say they want to be quiet, but when police catch a criminal, the criminal says they'll behave, and then they don't."

Luc wouldn't meet her eyes. He sipped his juice pensively and smacked his lips.

"You want to turn them around," he said.

"If I can."

"Then, what the Banks tried to throw at us hits them."

"Yes."

"But it's people."

"Yes, people who've been changed, to sometimes be quiet, and sometimes hurt whatever they're pointed at," she said.

"I like to be quiet."

She put her hand on his. "I know, *cousin.*"

"Are there more children being changed?" he asked. "Where are the children?"

"I think that these the weapons got away from the Banks, so now the Banks are going to make more and more, and be more careful with the people they turn into weapons, so that they don't run away, so that they attack us."

"Can you stop them?"

She shook her head. "I can't stop the Banks from turning people into weapons."

"What are we going to do?" Luc asked.

"I don't know."

"I want to meet these people," he said.

"I'll arrange it."

He smiled at her. "I'm happy you're here. I want to see you again."

CHAPTER FIFTEEN

August, 2515

Manafwa was the inner of two gas giants in the Bachwezi system. Belisarius watched its translucent blue methane clouds three hundred thousand kilometers below. They turned with deceptive calm. Manafwa's hot core churned the entire atmosphere into convection cells that mixed everything to near-featurelessness. When Belisarius adjusted his augmented eyes to catch infrared and ultraviolet, the wind streams appeared in blurred brushstrokes, converging on a south polar double storm system. Beautiful. Self-organizing. Logical.

Manafwa had captured dozens of moons, four of them sizable iron-nickel nuggets dozens of kilometers in diameter. In the distance, his telescoped vision could make out solar-powered mining and smelting operations on the nearest moon. All around the lunar orbits furious construction was happening in new shipyards, factories and orbital fortifications.

General Rudo had set up her military headquarters here, rather than at the capital at Bachwezi or its moon habitat Kitara. The Manafwa yards didn't need Rudo here so

Belisarius guessed that she headquartered here because of continuing assassination dangers.

The local magnetic field altered as Cassandra floated near and touched his arm. She watched the fluid dynamic artistry below, as he returned his visual senses to normal. False colors faded. Storms melted into the methane haze. The sounds in the room changed too. Voices impinged on the fragile, temporary tranquility he'd constructed: Anglo-Spanish, smatterings of Shona, and the strange dialect of *français* 8.3 that had evolved in the forty-year isolation of the Sixth Expeditionary. When the voices quieted, he rotated to face the room. General Rudo was floating in after her bodyguards. Some of the other guests began floating to seats.

Two Puppet representatives, Gates-15 and Rosalie Johns-10 huddled with a small bishop Belisarius had seen several times on the news in the Free City, Grassie-6. Rosalie, his friend once, eyed him furtively. It was unlikely she was his friend anymore. Three Bank representatives formed a similar cluster, their external AI and sensory augmentation shining against brown skin. Through his electroplaques, Belisarius felt the gentle white noise of computation emitting faintly in the EM. Iekanjika followed Rudo into the stateroom, her eyes sweeping the attendees with neutral evaluation, not lingering on Belisarius any more than on anyone else, although he saw her visual scan dip to the service band on his wrist that contained Saint Matthew.

Rudo made her way around the room, greeting each guest. A politician from Bachwezi followed, shaking hands. He was introduced as Foreign Minister Akuffo, Rudo's cabinet colleague. Rudo had the barest of smiles for Belisarius before she was introduced to Cassandra and Saint Matthew. When she came to the Bank representatives, four were introduced instead of three. They apparently carried an AI, one important enough to be introduced as a person. She sat at the head of the table. In the months since Belisarius had last seen Rudo, she'd aged. The sixty-two year old woman now looked her years, her black hair gone to gray, wrinkles etching deep into dark skin, her expression more stately and commanding. The uncertain, overcompensating twenty-two year old woman he'd met in the past, the one who'd ordered him beaten, was there too, but leavened with something more substantial.

Belisarius took a spot beside Rosalie, across from the Bank representatives. The foreign minister strapped into the seat beside Cassandra's and smiled amiably. A hologram appeared over one of the empty seats, outlining a dark volume into which part of an alien, gilled face drifted off center. Belisarius half-expected one of the Bank officials to speak first, as if this were their meeting. He didn't expect that Bank analysts put too much faith in the Union rebellion. He wouldn't have. And yet, here the Banks sat, waiting for the diminutive general of a tiny nation to speak. Rudo's eyes moved from face to face and she gradually constructed on her own a tight smile, straining at humor.

"Common enemies make for strange... acquaintances." she said.

Belisarius eyed the Bank officials. Gillbard carried an admiral's rank and seemed to be the highest-ranking one, but Luisa Pacheco, some flavor of technical advisor, spoke first.

"The Banks of the Anglo-Spanish Plutocracy see themselves as interested parties, General," she said, "and have empowered the four of us to discuss economic, military and political implications with great frankness."

"I am similarly empowered by the Episcopal Conclave of the Theocracy," the Puppet bishop said, thrusting out his jaw. A strap under his chin kept his mitre from floating away. Rudo maintained her precise smile and then looked to Belisarius.

"The *Homo quantus* came for information," Cassandra said.

"Hopefully there's more than information in the conversation," Rudo said. "The *Homo quantus* pose a threat to all of us."

Belisarius would have objected, but no one would believe him. The legend of the *Homo quantus* had obviously grown large. Attempting to turn the attention away, Belisarius gestured to Stills.

"Don't look at me," Stills said in his mechanical monotone. "The mongrels don't got an economy, politics or a military." The tone his translator inserted into his voice suggested he wasn't finished. The table waited as his dark fish face left the camera view and his blubbery arm came into view, a single finger extended.

"Of common interest is the weaponization of the *Homo quantus* by the Congregate," Rudo said. "Some mix of genetic and electronic augments are flying combat missions. We don't know if *Homo quantus* assets have been deployed to other uses by the Congregate, but their presence in a theatre of war poses a risk we can't yet quantify."

The general's look went to the Bank officials rather than Belisarius and Cassandra.

"The *Homo quantus* were never meant to be front-line combatants," Pacheco said. "The project designed them to be strategists, tacticians and forecasters. Our first concern is assuring the safety of the other *Homo quantus* and the immediate end of Congregate violations of our licences and patents, ideally by the rescue of the captive *Homo quantus*."

That was very interesting. A rescue. If the Banks moved directly against the Congregate, it might force even the other patron nations to choose sides. There had never been a real war between the patrons; their cold war smouldered in small flames here and there, in plausibly deniable skirmishes and client nation proxy battles.

"Failing that?" Iekanjika said.

Pacheco made a gesture of indecision.

"For less ideal circumstances, there are less ideal solutions," Admiral Gillbard said.

"We don't know where the captive *Homo quantus* are," Belisarius said.

"They're being held at one of the Ministry of Intelligence globes in the clouds of Venus," Gillbard said.

Cassandra met Belisarius' eyes, but there was no hope in them; her expression mirrored his inner turmoil. Despite all that she'd said about blame and choices, his choices had hurt his people. He'd brought suffering to them.

"We have more details," the admiral said, "but they would need to be revealed in a smaller meeting." None of the Bank representatives looked at the Puppets, although Gillbard might have meant Stills.

"We're part of this," Grassie-6 said. "We have more than a stake. The Congregate will regret making enemies of the Puppets."

Iekanjika quirked an eyebrow. Belisarius didn't know Iekanjika to ever waste time. He didn't understand why the Puppets might be here. On the surface, they had nothing to offer the Union, or anyone.

"How do you hope this matters to the table?" Gillbard said.

"We're going to send a Puppet assault force to Venus, to rescue a person of great importance to us," Grassie-6 said without a hint of irony or doubt. "Antonio Del Casal, a genetic engineer, was helping us address serious medical concerns in the Puppet theocracies. Congregate agents stole him from the Free City."

"We saw the Congregate take the geneticist," the third Bank official said, the Teixiera woman, "although at the time we didn't know his identity or significance. Since then, Bank intelligence operatives in the Venusian cloud cities have co-located Del Casal with the *Homo quantus*. He's an extraordinary geneticist."

"Extraordinary enough to try to reverse engineer the *Homo quantus,* perhaps," Gillbard said.

"He's starting from scratch?" Rudo said.

"We fled with the *Homo quantus* in a hurry. There was no time to erase the backups," Belisarius said. "And to get Del Casal to help us, I offered him a chance to look at my biology."

"And because you violated your NDA around your IP, he may have a chance to provide assistance to the Congregate," Gillbard said angrily.

"I'm not IP," Belisarius said. "This is my body."

"You have a poor understanding of the law," Pacheco said.

"None of the captured *Homo quantus* are capable of entering the fugue," Cassandra said.

"Could he fix them?" Iekanjika said. "Could he make those *Homo quantus* fully functional?"

"The resources of the *Homo quantus* project couldn't," Belisarius said.

"The project ran within some ethical guidelines," Teixiera said with a disturbing silkiness in her voice "And the project wasn't rushing to product with manuals and prototypes in front of them."

"The Congregate are strongly resistant to genetic engineering," Rudo said.

"With respect, General," Gillbard said, "they were until you took away the Freya Axis. Their House names have changed. They've lowered the ensign of the House of Saints and raised the standard of the House of Styx for the first time in sixty years. Their wartime criminal, security and civil codes now apply."

"Our own autopsies of *Homo quantus* pilots were revealing," Teixiera said, her long fingers stroking her jawline.

"How many have they killed?" Cassandra demanded.

"The Congregate aren't relying strictly on genetic engineering," the risk analyst said. "They're using our AI tech and internal nano-wiring to supplement the neurological pieces that aren't functional."

"AIs?" Belisarius said, looking with a queasy horror at the bulbous metallic lumps growing out of the heads of both Gillbard and Pacheco. His feelings were illogical. He'd been wired and built and designed as much as they, probably more, but all of the changes to Belisarius and Cassandra and the *Homo quantus* were biological.

"You think they're achieving the fugue by supplementing with AIs?" Belisarius said.

"We don't know what they're achieving," Gillbard said. "The *Homo quantus* aren't the only path we've been investing in to develop superior perceptions in humanity. We know you're carrying a prototype of ours, Mister Arjona."

Belisarius kept his eyes on the Bank admiral, but his hand brushed the service band. After a moment, the hologram of Saint Matthew appeared, rendered in the scultped limestone style of pre-contact Mayan.

"He chose to leave," Belisarius said.

"That's not something he can choose," the admiral said, "nor is it something you can possess, under Plutocracy law, but everything is negotiable."

"No one possesses me," Saint Matthew said.

"Our primary concern for the rest of the *Homo quantus* is

their safety" Gillbard said. "We have the resources to set up a new Garret almost anywhere you want, with all the resources you want, so that you can return to lives of study and peace. Even your... Saint Matthew can negotiate new licensing terms."

Beside Gillbard's head, on the side where the chrome-reflective dome emerged, a hologram appeared, lit only in yellow light, its features those of a hairless, androgynous human head.

"That's your new general artificial intelligence," Belisarius said.

"Yes, the Aleph Class AI, like your AI but without the instabilities," Gillbard said "and integrable with human neurology. We can lease you one if you want. Yours is clearly broken."

"No thank you," Belisarius said.

Gillbard's shrug was insouciant. He and the AI holographic face looked to Rudo, but she gave no encouragement. Iekanjika had already shown herself to be wary of Saint Matthew's capabilities. A hungering Bank AI wouldn't get a warmer welcome.

Teixiera still watched Belisarius and Cassandra. "We've been running projections since the break-out of the Puppet Axis," the risk analyst said. "No model has shown the Congregate ever relenting in their pursuit of the *Homo quantus*. They can't afford to, given your role in all of this. We're responsible for the *Homo quantus* and we'll protect you, but that needs to start soon. We're massing Bank naval forces in Epsilon Indi, but so is the Congregate. We can pick up the hidden *Homo quantus* and we can fend off anti-matter warheads, but we can't do both for long, and doing it at the same time is risky."

"We're safe," Cassandra said. "We're concerned about the *Homo quantus* in captivity."

"The problems are related," Grassie-6 said in his clumsy

Anglo-Spanish. He switched to his native Anglo patois. "Antonio Del Casal needs to be safely among the Puppets. We will protect him and keep him from ever falling into the clutches of the Congregate."

"You couldn't this time," Pacheco said dryly.

The little bishop's pink cheeks flushed in blotches. "Had we known he was a target of the Congregate, he would have been as secure as the divine themselves. We know how to protect what's ours. Their interest in him came without warning."

Teixiera's expression shifted, the geometry of the scarlet tattoo lines on her bare scalp and forehead became eloquently dubious.

"Puppet troopers are willing to break Del Casal out of wherever he is in the clouds of Venus," Grassie-6 said, pointing at Iekanjika emphatically. "That will stop part of your problem."

Cassandra leaned around Belisarius to look at the bishop. "In your rickety ships? Against Congregate dreadnoughts?"

"I wouldn't gamble on the Puppet navy," Belisarius said, "and under normal circumstances, I wouldn't bet on the typical Puppet, but when they sense some danger to the Numen, Puppet troopers can be vicious."

"We're prepared to send in a war Numen," Grassie-6 said.

Cassandra was about to ask, but Belisarius signalled her to wait with the faintest of electrical discharges from his fingertips. She wouldn't like the answer and whatever the Puppet plan, it wasn't the rate limiting step.

"It doesn't matter that the problems are related or not," Belisarius said to the Puppets. "Venus is Venus. It's more fortified than any Axis. The bulk of the planet and the immensity of atmosphere not only shield it from covert entry, but we literally have no way to know where anything is. It doesn't have a fixed geography. Like every other part of Venus, the Ministry of Intelligence follows the winds. We wouldn't even know which altitude to begin searching for it."

"That's not entirely true," Gillbard said. "We have, with extreme difficulty, placed some agents within Venusian society. We know where the Ministry of Intelligence globes are."

"Are you able to move weapons through customs?" Belisarius said. "Can you get drones through the defense net? Are you able to get warships into any orbit? It not, this conversation is academic."

"No one thought anyone could get the Sixth Expeditionary Force through the Puppet Axis," Rudo said. "And yet..."

"I lived in the Puppet Free City for years. I knew the Puppets, their passions, their blind spots."

"Are you saying the Congregate has none of these things?" Rudo said.

"We're not dealing with a wormhole with public access," Belisarius said. "A Ministry of Intelligence globe is a fortification. None of the *Homo quantus,* even me, were ever successful military analysts."

"We didn't hire a military strategist to get the Expeditionary Force across the Puppet Axis," Rudo said. "We hired a con man. A magician. Your people need your magic as much as mine do."

"Nothing but the Plutocracy's entry into the war will be any help to you," Belisarius said. "If you're not clear on that, you're in trouble. Cut a deal with the Banks and save yourselves."

"We didn't come through all of this to trade one yoke for another," Rudo said.

"Neither did we," Cassandra said.

"The captive *Homo quantus* are not the only ones paying for your freedom, Arjona," Gillbard said. "The Union will pay and the shareholders of the Banks will pay when the Congregate perfects its own *Homo quantus* technology."

Belisarius unstrapped himself from his seat.

"The Banks made the *Homo quantus* to do exactly what they're doing," Belisarius said. "The Banks made hard AIs as weapons. It sounds to me like you're reaping what you sowed."

CHAPTER SIXTEEN

The Trial of Timmy Hill-9
Parish Notes

TIMOTHY HILL-9 WAS borned into the Hill family in Hill Town, and was immunologically compatible with both the Hill and Carter families. At age twelve, Timmy started his puberty with the right symptoms. On testing, I found he properly saw, felt and smelled the Numen of Hill Town (Cindy Hill, Bethany Hill, Roger Hill, and Samantha Hill, hallowed be their names, I love you) with no special features. Timmy was entered into normal schooling to be a welder. At fourteen, Timmy was brain-chipped with a normal worker one and at fifteen, Timmy began to see visions. I conducted standard scriptural tests for vision orthodoxy (the Blackmore test, the Triple Color test, and the Hose test, but not strapping). Timmy's visions were unconsistent to the canon, even after deepish searches into the *The Book of Unverified Notes*. Timmy was punished according to *The Book of Assessments* and put into corrective school. Timmy kept having visions, abstract images with nothing to do with the Numen. His chip was removed and destroyed and a new one put in, but the visions didn't stop. At age seventeen, following procedures in the *Book of Assessments*, Timmy was tried for thinking of heresy and nonsense, and sentenced to death by stoning. A small stoning festival was set up. Cindy Hill and Roger Hill, hallowed be their names, I love you, were wheeled out so it was a wonderful day.

Dennis Hill-3, Priest
Parish of Hill Town

ROSALIE JOHNS-10 FLOATED in the back cabin of the Puppet warship *All the Blackmores Punch Hard*. Although the cabin was pressurized, she wore her vacuum suit. This was a special communion for her, so none of the other envious Puppets around her would be allowed to smell His Holiness Lester. The War Numen was safe and secure and really strong inside his battle cage and hidden by the curtains behind the shock-proof glass. A frisson of anticipation tickled up her spine.

Bishop Grassie-6 attached the hose to her helmet. She already breathed deep and heavy in anticipation. Her bodyguard Jill floated near and watched Rosie's face with eager trepidation. Jimbo had somehow squirmed just behind Jill and steadied himself by holding onto her shoulders. He watched Rosie's face with fearless envy. Idiot.

Rosie's visions were getting stronger. Her visions had been tested multiple times and had been the subject of a study during her time in the seminary. A couple of times she'd come close to being kicked out of the seminary or to being tried for them, but some of the bishops, Grassie-6 included, had been waiting to see what came of her visions. Until she was convicted of heresy or nonsense, the Puppet warriors and troopers treated her as a sort of religious talisman, a priest with one eye seeing another world.

There were no Numen in her visions, no odor of the immaculate, no feeling of the consecrated, and that was the problem. By definition, visions without the holy were profane, false images and knowledges meant to draw the faithful away from the Numen and into the absence. Some of the examining bishops wondered if she might be seeing the souls of the Numen. Others thought the nature of the Puppet Axis was being revealed to her, although her drawings didn't mean anything to anyone. Some of the doctors looked to see if she had an enzyme or neurotransmitter loose somewhere. And until told not to, the watching Puppets thought she was special, possibly oracular, hopefully lucky, probably not heretical.

Bishop Grassie-6 turned the spigot and air flowed through the two channels of the hose. Stale, hot air began to fill her helmet, rich with the scent of old sweat and unwashed body, laced with the tang of urine and the pungent rankness of feces. Air from her own helmet and suit pumped outward, to the Numen's War Cage. She and she alone shared air now with His Holiness Lester.

She sighed as a feeling of overwhelming connection stole over her, a contact with something larger than herself. She shrank to insignificance in the face of an immense, cosmic truth. At the same time, she grew large and important, because *she* was connected to it, through Lester, blessed be his name. She may have released a groan of spiritual satisfaction, a kind of sacred ecstasy. She controlled her journey though. She could think in this connected world in ways other Puppets could not. The tide of divinity sometimes just swept the workers, the warriors and the servants away, but priests could hold against it to find new truths. Jimbo slapped his hands excitedly on Jill's shoulders, beside himself just from seeing Rosie's communion.

Rosie's eyes widened, painfully, with unblinking dryness as the powerful, beautiful taste of the Numen pulled her along in an alien dreamscape. The colors were wrong, nonsensical. Light didn't shine into her eyes; it was already inside them, behind tightly squeezed lids. Pale greens shifted to somber reds or watery blues, switching from second to second, struggling to emerge from a gray mist. Shapes hid in that mist, like great lumbering animals, but seen only through impressions. They weren't really animals. She knew from other dream trips with the Numen that her thoughts made patterns. Oracular priests received something too large and sublime to understand, so the Puppets translated it down to something they could hold onto, like holding on to just a snippet of a song.

There was so much to apprehend, but her arms were too small, her mind too humble. And the world squeezed her. A claustrophobia made her heart thump, as it had when tied up as a child for training, when it was so tight it was hard to breathe. She didn't panic, because she knew the knots were as tight as they needed to be to teach little Rosie a lesson. She didn't panic because little Rosie had known that she could be the Good Boy. But there was something in the grayness; looking upon it stoked up fleeting, alien fears.

Puppets knew only one real fear: the absence, the unique Puppet terror of being away from the Numen. Others were just shadows of the absence. That was why this fear of being lost came to worm beneath her experience and confidence. It wasn't a fear she knew how to handle. She translated it into her kind of fear, a fear of being in the absence and not being able to find her way back to divinity.

Shapes in the gray shadows, outlined in uncertain, stippled

light, made no sense to her and she heard her own voice in her ears, her voice yelling into her helmet, saying nonsense. She opened her eyes. Jimbo cowered behind Jill, hugging her neck, staring wide-eyed at Rosie, no envy in his eyes at all. Cold, dry air blew into her helmet, flushing out the taste of Numen, but Lester permeated her body now, her soul, and would until the experience decayed. The visions weren't going away. Even with open eyes she saw the shapes, the strange architecture overlaid on the inside of the bay of the war ship. And she cried because she didn't know what it was happening to her and the idea of speaking heresy and nonsense terrified her as much as the visions.

CHAPTER SEVENTEEN

IEKANJIKA HAD GIVEN her and Bel a small suite. The right angles and gray plastic walls of their suite here felt cramped and uninviting compared to the rolling hills they'd carved out of the ice of the Garret, but it was an improvement on the conditions in the freighters with the other *Homo quantus* refugees. She let herself feel those unpleasant thoughts, even a bit of guilt. In part she might owe it to the other *Homo quantus* as the mayor. She allowed the unpleasant feelings too in part because of Bel. He let himself or made himself feel all the guilt, earned or unearned, for what happened to the *Homo quantus* and the *Hortus quantus*. She still took some cues from him, but that had to stop. She'd learned so much since leaving the Garret, about the wide world, about herself, that she sometimes felt she was handling things better than Bel.

In the sleep sack next to her, he had a distant, thinking stare, as if disengaged from the here and now. She doubted he was thinking healthy thoughts like new theories of space-time geometry. Unseeing *Homo quantus* eyes could examine the past with perfect memory and every blink could flicker the torn bodies of Martín, Ana Teresa, and Edmer into view. Like a nightmare. More than enough reason not to blink.

The tearing of their bodies, by Stills' pilots, by imbalanced accelerations and explosions and shrapnel felt like an accident, a downstream consequence of a far greater violence. Their bodies had been violated by wires, their skulls invaded by AIs, their pensive, pacifist personalities disengaged, like Bel's eyes while he thought. It was like the Congregate engineers had illustrated a fully complete and self-consistent theory of bodily violations and it was hard to stop thinking about it. Her brain was very good at visualizing space-time configurations in four, six and even seven dimensions. The footpaths of electronic invasions in the corpses in three dimensions was so childishly easy that left on its own, her brain began to optimize design, finding more efficient ways for Congregate engineers to have enslaved her dead cousins.

Someone knocked at the door. She and Bel looked at one another questioningly and then began unzipping their sleep sacks.

"Should we be worried?" she whispered to Bel at the door.

"The Banks want us, but we're worth more to them cooperating than not."

"That's not reassuring, Bel."

The knocking sounded again, impatient. Cassandra unlocked it and pressed the release to slide it open. Two Puppets floated in the hallways, beyond the two Union MPs who'd been guarding their room. Coulibaly was there too, one of Iekanjika's staff.

"The Puppets wanted to see you," Coulibaly said. "The major-general didn't know if you'd want to see them or not."

Cassandra's first reaction was just to close the door. She didn't care about the mad wants of the Puppets, but the woman, Rosalie, had a look of hopefulness. The bishop was with her, with his tall green and gold hat.

"Rosalie," Bel said. Cassandra didn't know what emotion colored the way he said her name.

"Hi, boss," she said with a tentative smile. "You, uh, you said to tell you if I ever had more of the dreams."

"Come in, Rosalie," he said. He paused one point one seconds, looking over the bishop. "Come in, Your Grace."

Coulibaly appeared uncertain about something in the hallway.

"There isn't much room in here, lieutenant," Bel said, "but I imagine that you have orders."

Coulibaly floated to the doorway and held herself pointedly there so that it didn't close.

"What dreams, Rosie?" Bel said, smiling kindly.

The Puppet woman drew folded papers out of a suit pocket.

"You burned reaction mass on your way here to transport paper?" Cassandra asked.

"No one will intercept the transmission," Bel said wryly.

"The Numen themselves enjoyed paper and pencil," the bishop said, adjusting his hat. "We follow their example."

"I like to draw," Rosalie said.

Cassandra didn't chase the flaws in their reasoning. Rosalie unfolded the pages. The abstract drawings didn't mean anything to her. She needed only a glimpse for her brain to render the images in her thoughts, giving a dimensionality absent in the lead lines on paper. She visualized in three, four, five dimensions, looking for patterns. Bel examined the papers, holding each one so that for a brief moment Cassandra could also see and memorize each. They were all drawings that looked vaguely similar to solutions to space-time structure theories that Cassandra had worked on, but ones that had no physical meaning, not representing anything that could really exist. But vaguely similar wasn't enough. *Homo quantus* pattern recognition had been amplified so she had to be suspicious of similarities.

"What is this?" Cassandra said.

"Rosie has strange dreams sometimes," Bel said, "since puberty."

"That's when I could first taste and smell divinity," Rosalie added helpfully.

"All Puppets have dreams and nightmares," Grassie-6 said. "The dreams of priests can be quite potent. Hers are different. Mister Arjona has looked at them before, but perhaps never with a tongue free to speak. We're under far different conditions than when you lived in the Free City, Mister Arjona. Can you tell us what this is? Are the Numen giving us new technology through her dreams? Weapons? Propulsion? Induced wormhole tech? Maybe coordinates to other Axes?"

Bel gently folded the papers and pressed them into Rosalie's hands.

"Are you able to send me the chip recordings?" Bel said.

The Puppet woman nodded and started manipulating a service band on her wrist before Cassandra realized what Bel was talking about.

"She has processing chips in her brain and you're going to upload from her?" she demanded.

The *Homo quantus* couldn't have chips in their skulls; they interfered with quantum coherence in the fugue, but each of them had a sophisticated innervated input jack on the outside of the skull. It had some storage space and theoretically, its algorithms could be infected with a virus. Bel held up his wrist and Saint Matthew's service band.

"Saint Matthew can project the dreams so we can both see."

Cassandra couldn't name her misgivings, but no one else seemed wary. The little bishop gulped briefly at the air, a strange movement, before smiling at her and floating nearer.

"I believe that I should address you as Your Worship, shouldn't I, Mayor Mejía?" he said.

"What do you want?"

"Although this meeting is unexpected, it may be an opportunity to advance bilateral issues," he said, before looking pointedly at Lieutenant Coulibaly. "Or trilateral issues."

"We don't have any issues with the Puppets," she said.

"As I understand more and more the interactions between the Reverend Johns-10 and Mister Arjona," he said, "I see hidden commonalities between the Holy Puppets and the *Homo quantus*. Our people each have access to parts of the cosmos that are inaccessible to all other beings, and possibly insights to offer one another as we are doing right now. And at the very least, the *Homo quantus* obviously do not want to be under the thumb of the Congregate or the Banks. Through the Holy Axis, the *Homo quantus* could make a home at Port Stubbs, away from both powers."

Cassandra didn't know where to begin with her offended retort and before she could decide, a set of weird holographic images bloomed above the service band storing Saint Matthew. The abstract shape looked like some kind of multidimensional manifold, more complex than the Puppet woman had been able to put into her pencil drawings. It had a basic structure that Cassandra would have associated with space-time curvature. She'd studied the six-dimensional tesseract architecture of the Axes Mundi throats, and the temporary structures of induced wormholes; this looked to be of the same class of topologies, but she'd not seen its like before. It was incomplete. Her brain tried to interpolate the missing parts, to guess what kind of fields or forces this might describe.

"What is it?" Grassie-6 asked. "It's important, isn't it? A secret."

"I don't know what it is," Bel said. "It reminds me of things that Cassandra is better at than me."

"What do you think it is?" Cassandra said.

He shook his head. "If I didn't know better, I'd say it's a space-time model, but...."

"But it doesn't correspond to anything real," Cassandra said.

"It is important," the bishop said, "and you're holding back because you know it's important. You've looked at her dreams before."

"She's had these dreams before," Bel said. "The shapes are always intriguing and suggestive, but I've never found any physical meaning in them. Is there anything else to it, Rosie?"

The Puppet woman blushed and shook her head.

"Have you looked at the audio component?" Saint Matthew's voice said.

"What audio component?"

"Some repeated patterns in here could be taken as a dimension of space-time," the AI said, "but if you're trying to interpret this as a space-time diagram, one portion of this looks like gravitational waves. I can render them as sound."

The diagram shrank as if one of its dimensions had vanished, and the lines throbbed or pulsed on a loop as a low thrumming sounded in the tiny room. Bel frowned. Grassie-6 squinted.

"What is it?" the bishop demanded.

"Did you hear this sound in your dreams, Rosie?" Bel asked.

"I don't know," she said.

"What is it?" Grassie-6 repeated.

"I don't know," Bel said. "I've never looked in her other dreams to see if there was an audio component."

"It means something to you? Space-time you said. Is it a map? A technology?"

"It could be a very vivid and very innocent dream," Bel said. "Puppet neurology, like *Homo quantus* neurology, is very new. It hasn't been tested by tens of thousands of years of selection.

My dreams, waking and asleep, are just my brain coming to terms with my waking life. It's very probable that Rosie's are too."

"Is she talented in mathematical and geometric thinking?" Saint Matthew asked, turning off the projection of the Puppet woman's dream and showing his own strange carved face.

Bel shook his head. "I don't think so. The opposite, isn't it, Rosie?"

She nodded.

"Johns-10 scored quite low on mathematical aptitude," Grassie-6 said. "Destiny chose her for the priesthood."

"This isn't—" Cassandra began.

"If this is a religious vision," Bel said, "you're really best placed to help Rosie understand it, Your Grace. The geometry is interesting in an academic, abstract sense, but this dream isn't very different from other dreams she's shared with me over the years."

The bishop didn't seem at all satisfied with this answer, but smiled diplomatically and repeated his views on the benefits of an alliance between their peoples. He backed out, pulling possessively on the priest's arm. Lieutenant Coulibaly saluted and closed their door.

"What was that, Bel?"

"I don't know. Rosie really has been having dreams like this for a long time. They changed her chips a couple of times. It's not the chips. I've dialed into them."

"You connected to her thoughts?"

"I've never found out what the dreams mean, if they mean anything. I've also tried not to let my brain run away with her dreams. I've tried to look at my reactions to them as false positives. It could be just biochemical imbalances in the Puppet brain. Do her dreams mean something to you?"

"She's creepy, Bel," she said in frustration. "They all are. What do you want from her?"

"They're different, Cassie," he said cautiously. "They've been used in the most fundamental ways, at the cores of their beings. Their abusers changed them. We can't judge them for how they were twisted by others. She's not normal, to the Puppets or to us. I reached the Free City when I was nineteen. I was... kind of running. I hadn't found a place to belong in three years with Will Gander. I wasn't sure how much longer I could resist entering the fugue. The Free City was different from anything I'd seen. Nothing made sense. For me, the Free City was all questions, each one with contradictory answers. I met a lot of Puppets, including some pre-seminarians, like Rosie. She wasn't like other Puppets. She was kind of isolated because she made them uncomfortable. She was curious in ways that most Puppets aren't. She had these dreams."

"They don't all hallucinate?"

"The Puppets think she's oracular."

"What if you'd gotten infected with something from her neural chips?" Cassie said. "Did you? Is that why you like them?"

"I don't... like them. I sympathize with them. I pity what they've gone through. I respect that they haven't just crawled into a hole and died. And I'm not stupid, Cass," he returned with a bit of heat. "Do you think a computer virus could get into our brains? There's certainly something objectively there in her visions. Her neural chips record her brain chemistry and activity during these episodes and they found something to measure, so she's not making it up."

"You talk about her like you're close," Cassandra said.

"We're friends."

"Were you more?" she said.

"What?"

"Were you more than friends with her? Was she... a lover?"

Bel frowned and pushed off the wall to come closer. She moved out of the way and came to a stop at the next surface.

"What is this about, Cassie?"

"You spent years among the Puppets and now I find out you tried to connect to their brains, maybe an intellectual connection. Am I going to your bed after some Puppet was there?"

"Where is this coming from?"

"Stills!" she said. "Stills! He called you a Puppet poker."

"What? When?"

"Months ago."

"Why didn't you say something if it bothered you?"

"It didn't matter," she said, huffing and crossing her arms. She felt like she wanted to hit something. "We weren't going to see any more Puppets or Congregate or Banks or anyone ever again if we got far enough away. It was one thing to bury the past. It's another to have her come to your bedroom at night to share her dreams while I'm here and find out this isn't your first intellectual intimacy."

"Cassie, no Puppet was ever my lover. It couldn't have worked even if I'd wanted to. The Numen were jealous gods; they didn't want their slaves to experience any pleasure except through them. They wanted their biological cult to be inescapable. Puppets don't experience sexual arousal or pleasure away from the Numen. Without a Numen nearby, sexual advances toward a Puppet trigger a fight or flight response. Puppets aren't even fertile without the Numen. In their presence, Puppets experience a kind of estrus along with the religious awe effect, and that's when they become fertile. There's no such thing as a Puppet lover to an outsider, even if that's what I would have wanted. Sexual arousal is another deeply personal experience that the Numen twisted in the Puppets."

Cassandra's hand had tightened painfully around the grip bar. She had relief, and disgust, and the tiniest bit of pity, the kind that maybe Bel felt. Bel neared, but not too close. He met her eyes, smiling hopefully.

"I've always loved you and only you, Cassie."

He offered his hand. She clasped the warm fingers.

"I've been thinking about what we should do," he said.

"Is there anything we can do?" she asked. She pulled him closer, changing their moment of inertia, but both of them instinctively adjusted the angles of their legs and the bends of their knees to keep them rotationally still in the zero-g, perfectly synchronized.

"Venus is a fortress," he said. "There's no way to get conventional forces there, even if the Banks threw all their fleets at it. And if the Congregate thought the Banks were close to taking the *Homo quantus,* they would move them through the Axis Mundi in Venus' crust."

"To protect our own refugees, we should move them deeper into the Axis network, where no one knows where we are, not even Stills," she said.

"There might be unconventional ways to get unconventional forces to Venus," Bel said. "The problem is we still wouldn't know where the *Homo quantus* are. We need some kind of marker or beacon. We've used markers before."

They had. To navigate the Union break-out, they'd left entangled particles within the Puppet Axis. And from within the fugue, Cassandra had been able to follow the lines of entanglement from the particles in her possession to the ones floating in the Puppet Axis. She'd been able to locate that wormhole within all of the vastness of space-time.

"How would we get entangled particles to where the *Homo quantus* are?" she said. "Would you put some in the corpses of the dead pilots, and let them be recovered by the Congregate?"

"The *Homo quantus* are valuable test subjects, but dead ones might not be valuable enough to bring all the way back to Venus. Or they might be stored somewhere different from the captives. But an injured *Homo quantus* is a different story. To fix an injured pilot, they would bring him back to their specialists at Venus."

"The chances of us finding a pilot who survived meeting Stills' people is tiny, Bel."

"Unless we make one."

A sense of disaster crept up her spine. She pulled away, setting them both to very slow rotation.

"It wouldn't work," she said. "It's throwing your life away for nothing."

"They're our brothers and sisters and cousins. I spent half my life alone. Now that I'm back, I feel what I've been missing. They're frustrating, narrow-minded and impractical, but in the most important ways, they're real family and my choices put them in danger. This isn't a question of just me. It's about what I owe to my family."

"Throwing your life away isn't what you owe, Bel! Living for them. Leading them together is what we owe."

She caught a grip bar and stopped her rotation. So did he. They faced each other from opposite walls.

"The real risk of Congregate *Homo quantus* isn't to the Union," he said. "The Union has already lost; it's only a matter of time. But if the Congregate can make *Homo quantus,* they might have the ability to find new axes like we did. They could follow us, Cassie, no matter where we went."

"They already have all the project notes. They'll have

copies scattered safely. Even if we got the captives back, the Congregate can always replicate the project's work."

"Over decades," he said, "and by then maybe our trail would be cold. But they're starting with more than a hundred *Homo quantus* of generations nine, ten and eleven. They might be trying to create new embryos even now, with all the resources of a motivated imperial power."

"What about the *Hortus quantus?* What about resurrecting that species?" she said.

"I want that, more than anything. But right now, the *Hortus quantus* are dead and our captive people are alive. I've given everything I know to our people. They might make a breakthrough. If our people live, they can try to recreate what I destroyed. But if in decades or centuries we're all just captive subjects of the Congregate, we never will."

Words stuck in her heart. Maybe there weren't even words to express what she felt. Or even experience to know what emotions these were. Bel neared along the wall, but didn't touch.

"There's a chance I could live, Cassie, but that doesn't have to be part of the calculation. Sometimes one person has to cover the escape of everyone else."

CHAPTER EIGHTEEN

April 2515

THE YACHT SHUDDERED as the first wisps of Venus' skirts brushed the ship. Seventy-five kilometers above the surface was far, even for the goddess, but as the saying went, Venus was a grasping bitch. Marie took it as a good omen. She was strapped in her seat, looking out the window at star-spotted black space over fluffy clouds lit white by the hard sun behind her. Colored lights high above showed orbital traffic, approaching, leaving and orbiting. They were too high yet, and Venus too expansive and secretive for her to see any detail of home yet. While a good fraction of Venus' people floated in the sun above the clouds, a larger portion lived within her diaphanous, stormy skirts, hidden from orbit. Marie did see something though: a tiny, distant flyer matched their trajectory, rising as the yacht neared aerobraking.

"*Tabarnak*," she said, unstrapping.

"*Mademoiselle*, please stay in your seat during descent," a waiter said, strapped into his own seat.

"I'm gotta hurl," Marie said as she moved back through the games room and bar. He called after her. She wobbled as the yacht hit the atmosphere hard and unevenly. The bar's glassware was packed snugly and nothing got damaged, although she might be when the turbulence got worse. She found her minder in his utility seat at the back. He wore a yacht uniform and his badge said "Social Convenor." He'd been keeping them all entertained for the last six days.

"Get in your seat!" he said.

Marie's hard fingers gripped the bar rail.

"There's someone coming up," she said.

"What?"

"There's a goddamn flyer coming up. You said we wouldn't have any trouble with border services."

"Maybe it's customs," he said, "or a coincidence."

"You're not being paid for coincidences," Marie said.

Strictly speaking, she wasn't paying him though. As best she understood, her aunt's clean up lawyers had hired a refueling logistics company to pay a hefty fee to a service consultant who was really a people-smuggler. And Marie wasn't Marie anymore. Well, she was, but she was carrying the passport chip of a woman called Andrée Fortier. The passport was legit and just enough of Fortier's blood and DNA was in a special sack implanted in Marie's arm that the chip would transmit an identity match signal when queried by automated systems. But Marie didn't look anything like the tall, willowy Fortier and if asked for a DNA sample from a real person, well...

The social convenor called up external sensors in a holographic display as the yacht bucked again. A long rumble accompanied their atmospheric braking and Marie held onto the bar rail hard. The hologram showed their descent vector and the flyer below keeping pace with them. Its identification was Border Services.

"*Crisse. Câlisse,*" she swore.

"It might be a spot inspection. They might not be here for us," he said, but his cheeks had paled.

Marie didn't know the law very well, but if it was more than a coincidence and Border Services found the four illegals, the law wouldn't be throwing the people-smuggler a party, that's for sure.

"How hot are the other three?" she whispered. Had she wound up travelling with some spies or war criminals?

"They shouldn't be hot," he said. Then he frowned and looked at her.

"I have tax problems," Marie said. ""Nobody important wants me."

"I know the others. They wouldn't have drawn attention."

"Why the hell would I?" Marie said. "Listen. We're gonna be bleeding speed until sixty-eight kilometers. I could drop out the back if I had a pair of wings."

"While the Border Services flyer is out there?"

"All four of us could drop out. They can't catch all of us."

"What did you do?" he said. "Who are you?"

"I'm nobody! I owe a lot of taxes, but Congregate Revenue doesn't send out accountants in intercept flyers. And let's get one thing straight, mister coincidence. If they ask me how I got someone else's passport in my arm, I'm not going to be shy about getting them to think about you. So how do we get me off this yacht?"

"They're outside! If they're boarding, their ship will be under us the whole time."

"I wonder if I could go outside the yacht, onto the roof or get behind the thrusters?"

"The yacht sensors will know when an airlock opens. Just go to your seat. The passport will work. Stay cool."

"I'm always cool," Marie said, stomping to the door beside

him leading to the cargo areas and engine rooms. "Emergency suits and wing packs are back there, eh? Open this," she said.

The yacht descended into thicker cloud and the sudden deceleration flung Marie onto her back and dragged her to the door back to the passenger cabin. She caught a floor bar and then hauled herself back to her feet. She staggered back to her stupid social convenor and the sternward door.

"Go back to your seat!" he said. "You're going to draw attention to yourself."

"I told them I was puking. Open the door."

"If Border Services boards, they're going to see one passenger is unaccounted for."

"If I fall, I'm falling on you. So trust me. I have a plan and my plans always work."

He didn't move so she gripped his wrist hard enough for him to understand he was playing with fire as she scanned his service band over the door control. The door slid open.

"See?" she said. "We're a good team. We'll get out of this fine."

He cradled his wrist. Wimp. She hadn't even squeezed that hard.

Marie almost fell backwards again as the yacht descended and its deceleration peaked, but she clung to the door frame and pulled herself sternward.

"Show me a smile, sweetie," she said. "It's going to be fine."

She struggled against the deceleration and shut the door behind her. The utility area was packed with food stuffs, empty wine jars, and emergency vacuum and atmospheric suits. The atmospherics weren't high end, just enough to abandon ship, blow an emergency balloon and wait a few hours for pick up. There were some wing packs though, and no cameras here, which was promising.

The yacht had slowed and flew level now. The bumps and hops of turbulence might have been deeper storms bulging up beyond sixty-five kilometers, or airlocks opening. She imagined the Border Services agents in their armor, looking around, checking passenger manifests. Hopefully someone was hotter than her and they left, but she doubted it. She would have loved to have known how many of them were coming sternward, and how heavily armed they were. Marie was tough, but lots of weapons would still make a big hole in her guts. Luckily, those weapons would also hole a yacht hull and wouldn't be anyone's first choice.

After a while, she started getting bored. It had been forty-five minutes and nothing was happening. She found a head and went pee. She didn't go back to her hiding place yet and pressed her ear to the door. She couldn't hear anything. The view out the portholes further back didn't hint at what the hold-up was. Maybe they were gunning for someone else? Maybe they'd netted the other three and no one had ratted her out. She was about to go back to the door to listen again when it chirped and opened. She darted back into the head and slid the door shut. She wished she'd gotten back into her real hiding spot behind some crates. This head was for crew and she wasn't sure how much they cleaned it.

There was a knock at the door.

She flushed. Turned on the water. Washed her hands.

"*Services frontaliers,*" an electonically-amplified voice said. "Come out."

"Almost done," Marie sang, turning on the air dryer.

The door shook as a fist hit it.

"There's another head!" she yelled through the door. "Don't be a dick."

She flipped off the lock, smiled sweetly and slid the door

open with one hand as her other shot out grasping the agent's throat tightly. He struggled and tried to draw a sidearm, but Marie grabbed his wrist. She leaned out of the head and looked forward. No one was there, but the door to the passenger area was open. The yacht rocked with turbulence.

Marie carried the flailing, punching agent sternward by his neck. She didn't want to kill him, but she couldn't afford him to speak a single command into his radio. If she remembered right, it took a minute knock someone out by choking. Or was it less? She might not be able to squeeze his carotid arteries through the neck of the suit.

"Shut up," she whispered, shaking him. "If you make noise, everyone's coming back here and you already found three people on false passports, right? And a people smuggler. Did you meet the social convener? He sold fake passports to those people. And he's not even entertaining. I had to drink myself stupid on this trip."

After a while, the border agent stopped wiggling. She flipped the clasps on his helmet and took it off. He was still breathing shallowly. She stripped off his suit. He was a bigger than her, but it wasn't the first time she'd found a suit designed without the petite soldier in mind. She moved briskly, and in about two minutes she was locking the helmet into place. French messages and commands were coming through.

"Nothing back here," she texted back.

She darkened the faceplate further and headed forward. Four border agents were checking passports and visas in the passenger area. Two of the people Marie had been smuggled with were standing in handcuffs at the front of the passenger area. So was the social convener. No one paid her any mind and she mounted the stairs to an observation deck and the opening to the airlocks. Two wingpacks were near the airlock. Good ones too, government issued, made for chasing contraband someone might dump into the atmosphere when customs enthusiasts came close. She strapped one on and plugged the command feed into her helmet. The airlock wheeled open easily, and she closed herself in and blew the air. Someone signalled the airlock panel through the yacht comms. She gave a thumbs up.

Messages started showing up in her HUD: "Bélanger, what are you doing?"

Someone just went through and is making a run for it, she texted. *They bypassed the airlock alerts but I saw them go.*

A flurry of activity filled her message screens and earpieces as she emerged onto the roof. The wide black bowl of the sky took up half the world, while below yellow-white clouds reflected blinding sunlight from horizon to horizon. The yacht rocked, passing from one pocket of high weather to another. She was home. All-points-bulletins and alarms filled the helmet displays.

I think I see him! she texted to the other border agents. *In pursuit.*

She ran along the top of the yacht, extending her wings. Their buoyancy was already set for high-atmosphere flight. The engine on her back whirred to life and showed green as she leapt out over the turbulent, fickle goddess who had raised her.

CHAPTER NINETEEN

August, 2515

THEY MET AGAIN in the same stateroom and assumed the same seats, Rudo and Iekanjika at the head of the table, the Puppets to their left, followed by Belisarius and Cassandra, with Foreign Minister Akuffo at the foot of the table. To Rudo's right sat Gillbard, Pacheco and Teixiera from the Banks and the hologram transmitted from the interior of Stills' pressure chamber, showing a fluke or fin from time to time, but nothing else. Manafwa Station had continued its orbit around the stately gas giant so that Bachwezi's star was not shining through the stateroom window, but the full face of the cloud tops cast a blue light on them.

Cassandra had fought with him through most of the hours since Rosie and the bishop had come to their door. She didn't like his plan, not her role in it, nor his, nor did she think it could work. She wanted their people back, but not at the cost of him. That touched him, deeply. They could still just leave and lead their people away, far away, to the other side of the galaxy if they wanted, following the Axis Mundi network as far as they could from civilization, where even other *Homo quantus* might never be able to follow. But he couldn't. Somewhere along the way, he'd just lost too much and couldn't lose anyone else, could not carry the idea of suffering on his hands anymore. He couldn't live in a world with victims, and his life seemed like a small price to pay for even a slim chance of setting the captive *Homo quantus* free.

"Nothing can stop the patron nations from making more *Homo quantus*," Belisarius said to the room when it was his turn to speak. "We *Homo quantus* are a technology, and each of the patron nations is entering an arms race to weaponize us. The Congregate's capture of a hundred and fifty *Homo quantus* may give them a twenty-year head start. Talk of alliances have come from every direction. Bank-*Homo quantus*. Puppet-Union. Bank-Union. Puppet-*Homo quantus*. But real partnerships aren't on the table."

"We offered full protection for the *Homo quantus* and military assistance to the Union," Teixiera said in a soothing, slightly eerie voice.

"A real commitment to partnership would have anti-matter on the table," Cassandra said on cue.

"The Banks have their hard-earned antimatter stores," Admiral Gillbard said. "That gives antimatter a measurable peso value that can be weighed against desired strategic outcomes. But absent solid alliances, the strategic outcome we want—the checking of Congregate growth—doesn't seem possible, which means our antimatter stores are more valuable as a deterrent."

"The Congregate are using antimatter right now," Rudo said.

"Is that an argument?" Teixiera said. "The more they use here, the less they have to use in a potential conflict with the Plutocracy."

"Antimatter is a measure of commitment," Belisarius said.

"The Union are quite obviously committing everything to their war of independence. The Puppets don't have much, so their small contribution represents a lot. In these times, for *Homo quantus* to be seen at all, even to those around this table, is risking everything. So the question is are the Banks really in, anti-matter and all?"

"We three are authorized to consider even antimatter if the alliance is right, but it is far from right," Gillbard said. "We've outlined various viable offers and we haven't seen any real counter-offers."

"Will the Banks match the amount of antimatter the *Homo quantus* put on the table?" Belisarius said.

"What do you mean *you* have antimatter?" Gillbard said. "Where did you get it?"

One of Stills' big eyes drifted into the hologram over the seat beside the foreign minister. It came close enough to expand the projection until the eye was fifty centimeters across, but didn't hint at expression.

"The *Homo quantus* have antimatter, and we'll commit it to an alliance," Belisarius said.

"Considering that a year ago," Pacheco said, "the *Homo quantus* lived in the Garret with no industry other than research, it seems unlikely that in the intervening time, in hiding, they built the solar arrays to power the accelerators to produce anti-matter. I hope your confidence schemes relied on more plausible stories."

"I'm not a con artist," Cassandra said. "As mayor of the *Homo quantus*, I ask again: Are you ready to commit anti-matter one-to-one?"

"How many grams did you have in mind?" Teixiera said, the smoothness of her voice humoring them.

"Ten to twenty kilograms," Belisarius said.

A kind of strangled, disbelieving silence stopped the room cold. Half a gram of anti-matter hit with the same force as a megaton thermonuclear bomb, which was more than enough to cripple even a fully armored patron warship. The major powers had huge moon-sized accelerators that produced grams of antimatter every month. Entire peacetime Bank navies probably didn't have more than a few kilos of antimatter, with strict use guidelines.

"This is absurd," Gillbard said. "Five to ten kilograms is the same as we would commit to a full-scale conflict with a patron nation."

"A partner who isn't committed is no partner at all," Belisarius said.

"The Union isn't set up for antimatter combat," Gillbard said.

"Precisely. The Congregate is not expecting the Union to have antimatter, and certainly not to be capable of deploying it in quantity," Belisarius said. "I have a few thoughts on the rapid retooling of Union weapons systems and we're sitting beside a shipyard."

"Fuckin' anti-matter," Stills said. Then his eye retreated from the image over the seat.

"Mister Arjona," Pacheco said, "it may be that your theories are quite advanced, but there are basic engineering problems that are only overcome with experience. If this is the first time you're deploying... kilograms of antimatter, you're as likely to blow up the Union fleet as equip it."

"I'm no engineer and have no experience with anti-matter weapons systems, but the Banks trained Saint Matthew to consider engineering problems as parts of larger military and economic strategy," Belisarius said. "And it's lucky you did because he's possibly strengthening your allies."

"If," Teixiera said, the hard edge in her voice discordant with its earlier silkiness, "the *Homo quantus* have antimatter in these quantities and we are committing antimatter in those quantities, we are going to need a different conversation, one about full integration of both the Union and the *Homo quantus* into the corporate structure of the Plutocracy, with a significant amount of power and influence, possibly even involving the creation of a major new Bank."

"The *Homo quantus* are offering a short term alliance," Cassandra said.

"Without a full partnership," Teixiera said, "our projections do not foresee either the *Homo quantus* nor the Union surviving in any form that leaves them with influence and agency in even the medium term. A short term alliance turns both peoples into a lost cause, and as you sink, you may drag us down with you. If you really have antimatter, many good options are available to you in a long term alliance."

"We don't need an alliance because reinforcing the Union is a distraction," Belisarius said.

"For what?" Gillbard demanded.

"For our move against the Ministry of Intelligence at Venus," Belisarius said.

"You can't strike a Ministry of Intelligence globe at Venus," Gillbard said. "We wouldn't be able to reach it."

"No one thought I could get the Union fleet across the Puppet Axis," Belisarius said. "We all have different goals, but as long as Del Casal is re-engineering the *Homo quantus* in Congregate captivity, we're all living under an existential threat. Cassandra and I will get the location of the Ministry of Intelligence globe in the atmosphere of Venus."

"How?" Pacheco said.

"It will mean me getting a lot closer to Venus."

"And how will that help?" she pressed.

"I'm not flying you to Venus, *patron*, if that's what you were thinking," Stills said.

"You can't get them out," Pacheco said. "Do you intend to kill them there?"

"This is a rescue mission," Belisarius said. "The Union will give me an inflaton ship big enough to carry a hundred and fifty passengers, equipped with some Bank tech, weapons, and the best magnetic coils for inducing a temporary wormhole."

"You can't induce a wormhole in the atmosphere and Venus' orbital defenses will see and stop any ship leaving without authorization," Gillbard said.

A set of tiny rings irised open in the silvery globe bulging from his temple, projecting a hologram. A schematic of a planet with orbital traffic showing in rings and loops glowed yellow, while defensive stations with arcs of fire and missile and laser ranges shaded in different colours. It was a depressing set of obstacles.

"The Puppets are probably best-placed to provide troops to assault the Ministry of Intelligence globe where the *Homo quantus* and Del Casal are being kept," Belisarius said.

"Even if you could get them there," Gillbard said, "Puppet troops are unreliable and of questionable competence, facing fortified Congregate positions."

"Our episcopal troopers aren't afraid to die!" Rosalie said.

"They will die!" Gillbard said. "Even if they could be transported there, which they can't, zealotry is no substitute for the military training and equipment of a patron nation. However much we dislike the Congregate, we shouldn't underestimate them."

"The Puppets will do anything to bring back Del Casal," Rosalie said.

"It doesn't matter how brave or motivated the soldiers are if they enter battle with horse and lance," Pacheco said.

"Then equip us!" Rosalie said.

"This is not the time for embargo-breaking," Gillbard said.

"Keep it all," Rosalie said. "We can do it. Del Casal is more important than equipment."

"The set of available tactics is different with fearless fanatics," Belisarius said. "No offense," he added to Grassie-6 and Rosalie.

"We find most Puppet choices repugnant," Gillbard said.

"I wouldn't make their choices for myself, and I wouldn't pick it for anyone else, but it's not mine to choose," Belisarius said. "Each Puppet has a certain amount of time in this world. What they do with it, whether we agree or not, is their choice to make. They believe they're contributing to something larger and more important than themselves."

"You're very blasé with Puppet lives," Pacheco said.

"The Banks have nothing to teach me about human dignity," Belisarius said. "If the Puppets are ready to die for a cause, there are ways of dying that advance the common good."

Gillbard and Pacheco seemed ready to argue further, but Teixiera uncrossed her long arms, a languid, slow gesture in the microgravity. She knit her slim fingers together thoughtfully.

"Arjona has thought this through," she said. "Let's hear him out. We shouldn't let morals get in the way of a profit line."

"I think I can locate the Ministry of Intelligence globe, get the Puppets, Saint Matthew and Stills to Venus, and get us out through the orbital defenses," Belisarius said. "Once out though, it's true that Congregate forces will be following. Can a Bank fleet protect us and bring us back to Epsilon Indi?"

Gillbard became pensive. The holographic Venusian orbital schematic shrank to include the inner solar system: the Earth,

Mercury, as well as the Atiras, Aten and Apollo asteroids whose orbits brought them close to Venus. Many of those asteroids were fortified military or mining bases; some would be astronomically close to Venus now.

"It's possible," he said. "It's an act of war. The Board of Directors would have to authorize it, but it is tactically feasible. Your chance of success is negligible."

"After we're released from your protection and a bit more trust has been established," Belisarius said, "a more comprehensive treaty between the Banks and the *Homo quantus* might be negotiated. But we're not going to be IP and we're not going to be deprived of our rights to choose our own way."

AN HOUR AFTER the planning session had wound down, Belisarius, Cassandra and Saint Matthew were circuitously escorted to General Rudo's private suites. Rudo was finishing some kind of bread he didn't recognize. They strapped into comfortable chairs around a small meeting table and bulbs of wine and juices were offered. Iekanjika was there. The foreign minister was not.

"Your idea of going to Venus," Rudo began. "You're playing with fire and impossibilities?"

"There seems to be no way not to," he said.

"It seems like an elaborate trick, on me, on the Banks," she said.

"No lie. I have to go to Venus," he said with a sinking feeling in his chest.

"How?"

"The hard way."

He explained. Her eyes widened, but she didn't tell him not to do it.

"You almost don't need me for this plan," she said finally.

"If we succeed, the Congregate won't be able to make more pilots. That won't really change how long you last against the Congregate onslaught."

"Your antimatter might," Rudo said.

"I'm not a military strategist, but I don't see antimatter being more than a short term gain," he said.

"Probably," she said. "The Banks weren't lying. The infrastructure to keep antimatter from detonating on our own ships isn't a small thing, and the warheads to carry antimatter are much bigger. Our missiles will be slower, easier to intercept. You really have kilograms of it?"

"In a few weeks, we'll be able to bring you kilograms of antimatter," he said. "And you won't need to retool your systems. We wouldn't be giving you anti-hydrogen or positrons in a gas or plasma, or even flake of anti-lithium. We'll bring anti-iron. It's stable and dense and can be manipulated by strong magnetic fields."

"How did you make anti-iron?" Iekanjika said.

"Cassandra's part in this plan means she has to stay here, to be in contact with me," Belisarius said, ignoring the question. "Neither of us trust the Banks to ever let her go."

"I'll guarantee your safety as far as I can," Rudo said to Cassandra. "If we're overrun I won't have much influence anymore."

"THE PUPPET TROOPS will have to be prepared to be shipped like cargo," Belisarius said two hours later. "Even with sedation, it won't be pleasant. For some, it'll be fatal."

He floated outside *The Calculated Risk* with Cassandra, Grassie-6 and Rosalie. Beneath the feet of their vacuum suits loomed the blue gas giant. They'd plugged themselves in to a four-way conversation that couldn't be intercepted.

"Hardship is not relevant to the Puppets," Grassie-6 said softly. "We're made to endure."

"Will they know most of them won't coming back?" Cassandra said to them. She rarely addressed the Puppets directly.

"They might," Grassie-6 said. "They might not. It's not the knowing that's important. Johns-10 will know. She'll decide what to tell the troops."

"Rosie is going?" Belisarius said. "I didn't think... You have military training, Rosalie?"

"Some," she said.

"She'll learn what she needs to," the bishop said. "This is a religious mission, a fated one. This will be decided by heart and soul more than by platoon tactics. And Johns-10 knows you. She's worked with you before. She's essentially our *Homo quantus* expert."

Rosalie smiled encouragingly at him through her face plate.

"I can do it, boss," she said, with the exact tone she might have used when he'd given her a part in a confidence scheme in the Free City.

"I know you can," he said. He didn't want Rosie to die. Despite her being driven by alien urges and needs he could only understand by analogy, he knew her to be kind and intelligent. She didn't deserve to die, any more than the *Homo quantus* did. "We'll meet back here soon."

CHAPTER TWENTY

August, 2515

"FOR THE RECORD, I don't want to be here, I don't want anything to do with this and I object categorically to everything. I also don't want to go to Venus."

Getting no response from either her or Belisarius, Saint Matthew's holographic face rotated away with a stately grace. The simulated stony finish and the elaborateness of the headdress were fascinating to watch. Around a kind of papal mitre with artistic abstractions of maize wound a two-headed snake representing infinity. Saint Matthew's head turning pique showed the imagery of blood-letting on the back of the stony headdress.

Saint Matthew's recent visual choices meant something, although Cassandra didn't know what. She'd found encyclopedia articles on the Neo-Copanic Papacy, the unnoticed schismatic end to the Catholic cult. Saint Matthew had gravitated to the symbology of this last period of his church for some reason, but he hadn't shared it with them. The Neo-Copanic popes had been a last return to philosophical roots: poverty, generosity, purity of intent, even some extremes of asceticism. She'd become accustomed to Saint Matthew's delusions, and she hoped his attraction to this phase of his church didn't signal some deeper pain. Wishing some kind of happiness for the the AI was irrational, but in many ways, the AI and the *Homo quantus* were emotionally and intellectually closer to each other than either was to baseline humanity. If he found some happiness, maybe they could too.

"I left weapons design on purpose," the holographic image said, turning gray stone eyes on them again. "They built me to work on anti-matter weapons. I left on purpose. I called for help. Mister Arjona heard me and got me out. How is this better?"

Bel didn't look like he was going to answer. In savant, he might be ignoring Saint Matthew.

"Someone else is calling for help now," she said.

He hmphed performatively.

Beyond the cockpit window, the weird eleven-dimensional space glinted with light and colors in strange directions that upset perspective. Purples and greens and luminescent grays radiated from nowhere. The weirdness wasn't just outside *The Calculated Risk*. Magnetic fields and electrical charges pressed on her magnetosomes in a dizzying kaleidoscope of discrete electromagnetic textures. She'd begun to understand that this hyperspace was her experience with something transcendent, and that perhaps let her imagine Saint Matthew seeking a similar experience, but one meaningful to him.

"I've done the projections," she said. "Without some change, the Congregate wins every time."

"You should pay attention to your projections," Saint Matthew said. "We were both built to think military strategy. We don't like it, but we can be good at it. If we both see that the Congregate always wins, then we should act accordingly. The same logic says that the captive *Homo quantus* are already lost.

I hate military thinking."

"We change the field," she said.

Saint Matthew's stony eyes narrowed dubiously. "We're putting many more people at risk, including you and Mister Arjona and me, and only shaving percentages."

Bel had been doing the navigational calculations and had displayed them on the cockpit screens. They weren't in a rush. They were being careful and programming all the navigational shifts in this hyperspace deliberately. Saint Matthew looked away as if frustrated.

"The angles look right," she said.

"Rotating one hundred and eighty degrees around the r-axis," she said, "and one hundred and eighty degrees around the u-axis."

Inertia changed in naked hyperspace. They could feel like they were tilting when they were actually still. They might feel nothing during acceleration, depending on whether they were rotating around an axis that was more spacial or temporal in character.

"I hate this," Saint Matthew volunteered, as *The Calculated Risk* completed its rotations. The hyperspace of the interior of the time gates still looked the same. They were anti-matter now: themselves, the shuttle, their iron cargo, actually, their anti-iron cargo now.

Bel activated the next part of the program. The shuttle reversed itself a few meters, letting fifty nanogram specs of anti-iron float out of open ports below the cockpit.

"Rotating back one hundred and eighty degrees around the r-axis," she said, "and one hundred and eighty degrees around the u-axis."

"This would be a stupid way to die," Saint Matthew said.

"Get started please," she said.

"Do this. Do that," he said. "Every soul around me is corrupting and we're making explosives."

The AI continued complaining as he reversed the rotations across the dimensions that had translated them into anti-matter, reversing charge, time and symmetry until they converted to matter again, floating before ten flakes of anti-iron. Striking with the right velocity, fifty nanograms of anti-iron would make a mess of *The Calculated Risk*. A glancing touch would annihilate surface layers of the anti-iron and the shuttle, but the force of the annihilation would send the flake of anti-matter away at high speed. Without some kind of detonation structure, they weren't explosives yet.

And in this, Saint Matthew was a genuine, if sheepish expert. His artificial intelligence had been grown by machine learning on vast military and economic data sets, among them, experimental ideas for creating anti-matter at industrial scales. The Banks had grown his intellect to be one of the most advanced AIs in civilization, fully conscious. And they'd succeeded, but some quirk of the hyper-advanced machine learning had given him empathy, made him believe he was a reincarnated Christian saint. Fortunately, that didn't make his technical knowledge any less useful.

Saint Matthew tracked the locations of the ten flakes of anti-iron with radar pulses as ten small silvery medical chips floated out of the ports under the cockpit. A manipulator arm held the first chip, opening it like an alligator clip and neared it to the first flake of anti-iron. The chip's magnetic field activated, catching and cradling the anti-iron as the two halves of the chip hinged shut. Cassandra let out a breath. The AIs expression remained calm.

"How stable is it?" Belisarius asked.

"Anti-iron is as ferro-magnetic as iron," the AI said. "A

magnetic field in a vacuum-sealed chip will be stable. The bigger ones will be more of a problem. Hush. I need to concentrate."

"*You* need to concentrate?" Bel said.

"I would like to concentrate on something other than answering technical questions."

Saint Matthew repeated the procedure on the other nine flakes of iron. A strange sense of success and terror came over Cassandra at having harnessed anti-matter. It wasn't something she'd ever considered doing before; it had been a throw-away idea born out of her experiences with Stills in the hyperspace of the time gates. Stills had hurriedly improvised a weapon to save their skins; she was now deliberately engineering weapons to help get the captive *Homo quantus* back. They repeated the process five more times, making a total of sixty chips. Each was loaded with fifty nanograms of anti-matter, with an explosive yield equivalent to about two kilograms of TNT.

They stowed these safely away before beginning the really dangerous part. Bel ran them back through navigational contortions to turn them into anti-matter, but this time, while in that state, they released fifty-gram pellets of iron to float in the hyperspace before them. A gram of annihilating anti-matter had the same yield as a small nuclear explosion. Fifty times that would incinerate them and possibly the time gates themselves.

They retreated very slowly and went through the rotations to translate themselves back into matter, leaving the first batch of ten fifty-gram pellets to float peacefully as anti-matter. When they were sure that everything was stable, Saint Matthew began bombarding each pellet with electron beams. The electrons annihilated with the anti-electrons in the iron. The explosive effect was too minute to propel the fifty-gram pellets, but after twenty minutes, the beams had given each pellet a strong negative charge.

Saint Matthew had built containment casings for each pellet, about a meter long with openings like alligator clips. Tightly wound electrical coils inside could generate powerful electromagnetic fields that would hold each charged and ferro-magnetic pellet in place. Cassandra stilled as the first casing gently floated around the first pellet of anti-iron. She flinched as it closed. The screens showed its electromagnetic field strengthening while internal electron beams continued to increase the charge of the pellet. With a kind of held-breath fascination, she and Bel watched Saint Matthew repeat the process.

"This is the road to damnation," Saint Matthew said quietly.

"We're selling weapons," she said. "We getting paid in support for getting our people rescued."

"That's not what I mean," he said. "We weren't strong enough to escape the gravity of our programming. Maybe it means we'll never escape it."

Cassandra disliked the idea of having been programmed. It was a very Belisarius way of thinking about self.

"Maybe you have programming," she said, "but you can't believe that your programmers intended to make a saint."

"The three of us were built by different methods to serve the interests of war, whether on the battlefield or on the economic stage," the AI said. "We saw the paths before us and tried to move away from our natures, reaching for something higher, and maybe we deluded ourselves for a time into thinking we'd escaped. Yet here we are, the three of us making the most advanced, powerful, experimental weapons humanity has ever seen, and they'll be used with terrible purpose. We failed to redeem ourselves. We're marked by an original sin, by flaws in our nature introduced during our creation."

The second casing enveloped the next pebble of anti-iron.

"Sin doesn't exist," she said. "Engineers inserted genes into us, changed the patterns of information flow in our bodies and brains, and made new phenotypes, but we choose."

Bel seemed on the edge of saying something, whether in retorted defense or remorseful confession, she didn't know. The friendly fire of Saint Matthew's self-accusations applied equally to anti-matter weapons, the terrible sacrifices the Puppets would make, the captivity of the *Homo quantus* and the destruction of the *Hortus quantus*. She didn't need an original sin. The very act of interacting with the world seemed to have triggered a set of catastrophes.

"Is it worse that we failed to escape our natures," the AI said, "or worse that we're now choosing to wreak this destruction upon humanity? At least in one instance, we're trying to do right."

"We didn't ask the Congregate to blow up our home," she said. "We didn't ask them to steal our people. We didn't ask them to turn our cousins into fighting machines. If you want to look for sin, go pester the Venusians."

The holographic face in repose could often appear stiff and mask-like because of the deceptive weight of the thick carved features, the stylized abstractions in motifs. This had been true when she'd met the AI wearing a face painted by Caravaggio. But powerful algorithms moved the projected face subtly, the movements designed to emote with the human subconscious. The shifts in tension of lip, squint of eye, and wrinkling of stony forehead communicated a kind of sadness and regret that felt like she'd profoundly disappointed a parent. The reaction surprised her. The third casing slowly maneuvered over the third anti-iron pellet.

She squeezed Bel's hand and smiled. His expression remained haunted.

"We're here, Bel, in a world of mysteries and answers. Saint Matthew can handle the anti-matter. Let's look around again, Bel, from the fugue."

He turned dark eyes on her and a hint of a smile quirked at the edges of his lips.

"What do you want to know?" he said.

"Everything. Come with me."

They unstrapped and floated to the dorsal hatch of *The Calculated Risk*. Their simple vacuum suits were built of dumb tech, mostly transparent to the electromagnetic fields through which the *Homo quantus* peered into the universe. They emerged from the metal and electrical systems of the shuttle into the naked surreality of the hyperspace within the time gates. Strange light dopplered into unnatural colors. Electromagnetic fields pressed at her magnetosomes from directions that weren't within the three physical dimensions in which she existed. The alien stimuli in this vacuum impacted even her auditory nerves, filling her with long, distant lowings. Yes it was alien, but this was her world, her observatory into the nature of the cosmos.

Saint Matthew manipulated the cases to carefully capture each of the pellets of anti-iron floating a hundred and fifty meters ahead. He would be another twenty minutes at least. She could probably stay in the quantum fugue unaided for about that long. She pulled Bel so that his face plate touched hers. His face was gently lit by the faint purpled light of the hyperspace.

"Come into the fugue," she said.

He nodded.

She triggered microcurrents of electricity from her electroplaques into her brain and she ceased to—

*   *   *

CASSANDRA CAME OUT of the fugue twelve minutes later, slightly breathless, feeling a bit hot. She took deep breaths. Her vacuum suit was cool and the chill air from the tanks helped with the beginnings of her fever. Bel floated close, looking at her.

"What did you see?" he asked.

She would have rather diagrammed it. It would have been more accurate, but they would both do that later. She told him of her expanding consciousness, of perceiving the cosmos through the lines of entanglement connecting the time gates to the larger Axis Mundi network.

"I saw lines of entanglement to thousands of axes of the Axis Mundi network," she said. "I'd been looking for positional cues, so I focused on only a few hundred of the closest and tried to locate them."

Her brain calculated and modelled and sorted all that had been seen in the fugue, comparing those probable locations to the locations of two thousand four hundred stars she'd memorized within the volume of space within fifty light years of them.

"I have more data that most of the axes are orbiting pulsars and pulsar binaries," she said. "Some are around what seem to be black holes, but some orbit very dim infrared sources that telescopes haven't characterized well. They have weird spectra."

"I looked at the same thing," he said, smiling. It almost didn't matter what happened in the outside world. As long as they had *this,* a window onto the cosmos, more learning to do, they could be happy. They spoke quickly, over one another in their excitement, before it became clear that it would be faster to input their observations into computer systems that could graph and compare what they'd seen. And Saint Matthew was calling them. Ten more cases hovered around anti-iron, holding the deadly explosives safe in powerful magnetic fields she could feel even from here. That was her idea. This was her world.

CHAPTER TWENTY-ONE

April, 2515

BAREILLES BROUGHT LUC to a windowless meeting room. He wore a different suit today, expertly pressed, a more traditional tie and collar to his outfit. His thinning salt and pepper hair had been recently trimmed. She'd had Santiago Gonzalez, ten years old, and Jeronimo Ballesteros, thirty-nine years old, brought to here too. They wore orange detainee jump suits, with their hands cuffed and wrapped in insulated metal mesh bags. Bareilles had also had the hallways and room Faraday caged. Even without the fugue, most of the *Homo quantus* could sense magnetic and electrical fields and she didn't want to give them any information she wasn't deliberately feeding them. Both *Homo quantus* looked bewildered and meek.

"Luc, this is Santiago and this is Jeronimo," she said in *français* 8.1. "They're *Homo quantus*. They can answer any questions you have."

"What's going on?" Santiago said in Anglo-Spanish.

"*Parle français*," Bareilles said.

The boy seemed to hesitate for a moment, and then repeated his question in clear, provincial *français* 8.3. Luc leaned forward and put on a pair of wire-rimmed glasses to examine the *Homo quantus* boy.

"This is *monsieur* Luc Deschênes, *un petit saint.*"

"Hello, Santiago," Luc said with his slight lisp.

"I want to go home," Santiago said.

"You were built to fight us?" Luc said.

"No. To learn. To understand the universe."

"But you did?" asked Luc.

"No. I didn't hurt anyone!"

"Belisarius Arjona and Cassandra Mejía were instrumental in an attack on the Congregate," Bareilles said to Luc.

"We have nothing to do with Belisarius," Jeronimo said.

"You can do what he does, or your children will be able to?"

"I don't know," Jeronimo said. "I don't know what he did."

"He used the fugue to develop new tactics," Bareilles said. "The Congregate now has ninety-four thousand dead in the last three months. One Scarecrow has gone missing. Arjona and Mejía made this happen with their *Homo quantus* abilities."

"We don't have any abilities."

"Ask them how fast they can think, Luc."

"How fast can you think?" *le petit saint* said.

Jeronimo hesitated, but Santiago finally said "About a thousand times faster than a human brain. Faster still in savant or the quantum fugue."

"Can you sense magnetic fields and generate electricity?" Bareilles said.

"Yes."

"Can you enter the savant state?"

"Yes."

"These are all abilities that baseline humans don't have," she said to Luc. "Their intelligence is the most dangerous. We do not have AIs that are yet comparable to their abilities. We don't know what weapons they may invent, nor what flaw in our defenses they may find."

"We don't think of weapons!" Jeronimo said. "We just learn about the universe."

A silence settled on them. Santiago and Luc regarded each other.

"What happened to your face?" the boy said.

"I born this way," Luc said, sitting a bit straighter. The question might have touched a nerve, because he stuttered and misconjugated his verb.

"Were they engineering you?" Santiago said.

"I have one chromosome extra," Luc said. His voice became more fluid, as if this were a phrase he'd said often.

Santiago's eyebrows rose. Depending on the boy's education, this might be his first experience with even the idea of trisomy-21. Such children were not born anywhere else in civilization, except in the kind of poverty that had midwifed the fragile Québécois colony in the clouds of Venus two centuries ago.

"You've got to let us go," he said to Bareilles. "We'll go home. Or wherever you want. We won't bother anyone. We won't make weapons or whatever you think we're doing."

"You're not meeting with me," Bareilles said. "I'm an observer. *Monsieur* Deschênes wanted to meet you."

"*Monsieur* Deschênes, please let us go," Jeronimo said.

"They told me that your people were changed before you were born, that you changed your own children, to make them do things that hurt us," Luc said. "If you promise to not make weapons anymore, I can ask people. I don't know if it will help."

Jeronimo and Santiago seemed to be processing more than Luc's words. Luc's grammar and pronunciation stumbled here and there. Finally, Jeronimo looked to Bareilles.

"Is he our advocate?" Jeronimo said. "Is he cognitively impaired? Can we have another advocate?"

"Would I have been born among your people?" Luc said.

The question seemed to startle the *Homo quantus*. Jeronimo shook his head slowly.

"Why not?" Luc asked. He wasn't angry, but Bareilles' indignation rose on his behalf.

"Only those useful to the project are born," Jeronimo said.

"I'm not smart enough?"

Jeromino shrugged helplessly. "I don't think you could contribute," he said.

"If I wanted to live with you, could you find a place for me in your people?" Luc said.

Jeronimo shook his head. Luc rose.

"Wait!" Jeronimo said. "Can you help us? Get us out of here?"

"As long as she says you're dangerous," Luc said, "you're dangerous. I'll keep asking about you though."

Santiago was crying and Luc squeezed his shoulder across the little table before the two *Homo quantus* were taken away.

"What did you think?" Bareilles asked.

"Is it that you don't know what to do with them?" Luc asked.

"I think I need to keep turning them around, make them stop being weapons against us and aim them at our enemies."

"Are they really enemies?" he asked.

"They strike through others," she said. "Without the *Homo quantus* the Union's rebellion would have been finished in the matter of weeks. They gave our enemies technology and strategic advice."

"You said they can think better than you?" Luc said, regarding her steadily.

"They're hyper-intelligent, as good as computers, except they have their own interests."

Luc seemed thoughtful.

"Among their people, I wouldn't have been born because I'm not smart enough."

Bareilles took his hand. She wished she'd met this cousin sooner. "Are you feeling alright?"

"You're not smart enough to be born among their people either," Luc said.

Bareilles' world seemed to tilt in a new direction. She didn't understand what she was seeing.

"Are you okay?" he asked.

"*Oui.*" she said although it didn't feel quite true. After Luc had left with his assistant, Bareilles wasn't sure what to think, or that she did think at all. She sat in a kind of stunned solitude. *I'm not smart enough to be born among their people.*

When she finally left, the corridors on her way to Del Casal's lab echoed with her boot steps. The geneticist was sunken-eyed. He saw her and straightened, not hiding his sullen, smouldering anger.

"What is this?" he hissed, holding up his forearm. A fine line of stitches two centimeters long reddened the skin.

"I had them add a chip."

"What chip?"

"A pain chip," she said, touching his face where the bruised swelling had faded, but he still flinched. "I can't beat you when I want. At some point it's going to do some cognitive damage and I need your brain."

He stepped back, out of her reach.

"Why don't you report this morning's progress?" she suggested sweetly. "And do it with a smile, won't you?"

Blotches of red appeared on Del Casal's face, but with sullen calm, Del Casal said "I rewired Vizcarra. He's the closest of any of your *Homo quantus* to the fugue. The new wiring based on the Second Bushido augment technology bypasses the parts of his neurology that don't work well for the fugue. I added a control chip, so I can... switch him, the person, off. When the *Homo quantus* shut off their consciousness and their subjective experience of the world, a quantum intellect is... booted up. When I shut off Vizcarra's consciousness the quantum processing system in his brain begins, ready to process, but there's no driving will. The quantum intellect that's supposed to take over the body doesn't."

"So what do you do now?" Bareilles said.

"Nothing," he said after a moment. "I don't know the trick to making the fugue active. The *Homo quantus* didn't know either, and they've been at this for a hundred and forty years."

He'd accomplished more than she'd expected.

"So you have a computational system that just sits there?" she said. "Everything I've seen suggests that a *Homo quantus* brain is one of the most advanced computational systems in civilization. Why can't it be turned to problems of combat? I'd like to fly them against the mongrels."

"There's no agency at all. There's nothing there. It's like a powerful computer with no software."

"So let's install a pilot," she said.

His eyes narrowed. "Connect a combat AI to them?"

"Just connecting one wouldn't take advantage of the *Homo quantus* brain. We could put in multiple AIs to run combat algorithms and problems through the *Homo quantus* neurology."

"I don't do AIs," he said with pique.

"You can finish wiring up my *Homo quantus*. You can reinforce their organs with something non-magnetic so they'll survive the accelerations of combat flying. You can install cooling systems to keep them from overheating and dropping out of their quantum processing state. We have AI experts here, the ones who build our own AIs. And the ones who are reverse engineering the Second Bushido fighters. Get started."

She grabbed his wrist and held his forearm up so that they could both see the stitches.

"If I haven't been clear enough before, I'll say it so you understand. I want something very, very soon, doctor."

She held up his other arm. He tried to pull away, but hadn't her strength.

"This arm will get the chip with narcotics," she said, very close to his face, making him flinch. "You don't like pain? Wait until you're addicted to something and begging me for a hit. If you can't motivate yourself, I'll motivate you."

Del Casal sagged. "Don't. I won't... I'm motivated."

He nearly collapsed when she released him. She emerged into the main pit. The transparent elevator carried her to the mezzanine where she found the Scarecrow at the railing. One of the camera eyes turned in its flaccid face until she was reflected in the lens.

"*Le petit saint* left your meeting looking troubled," the Scarecrow said.

That was bait, if she took it. She could ask the Scarecrow about her having brought in the one *petit saint* who was also family. She could ask what kind of test or pressure this was to be. But she resisted; the Scarecrow wouldn't answer properly until her own purpose was served, and by then Bareilles would have her answer.

"There are no saints' tears yet," Bareilles said.

"Turning the *Homo quantus* against the mongrels and the Union is a bold move," the Scarecrow said. "It will not be popular in all circles."

"Those people are free to take my job. I wouldn't mind being back in the field as a major again."

"I'm not the only Scarecrow watching you."

That sounded ominous.

"You're close to... getting it," the Scarecrow said.

"The General Staff are worried about what the *Homo quantus* can do militarily," Bareilles said. "We have no evidence that the Union can replicate their trick entry into the Puppet Axis. That must have been the *Homo quantus.*"

"They're worried," the Scarecrow agreed over the soft, eerie humming.

"The *Homo quantus* may be a technological singularity, as consequential as the discovery of the Axis Mundi network," Bareilles said.

"Fortunately, we were the first to the network, and the network has natural choke points, where variables can be contained."

"While the *Homo quantus* invalidate all existing military projections and assessments."

Bareilles gripped the transparent railing a bit tighter. *I'm not smart enough to have been born among them.*

"That's not why *you're* worried," Bareilles said.

"*Non.*"

Below, an orderly wheeled Vizcarra to the scanning suites at the end of the pit, to be probed and prodded, for his insides to be mapped again. Vizcarra, a single, broken *Homo quantus,* terrified all of the Congregate. Bareilles, the Scarecrows and all the intelligence services were reduced to analyzing leftovers to understand the new predator. Again the Scarecrow hummed. The sound reminded her of the moaning of trawler cables resonating in the winds of Venus, something she'd not heard since been learning to fly in the deeper clouds as a girl. She hadn't forgotten the sound; rather it had melted into the background of memory.

"We're thinking of having you join F-Division," the Scarecrow said.

Bareilles had never heard of F-Division, which, in a secret organization meant little. She'd worked most of her career with eyes-only and need-to-know information.

"You could have just had me assigned."

"We don't think we'd get the best out of you by conscription," the Scarecrow said, the humming running more loudly on some other channel within the weaponized AI.

"We wouldn't be having this conversation if F-Division was something simple," she guessed.

"We think we know what kind of person you are. F-Division is not focused on our strategic military needs. It's not worried about intelligence and insurgency. F-Division worries about the future of the Congregate. When you're further along with your *Homo quantus* work, I would like to talk about that future."

The Scarecrow thumped away with heavy footfalls, her humming having changed to something light and cheery.

CHAPTER TWENTY-TWO

August, 2515

"I WASN'T MADE to be a surgeon, you know," Saint Matthew said.

Belisarius didn't know if the AI had a point or was just making conversation to distract him. Saint Matthew had an array of surgical tools working within Belisarius' body, poking and tugging in some places, making nano-scale changes in many others. The AI didn't need powerful lights, so a soft glow lit the small operating room.

"There are lots of things we weren't made to do," Belisarius said.

Cassandra squeezed his hot hand with her cool one. Her eyes had dried. The strands of fine metal worming their way into his body didn't hurt really. Saint Matthew was building in Belisarius the same wiring they'd found in Martín, Ana Teresa and Edmer. He could reroute the bits of pain at the insertion points to the quantum objectivity, which didn't feel. The chips being inserted into his body were harder to ignore. Saint Matthew had removed the chips from Martín to implant into Belisarius. With his magnetosomes, he could feel them in his body, like a sock twisted uncomfortably in a shoe. Saint Matthew had put one in his brain and another along his spinal cord. So far, they weren't interfering with the quantum fugue, but could be shut off if that happened.

Cassandra touched Belisarius' cheek. It was swollen and sore from the last fourteen hours of calcium deposition and bone growth there, as well as along his jawbone and chin and forehead. They were building up his bone, changing the shape of his face. He did not look like Belisarius Arjona on the outside anymore. And inside, he looked like one of the rewired *Homo quantus* the Congregate had flung into battle against the mongrels. But the faint electrical language of childhood, the code he and she had shared by fingertips, was still there. *I love you,* he messaged. He closed his eyes and his brain could remember him perfectly, as hers would remember his, no matter the distance.

Saint Matthew's robots began withdrawing from within and around Belisarius.

"You're done?"

"I doubt I did it perfectly," Saint Matthew said. "We can't even be sure where all the pieces are supposed to go. Mister Stills' people were not gentle to them."

"They were fighting for their lives," Belisarius said.

"So were Edmer, Martín and Ana Teresa," Cassandra said, removing her hand. The message she'd been sending fingertip to fingertip vanished, incomplete.

Edmer, Martín and Ana Teresa hadn't been fighting for anything. They hadn't been people anymore. They wouldn't have reached the quantum fugue, but the wiring seemed to be set up to turn off the subjective consciousness. Their bodies had experienced a kind of psychic death, a pause on identity and self. They'd been nothing more than external processing units. The only people in that battle had been the mongrels.

"You're always on everyone else's side," she said. "The Puppets. The mongrels. Even the Union."

He felt at his face. Very sore.

"Everyone hurts," he said, "sometimes for things they didn't do. Including us. Including the *Homo quantus* on Venus. We'll get them back."

He didn't mention their back-up plan. If he couldn't rescue the captive *Homo quantus,* he would still need to stop or delay the Congregate from having *Homo quantus* of their own. Cassandra took his hands again.

"When you get back, we'll never worry about anyone else again," she promised. "We'll run, together, as far and as fast as we can, so that no one in civilization will ever find us. Not in a hundred years. Not in a thousand years."

His face hurt when he smiled, but he did smile. He wanted what she wanted.

CHAPTER TWENTY-THREE

August, 2515

THE DAWN SUN glowed beneath the horizon in the west. At the edges, towards the poles, the light dimmed to oranges and burnt yellows, but directly westward, the sun backlit the top of the Venusian atmosphere to a white and glowing arc that felt close. Guillaume, the young man sitting over Marie's forearm traced the stylus where he'd left lines of ink. The needle, despite reinforcement, stalled and caught on her skin, struggling to penetrate military-grade dermal augmentation. It sounded like he was clear-cutting dead brush rather than embellishing a tattoo. He smiled apologetically and withdrew the stylus to replace the needle for the fifth time.

He was fit for an artist, with blue eyes and short sandy hair. She didn't think much of his fashion sense, a bright red blouse, loose-fitting on the chest and arms. His pants were a bit like pantaloons with high boots. When she'd seen how hot he was, she'd thought of using her ladylike charms to seduce him. It would have been a bit expected. Venusian high society loved its galas and balls, its secret romances and illicit trysts, the licit ones too, if that was a word. And he might have said yes. But watching him labor over her tattoos made her self-conscious about being tough and unladylike. He might have broken if she'd gotten too enthusiastic anyway and that was the wrong kind of gossip. It would not do for a lady to break an important *artiste*.

Her aunt had shown Marie his work, gushed over his reputation and stature in the art world, a moody rising talent, a star pupil of the nova analytical cubist movement, politically subtle, physically attractive, shyly spoken, on the cusp of greatness, already widely in demand. But few people wouldn't clear their schedules when a high-house matron called, so Guillaume Beauchesne was in *Tante* Marielle's floating manor. The aging Madame Hudon came close, leaning on her cane. The young man blushed as she inspected his work.

He'd finished one of Marie's forearms, masking the old lines of the crossed out NCO tattoo, drawing within and around it a mosaic of fractured planes that climbed her arm and used her elbow and the movement of her muscle to give further strength to the illusion of multiple viewpoints. He'd gone past the elbow on her left arm too, but had been building that almost as a frame to inform the way he would approach the centrepiece of her forearm, which he'd been shaping into white-flecked planes of oceanic blue-gray, like ices under overcast skies. One of his patrons, not *Tante* Marielle, had funded his tour of Earth. The society columns talked about his visits to the galleries of Madrid and Beijing and Buenos Aires before he'd studied the winter ices of the Hudson Strait from Kangiqsujuaq and Niaqunguti. Since then, he'd been expressing himself with freeze-thaw motifs.

"*Très joli,*" *Tante* Marielle said in *français* 8.1. She patted Guillaume's shoulder, before addressing Marie. "I don't want to get you a dress that anyone could wear. I have a designer in mind. Françoise Côté will design something special to highlight the new tattoos and show you off. Finish. Finish," she said to Guillaume, walking away slowly. "We have parties to plan."

Marie smiled apologetically at Guillaume in the wake of her aunt's retreat. He returned to her very durable arm. This would have been the moment to invite him to whatever party *Tante* Marielle was referring to, but she became shy about it. *Tante* Marielle's parties were political soirées and salons, attended by ministers of state and industrial magnates. Artists might be there as curiosities. Would he feel any more comfortable than she would? Guillaume finished the last line and wiped away spots of blood and flecks of metal. He regarded his work, no longer looking at her as a person. She was a canvas again, something durable on which to draw.

"*Voila, mademoiselle* Amélie," he said, addressing her by her cover name.

Her first instinct was to flex, and so she did, gracelessly. She stopped herself, then smiled sweetly and held her arms in the showy manner of a delicate Venusian debutante. Or tried to anyway. She never seemed to nail graceful. He'd packed his tools and gave a bit of a bow as he excused himself. She inclined her head as if she were accepting the bow. He was a rising artist, but she was a *grande damoiselle*. She had to accept the proper, due courtesies, even if they felt silly.

His work was beautiful. Beginning at the sides of her pinkies, tiny planes, fragments of sea green and gray wound up her wrists, triangles and quadrilaterals of pale turquoise, edging up her forearms, interspersed with long rectangles of slate, angles shallow and deep giving the impression of weight and texture, of coiling vines that were neither precisely Terran nor Venusian. From close, the abstract shapes were charming, and from far, they suggested living growing things. Venusians had been decorating their bodies with whatever they could for two and a half centuries. *Tante* Marielle had thought that Guillaume's work would add to that tradition.

Left alone, she flexed then, swinging her arms, swishing the beautiful gown made in real silkworms. The diamond-laced window wrapped the full two hundred degrees of the forward observation salon, arching high above and she neared the glass, brushing its coolness with fingertips. The sun rose into black sky, and the streamers of vapor around the floating manor glowed more brightly. Lines of orbital factories and docks and mass drivers floated high above, distant colored dots. All very orderly. So very orderly.

An implant behind her ear buzzed.

"*Entrez,*" she said.

"*Bonjour mademoiselle* Amélie," Martine said.

Martine wore a gauzy pale green dress. She was a daughter of The House of Mists, called House of Shadows now that the Congregate was at war. As a minor family, the House of Shadows sought a closer alliances with the House of Styx. *Mademoiselle* Martine was the kind of Venusian everyone liked: smart, loyal, pretty, delicate, and yet tough enough to fly through the deep acidic clouds of the lower decks and wrangle wild trawlers. Although she was Amélie's lady-in-waiting and the junior, Martine seemed to be much more familiar with all the social courtesies and a couple of times had stopped her from making some real *faux pas*. Martine bowed shallowly and held out a package.

"For you, *mademoiselle.*"

The plastic box was about forty centimeters on each side, covered with interplanetary routing stamps and Congregate customs approvals. It also bore security stamps around *Tante* Marielle's Hudon family ensign, a House of Styx crest modified to indicate a cadet branch. Marie didn't recognize the sender, but the posting dates were recent. Someone had paid a lot of money to send this through space. Well, what she used to think was a lot of money. Martine waited politely, with the right shade of smile to not seem to be trying, but to not appear to not be trying to please either. Society was exhausting.

"Thank you," Marie said. Martine curtsied and left as gracefully as she'd come.

Marie sat wondering about a knife to open the box. She hadn't needed a knife since returning to Venus and didn't have the faintest idea where to find one, but finally found a one-time security pull tab. She broke the plastic around it and pulled. A wire came free, something clicked in the fastens, and the lid came loose. The room was private; it was a point of pride that Congregate citizens were trusted and not observed by the state, but she still turned to see if Martine had gone. Of course she had. She behaved *comme il faut*. Properly.

And the box contained... some junk, tumbled together by the long trip. An old Congregate marine uniform headdress lay bent around a casino ashtray. Some tourist knick-knacks from an old Middle Kingdom pilgrimage temple lay under a printed picture of a family standing in front of it. She didn't recognize the people hamming for the camera. A scholarship medal from forty years ago with the name Albert Rouleau didn't ring any bells. She pulled several cheap, folded-up novelty toys, but she didn't know the trick to open them. Whose garbage was this? Had someone cleaned out a lost and found and sent it to her? Why? No one knew that Amélie Hudon was here because Amélie Hudon hadn't existed a few months ago. She upended the box on the floor between her feet. The random bits of other people's lives fell out. All clues, she supposed. She didn't like puzzles. Actually, that was a lie. She hated puzzles. She toed the mess undaintily with her dainty yellow slipper, then fished something out.

A service band. The kind worn by working-level Congregate officials, the kind of bureaucrats who stamped forms and corrected tax filing information and inspected things. Actually, they didn't do those things. Not really. They carried sub-AIs in these service bands to do that work. Come to think of it, she hated petty bureaucrats as much as she hated puzzles. She turned the band in her fingers. It was beat up the way things get when they're used.

And it made the hairs on her neck rise. She was about to turn it on when on the tiny green and yellow status lights glowed in their own. The projector on its face lit and then a hideous, almost abstract miniature face appeared in hologram. It was all shades of gray, as if carved from stone, with heavy eyes and cheeks, prominent ears and a big headdress.

"Miss Phocas," said a familiar, annoying voice.

"Saint Matthew?" she asked in a hushed tone.

"Yes. I'm glad you're here."

"What are you doing? What the hell happened to your face?" Although the face appeared as stony as his old face had seemed painted, the AI's expression seemed more fluid, more mobile. The carved stone eyebrows rose, one higher that the other, judging.

"I changed my look," he said. "So did you."

She smoothed her silk dress self-consciously.

"How did you find me? No one's supposed to be able to find me. Why aren't you with Bel?"

"Mister Arjona and I did some modelling of your behavior. He thought you might be on the surface of Venus with your relatives in the House of Stone. I'd guessed that you'd make a new identity with your extended Hudon relatives."

"Wonderful for you," she whispered angrily. "You won the bet. Are you trying to blow my cover? There's a garbage chute in the service area. I should drop you and all this junk into the clouds."

His affront, as performative as Venusian art, was obvious.

"What would you tell Mister Arjona then?" he said.

"I don't have to tell him anything. He's not my father." She neared his face until the grain of the holographic stone resolved. "There's a two million franc bounty on me," she whispered. "He didn't tell me there would be a bounty on me! This is serious shit! I should turn myself in for the cash."

"Yes, your suffering is palpable," he said. "You're practically a martyr. Ring for a servant to bring your smelling salts."

"My what?"

"Your... nevermind. Mister Arjona needs your help."

"Did you listen to anything I just said?"

"No one listens to what you say. You never make any sense."

She felt her forearms flexing under her new tattoos, myofibril augments tightening like steel bands under almost unpuncturable skin.

"That's the problem! Bel needed a minion and I was it. Just like Stills. Just like Will. Just like you."

"What?"

"We're his tools! He makes us think we're useful and valuable and when he gets what he wants, we get the heat."

"He's gotten heat."

"Says his butler."

The thick eyebrows shifted to express cartoonish dubiousness.

"No one has a butler in this situation except the Venusian princess."

"*Mange d'la marde.*"

"I'd never made the connection, you know," he said. "Phocas.

The Phocas family, of the House of Saints."

"Yes, yes. It's a big house with thousands of members and enough black sheep to field a hockey team."

"So you're the goalie. I'm glad you're making the best of a rough situation," he said. "While you've been playing dress up, I've been riding in a shipping box trying to get to you."

"I'll ship you back with the other junk in a minute." "The Congregate detonated a nuclear device over the home of the *Homo quantus*. Mister Arjona managed to evacuate most of his people before that happened, but the *Homo quantus* are hidden now, refugees, being hunted by the Congregate and the Banks."

"That's on Bel's head."

"He's very conscious of that. Nonetheless, the refugees are a collection of innocents. Pacifists. Researchers. Non-combatants. Children."

"I'm very sorry for them, but I'm not involved in Congregate foreign policy or military affairs."

"We all chose to help Mister Arjona," he said. "Each for our own reasons. I don't think anyone understood what success might mean, not even Iekanjika."

"I'm glad she got what she wanted," she huffed. "Well, it's been really nice catching up with you. I'm sure you have to go."

"Mister Arjona needs your help."

"And he thought you were the right person to send to ask for it?"

"The Congregate did capture about a hundred and fifty *Homo quantus*," he said. "The Congregate and the Banks know that Mister Arjona and Miss Mejía did something to help the Union break through the Puppet Axis. The Congregate are experimenting on the captured *Homo quantus*. We think they're using some tech to run the bodies of the *Homo quantus* against their wills, like enslaving them. They're throwing them into battle against Stills' pilots."

"He did it? He really signed up to fight someone else's war?"

"Mister Stills seems happy. It's hard to tell with him. That's not the point. Mister Arjona wants to rescue his people."

"He's stealing people now, instead of money?"

"He's rescuing his people," he said, "and I'm helping him."

"You're a saint," she said, but she didn't feel like the sarcasm landed.

"We need your help."

"I don't need money."

"We're not hiring you. You have everything you need here, if I judge correctly. You're living the life of a Venusian lady under the wing of a non-conformist aunt who wanted a bit of daring in her old age. This is exactly what I expected Marie Phocas to want."

His sarcasm did bite, but she said "You judge correctly."

"Your help doesn't need to blow your cover," he said. "We need shipping help, mostly, to bring in what we need to reach the Ministry of Intelligence."

"They're in the Ministry of Intelligence?" she said in hushed disbelief. "You can't hack your way into MinInt."

"We don't mean to hack our way in." His expression, such as it was, betrayed nothing.

"When you get stopped and caught, the Ministry will interrogate your whole plan out of you, out of Bel, and out of anyone else stupid enough to get in on this. Then they'll trace it back to anyone who helped you, including 'shipping help.'"

"I came with a plan," he said. "Mister Arjona already owns a small Venusian import-export company under an assumed name. It's been doing regular, routine business. It doesn't have to right corporate structure to import what we need though, but with your help, we could establish several layers of shell companies and get the right exemptions to bring in what we need."

"You need a lawyer or a notary," she said. "I worried you were doing something stupid and needed explosives help."

"It's funny that you should mention that," he said.

CHAPTER TWENTY-FOUR

June, 2515

WHERE DOES A species come from? There is a causal answer and a teleological answer. The causal seeks to answer the question in events and forces pre-dating a speciation event. The teleological answer finds its response in the end result. The acorn exists to cause the oak to be. In most situations, Darwinian evolution does not depend on teleology at all; in fact evolutionary theory in most cases rejects teleology, relying on natural selection as a necessary and sufficient causal answer. Mutation, natural selection and genetic drift cause speciation in modern evolutionary thought. And yet, this answer is no longer sufficient.

The advent of genetic engineering reinserted teleology to evolution, driven by the intent of human minds. Bioremediation bacteria exist to clean pollution from the soil. Whole classes of yeast variants exist to vat-grow food to feed teeming millions. The *Homo eridanus* exist for a fragment of humanity to avoid extinction by migrating to the benthic depths of an alien ocean. The *Homo pupa* exist to serve slavemasters and slavemakers. The *Homo quantus* exist to understand and ponder questions beyond the ability of *Homo sapiens* to master.

Where does a species come from? Causal and teleological answers in the modern world are not mutually exclusive. Some strains of spilled yeast find new environments to colonize behind radiator vents, under cooling vats, in pipe junctions. Bioremediation bacteria may jettison ecologically expensive genes needed by humanity and thrive in reconditioned soils. The *Homo quantus* project has unleashed new genotypes upon the world that are finding ecological niches never imagined by the project engineers.

Philosophical Anxieties Keynote Excerpt
The 7th Scarecrow Congress on the Speciation Problem

THE SCARECROW MOVED cat-quiet, her humming inaudible. Every so often, she paused in her pacing to swivel a lens onto the lieutenant-colonel. Bareilles sat in one of the elegant hanging chairs of antique carbon-weave that the early *colonistes* had invented for their lives in the clouds. The Scarecrow had not really been able to tell her anything more of F-Division. She'd used elliptical wording and hints, but none of that helped the officer understand what F-Division really did or what her life might look like if she joined. The most the Scarecrow would admit was that the division managed the deepest of Congregate secrets. Within that inability to say anything hid a familiar career risk of the espionage world: sometimes one could only see the contents of a room by entering. But entering one room might close other doors, including the one by which one entered.

Her decision depended on how much Bareilles might or might not trust the Scarecrow. She would have followed her own Scarecrow, the vanished Epsilon Eridani one, on its simple say-so. They'd built an understanding over years of common mission. This new idiosyncratic Scarecrow felt like a headquarters operative who sough to shape her into a headquarters officer.

"Is F-Division connected to this assignment?" Bareilles said, swaying slightly in the chair.

The small lenses rotated, as if zooming in on her, down through her vulnerabilities and insecurities to her innermost thoughts.

"The dangers it presents, yes," she finally said. "F-Division deals with the largest possible threats to the Congregate."

The largest possible threats. More than the war? More than the *Homo quantus*? Insurrection? Revolution. Rebellion. Something that could threaten the connectivity of the empire through its access to the Axis Mundi? The Congregate was vast and strong and growing. What could threaten it? Whatever it was, it was larger than what she'd done before, larger than tactical and strategic espionage advantages. If the state needed her, in some place more important, was it even right to consider her own wants? As a younger woman, she'd put on a uniform to serve, to protect, and looking back on that decision, in the most important ways she'd made it without reservation. This irrevocable decision was perhaps no different than any other she'd faced in her life.

"*D'accord,*" Bareilles finally said. She had to trust the Scarecrow. Without trust, she had nothing. "I'll join F-Division. What do you need from me?"

The Scarecrow crept close, one big silent foot after another.

"F-Division is setting up conditions to evolve the humans of the Congregate," the Scarecrow said.

"What?" Bareilles said.

"It is not an asteroid impact or a trade war that will destroy the Congregate," the Scarecrow said. "The Congregate is large and healthy with no end in sight to our prosperity and strength. We touch our natural competitors only across the wormholes of the Axes Mundi, and yet we face an extinction level threat."

"For the last thirty thousand years, *Homo sapiens* has been the only intelligent hominin," the Scarecrow said. "Since the extinction of the neanderthals, we have competed only with other *Homo sapiens*, competitors who had similar abilities, competitors who shared the same genes. Before then, we shared the Earth with other lineages of hominins and we outcompeted them. It might have been direct conflict or we might have taken away their habitats."

"*Homo neanderthalensis* endured three hundred millennia before we drove them to extinction. *Homo denisova* endured for five hundred millennia before we drove them to extinction. *Homo heidelbergensis* endured for four hundred millennia before being outcompeted by ancestral species. These lineages competed with each other using relatively new evolutionary traits."

"*Homo sapiens* were able to symbolize, to abstract in sophisticated communication. We developed memetic traits, tools that could be shared horizontally, instead of relying on the sharing of traits by vertical genetic descent. Fire, clothing and language conferred selective advantages and were subject to incremental improvements, just like genetic traits, except that they spread and evolved faster. We've been competing with each other with rapidly-changing memetic traits for so long that we sometimes lose sight of the fact that this speed of change is not typical. Humanity has been in a period of accelerated evolution for a millennium and now our species is no longer alone."

"You're worried about the *Homo quantus*?" Bareilles said.

"Not just the *Homo quantus*. The Puppets, the mongrels, every meld of human and machine in the Anglo-Spanish Plutocracy, as well as experiments we hear about from informants in the Middle Kingdom. Every variant is a true competitor in fitness and every lineage competes for the same resources. We compete for Axes Mundi, for more advanced propulsion, for faster, more complex information processing, for more accurate predictive simulations and modelling. Humanity is evolving as we speak, and the Congregate is falling behind."

"We're the Congregate," Bareilles said as refutation. "If the Banks unified, they might be able to compete with us, but they're fragmented by greed. The Ummah and Middle Kingdom are dangerous, but they aren't our match."

"The Congregate lost the Freya Axis."

"We'll have it back soon," Bareilles said. "Months, not millennia."

"The Union inflaton drives and cannons are beyond our technology."

"For now. We're reverse engineering them. And in the meantime, we're overwhelming them with brute force," Bareilles said.

"The *Homo quantus* have senses and cognitive abilities we cannot replicate, nor even yet understand," the Scarecrow said. "Whatever they did with the Puppet Axis might be accidental or unique, but if not, if they find some novel use for those senses and cognitive abilities, the advantage will spread in the equivalent of an instant of evolutionary time. It won't matter how big or united the Congregate is. Our size may actually count against us. Evolution occurs slowest in large populations. However, we're taking steps to prepare the ground."

"What steps?" Bareilles demanded. The slow realization

that the Scarecrows had a vast, insane vision collided with the thought that they also had tremendous secret resources to bring to bear. "Did you do something to me? You're supposed to protect the Congregate, as it is."

"We are protecting the Congregate. We're loyal to the *Homo sapiens* of the Congregate and to the polity itself. *La famille.* For decades, the Scarecrows have been recommending laws to the Praesidium to increase the heterozygosity of the population. We've been migrating genetic material all over the empire to maximize variability, and we've carefully duplicated some genes in different sub-populations, to give even more canvas for evolution to write on. We've also genetically cut off certain Congregate sub-populations to increase the speed of spread of novel genes and possibly speciation."

Bareilles tried to grasp the genetic architecture the Scarecrows were constructing across nine billion Congregate citizens spanning forty nodes of the Axis Mundi covering two hundred light-years.

"Regular mutation and genetic drift are too slow for real advantages to spring up," Bareilles said.

"You're right," the Scarecrow said. "It's too slow for you, or even I to see in anything other than shifts in allelic frequencies, which are changing ten times faster than a century ago. If the Congregate lived alone in the cosmos, only some of us would need to survive the environment to avoid extinction. But with other lineages of hominins in play, we need to outcompete them, or millennia from now all of the Congregate will be a footnote in some other species' historical records. We're laying the groundwork for evolutionary change."

"You shouldn't have done that."

Holograms lit beside the Scarecrow, population graphs.

"If we were dealing with tool-less animals, it would be

relatively easy to measure the selection pressures of a single gene coding for an enzyme, but we aren't. We mastered molecular biology five centuries ago and we still have no system to predict or even measure forces like self-assembly, chaos and complexity theory stemming from traits like intelligence and abstraction. The Scarecrows don't fear a technological singularity. We can reverse engineer the inflaton drive in a few years. The existential threat to the Congregate is the evolutionary singularity, beyond which nothing is predictable. We're racing to create circumstances where *we* will create fire, where *we* will enter new habitats, where *we* will think new thoughts."

The graphs changed to show the adoption of AI against various metrics: GDP, patent registration, human health outcomes, education, lifespan, industrial and military capabilities. At every stage of AI adoption, humanity had experienced boosts in every metric, often by orders of magnitude.

"Even general AI, has reached a plateau," the Scarecrow said. "We're making no more progress with it. Bank experimentation with human-AI interfaces is innovating at the margins and their new Aleph-Class AIs don't change that. The *Homo quantus,* on the other hand, are capable of thinking new thoughts, things we can't imagine. They have new senses and they can potentially apply all the learnings and tools of humanity onto new things they can see and we can't."

"You want us to make our own *Homo quantus?*" Bareilles said. "The Banks lost control of their tools. The *Homo quantus* went on to find in the Sub-Saharan Union a useful weapon they turned on us and the Puppets, while ignoring their funders."

"Everything has been approved. The Scarecrow Core received policy authority to proceed seventy-five years ago when the extent of *Homo pupa* and *Homo eridanus* evolution became clear. F-Division reports annually to the Praesidium through *in camera* sessions. They are supportive because we're already in a biological arms race. We can either let these forces blow as they will, or we can steer the outcomes."

"But we're the Congregate. We're *de souche*. We've been protecting our culture and our identity from assimilation for centuries. You want to change us now without us knowing?"

"People can't know," the Scarecrow said. "Loyalty to the genes we have is hard-wired into the deepest parts of life; it's the deepest of biological confirmation biases. It's strong enough to drive kin selection, strong enough to power the tribalism that rejects the other as well as new ways of doing things. People instinctively reject the idea of change, as you are now. The Puppets and mongrels changed because they were forced. The *Homo quantus* were engineered gradually, at the embryo stage, generation by generation. The nature of the threats we'll face and the severity of the evolutionary selection factor will determine how fast we need to go and how much the people need to know."

"You're abandoning what makes us what we are!" Bareilles said. "What made the Scarecrows think of this?"

"The Scarecrows might have been the only ones capable of perceiving this threat to the Congregate. We're loyal to the state but detached from our own genes. That gives us unique perspective. We don't want to be *Homo quantus*. No one needs to be. We have molecular tools to engineer ourselves in any direction. The *Homo quantus* point at just one possibity. But we need to explore this new genetic space. The future struggle for survival will occur on the terrain of abstraction and symbolizing and cognition. We can match the *Homo quantus* and surpass them."

"The *Homo quantus* slipped the leash because the Banks didn't know how they would think," Bareilles said. "The

Banks didn't realize that the *Homo quantus* would want different things. If you change us, our children won't be human anymore."

"Human is a label," the Scarecrow said. "Species are labels. Each one of us, in every generation, is a combination of genes and mutations, a set of algorithms that collectively try to propagate themselves."

"We're more than that."

"You can believe anything you want. That is the luxury of surviving. Sixty years ago, I would have argued that we show every chance of surviving, but in just one decade, the evolutionary singularity has struck. In a millennium, humanity as we know it might not exist."

"A millennium?" Bareilles said. Her tone had been at the edge of scoffing, but something held her back, something worried at the possibility that the Scarecrows might be right.

"The enemies and threats to the Congregate separated by time are no different from those separated from us by space. The very fact that humanity has difficulty thinking on geological and evolutionary scales is an artifact of previous habitats we occupied. Our genes are adapted to summers past. We can change now, or we can become another branch on the evolutionary tree ending in an extinction."

In the silence, the Scarecrow waited like a machine. She was a machine, a vitrified, crystallized brain armed with terrible weapons. Unless they'd had children before the vitrification process, each and every one of the Scarecrows was already an evolutionary dead end. They were variant forms of human senescence. And yet they cared, if that was what it could be called. They thought thoughts so far from comfort that they edged on madness. And yet, she'd not been able to pick apart the Scarecrow's logic. The Earth had once seemed limitless, and yet at some point, *Homo sapiens* had found it easier to live without the neanderthals around. The galaxy was vast, but humanity couldn't break the speed of light. So they expanded through the Axis Mundi network, a scarce resource that any government would steal from any other if they could. And the Union had taken an axis from the Congregate, aided by unknown *Homo quantus* abilities and insights.

And all the *Homo quantus* were the result of a small project of modest funding over slightly more than a single century. The mongrels had gone from baseline humanity to *Homo eridanus* in three generations of punishing re-engineering and now they flew against the Congregate. What might the *Homo quantus* and the mongrels be in another century? What would the Congregate bring to next century's fight? The Scarecrow worried about what the competition of a millennium from now would be like. This was not the struggle she'd trained for. What she'd trained for, everything she'd accomplished in her career and life seemed now small and insufficient. And Luc, the *petit saint,* had been very insightful. She wasn't smart enough to be born in *Homo quantus* society.

CHAPTER TWENTY-FIVE

August, 2515

THE ACCELERATION CRUSHED Belisarius like a closing hand. Shock gel pressed hard on his skin, inside his lungs, in his throat and ears. Stills pulled wild, bone-bending maneuvers with twenty and twenty-five gravity spins, slides and breakaways. Congregate pilots, even those reinforced in bone and joint and organ, could endure about twenty. Stills could bear a lot more, but not without doing Belisarius an injury.

Belisarius' telemetry was limited to the emergency pilot module in which they'd found Martín's corpse. It had been patched enough to make it be space-worthy, holding shock gel and a few functioning sensors. They'd wrenched and screwed Belisarius into it and welded the whole thing beneath the hull of Stills' command fighter. The Union engineers had put a counterweight on the dorsal side of the ship, but Stills had been complaining for some time about the distribution of weight.

Belisarius tamped down the panic he could, his brain calculating the inertial differences and the center of mass changes that Stills would be fighting, with sub-calculations and probabilities attached to Congregate missile and enemy fire.

The mongrel squadron swarmed around them like wasps. The stars spun and tens and hundreds of kilometers away fighter craft and missiles blew past, without any apparent pattern, even to someone like Bel who saw patterns even when there weren't any. The utter, deadly chaos they brought to the battlefield was part of the mongrel strength. No one knew what they would do next, not even the mongrels themselves. Except for Stills, because he wasn't fighting. He had a mission. He was ferrying Belisarius to the underworld.

A pair of missiles neared, keen and persistent, hot targeting lasers licking at Stills' command fighter. A small mongrel fighter shot past on another orbit entirely and a fiery receding cloud of debris replaced one of the pursuing missiles. But as the other missile neared, gravity lurched so hard that Belisarius blacked out.

When he regained consciousness there was no missile, but accelerations above twenty gravities almost caused him to black out again. Wrenched into a spin, Belisarius saw, through the few electronic sensors jacked into his brain, three mongrel pilots chasing down a single Congregate fighter, quite obviously being piloted by another of the captive *Homo quantus*. Stills rolled, diving in and opened fire, two small missiles blowing it into shrapnel. Stills continued his arc, passing very close to the debris field as the explosive bolts binding Belisarius' capsule to Stills' command fighter blew. Belisarius tumbled through space in his damaged little pilot module, on a trajectory that would drift him closer and closer to the Congregate fleet. The capsule's distress beacon began pinging.

CHAPTER TWENTY-SIX

August, 2515

THE EARNESTLY *CORRECTE* young man went on to Marie about foreign policy and the war over the hum of winds pressing at the diamond roof. She sipped her wine. Streamers of white cloud threaded a bowl of stars above the candles of the ballroom. *Le beau monde* and their upheld fluted glasses formed a thin forest occluding the view of the band coming back for another set.

The war was exciting, really, he went on. A true client nation rebellion had never happened. Not like this. Marie smiled. Well, she wasn't really Marie here, and it wasn't a real smile. She was presented as Amélie to everyone now and if all went well, she would be Amélie to the end of her days. The young gentleman was dull though.

She caught the eye of a black-tied server and delicately gave him the champagne glass and plucked two more. The young gentleman, Lucien, handed back his empty glass too. He was handsome enough. Marie looked surreptitiously to see if anyone was watching, then chugged one glass, then the other. Lucien's smile tightened. The server's eyes widened slightly before looking carefully to the other guests, to the band, to the cluster of *petits saints* in their evening gowns and tuxedos. She wanted some reaction out of him. Some life. Blow up. Laugh. Get angry. Drink. The server continued to a different cluster of guests. Lucien couldn't disapprove of Marie; he was a social climber and she was a hill.

But this was boring. He was boring. The speeches hadn't even started and she'd been here an hour and a half. She could have grabbed Lucien and gone into the kitchens or a board room and see what his body could take. Well, not grab. This was *Tante* Marielle's party. Marielle was the black sheep of the family. Well, gray sheep anyway. *Tante* Marielle was eccentric, but had found places to fit into Venusian society. She'd been an ambassador, thriving among foreigners. She had a box. For everyone their box or category. Lucien came from affluent middle families, looking for a career and maybe alliances, like Martine. Maybe he'd get a promising bureaucratic career capped by a respectable term or two as a provincial assemblyman. Very *correcte*.

So bored. She wanted to scream. She wanted to say things, if society would let her. If anyone could listen. They might not be able to. Sometimes when people heard strange things, they translated what they heard into something familiar to avoid social awkwardness. She put a hand lightly on Lucien's chest and leaned seductively close.

"Those shrimp are going right through me," she whispered. "I'm going to find the can."

Marie as Amélie wove through the clusters of high society, attracting some interest. The story went that Marielle Hudon's niece had been raised in the far provinces of the Congregate by a diplomat sister. Two boxes then for Amélie: expat, high house daughter. That would make some of her rough edges almost acceptable to society; they fit her *story*. And some of the story was even true. Marielle really was her aunt, but Marie's mother was a flighty artist, joined to only one spouse, a minor member of a cadet branch of the Phocas family. The pair of *non-conformistes* travelled endlessly through the back provinces of the Middle Kingdom and the Ummah. Given their unconventionality, Marie's parents had had the good grace to at least stay out of sight.

Marie passed the toilets. She activated her jewellery containing passcodes that persuaded low level surveillance systems to look the other way. Most people of her class had them, principally for illicit political meetings and romantic trysts with the wrong kind of people. What couldn't be proven could be winked away with knowing and occasionally scandalized smiles. To these low-level surveillance systems, she was a ghost. Her bracelet opened the way to the service entrance, where she startled two caterers who artfully tooth-picked sautéed scallops on trays.

"Those look good," she said.

She scooped a handful and a stack of napkins. She chewed as she walked, keeping the napkins close under her chin to keep from dribbling on her dress again. She wandered down narrow service stairways to the less impressive parts of the *Thivièrge*, *Tante* Marielle's floating palace. She found the engineering access doorways and windows with views of the propellers and power plants.

Someone had left the door to a crane operator cubicle unlocked. The glassy diamond floor looked onto yellow, nighttime cloud tops. Marie moved the straps aside and sat in the operator's chair. Most of the time, dumb sub-AIs would run the crane, but sometimes humans did too; the Congregate approached artificial intelligence warily. They'd struggled for the independence of Venus too hard to hand it over to anyone, even machines. She watched the drifting cloud tops, dropping greasy toothpicks between her expensive slippers.

Her purse made a noise. The purse was too small to hold a gun, but was big enough for brass knuckles. She closed the cubicle door, slumped out of the posture of a high house *mademoiselle*, and reluctantly fished the service band from beneath the brass knuckles. The stupid stony head appeared in hologram. The thick features sniffed like he was better than her. The joke was on him. She had a cocktail dress and a handful of scallops.

"You know," he mused. "I expected you to hide someplace a little... further from the people who want to arrest you."

"You changed your face. I changed mine. Mine looks better."

"You look happy," he said ambiguously. She wasn't happy, but she didn't like him to say it.

"You go to ground with a two million franc bounty on your head! I did pretty good."

"Honestly, this is much better than I expected," he said. "I thought you would to end up in a ditch somewhere, riddled with bullets."

She retraced his argument, trying to decide if she should be mad.

"Look, I'm really glad you came," she said, putting air quotes around most of the statement with her clean hand, "but I don't need any more jobs. I've got a big job with my aunt's companies. I'm going to be a vice-president of corporate security."

His face, even graven from stone, seemed to find some new level of doubt in her.

"I'm going to do a good job! I'm executive material."

"Of course you are," he said dryly.

"I am!"

"I'm imagining you in board meetings right now. Enjoy

the quarterly reporting, the annotated agendas and everyone checking with their lawyer before they make their statements."

If he weren't a hologram, she might have tried out her brass knuckles. There'd been no chance to practice with them in the clouds. The clouds had different kinds of fights she didn't enjoy or understand.

"But what about the captive *Homo quantus*, Miss Phocas? We need help. They're innocent."

"No one is innocent."

One stony eye looked at her askance. "The world has many innocents. Some of us get our hands dirty for money, and in the past, Mister Arjona's plots have made me very uncomfortable. But this feels different. It isn't what we used to do. It feels right."

"Oh, please..."

"What could be better than freeing innocents taken by a hostile power?"

"It's not *a* hostile power. It's *my* hostile power! You're talking about hitting my people."

"When did you become a patriot?"

"I was a goddamn NCO!"

"Cashiered! Thrown in jail."

"I'm still Venusian."

"And you support your government kidnapping and enslaving people?"

"I've only got your word on it."

His face shifted, and melted away, and an image of three corpses appeared.

"*Ouach!*" she said in disgust.

"These are *Homo quantus*," he said. The image zoomed in on broken tissue and shiny wiring. "The Congregate added in chips and circuitry to run them like robots. Your people did this and they might be committing these same crimes against another hundred and forty innocents here in the clouds."

"What do you want me to do?" she demanded. "Say I'm sorry? I'm sooooo sorry I'm a citizen of an imperial power. There. Feel better? Or do you want me to go talk to someone and have all this fixed? I'll just walk up to the Praesidium and tell them not to be a bunch of assholes! That sounds promising. This is foreign policy, *espèce de cave!* I don't get a say."

"I'm not asking you to storm the government," he said, leaving the corpse images glowing in her hands. "There are a few things you could do where you are, as you are. Shipping and import orders. Setting up a few civilian sensor floats in the clouds. After that, we won't bother you."

"I don't owe Bel anything."

"He broke you out of prison."

"And I don't want to go back!"

"We've started," the crazy AI said. "If you don't do this little thing for us, Mister Arjona is a dead man."

She groaned in resigned frustration.

"You're doing the paperwork," she said. "I hate paperwork."

CHAPTER TWENTY-SEVEN

THE ROW OF excited, eager Puppets in the metal storage area looked at Rosalie Johns-10 with wet, shining eyes. Their looks darted often to the unmoving, lumpy shape in the bullet-proof glass behind her. Their mouths were open, looking for some stray scent of the war Numen, but the hermetic systems that separated episcopal troopers from His Holiness Lester rarely leaked.

"You deserve everything I have to give," Rosalie chanted. The Puppets repeated, and then inhaled deeply.

This cargo container was their home, for as long as it took to get to the Venus system. It might be their tomb, but they weren't in the absence. They'd brought a Numen with them, a candle in the dark, divinity to light the darkness.

"My body is your body," she said.

Some of them mouthed the words as she recited them before they all repeated them with an urgent expectancy. Two rows of eight Puppets squiggled closer to her. Each wore a badge that showed a little yellow panel. They followed her with their eyes, drinking in the *idea* of the Numen she would soon connect them to. Rosalie floated on sacral stilts with magnetized feet. Her sleeves flapped in the too-big clothing of a real Numen.

Over the years, the old sweaty work shirt had lost every scent of divinity, but the chest pocket had a fragment of old chewed gum and two of the stains on the shirt were definitely dried saliva. The rest was spilled food, but food that a Numen of the pre-Fall era would have been putting in his mouth.

"My organs are your organs," Rosalie said. They chanted the line with deep feeling.

The right sleeve was rolled up and pinned so that Rosalie could hold an uncoiled whip. She didn't need it, because they were being good, but a pre-Fall Numen without a whip didn't make a lot of sense to the common Puppets, even though it was a holy fact that the Numen often hadn't needed whips.

"Please take them!" one Puppet cried out, unable to contain himself. He bounced up and down on the wall rail where he'd anchored his legs. He was among the Puppets farther back with green panels on their badges. He eyed the bulletproof glass behind her, although the inner curtains obscured His Holiness. Rosalie snapped the whip.

"Interrupting is *bad*," Rosalie said in the tone of a displeased Numen, quoting from from *The Book of the Good Boy*. The whip crack and her tone made Jimbo Tyler's attention come back to her. "Bad boy!" someone said from the back row.

"Please take them!" Rosalie implored, raising her arms.

"Please take them!" the Puppet worshippers said.

She turned on her stilts until she faced the Numen's War Cage. She couldn't smell him, but she felt a frisson of side-excited, the knowledge and idea that a Numen was close, even if they couldn't be smelled. A Numen behind glass was magically unreal and half-real, like an epiphany just beyond understanding, grace just past seeking hands. Side-excited was about the delicious impendingness of the touch imbued with the quality of frantic almost there soonness.

"I love you," she intoned.

The Puppets behind her repeated the scripture, as did the sixteen armored Puppets near the War Numen's War Cage. Each of their badges showed a red panel and hoses connected their helmets to the chassis of the War Cage. Douglas Gold-4, the other priest, waited with his hand on the spigot for the main hose feed.

"Will you obey?" Rosalie said, from *The Book of Behaving,* Chapter of the Parable of the Behaving Puppet.

"Yes!" the Puppets all shrieked, even Doug.

"Will you obey?" Rosalie said. They only whispered their response this time, fearful of the last part of the liturgy even as they ached for Communion.

"Even in the absence?" she said in a low voice.

No one answered. Robbie whimpered near her. He made as if he would reach for Rosalie, for protection.

"Even in the absence?" she repeated, pinning Robbie with her stare.

"Yes," one of them said.

"Yes," another said.

The yesses started to become a chorus, an affirmation, an oath to walk away from the Numen themselves if so ordered. Some of them, especially the reds who were connected by hose to the War Cage, reached their hands out, trying to feel through steel and glass, to touch divinity.

"I bless you, for now," Rosalie said.

Doug turned the spigot on the hose. A hiss of sharing air sounded. The connected Puppets stilled, muscles tensed, waiting. The Puppets behind and around her bounced on their knees in envious excitement, drowning the sound of whirring fans. The aching anticipating stiffness of the Puppet troopers connected to the hoses softened. Some of their postures melted, relaxing bonelessly in the zero-g. Others hugged themselves. Others spoke in tongues on the common channel where it could be recorded and analyzed later for visions and snippets of wisdom from the divine channelling through the faithful. A few Puppets tentatively approached the thick windows of the War Cage. Some pressed their faces to the glass, trying to glimpse His Holiness between the folds of curtain. Its interior was about a cubic meter, and behind closed interior curtains the War Numen was safely strapped down against zero-g. After five minutes, Doug closed the spigot and the hissing exchange of air stopped.

"I love you," Rosalie intoned.

The Puppets repeated. Those who'd communed repeated with a depth of feeling that inspired an envious longing in her. Every communion, every bathing and feeding of the Numen, every brushing interaction with them was a deep mystery, a window into the cosmos that overlaid and warmed the experience of the cold hard world.

"I suffer through the world, but care not for the suffering," Rosalie said, raising her hands. "I live in a world of mysteries and miracles."

The Puppets repeated.

"Be the good boy," she said.

Some of the Puppet troopers began to weep openly. They wanted so much to be the good boy. *She* wanted to be the good boy. So badly. She cracked the whip, finishing the communion.

The Puppets remained silent and overwhelmed, those attached by hoses by their contact with divinity, those with green and yellow badges by the witnessing of it, each no doubt dreaming of an Edenic world where the Numen outnumbered the Puppets. Doug unhooked their hoses and blessed each. He also slipped an overseer key into each badge, turning reds to green, the worst colour, because it that colour had to wait the longest for their next communion.

The Puppets behind Rosalie perked up, pointing at their badges, trying to draw her attention. The sergeants organized the yellows into a line and the greens into another. Rosalie used her overseer key to turn each green to yellow and then in the next line, each yellow to red. Reds were eligible for next communion. Partway through this rite, one of the sergeants caught Robbie trying to sneak from the new yellow line to the yellow line being keyed to red. Rosalie whipped him once, while the other Puppets yelled and shoved at him. In the confusion, Jimbo made a furtive leap for the yellow-to-red line, but lost his nerve and raced back to his place in the green-to-yellow line. All in all, it was a typical communion.

CHAPTER TWENTY-EIGHT

BELISARIUS WAITED IN space with only the stimulus of his tumbling spin, as air and shock gel leaked out of the pilot capsule. His brain thought quickly enough that he had the time to reflect on how the sum of his choices and those of his makers had brought him here, to the pilot seat of a dead cousin, haunted by the imagined ghosts of a whole species he'd killed.

He tried making algorithms to steer his thoughts off those tracks. He directed them to puzzling at the philosophical implications of what he was now, in informational terms. He shared many characteristics with the baseline humans, the kind that might have hunted and gathered on the savannas of Africa a hundred thousand years ago, but with many additional genes added, by his own people, building him into a new species of the genus *Homo*. But informationally, he'd become more that too.

He carried metal and wiring and chips in his body now, dense with their own informational histories. Wired into the pilot capsule now, he saw through its senses, listened through its sensors, felt the radiation of space through its detectors. He was a hyper-creature, a conglomeration of already-complex evolved information-processing systems capable of reflecting on their own evolution, pastward and forward. Within this complicated intellectual frame, his brain invented all the musings, projections and interpolations it wanted, testing logical connections. These thoughts occupied him for minutes and hours, backgrounding his ghosts as he drifted closer and closer to his own underworld.

The Congregate recovery drone neared Belisarius' drifting capsule twenty-two point three one hours later. Just a small engine under a block of ice for reaction mass, the drone's spider arms telescoped to hug the capsule before it began to thrust at about a tenth of a gravity. Soon small paramedic bots crawled free of the drone. They filled some of the fractures in the capsule with foam, insulating where the shock gel had solidified in contact with space. The sinking, fearful feeling of being trapped gripped him more strongly, as if the gravity of the Congregate had gripped the orbit of his life. He neared a Congregate ship inexorably, filled with the people who had been hunting him and his people for months.

The capsule vibrated when grappler cables caught it. Other vibrations began, sounding like crawling insectoid feet. The tac-tac-tac of maintenance drones and security sniffers moved around the outside of his capsule. He felt the magnets of their feet through layers of plating. Short bursts of x-rays shot into the capsule, pixellating his vision. The capsule jerked as the grapplers pulled it into a hold. His heart beat faster.

The bay pressurized and the paramedic and maintenance drones crawled with magnetic feet over the capsule shell, removing the plating and armor. Through the jack connected to his brain, he felt the moment they plugged into the black box system. The flight recorders had been plausibly radiation-burned by Saint Matthew to destroy data that might have been valuable to flight investigators and telemetry that would have shown the capsule in Union custody. Hoses vacuumed the shock gel from around Belisarius as the inputs from capsule sensors abruptly stopped, one by one, leaving him with only his own senses. People entered the bay, just impressionistic shapes and colors intuited through gel-gooed eyes. They pulled him from the protective capsule, the gel slurping at his body. The tubes running into his lungs began to inject oxygen and suck away the gel. His body's choke response re-engaged and his chest heaved painfully. Through the half-solid gel packing his ears, he heard French.

"Internal bleeding."

"Processor two is down as well. Black box shot clean through."

"Piece of shrapnel just missed the artery."

"Chronometer's good. Four hours of drifting before the drone got to him."

"Could be neural damage."

"Half the chips aren't pinging. Might have gotten too close to an EMP."

They pulled waste and feeding hoses from numbed body parts and strapped him to a stretcher. One of the drones finally wiped his eyes of gel. He blinked, not needing to pretend disorientation.

"Running a fever. Dose him with anti-pyretics."

They shone light in his eyes.

"Lucky guy. Glad I wasn't fighting the dogs."

"I don't know how lucky. I don't know what we can salvage out of him. A lot of the internal control systems won't respond. He might be a write-off."

He'd expected an anti-pyretic in the next injection, but a powerful lethargy dragged him into sleep. He could probably have fought it, by stimulating the right parts of his brain to remain groggily awake, but he couldn't show his hand yet. He left instructions for the quantum intellect to record everything his body heard and felt and then let the sedation--

NINETEEN HOURS LATER, Belisarius came to a partial, drunken consciousness. He'd tried drugs before. After he and Will Gander had been working for about six months, he'd felt safe enough to try Waking Dream and Triptonic. He hadn't taken well to either one; the sense of dispossession and alienation from his body and thoughts terrified him. He'd experienced weird synaesthesias and inescapable frightening imagery. For a mind as powerful as his, so computationally fast and strong, it had been like watching a sped-up rollercoaster video for an eternity.

The sedation had not started like this; it had simply shut him down, like a robot being turned off. In this semi-conscious state, he could receive information from the quantum intellect: time, inertial navigational tracking, orientation to the prevailing magnetic field, even snippets of conversation and reporting around him. But he couldn't process. His mind seemed to be stuck, experiencing and calculating and reliving sensory input over and over, the experience unrooted to anything.

His mind followed weird *Homo quantus* dreams, exploring a space like the interior of the time gates. Electromagnetic sensation dopplered, making weird psychedelic colors of things he shouldn't have been able to see. He dreamed and processed and calculated a ghostly world that terrified him. He looked for Cassandra, but couldn't find her anywhere. He wasn't anywhere either. He was disembodied.

He reached out with his magnetic senses, but instead of feeling the world through his magnetosomes, he bent the world, shaping space around him. And he relived images of the *Hortus quantus* on Nyanga, not as he'd seen them moving and living their slow, collective lives and society. Instead, he kept seeing himself observing them, destroying the most vital parts of them, the most unique, most precious. And he cried in that timeless psychic loop.

"What's wrong with him?" a voice said in French. The sound warbled.

"This dose should have knocked him out. I don't understand their brain chemistry."

"Autonomic response?"

"Search me. They're rewired so many ways that all his reactions could be jumbled. Put him under again."

He dreamed of trying to escape the strange, empty space, but--

CHAPTER TWENTY-NINE

Introduction to The Speciation and Extinction Studies
White Paper

The Scarecrow Corps

ONCE VISIBLE THREATS to the Congregate are tracked and
managed, prudence requires us to seek the invisible and
unmanaged. This is less an arena of spies and insurgents
and economic and military threats, but instead a world of
statistics, trend lines, systems, complexity, and evolution,
all areas where human vision has difficulty focusing. The
human mind has evolved to use the past to extrapolate
into the future, but the true range of human vision, even
assisted by external computation, is measured in units
of centuries, a window that under normal circumstances
can barely perceive evolutionary change.

The major lessons from the extinctions of
hominin species like the *Homo rhodesiensis, Homo
neandethalensis, Homo denisova* are that failures to
keep up with even small changes in intellectual capacity,
technology, behavior and social systems can lead to

species-wide death. This is most clearly seen in the neanderthals, where *Homo sapiens* better exploited the archaic environment with superior abilities to abstract and communicate, which led to new technologies. Even without direct conflict, the simple shrinkage of neanderthal habitat due to *Homo sapiens* encroachment would have begun and completed a mathematically precise process of extinction.

In the last century, three major hominin speciation events have occurred. The addition of thousands of new genes, deletion or transcription-level control of thousands of others, all directed over a few decades by human intent using genetic technology, indicate that evolution itself is a new and immediate threat to be considered by the Scarecrow Corps.

The Puppet/Numen symbiotic pair of sub-species does not represent a threat to the Congregate. They appear to be an evolutionary dead end with a species lifespan on the order of centuries. The *Homo eridanus* are a more drastic departure from *Homo sapiens,* and sound arguments propose considering them a new genus. They appear to be genetically stable and adapted to their current habitat, but incapable of expanding into others. Their ferocity in combat is causing loses in the Congregate, but their contractor relationship with the Union will not endure longer than the rebelling nation does.

The *Homo quantus* is the exemplar, however, of the need for F-Division and the attention of the Scarecrow Corps. Their evolved intellectual and perceptual abilities, once considered trivial, have proven to be qualitatively and quantitatively different from the kinds of processing offered by artificial intelligence. They may present an existential threat to not only the Congregate, but to humanity itself, not on the scale of centuries, but certainly on the scale of millennia.

May, 2515

DEL CASAL HAD GENE maps on one holographic screen, shades of yellow, ochre, and orange showing subtle shifts in interaction networks. Another screen showed neural connectivity diagrams of the *Homo quantus* brains in three dimensions in soft holographic blues. The last, in green light, displayed a complex proteome profile, every small molecule associated in and around the neurons, at this magnification merely a misty cloud.

The Ministry of Intelligence doctors and geneticists worked around him on their own pieces, speaking softly to one another in French, sometimes looking his way. Some of them met his eyes, some didn't. They knew the field deeply, but they were spies too, spies for the Congregate in general and spying on him specifically. His need to escape was becoming all he could think about. Day and night. And some plans had started to form. He had trouble focusing on the devilishly complex problem of the *Homo quantus* and that was upsetting Bareilles.

Bareilles. Bareilles. Bareilles. She watched him all the time. Through cameras. Through her spies. In person. She recorded every gesture, every database request, every glance and eye movement. He'd been chipped again. She'd threatened it and now he had a deep ache under a short scar on his other arm. She'd only used the pain chip on him once, only for a second, an excruciating demonstration. He didn't know what the other one did, but she'd threatened to addict him to something.

The palate of his mouth also bristled with stitches. If they'd put a listening device there, they would hear everything he said, every whisper. But it might be something else. Another pain chip. A tracker. But Bareilles was also fiendish enough to have him operated on in his sleep and not put anything in, just to drive him into paranoia. She thought she could break him.

She needed him though. That was the key. She couldn't hurt him too badly, for all her threats. She couldn't drug him. Addictions impaired cognition. They'd gone to all this trouble to bring him here because they couldn't crack the neurology of the *Homo quantus* themselves. Even with the vast resources of empire, they couldn't crack it, and he could hold that over them. That was his leverage. Once he cracked it and told them, he was done for.

Del Casal turned suddenly, almost jumping. Bareilles stood in the doorway. He'd... felt her. Not really. He hadn't felt her. He hadn't. Her appearance in the doorway had changed the timbre of sound in the lab. She had a tiny smirk of satisfaction. He returned to his work, but his hands were shaking.

"*Docteur,*" she said, right behind him.

He swivelled in his chair and looked up innocently. He rose warily. She'd crossed her arms over her chest, as if to display the service band on her wrist. That was how she'd demonstrated the pain chip. His thoughts made an unbidden litany of *please don't turn it on, please don't turn it on.*

"It's not ready," he said, an edge of resentful defiance creeping into his tone. He crossed his own arms and spoke more quietly. "You'd better lower you expectations."

"Odd negotiating position," she drawled.

"Humans became behaviorally modern over the last 120,000 years, but it wasn't just a single gene change. Our behavior is the result of hundreds of changes at the gene and regulation level. It has to do with a number of neural connections so large that we need statistical mechanics to understand."

Her expression cooled, like someone across a poker table who intended to break his nerve. He'd played a lot of poker. He'd broken the resolve of many players. He'd only rarely been deceived. And he'd never been broken over cards.

Please don't turn it on, please don't turn it on.

"Marie Phocas once told me once that when she met Arjona, they argued, and that he said, perhaps in jest, that he was made of statistics," Del Casal offered. "I thought the story just showed more of Arjona's nonsensical, arrogant wordplay. But as I look into the *Homo quantus* brains, I realize he'd been telling a joke only he could laugh at."

"I'm not laughing," Bareilles said.

"Mental ability is the pattern of connections. Those patterns are partly genetic and partly developmental, and they're different in each person. I can't look at your captive *Homo quantus* and tell you which pathways are missing and which need to be removed. They're different in each one."

"You didn't have any successful Numen either."

Her expression kept hardening with disappointment, but the dull gun-metal of the service band kept drawing his attention.

"Making Puppets and Numen is an order of magnitude easier than trying to make an individual *Homo quantus* brain work."

"Let's be honest with each other," she said, her hand went to the controls on the service band. The feeling of utter powerlessness gnawed at hope, happiness, and self. "I went to a great deal of trouble to bring you here with the understanding that you would be of some use. Let's clarify. In forty-eight hours, one of two things is going to happen. You're going to show me meaningful progress, or I'm going to try new methods of motivating you."

"Forty-eight hours isn't enough! Not for anyone. I'm good, but no one is forty-eight hours good."

Her musing stare transfixed him, stilled his breathing.

"I don't feel you're properly focusing, doctor," she said. "I feel you're not trying hard enough. If you have nothing to show in two days, you'll regret it."

CHAPTER THIRTY

August, 2515

BELISARIUS TRIED TO wake from a sticky unconsciousness, but straining felt futile and exhausting. When his struggling stopped, his still mind floated in a kind of stasis, directionless. The objectivity running in his brain, hot and persistent and uncaring, fed him information he didn't understand, like readings from an uncalibrated instrument, in the language of fields and waves and interferences. He couldn't make sense of any of it. His thoughts stuttered over non-linear tracks within powerful sedation, ethereal, disembodied.

Between doses of the sedation, he'd had moments of lucidity, when he could make sense of fragmentary information. The objectivity had a precise inner time sense. He'd been sedated for days. He'd crossed two mouths of the Axis Mundi network. They'd crossed the second Axis in a smaller ship, something more maneuverable, and had come into an environment with gravity, a lot of gravity, nearly Earth-like. The data suggested he'd been transferred to an atmospheric vehicle and that he'd risen through the thick, burning atmosphere. Which meant he'd entered Venus through her heart, through the first Axis ever found. The historical gravity of that Axis had inflected Venusian history two hundred and fifty years ago, turning her from a failing backwater colony into an interstellar power. Now it was directing his history.

"I'm getting some conscious responses," one voice said in *français* 8.1.

"There's not a wire in him that hasn't been damaged or displaced. He got beat up pretty bad."

In a kind of bed. Strapped down. The sedation slowly wore off. He was meant to wake, so he gave them what they expected. He groggily opened crusty eyes and saw hard white lamps and a ceiling set with cameras. Two figures in green hospital gowns looked down at him.

"Can you speak?" one of them asked in accented Anglo-Spanish.

His disused throat didn't let him, saving him from faking through an answer.

"Mister Revilla," the other said. "Do you remember what happened to you?" Her Anglo-Spanish was less accented, like she'd spent some time speaking it.

Belisarius swallowed around a dry mouth. He turned his head side to side, very slowly. "In a capsule," he answered. "In space. Hurt."

He didn't need to pretend exhaustion. The *Homo quantus* were not built for toughness or endurance. The punishment of travel and sedation and the surgeries felt like a long slow beating. As he gradually became more aware of his surroundings, he realized his body was hotter than his normal low fever. Had he caught some infection? Or his body was rejecting some of the wiring and chips and other things that had been implanted in him. They switched to French.

"There's too much damage," she said. "Del Casal will want to do his own assessment anyway."

Belisarius croaked out the next words, swallowed, then said "Can I see the others?"

"We need to fix you first," she said. "You're still feverish."

"Are they safe?" Belisarius said.

"Nothing will get them here," she said.

He exhaled slowly. His lungs still ached from the shock gel and the beating he'd taken as a piece of Stills' cargo. He closed his eyes, cutting away stimulus, sinking first into savant, and then into a kind of meditative state.

Some of the chips Saint Matthew had put into him were replicas of those found in the dead *Homo quantus*. Some had been retrieved from the dead *Homo quantus*, the damage they'd sustained more authentic than anything Saint Matthew could have faked. But an entirely novel one didn't look like a chip at all. During the calcium deposition to change the shape of his facial bone structure, they'd embedded a chip in the growing bone and connected it to the internal *Homo quantus* wiring. It had no metals in it, so as to be invisible even to complex scans. Graphene and carbon nanotube wiring led to hundreds of particles entangled with pairs held by Cassandra. They had used entangled particles before, to send a single one-bit signal to a suicide switch inside Will Gander, and to navigate into the Puppet Axis. From within the fugue, he and Cassie could use the lines of entanglement between particles to map locations, as they had to find the locations of the Axis Mundi.

He gave a micro-current from one of his electroplaques to one of the entangled particles, enough to change its state, and by consequence, the state of its entangled partners, many many light-years away in Bachwezi, near Cassandra.

The sedation swallowed him again.

CHAPTER THIRTY-ONE

CASSANDRA EMERGED FROM the quantum fugue in a well-furnished stateroom aboard Manafwa Station. She'd chosen this room for her fugue diving. It could be Faraday-caged from the electromagnetic signals of the rest of the station and the crystalline regularity of its single large diamond window could make her feel for moments like she was by herself, alone with the cosmos.

Colonel Kuur, the wiry young Chief of Staff to Iekanjika watched her, almost protectively, possibly because the Bank admiral, Gillbard, fixated on her with more predatory interest. The mirror-finished bulge on his head emitted no EM, so he'd shut down his active sensors, but she had no idea what sort of sophisticated passive sensors he'd trained on her.

She normally entered the fugue for only a few minutes, just long enough for the quantum objectivity's senses to expand and sharpen, peering not at the particles that Belisarius had given her, but at the lines of entanglement that linked them to him. She'd been doing this every waking hour every day since he'd flung himself into the hands of the Congregate. On this two hundred and fourth time, it had been different. She'd been in almost an hour. Both men waited for her to speak. It took time for memory of quantum observations to be translated into classical, grounded information, and a good deal of her brain's processing capacity. Position. Velocity. Time.

"Belisarius signalled," she said. "He changed the entangled particle that..."

Wide solar system-spanning geometries filled her thoughts, things that were hard to translate into Anglo-Spanish. She activated the display beside her and entered a series of coordinates. Altitude with respect to the Venus Axis Mundi. Latitude. Longitude. Speed. And time. She transmitted to both men.

Gillbard smiled at her as he unstrapped himself from his chair. Kuur opened the door for him. A pair of Union MPs escorted the admiral off. The young colonel closed the door, and as he had hundreds of times now, dimmed the lights. He floated close enough for his smooth face to come into shiny focus. He offered her a bulb of water so cold that condensation trembled on its round sides. Her fingers shook. She had a low fever, but that wasn't why.

Bel had reached Venus. Bel had violated his body to disguise himself and now he was ringed by people more greedy than Gillbard, in the fortress of monsters. Her hands shook so hard that droplets of condensation floated off, carrying her anxiety into the air. Kuur's calloused fingers steadied hers and moved the straw to her lips. She swallowed the water down, its iciness forming an axis within her, something that didn't tilt and precess.

"How long will it take for the message to get there?" she said in his language, the Shona she'd memorized.

"The Bank has several fast scout ships waiting at the mouth of the Freya Axis, ma'am," he said with a respectful awe. "Maser transmission to scout ship is only minutes, as is the crossing.

The scout will duck out the Epsilon Indi side of the Axis and transmit to scout ships around the Anglo-Spanish Axis in system. That's another forty light-minutes. That scout will cross that axis to the Earth system, and transmit to Bank assets near Venus, which I've been told is ninety-five light-minutes away."

Three hours maybe, if everything went properly. And that would only tell them which habitat in the vast atmosphere of Venus held the *Homo quantus*. Then their plan, which Cassandra didn't even think would work, had to roll into motion. She clung to the cold bulb more tightly.

"May I ask you a question, ma'am?"

She looked up at him and nodded.

"General Iekanjika said that your species is designed for strategic and tactical abilities."

"I don't know if that worked."

"General Iekanjika said she trusts you."

"Really?" Cassandra's surprise was genuine.

"I've been asked to think through everything we could do to slow down the Congregate advance. Things aren't going well. My analyses give us only two to four weeks before the Congregate navy breaks into the Freya Axis."

"I'm sorry," she said.

"I'm thinking of mining the mouth of the Axis," he said. "Ships almost have to advance through the axis in single file. A weapon within the axis could do a lot of damage to them."

It felt good to have a physics problem, a quantitative problem.

"The wormholes of the Axis Mundi network are permanent," she said, "but not that permanent. Explosive energy still has to be absorbed somewhere, and too much energy could alter the hyper-conformation of the axis."

He looked at her without understanding. She put a hand on his arm.

"I don't know what would happen if you used heavy lasers or nuclear weapons or masers in the axis. No one does because no one has ever risked finding out. I wish I had some strategic insight for you. We're all just shooting in the dark."

"Yet you saw all the way to Venus."

She nodded slowly. "I think I'd like to be alone now."

CHAPTER THIRTY-TWO

May, 2515

DEL CASAL LEANED over subject ninety-one in the soft light of the medical lab. *Homo quantus*. Female. Forty-three years old. Healthy. Capable of entering the savant state. Full control over electroplaques to within micro-ampere precision. She'd been hardwired following his specification, fine metal and carbon nanotube filaments webbing her inside now, from the new control chips to the parts of the visual cortex where *Homo quantus* processed mathematical and geometric abstractions. She was like a marionette now, with all the strings inside. He could turn off her personality, her subjectivity, the person who worried about *I*, the person who felt pain, joy, fear. He could make her progidious brain process information, faster and more creatively than all but the most advanced AIs.

But his every attempt to induce their fugue state had failed.

One of the doctors barked a laugh across the room, startling him. Del Casal was trying to observe his symptoms, to diagnose himself. He suspected he was suffering from some paranoia, among other things. In the last forty-eight hours, he'd slept for only hours at a time, but woke up tasting blood and his thoughts feeling sticky, like they'd done something to him in his sleep. The stitches in his palate felt the same.

He'd had new dreams with their strange longings. He'd loved and feared in these recent dreams, usually without any object of affection or terror. The emotions just existed, pinning him like an insect in a display. Sometimes he dreamed of Bareilles and the other doctors, and in other nightmares, of the Scarecrow he'd seen in the distance. In one dream, he ran towards Bareilles, like she was safety and refuge. He awoke from those manipulated dreams angry, trying to guess at how the bitch had gotten into even his sleep. There were suite of hormones and neurotransmitters in animal patterning, sets of neurological effects that made infant animals and humans follow and imitate and love the parents. The effects weren't species specific – a newborn kitten could pattern to a dog and treat the dog as a parent. He wondered if she'd resorted to those, clumsily trying to cement his loyalty to her when he would happily put a bullet through her chest.

The cruel bitch held his life in her hands. He hated her to his bones, but some faltering part of him longed for a moment of pity and mercy from her, and he loathed that weakness. He wanted to hit something, and not just because of the situation. These directionless flashes of anger were real, like riding testosterone surges as an adolescent. What had they pumped into him?

Idiots! Idiots, idiots.

How could they treat him like this? The hard laughter spooked him again, made him cringe before he realized it. Laughing at him? He leaned over his patient. She was a mindless, empty shell until he switched her consciousness back on, utterly helpless. But unlike this *Homo quantus,* he might be able to control whatever Bareilles was doing to him. He could understand and then master these symptoms.

His anger.

His depression.

He could endure. His captivity would eventually end. Either he would engineer an escape or she would be replaced with someone more reasonable. And some sort of deal could be made when the politics improved, once the Congregate had obliterated the Union. Del Casal might not live freely back in the Plutocracy -- he knew too many military and industrial secrets now -- but some new equilibrium might be reached. A villa and a research lab in the clouds of Venus might be his. A university professorship. Some rank of respect within the Congregate intelligence services.

The glass doorway sounded behind him and he spun. Bareilles stood there. She'd shucked her tunic and wore a dark v-neck service shirt beneath, utility boots and dark fatigue pants. Her bare arms were lithe and muscled. Was she trying to use her femininity on him? She was attractive, yes, but he'd seen better. He wasn't one to fall for a passing pair of legs. She neared. He retreated, his breath coming shallow.

"Forty-eight hours," she said. "I'm disappointed."

She followed his retreating steps, not even glancing at subject ninety-one. A doctor beyond her shoulder looked up and very briefly his eyes met Del Casal's, smirking.

"I have to confess something. I've never been a good interrogator. I've never been good at prisoner management," she said, the last part coming out as a euphemism he didn't want explained. "I've worked with very good interrogators though. I respect the vocation and I'm not ashamed to ask for help."

She pinched at the muscle of his shoulder, as if calculating the depth of sinew.

"But you and I and all of this are eyes-only and need-to-know, so I can't delegate your daily... motivation. So you're stuck in my inexpert care."

He shrugged off her touch and stepped back. He was done being intimidated by her.

"You need me," he said, but his voice edging on shrill. "You need me healthy, lucid, aware, undistracted. Anything else is counter-productive."

She shrugged.

"I think I need you, but if you can't deliver anything useful, do I really? You haven't delivered. And I just don't know why, do I? It could be you're not good enough. It could be you're not trying hard enough."

"The problem is fiendishly complex. Even the best need time!"

"I think we're at a crossroads and I'm going to have to motivate you, but fair warning: my inexpertness might lead to mistakes. I wanted you to know that some of the permanent damage I'm going to do is intentional, but some is not."

"I'm not an idiot who needs convincing! I'm a genius with unique skills! I respond to partnership! And money!"

She continued advancing, her manner almost alluring, but that made her seem more threatening.

"If I thought your loyalty was for sale, don't you think I would have bought it by now? It's never been for sale. You work for multi-nationals one day. A casino the next. A terrorist the next. And then the Puppets. You know what those all have in common?"

She caught his wrist. She was strong. He couldn't pull away.

"You weren't loyal to any of them. A man is his character, doctor, and you are only loyal to Antonio Amador Nariño Del Casal." Her slim fingers poked at his chest with each name.

"I can be loyal to you if I'm treated with respect."

"Not even a little," she said, smiling as if chiding a naughty child. "I met you while you were selling out Arjona. Since you've been here, you've spent more time thinking of escape than you have of my needs."

She released his wrist and he cradled it, even though she hadn't hurt him.

"No," he whispered but he didn't know anymore what he was denying.

"Let me explain *my* stakes, why I'm disappointed in you, and why I've decided to do permanent damage."

The lab tilted around him and he stumbled back around patient ninety-one's bed.

"A new weapon has been invented," she said, standing twenty centimeters from him. "Thousands died on the dreadnought *Parizeau*. Thousands more died in putting down the Union rebellion. Those numbers are baked into the stakes already. Military, economic and reputational costs are still being calculated. We have enough pieces of Union ships to reconstruct their inflaton drive and inflaton cannon. Two to four years to prototype, five to seven for a full roll-out to every part of the Congregate. We don't think the Banks can match that timeline and our intelligence suggests that neither the Ummah nor the Middle Kingdom even have samples to reverse engineer. The immediate future is expensive, but it's still a bargain in the long run, despite the costs."

"You don't need me then," he said.

"We can't cost the unknown," she said with a lilt in her beautiful French, like she was speaking at a party, entertaining other socialites. "Who else has the other new weapon? This *Homo quantus* mind? One Bank? Three Banks? The fleeing *Homo quantus* certainly do and what do they want right now? What will they want in a century? Our short term win on inflaton technology isn't much of a bargain if in a few decades we lose a biological arms race."

Her nose neared his.

"And the good Doctor Antonio Amador Nariño Del Casal," she said, punctuating every other syllable with a hard poke to his chest, "is not enthusiastically on my side."

He wanted to swat her hand away, but he realized that she terrified him. Bareilles ran a fingertip along subject ninety-one's face.

"They're beautiful, aren't they?" she said. She looked back at him playfully. "I have nothing against foreigners. You. Her. The Puppets. We live in a world where we have to get along with one another."

She came around the head of the bed, putting her hands on the rail above the monitoring equipment.

"We can't seize Oler by frontal assault," she began and for a moment he lost the thread of her meaning. "Even with primitive tech, the planetary batteries of the Puppet Free City could hold us off prohibitively long. And the larger danger is that another patron nation swoops in and takes the Puppet Axis while we press the assault. So for decades we've relied on infiltration and espionage. We capture Puppets and interrogate them. They're even less forthcoming than you, but you know what makes them talk?"

"You have Numen," he said, retreating to put the bed between them. His voice wouldn't resonate with the strength he knew he could project. She shortened the space between them, step by step. "We began with refugee Numen and some early escapees," she said. "We despised the Numen. They were monsters. Every single one of them was guilty of crimes against humanity, but taking them in presented some long term strategic advantages. The escaped Numen are the best interrogators of Puppets, who don't feel pain the way baseline humans do and can't be coerced. The escaped Numen were also the best infiltrators and spies, even if they sometimes only obliged us at gunpoint. So we held our noses for state and empire. That sparked my interest in you. If you were making new Numen, why should you be making them for the Puppets? We have a few, a very few Numen who still fully express the Numen pheromones. Imagine what we could do with a platoon of Numen, though. A company of them. Or a regiment. We wouldn't need very many to capture the entire Free City and therefore the Puppet Axis."

"I'll do it!" Del Casal said. "As a partner!"

She shook her head, barely enough for him to notice. Despite his resolve, he retreated.

"No one in their right mind would trust you, doctor. I need absolute, enthusiastic obedience."

She touched her service band and he braced himself for pain. Instead, a weird dizziness bloomed behind his eyes, a strange taste on his tongue. His skin crawled. "Psychotropics in a chip?" he said, stabbing a finger at her. He blinked around the subtle shift in perceptions, the beginning of a light euphoria. How many remote-controlled quick-release drug packs had they placed in him? "That's the best you've got?"

She shook her head, smiling. The euphoria strengthened. He felt strange things for her. She was impressive. Sublime.

"Your notes on Puppet physiology were very useful, doctor," she said. "They're really a map for us to follow."

The universe expanded around her, became richer, meaningful, and so, so wonderful, magical, more than could be contained in words or thought. His growing awareness and awe of the truth of the entire world could only be contained in a soul. He'd never thought thoughts like this. He'd never felt his soul before.

"You've committed crimes against humanity, doctor," she said. "I can imagine few fitting punishments. You're a slaver, pure and simple. You didn't do it for the survival of your nation. You did it for money, for the pride of puffing yourself up, to tell yourself you were the best, that you did what no one else could do. Justice sometimes moves slowly, doctor, but we take it very seriously."

His feet rooted in place as she approached. He panted through his mouth, imbibing the richness in the air, tasting the truth of the world. The overwhelming awe and majesty of the universe washed into every part of him, like the wonder of the world was wicking into him. He'd never experienced a drug like this, so powerful, so real. The elation swept him up. She touched his cheek, ran her fingers along his jaw line and he was so happy, fulfilled.

"You didn't have accessory olfactory systems," she said "because you're not a lizard. We had to engineer those sensory tissues and build in electronic connections to the awe centers of your brain. There are many more changes to Puppet physiology, but that's the main one. That's the doorway for Puppets to reach their dreams of majesty."

Dimly, her extraordinary, terrifying words penetrated the wonder. She was godlike. She could change him. It was *right* that she could change him. She could do anything she wanted to him. She was more than human. He'd never seen it. He'd never been capable of seeing it. Before these revelatory moments, he'd been part of a soulless, material world, blind to the vast truth of the cosmos. And in the deepest part of him, he knew that *she* was the doorway to everything important.

"I'm the granddaughter of a Numen refugee," she said. He hung on the timbre and tone of each exquisite syllable. "My grandfather was an intelligence officer, and he loved the Congregate enough that he made children with a callow, stupid war criminal, one of the short-sighted, immoral Numen who'd succeeded in fleeing the consequences of the Puppet rebellion. Producing some Numen for the Congregate was so important that he mated with that monster."

"It should have been a clinical *in vitro* process, but we learned early that physical presence helps the specific Numen microbiomes to persist in the long term. It was not a pleasant thing for my mother to be raised by that kind of a monster, to spend day after day with her. Nor for me. I knew my grandmother. By then she'd learned enough of Congregate culture and language to not embarrass herself and the family, but her roots were still very evident. I don't know if I would have been strong enough to do what my grandfather did. I don't think I'm committed enough to have mated with one of those slavers. But the Congregate needed Numen."

"Numen physiology isn't always stable, but I'm one of the stable ones. I can make you *want* to do anything with my presence." Her voice seemed distant, as if coming near enough to her was impossible. "And I can torment you with Puppet dreams and Puppet needs with my absence."

He knelt, unable to apprehend the majesty and depth of her. She leaned closer. The experience of her smelled more powerful.

"Make me more *Homo quantus*," she said in a hard voice that terrified his soul. "Right now."

He quivered with awe as what she needed sank in. *She* wanted more *Homo quantus*. And he had to give them to her. He squirmed backwards, away from her magnificence, pulling himself up the side of the bed. He didn't want to leave her. He didn't want to the lose sight of her, the smell of her, the taste of her on the air, but she wanted *Homo quantus*. She stood before him, vast, august, terrifying, the doorway into a world he'd never known, making all his life before this seem tragically small.

CHAPTER THIRTY-THREE

August, 2515

EVOLUTION AND SPECIATION were at first conceived as a tree of life, with clear vertical descent through discreet branching points, with no genetic transmission between branches. It took time to realize that genes move quite freely between species. Bacteria trade genes among themselves promiscuously. Significant fractions of human DNA are viral in origin. Complex eukaryotes are derived from no less than sixty-five separate events of a single prokaryote swallowing another whole.

And eukaryotes with their cellular nuclei and mitochondria and chloroplasts filled a new ecological niche: they became the life forms capable of inhabiting life styles requiring high-energy metabolism. Armed with energy budgets beyond anything bacterial metabolism could match, eukaryotic cells grew bigger and performed new and complex feats. And they continued to exchange genes.

Homo sapiens and *Homo neanderthalensis* diverged over millennia, each collecting mutations and adaptations to the rapid environmental changes of the Pleistocene era. Biochemical changes altered metabolism, cognition and socialization of the two species as they competed with each other in the similar ecological ranges. But modern humans and Neanderthals also interbred. Important genes in modern humans originated in the Neanderthal lineage. And once modern humans had acquired those genes, the Neanderthals were outcompeted to extinction. This is a cautionary tale and a model.

White Paper on the Evolutionary Future of the Congregate, Chapter Four
F-Division, Ministry of Intelligence
Venus

BELISARIUS WOKE INCOMPLETELY in a small hospital room, only a few meters on a side, with softly-lit plastic walls. The faint electromagnetic buzz of medical devices pressed against his magnetosomes. He felt weak, starved. He'd been sedated so many times even he had lost count. Several times, the sedative had disrupted even the quantum objectivity running in parallel with his thoughts.

He shifted the white covers. His body still ached, but his fever was low. Bandages wrapped his arms and neck, and two spots on his chest. His sinuses were stuffed and aching. His fingertips scraped along the bristles on his head where it had been shaved for sensors to be taped to his scalp.

The front wall of the room was transparent plastic, two doors, looking onto a walkway ringing a lower plaza within some kind of medical facility. Many sets of transparent double doors lined the ring on his level, all little rooms like his. Some were occupied. Others were dark. People in medical gowns moved along the walkway. They were mostly light-skinned, like most Venusians.

With some difficulty, he activated the augments in his eyes. The lenses telescoped, resolving the bed and its patient room across the way. The head had been shaved, but he recognized the sleeping or sedated face of Mariana Jiménez. He'd never spoken with her, but he'd seen her face, uncertain, fearful, resistant, when they'd evacuated the Garret. She'd stayed behind. She hadn't believed him.

The two figures stopped in his doorway. A Venusian woman wore dark service fatigues, with lieutenant-colonel bars, but no unit insignia. Not a good sign. Her blond hair was tied back into a braid, revealing delicate cheekbones with only the barest of acid spattering. The glass of the double doors fanned open as Belisarius' groggy brain finally recognized the man.

Antonio Del Casal.

The doctor held himself proudly, but the gray had spread at his temples. The muscles in his face betrayed anxious exhaustion. Belisarius had spent a lot of time observing baseline humans, and his brain could track and analyze the degree of tension and relaxation in the forty-two facial muscles and interpret emotion as well as an AI. Del Casal's careful expression couldn't hide the fight or flight response. They entered. With feigned clinical indifference, Del Casal rubbed his thumb over Belisarius' cheek.

"Clumsily done, Arjona," he said in Anglo-Spanish. "You've lost your touch, I think. Did you think we wouldn't check your DNA?" Del Casal said. "Very stupid."

The woman wheeled over a black stool and perched herself on it.

"We all know *Monsieur* Arjona isn't stupid, don't we?" she said. Her *français* 8.1 was beautiful, with the hint of a lower cloud drawl accenting her mid-house diction. "Do you fancy yourself a Trojan Horse? A hero to rescue my *Homo quantus*? An assassin to balance the scales?"

"You haven't learned much of the *Homo quantus* I guess," Belisarius croaked.

"I've learned little about the *Homo quantus*," she said, her stare intense. "Since mine are all broken, I don't know anything about your quantum fugue. I don't know how the Union entered the Puppet Axis. I don't have any details on this story of a time travel device." She leaned forward. "This is the opening of negotiations, *Monsieur* Arjona. I'm telling you what I want. Now you tell me what you want."

"The *Homo quantus* aren't soldiers," he said, clearing his throat. "They're not fighters. You've seen that. They're fragile and you're using them as external processing systems. They'll never do more for you. You've captured some innocent, inept researchers. You can create suffering, but the research is a dead end. Your spies must have known this, otherwise you would have moved against the *Homo quantus* before now. If we actually had been useful, would the Banks have left us unprotected in the Garret?"

"And yet," she said.

"There is no yet. You've studied us. We're researchers, yes. Contemplatives, yes. Economic geniuses, no. Strategists, no. Soldiers, no."

"I like the results we're getting from the pilots," she said. "They're better than ours. They're not as good as the *Homo eridanus*, but I don't need them to be. If one of your *Homo quantus* can save the lives of three of four *pur laine* Congregate pilots, it's a reasonable trade. Your people started this."

"I don't know what happened at the Puppet Axis," Belisarius said. "I don't know how the inflaton drives actually work. I don't think that the Union does either. But they made an induced wormhole within an inflaton field. It opened into the Puppet Axis. They haven't been able to replicate it since. They had me look at the geometry of the process, to try to figure it out, but I didn't understand it either. They weren't going to let me and Cassandra go if we didn't figure it out. That wasn't part of the deal. So we escaped."

"You can give me all the information you have on this process," she said, handing him data pad. "Your *Homo quantus* memory is perfect isn't it?"

Belisarius set the pad on his lap.

"My memories are good, but they're not free. I want half of the *Homo quantus* released from here. I don't care where they get sent. The Plutocracy will at least care for them, but the Ummah or the Middle Kingdom would give them asylum."

"Only half?"

"I didn't think you'd bargain for all, so I didn't want to insult you by starting there."

Her half-smile bordered on mischievous. He held out the pad to her, but she didn't take it.

"Half," he said to the woman, still holding the pad to her.

She smiled more widely.

"You don't want to make me angry," she said, taking back the pad. "Talk."

"We deal first," he said.

The officer smiled, a predatory joy in the expression. She tapped her service band. Moments later, five *Homo quantus*, hands bound in front of them, were shepherded through the doors. Belisarius' room wasn't meant for so many so they crowded shoulder to shoulder. Sofía Scanavacca, Maria Angelica Juez, Paola Isaza, Carlos Niño and César Tovar. Terrified, they looked at him without recognition, because he looked different. But he knew them. Some just by name. Some he'd grown up with.

"That one is our next pilot," the lieutenant-colonel said, pointing at Maria Angelica. "Wire her up." The woman froze as Belisarius' heart froze.

"No!" he said. An orderly was pulling Maria Angelica back. She screamed.

"Stop!" Belisarius said.

"You refused my first request. And my second," the officer said. She pointed at Paola. "Her too."

A different orderly pulled Paolo away. She followed, crying.

"Stop! I'll deal!" Belisarius said.

"We deal when I say we deal," the lieutenant-colonel said. "I've told you what I want. The cost in *Homo quantus* to you is entirely dependent on how put out I feel."

"Bring them back," he said.

The lieutenant-colonel leaned forward. "They're never coming back, *cheri*, because I don't like your games. I've been honest with you. I need more pilots to counter the *Homo eridanus* flying for the Union. If you give me something more strategically useful than a hundred and fifty pilots, there's plenty of room to deal. You told me you'd studied the interaction between the inflaton drive and induced wormholes. Put it all in here."

He took the pad and began configuring it for more efficient input. He felt the terrified stares of the three prisoners.

CHAPTER THIRTY-FOUR

Université de Vénus
Lecture and Event Series

THROUGHOUT THE YEAR, the Faculty of Foreign Affairs holds a variety of lectures and events to showcase accomplished academics, diplomats and professionals to advance public debate and understanding of foreign policy issues.

The 2515 Simone Bilodeau Lecture Series on Foreign Policy will feature Vincent Rodriguez, Foreign Policy Advisor to the *Homo eridanus* Moot at Indi's Tear. In a series of eight lectures, Professor Rodriguez will discuss the governance systems of *Homo eridanus* society, trade and foreign policy questions, the unique diplomatic and military approach of the *Homo eridanus,* with a focus on the policy drivers behind their recent decision to contract military specialists to both the Congregate Navy and the rebellion of the Sub-Saharan Union. *L'université de Vénus* gratefully acknowledges the generous support of the House of Styx and the House of Storms.

MARIE SAT IN her palanquin and tried not to fidget. She wanted to look at the immigration officer, and maybe give him a good whack, but as a *grande dame*, she had people to do this for her. She could nonetheless make her face look annoyed, which it sort of did anyway.

The Immigration headquarters orbiting Venus was a colossal station, built of steel and diamond and plastic, designed by some of the finest architects and artists in the Congregate. Sunlight angled across mirrored arrays, focused and defracted into the right colors to softly illuminate sculptures of diamond and emerald. Marie's palaquin was similarly artful, flimsy some might say; it had negligible ramming mass. The immigration officer's bureau took advantage of the microgravity to be airy and bright with many transparent panels. The only unsightly thing in the immigration hall was a big steel tank holding about five or six cubic meters of water under eight hundred atmospheres of pressure. Martine, Marie's.... lady-in-waiting, floated before the immigration officer gracefully.

"*Mademoiselle* Caillouette," the officer said, "I am not arguing with you or disrespecting *Mademoiselle* Hudon."

Marie was careful to not turn at the sound of her name.

"Professor Rodriguez' visa and DNA information have not arrived yet," the officer continued. "I can't clear him on security grounds because I don't yet have the information from the Consulate at Indi's Tear."

"*Mademoiselle* Hudon is not responsible for your communications problems," Martine said with growing affront. Marie liked her. She could be feisty. "Professor Rodriguez' visa is in order and *Mademoiselle* Hudon has made the trip here as a donor to the Foreign Policy Council of the university."

"I'm sure the message from the Consulate will arrive within

the next day or two," the officer said. "Professor Rodriguez will be a guest of immigration during that time."

Marie made an impatient gesture and sound, probably not a graceful sound. The immigration officer and Martine quieted. Then Martine leaned in.

"*Mademoiselle* Hudon came to receive her guest, who is carrying a properly issued visa. Her aunt, Marielle Hudon, is an old colleague of the Minister of Immigration. She is also waiting on the arrival of *Mademoiselle* Hudon's guest, and if there are delays, she'll feel obliged to contact the Minister."

Marie looked their way now. The officer looked uncomfortable. Martine had told the truth and the officer's AI could quickly scour the celebrity and political reports to find accounts of *Tante* Marielle's Cabinet contacts easily enough. He coud make the calculations about how much he wanted to explain to his supervisor, especially if the Minister got involved. The officer might be thinking whether he wanted to risk his name being on some House of Styx naughty list.

"I'll issue an exemption code for now," he said finally. "If we don't receive the confirmation from the consulate, we'll have to do additional interviews."

"Fine," Martine said. "Do it quickly. *Mademoiselle* Hudon has been waiting long enough."

Soon, robot servitors carried the big tank out of immigration. Marie's robotic bearers bore her beside it.

"I'm Amélie Hudon," Marie said sweetly. "It's so nice to finally meet you, professor."

A familiar, atonal voice spoke.

"Bite me."

CHAPTER THIRTY-FIVE

IN THE CRAMPED cargo bay, the Puppets clung to the reorganized crates before their final entry into Venusian orbit. Rosalie motioned Jimbo to back up a bit. Several troopers had scooched closer, inhaling the divinity of His Holiness Lester. A peaceful glow of meaning had settled onto all of them, a wondering disbelief at the size and beauty and rightness of the cosmos.

To care for His Holiness, they'd unsealed the bulletproof glass, revealing the old shrivelled body inside, releasing the stale, concentrated smell of him. The Numen flinched from the soft, eager hands as they washed him. Doug led the process and today Erin got to climb into the War Cage with Lester. She nearly vibrated with excitement. She'd been the best good boy. The feeling of contentment ran deep in them all. They knew where they were. They knew what would happen. It was all part of a hallowed destiny they couldn't apprehend because of its vast wonderity.

All cargo tankers entering Venusian orbit were dosed with sterilizing x-rays, for contagions, to scan the interior of the tankers, and to prevent smuggling. The bathing of His Holiness Lester was like their last supper, the final picnic, the end of peace before they girded themselves for their final battle. The

Numen had created the Puppets to replace the Numen in jobs too dangerous for fragile divinities, so additional pigments already permeated their bodies. The pigments absorbed many kinds of hard radiation and their DNA repair systems were aggressive, but they would still probably all take fatal doses, even the War Numen. They would begin to die, but the automated customs systems would probably not register their small sizes as biologicals and the radiation shielding in their pods would further camouflage their outlines. They might live long enough to finish their quest.

Robbie hadn't been the best good boy, but he'd tried hard. Rosalie chose a spot close to the War Cage for him because he was young and after this everything would be harder. They'd tied him to a strut and he wriggled in his bonds, smelling at the air, urging on Erin and Doug.

"Make him smile," he said with a barely controlled shiver.

Erin sponged the wrinkled face and papery eyelids of the dying Numen, her expression revealing a distant, disbelieving reverence in the experience. His Holiness Lester was over seventy years old; most Numen didn't survive past fifty. There was something prodigious and holy in this Numen's endurance. Doug smiled indulgently and dabbed his fingertip in red paint and smeared a smile onto Lester's slack lips and cheeks. Jimbo scooched closer, not to the Numen precisely, but to Rosalie. He trembled, staring, inhaling heavily through his mouth. He hugged Rosalie's waist tightly.

"He's smiling," he said breathlessly.

As Jimbo squirmed against her, she noticed his badge was red. They were all feeling the Numen now anyway, before they went into their life shells, so colors wouldn't matter for a while, but his was supposed to be yellow. She didn't want to spoil this moment, her moment of communion with the Numen. But she turned and did a quick count, finally spotting one of the troopers who should have been wearing a red badge, but hers was yellow.

Rosalie took the whip from her belt and hit Jimbo with the coils. He let go and floated back. She had everyone's attention except the Numen's. This was the harder part now. In the glow of divinity, some messages penetrated deeper, some shallower. Priests learned how to pitch their voices to the right tones, to match the recordings of the pre-Fall Numen in all the television shows and movies.

"You!" she accused, as if she were the Puppets and she the betrayed. "You!" She stabbed her finger at Jimbo. Deep in the embrace of divinity, all of the Numen cowered back.

"You stole a different badge color," she said coldly.

She wasn't wearing her stilts nor her holy Numen clothing, but the Numen was present. Rosalie stood like one of the overseers of old, the herders and movers of the divine servants. Jimbo bolted towards Jane Mulligan-16, to give back her badge. Mulligan-16 flinched away from the bad boy and the badge floated, spinning in the zero-g. He pushed it awkwardly and it bounced off Mulligan-16's forehead.

"The Numen is very mad!" Rosalie said in her most booming voice. The Numen stayed still, too holy to uncurl from his fetal position. "The Numen is communicating with me," Rosalie said, "and asking me whether I think everyone's color should be reset to green."

Low moans of despair sounded. Someone shrieked "Bad boy, Jimbo!"

Rosalie moved along the rail with just her toes, raising her arms, making herself look bigger.

"Do I need the airlock, Jimbo?" she demanded. "Do you want to be like Jeffey?"

In his panic, in the sudden turn from divine joy to divine anger, Jimbo had let go of the rail and now rotated slowly in the air. He was shaking his head, breathing hard with his mouth, smelling.

"I don't want to, Jimbo," Rosalie said, "but Lester can order me to do anything. He can tell me anything he wants."

They gasped. "No, no, no, please," Jimbo whispered.

"Take him into his pod now," Rosalie said. "That is what the Numen wants."

"No!" Jimbo shrieked.

The punishment was severe. They had to enter their pods in about ten minutes, but Jimbo would miss ten minutes of the presence of divinity, miss the washing and caring of the Numen, maybe right before he died. But she needed to be severe. This mission, soaked in such holy consequence, needed them all to be the Good Boy all the time because they were marching into the dark, carrying a fragile candle.

Jimbo wriggled and resisted as fearful hands grabbed and punched him. He cried and screamed "no, no, no!" Rosalie's hands shook. She didn't like being the parent. She hadn't asked to be the responsible one, who loved and disciplined the Puppets, taking a role that should have been the Numen's, but for the Fall. She hadn't wanted to decide for the Numen; she ached, like all the Puppets did, for the gods to be the way they were before. And she was young, very young in the hard journey of a priest. It was a hard thing to be a parent, deciding for others. But maybe, if they succeeded, if they brought back Del Casal, they really would enter a new age, a new generation and era of gods walking among the faithful, taking back the roles that the Puppets had shouldered for them. Strong, nimble hands shoved a screaming Jimbo into his safety pod. They strapped him tight and closed him in. Jimbo beat at the inside of his pod, blunt distant sounds.

Rosalie felt a kind of dazed satisfaction. In the presence of divinity, the cosmos could make strange bridges between past and present and future; moments of the Edenic past could live in the present. She felt like one of those moments of the past had reached out to them. Thick in the scent of the War Numen, something deep and important visited them today like the fingers of fate brushed them.

And weird images slithered into her thoughts, waking dreams laying a surreal transparency over the cold hardness of the cargo bay. A keening pried its way into her thoughts, a high-pitched vibration accompanying the unreal colors dyeing her soul. The blunt thudding of Jimbo's fists inside his pod receded.

"I'm lost," Rosalie intoned in the voice of sermon. The troopers, and even Doug, froze, listening. "I float, adrift in a world that isn't mine, carrying a tiny light against the absence."

Except it wasn't the absence. She'd endured that many times, but she didn't have other words for this vision of some other cosmos. The Puppets huddled in place, tasting the air, trying to see what she saw, recognizing the touch of divinity in this moment. They whispered about her supposedly oracular visions when they didn't think she could hear them. Some averted their eyes. She wasn't quoting any part of the Puppet Bible. She ranged beyond scripture. She'd experienced abstract visions like this for years, with a sense of strange space and shape, but clearer now, more tactile and cold. What were the Numen trying to tell her? What part of divinity was this? She shivered. Doug came close, recording with his service band.

"The world is transparent, not real," she said. "I'm alone. I'm a ghost. Trapped."

Nearby Puppets started moaning. "Stop it, stop it, stop it, no," Joey whimpered, covering his head with his arms.

Rosalie couldn't. The vision strengthened. The fog of that

other world made this one seem indistinct, as if the other Puppets existed behind a veil, even Doug, right beside her. But the world had expanded. Doug seemed bigger. No. Not bigger exactly. He had more depth. She could see parts of him that weren't the meat parts of him. She squinted to see Joey and pushed off the wall, coming close. She laid her hands on Joey's head. The touch felt removed from her, only half of an experience. Rosalie's hands shook. Her visions had never intruded so deeply into her world.

"You're safe in this world, Joey," Rosalie said. "This is not your journey."

Rosalie pushed away to float to the Numen. Lester's thin eyelids slitted open. At her approach, he squeezed them shut and pulled blankets over his naked wrinkled body. She rested in front of him, smelling deeply, then breathed through her mouth, filling herself with the holy spirit. The thin transparent world without shape, with too much shape, holding only a vague fear and hopelessness left her. Her nearness to the Numen brought a familiar elation that banished misgivings. Doug came close.

"His Holiness banished my vision," she said.

"If His Holiness banished it, was it profane?" Doug said with a queasy expression. She didn't blame him. He was the junior priest on a mission of destiny and now his superior saw possibly profane visions? What would she do in his shoes? Convene a heresy trial? Court judges were all bishops and they had no bishops. Could he somehow prod the War Numen to take up the role of divine assessment? If she couldn't lead them, could he? Rosalie had never been sure she could do it herself. She breathed of Lester more deeply and the world seemed to solidify further, to make sense, even if she couldn't grasp the subtlety of its logic.

"I think I saw a deeper absence," she said. Jill, Marigold,

and Reggie heard her and started crying. "It's a faint vision of a world that might be." Lester shrank from her stroking touch and close-sniffing nose. He made it right. Lester made everything right. "I don't think it's a world that has to be," she said to Doug. "It's only our world if we don't succeed."

"We'll do it," Sammy said. "We'll do it!" Others repeated, pumping their fists.

Rosalie caressed Lester's flaky cheek. He didn't understand how special he was. He didn't understand that he didn't have to be afraid anymore. He was their candle. He would light their way through the darkness. He was an island of divinity, a raft they clung to with all their hearts, hoping they had the strength to save all their people. Through him, they would rekindle light and wonder in the world.

"I love you," Rosalie whispered to him. Lester trembled and pulled the blanket to completely cover himself.

"Strap His Holiness Lester safely," she said. "Add the radiation shielding. Then take your good pills and get into your pods."

CHAPTER THIRTY-SIX

BY CHARACTER, THE *Homo quantus* lack aggressive qualities that are sought in even the most peaceful of military units. They are pensive and retiring, disliking sudden movements or loud sounds. They neither enjoy nor seem particularly good at tactics or strategy, on the naval battlefield nor in the economic state space of corporate warfare. These results seem to have discouraged the Banks, despite the stupendous cognitive advances in the *Homo quantus*. Even those *Homo quantus* who cannot access their fugue state possess capacious memories, exabytes in the eighth and ninth generation, with some assessments suggesting zettabytes of memory capacity by generation twelve. Paired with abilities to analyze and process data quantities in the hundreds of petaflops and possibly exaflop range, everything but temperament seemed to have fallen in the *Homo quantus* Project's favor. The Banks however entirely missed the point in what they'd created in the *Homo quantus*.

New gene sets may face the same environments as baseline humanity and perform no better than their forebears. But novel genotypes are gateways into new environments and ecosystems. Increased social cooperation had some minor immediate survival impacts for the first hominins, but found its full impacts as a gateway to agriculture, architecture and chemistry. The Banks invest on a variety of scales, from seconds to centuries, but in the *Homo quantus,* they created novel benefits they could not understand because the full impacts will be felt on the scale of millennia.

Scarecrow Musings on the Garret Notes
F-Division

THREE ORDERLIES IN white and green medical uniforms moved Belisarius from his small room. He managed to peek through some of the glass doors and recognized four other *Homo quantus.* They brought him to a room off the floor of the central pit. His last room had been equipped like a low-care unit. This one was an operating theatre. The ultraviolet sterilizing light shut off as they entered.

The world pressed at him, but not in a way he could measure. He couldn't feel his magnetosomes. He couldn't feel his electroplaques. They felt like numb feet, like the quantum objectivity he couldn't feel in his mind. He'd long resented the *Homo quantus* part of him, a feeling that had sharpened with the tragedies that had followed him, but being severed from the quantum objectivity was alienating. The world felt insubstantial. What had they done to him?

Del Casal limped in shortly, accompanied by a thick-muscled and blond-bearded nurse. Swollen bruises yellowed Del Casal's cheeks at the back of his jaw, like he'd had dental surgery. The nurse didn't appear to be paying much attention to Belisarius. Del Casal scowled.

"Your minder?" Belisarius said in Anglo-Spanish, which strictly speaking wasn't politic within the Congregate. A bit of Del Casal's old arrogance showed and he glanced meaningfully at the man.

"He's a real nurse," Del Casal replied in Anglo-Spanish. "We're all minded here." Del Casal gave a few instructions in French and the man moved around the small room, preparing instruments.

"You really messed this one up, Arjona," Del Casal said mildly. "The most hunted man in civilization tries to sneak into the most guarded security operation in civilization." Del Casal shook his head. "I would have run far away from here if I could."

"What have they done to my brain? I can't feel my magnetosomes. Or anything."

Del Casal limped around him, checking on readings.

"We missed you when we were passing out the shares of the haul," Belisarius said.

Del Casal put down his pad and regarded him with blood-shot eyes.

"I jumped ship when I saw the plan heading full speed towards a wall."

"But we did it," Belisarius said.

"You started a war that's getting us all killed. Your people. You. The Union. Me. That's all you did."

"No one could have known that the Union would have lasted this long. I thought they would get the fight they wanted and get wiped out, along with all information about us."

Del Casal shook his head, turning away as he wiped his eye. The nurse applied alcohol to Belisarius' arm.

"What's this?" Belisarius said.

"I've been trying my damnedest to do what they want," Del

Casal said as the nurse put the needle into Belisarius' arm. "They want their captive *Homo quantus* to work. I had all the notes from the Garret, but not a single working *Homo quantus*."

"What did they break in me?" Belisarius whispered, looking from the needle to Del Casal who wouldn't meet his eyes. "What did you do?"

A figure appeared beyond the glass doors, the lieutenant-colonel. The doors slid open. Del Casal's muscles tightened very slightly. Belisarius only noticed it because he'd spent so much time watching other players in casinos. She tossed a pad onto Belisarius' lap.

"Trash," she said. "You gave me trash. I've sent the other three *Homo quantus* to be surgically altered. Pilots it is."

"I gave you the answers I have! I gave you the truth!" he lied. "You didn't understand it."

She might believe him. It might not matter. The scope of what he'd offered was too small. Her questions revealed her suspicions about his deepest secrets. And now Sofía, Carlos and César were gone, to be mutilated by Congregate doctors and chewed up by the war. Like Martín, Ana Teresa, Edmer.

"*Your* people didn't understand it," she said. "You have some pretty sharp minds among the *Homo quantus*. They found all sorts of 'flaws in the reasoning, conclusions and assumptions,' end quote. Let's return to my questions."

"What did you do to me?" Belisarius said. His words sounded slurred and his thoughts fuzzy. "I can't feel my magnetosomes. Did you break me?"

He heard a rising panic in his voice. He resented some of his *Homo quantus* nature, but it was still who he was. He reconciled himself to being a person built at someone else' instructions, down to his instincts and wants being determined by corporate interests. Good or bad, he inhabited this set of wants and needs, the burning need to know, to understand, as all *Homo quantus* did. But his magnetosomes were his principal means of navigating and querying the world. The loss bit at places selfish and irrational; he'd come here to save his people. Of course there were costs.

Del Casal moved the covers, exposing some wiring emerging from under the bandaging on Belisarius' chest. The lieutenant-colonel smiled. Belisarius' perceptions seemed to liquify. Sound muffled. Some things became sharp and clear, while others fell out of focus. Was his brain processing things incorrectly or were his ocular augments damaged, focusing at random distances and wavelengths? Del Casal limped closer.

"Your brain is a highly-engineered tool with unique pathways," the doctor said. "Your thoughts can activate parts of your brain, parts of your body, with exquisite precision, according to very intentional neural plans. And I have the blueprints. That made it very easy to rewire you, Arjona. Enjoy the hell you've made for us."

The doctor shuffled away. The lieutenant-colonel smirked, pulling at something on the sheets that tugged in his chest. He found fine wires emerging from swollen skin on his chest.

"Your *Homo quantus* family taught us how to turn on and off your consciousness, how your brain is partitioned, how to connect the parts, how to switch pieces on. That told us where to read your thoughts," the lieutenant-colonel said sweetly.

She didn't look like she was bluffing. Limited thought reading was possible. That's how some augmentation worked. Sensors fed into the human brain, translating into something neurons could process. By the same token, chips in the brain had to translate neural signals into semiconductor potentials. These were simple, straightforward connections and processes. True thought and memory reading would be complex, limited and take enormous processing power.

"Thought reading can do some damage if we get it wrong," she said. "First, tell me everything you know about the Union break out of the Puppet Axis. Second, tell me everything you know about any rumors or truth to a time travel device. Third, tell me everything about your plan for disguising yourself and handing yourself over to Congregate custody."

The world blurred and came in and out of focus. His brain was accustomed to summoning and sorting facts and knowledge; used to processing some questions in the background while other tasks occupied his attention and the bulk of his mental processing. The cables from his chest lit as the screens on the walls came to life, displaying cascades of luminous data. He didn't recognize it, but they were reading his thoughts?

The sheer volume of information on the screens gave him some hope. His brain, the brains of every *Homo quantus*, had to be able to hold and retrieve far more information in a day than the human brain would normally hold in a lifetime. The *Homo quantus* stored information more densely, using nested sets of compression algorithms and indexing systems. Every element of that was different from the way baseline human memory worked, or computer storage. Even with months and years, even with access to all the Garret research files, even with access to *Homo quantus* with brains built like his, the Congregate might not figure out how to read something so alien.

The data on the wall screens, incomprehensible, unfiltered, moved in and out of dizzy focus. The drug they'd injected melted bits of reality, patch by patch. The glass doors sounded and he bonelessly turned his head, blinking to make sense of the shapeless figure who entered. No face. A bag of metal mesh over the head, tied at the neck under a painted mouth and a pair of small, roving camera lens eyes. The metal weave material in the gloves seemed overlong in the fingers. The gloves folded clumsily at fingertips as they took the cable from the lieutenant-colonel, fitting it into raw wires sprouting from between sleeves and glove.

Belisarius' perceptions weren't working. False positives everywhere. His brain knew that. He tried to engage the normal batteries of error correction and verification algorithms, but his brain limped within a drugged haze. The chips Del Casal had wired into his body could turn on and off parts of him. As if remote controlled, they engaged his recall, accessing all kinds of memory, all flavours of knowledge, all kinds of encryption.

The hulking figure neared, machine joints and movements whirring. Belisarius couldn't feel anything with his magnetosomes, making the machine feel dubious and ghostly rather than monstrous. False positives and false negatives. He couldn't think. The crude painted face loomed over him, and camera lens eyes focused as Belisarius' consciousness finally failed.

CHAPTER THIRTY-SEVEN

Rosalie barfed into the bag again. She thought she'd finished, but her nose-bleed restarted too. Three medics crawled around His Holiness Lester. The scent of him permeated the bay, giving the waking, suffering Puppets a feeling of drowsy rightness. Lester barely lived. The Numen were not hardened against radiation. That was a core mystery of the divine. Why hadn't the Numen been made more durable when the Puppets were being created? Puppet theologians theorized endlessly about that question.

One of the sergeants approached. Hibernation drugs and radiation sickness still fuzzed Rosalie's vision, so she didn't recognize Erin until she came close. Her bristly hair was matted on one side where her helmet must have been pressing during orbital insertion.

"Four dead, ma'am," she said. "Timmy, Ralph, Michelle and Louis. Michelle was a machine gunner. I'm giving her equipment to Robbie. He'll have to do."

Rosalie held onto Erin's shoulder. "Help me put on the stilts."

Erin did more than that. She fussed with the laces and straps, so that despite her aches, Rosalie could put on the baggy Numen shirt and roll the sleeves up until her hands were visible. Doug came over. His lips were red; many of the Puppets bled from the gums.

"His Holiness is alive," Doug said. "Eight sieverts got into the War Cage."

They'd only been able to pile on so much shielding. Anything more or denser and the scanning AIs would have flagged the unpenetrated spots for secondary inspection. Rosalie's radiation meter had measured over twelve sieverts of ionizing radiation, even after the shielding had blocked much of it. Ten sieverts was almost certain death for humans and Numen.

She cleared her throat and said "Bring Timmy, Louis, Michelle, and Ralphie. They've quested far, but have far yet to go."

A few gasps among the Puppets interrupted some soft, mournful crying. Lloyd, Norma, Jill and Fred, gray-faced and weak, brought the four dead Puppets to the War Cage. They stroked slack cheeks, straightened brittle hair, decorated them with ribbons. Rosalie had been waiting for this moment, the first losses, the first blood, to invoke the quest stories.

Rosalie went to the War Cage and brushed her fingers along the slack skin of his Holiness' cheek. She signalled Doug to move into the cage and behind him. Rosalie raised her arms, standing on her stilts, with the scent of Numen diffusing into the cold bay.

"When old Dennis Creston commanded Teddy Creston-13, his most trusted servant, to recover the relics of his son," Rosalie said, catching their eyes on the pause, the open-mouthed expectation, "that was a good day."

"Yes, a very good day," Jill said.

"Sometimes fate is hard to see," Rosalie continued. "We don't know where we're going. We fetch water. We fix things. We count the minutes to the next time we'll see a Numen while the world seems to wind down."

Freddy wiped at his eyes and then hugged two of the dead Puppets under his arms, like a last encouragement.

"But when old Dennis Creston told Teddy to go get his boy, he painted meaning onto the darkness," Rosalie said. "He revealed the hand of fate."

Doug nodded vigorously.

"Teddy gathered to him three trusted Puppets who understood the moment," Rosalie said.

Robbie sobbed.

"A Numen had died," Rosalie said, as a few more Puppets began to cry softly. "Ronald Creston. Only thirty years old. Divine. Godly. Unique in all the universe. Irreplaceable. And old Dennis Creston told Teddy, his most trusted servant, to go bring his son's body home."

She felt like her words hammered her own heart. The Puppets couldn't look at her anymore.

"Teddy's three trusted companions didn't survive," she said. "They gave themselves for the recovery of something greater than themselves, for something divine, something his Holiness Old Dennis Creston wanted. They walked into the absence at the call of fate and they were joyous."

With wide open mouth, Jimbo inhaled the divinity of Lester and puddles of trembling tears collected around his eyes in the micro-gravity.

"Teddy quested and returned," Rosalie said. "He brought Ronald Creston home before he himself succumbed to the cost of his quest. He died happy at the feet of a grieving divinity."

A loud sob came from the shadows at the back of the cargo hold.

"We've been given a quest," she said, her voice taking on a deeper resonance as she felt the words in her, what Teddy Creston-13 must have felt, "a much larger one and more dangerous. The arrow of time follows the decay of the world. Every year, less Numen are born. Their numbers dwindle. And we don't know how to stop it. The absence crowds against shrinking candlelight. It threatens to end divinity."

Norma wept full-throatedly and Reggie hugged her.

"We don't know how to keep the divinities alive. We don't know how to make more of them. But one man does, a man like the creator of the first Numen. Only one such man lived and then died. Since then, the world has been winding down from the Edenic Age he made. But now there's another. A new man has made more Numen. He can turn back the clock of the cosmos, and return us to an earlier age."

Some sniffled loudly, but they looked up one by one, as if seeing if the hope she offered were true.

"We quest for a new age."

"We quest for a new age!" Lloyd squealed.

"Today, we lay to rest Michelle, Timmy, Louis, and Ralphie, who, like the companions of Teddy, laid down their lives for the Numen. They finished in this life but their worship will not end. The Numen who have passed need new servants. Michelle and Timmy and Louis and Ralphie will attend the Numen who have passed, while we honor them and carry on in this world. Many of us may already be dying from the radiation. Many of us certainly will follow them, but we will bring home the man who will rekindle the Edenic age. Today, we are all Teddy."

Jimbo whispered to himself in a trembling voice. "I'm Teddy. *I'm* fucking Teddy."

Rosalie guided the Numen's unresisting hand to touch Michelle's beribboned forehead.

"You are a good servant," she said in a gruff voice, imitating a Numen of old. "You accompanied Teddy. Serve my fathers and my mothers in the next life."

Freddie wept louder as Rosalie repeated the rites with the other three and committed them to the Numen of old, wherever they were in the cosmos.

CHAPTER THIRTY-EIGHT

BELISARIUS' SYRUPY THOUGHTS followed themselves in nonsensical loops. Humming clouded vision. Taste prickled like the brush of gauze on skin. Smell brightened. Sweat pasted sheets to hot skin. And then, sense of place vanished. Bodiless, he floated in foggy grayness, behind a pane of glass, in a suit. He wasn't anywhere. The patterns of entanglement confused him. Then, he was on the *Mutapa*, months ago, feeling the powerful electromagnetic fields of the warship around him, back around the Stubbs pulsar. But the time felt wrong in a dreamy way; he felt *forward* in time, not backwards, because the stars had changed. And without a discreet break, he felt himself really existing under the sullen orange glow lighting Nyanga, in the past. He didn't want to be here again. He didn't want to feel this again. He struggled, pushing against the sponginess holding him. He heard crying. Was he crying?

He blinked in sight of soft lamps, surrounded by the hum of processors, the gentle glow of holographic displays switched to dim red. A figure hunched over him, whispering.

"Arjona. I can't take it anymore. Arjona."

Hard hands shook him, disturbing the silt in his mind. Del Casal's tear-streaked face neared in the gloom. They were alone, in the surgical room. Wires led from his body to banks of thought reading equipment, dim screens scrolling through terabytes of encrypted compressed memories every second.

"I'll pay you anything to get me out of here, Arjona."

The gummy synaesthesia loosened its hold. The gloom clarified, but he was still strapped down. Del Casal gripped his hospital gown, weeping over his chest.

"What did you..." Belisarius' throat was raw, like he'd been screaming. He tried swallowing. "What did you do to me?"

"We don't have a lot of time," Del Casal said.

Del Casal worked at the restraints on Belisarius' wrists, but they resisted his efforts.

"What's wrong with my brain? What did you do to me?"

Belisarius' words seemed to penetrate the doctor's frantic terror.

"Keep your voice down," Del Casal whispered. "The centrifuges. I've got them all spinning. White noise for the microphones, but it's not much. The lights are dimmed for the cameras. The processors are going to be slower for a bit. I have them computing genomic problems."

Was Del Casal an idiot? Belisarius made out the centrifuge noise and trusted that Del Casal thought the other measures were in place. Maybe they were, but they wouldn't fool any decently secure facility that had backup cameras, multispectrum sensors and listening bugs.

"Tell me what you did," Belisarius whispered, "or I'm not helping you."

Some of Del Casal's old prickliness briefly emerged from his twitchiness.

"I added some wiring to your brain, in places where small, steady microcurrents can depolarize major neuronal pathways, to interrupt signalling. Like the inputs from your magnetosomes and the neurons leading to the conscious control areas. Some cognition. You're not broken, but I inserted some off switches."

"Then how am I supposed to help you?"

"I don't know," Del Casal said right beside his ear. "You have to get us out. You know how."

Del Casal's fingers felt cool. Was Belisarius still feverish? He'd had the same fever for months and almost didn't notice the low ache anymore.

"Did you shut everything in me off?" Belisarius said.

Del Casal yanked on Belisarius' restraints, as if somebody would come in any second. Or this was orchestrated? They might have drugged Del Casal with something to make him paranoid to see what Belisarius would do. Or say. From what he saw on the screens, they couldn't decrypt his thoughts yet.

"You shut off all my *Homo quantus* changes?" Belisarius said.

Del Casal momentarily gave up and wept over Belisarius' chest.

"Antonio. Antonio! We have to keep moving. Tell me if you shut off everything in my head. Can I reach the fugue?"

The doctor's eyes darted to shadowed parts of the room where nothing moved.

"Antonio, focus. We're both stuck here."

"Your brain is all jumbled," Del Casal said. "The parts that should be active during the fugue are on all the time. You're broken, but I didn't do that."

On all the time. Then the quantum intellect was still operating in his brain, but he was cut off from it. Temporarily? Permanently?

"Why am I still here and conscious? What do they want?" Del Casal looked at the displays suspiciously. One of the centrifuges came to the end of its cycle and its long whining note deepened. Del Casal crouched, snuck over to it and set it for another ten minute cycle. When he returned, he stayed behind the head of the bed where Belisarius couldn't see him.

"Antonio!" Belisarius whispered urgently. He heard wrenching sobs.

Del Casal came around. He knelt and draped his arms through the rail.

"Save me," he whispered. "I'm all gone."

"Antonio, they drugged you. Help me if you can. I'll help you."

The doctor's expression melted in a kind of anguish.

"You can't help me. There's no more me. It dissolves in front of her." Del Casal's face slackened and his mouth opened like he was going to vomit. He gulped like a fish in air, as if grasping for an elusive taste. Or smell. Like a Puppet. A shiver tickled down Belisarius' back.

"Who is she?" Belisarius said.

"I missed so much before," Del Casal said, a tear running on his face. "There's so much I didn't see. How could I have been blind for so long?"

"Antonio, focus. Part of the awe effect in the Puppets amplifies pattern recognition. You're filled with false positives right now. You see meaning and revelation in everything. It's all false positives."

"How do you know?"

"*Homo quantus* pattern recognition is dialed higher too. The false positives are tempting, but they're all mirage. I struggle to tamp down signals in the data that aren't there. It's hard, but it's possible."

Del Casal shook his head. "This is more real than anything I've ever felt. My life..." He seemed to stumble over some feeling that overwhelmed him. "Everything that came before is so hollow, so empty."

Belisarius shook the bed in his restraints, trying to get Del Casal's meandering attention.

"The awe effect is a very sophisticated hallucinogenic experience, Antonio. Take the science you lived with before and deconstruct what you're feeling. It's possible to see this in another way."

"You think I'm not trying?" he whined, regarding Belisarius with angry, red-rimmed eyes. "But I'm small and this is so big. I can't escape it anywhere. It's in every thought. Every feeling." Fat tears fell now. "You killed Gander. I was there."

Belisarius stilled. He'd understood that Del Casal had gotten cold feet and bailed on the con, that he hadn't even gone to meet them later for his cut. At the time Belisarius hadn't thought through everything. He'd thought maybe Del Casal had run afoul of the the Puppets. But... *I was there.*

"I couldn't know what I had made then," Del Casal said. "I didn't have the capacity to... *see* what he was, that he was genuinely divine. But now I know. I saw the reactions of the Puppets. I can imagine now what it would have been like to breathe him, to bask in his presence, to feel his divinity. He was angry. So angry with me because I was with the Puppets and he was strapped to the table."

Belisarius felt faint.

"When did you go to the Puppets?" Belisarius said.

"His last words were to me and I couldn't even know their holiness at the time. He cursed me, Arjona. A divinity laid a curse on me! He said *Enjoy hell. You can have my spot.* But I didn't take his spot. I entered the world *he* touched, the world *he* walked, that he himself couldn't feel. I made divinity, but I couldn't feel it and neither could he. Can you imagine so much blindness? But now I know and it hurts so much."

Del Casal sobbed hopelessly.

"I'm not made to be powerless," Del Casal said pleadingly. He focused on Belisarius, patting his arm, then clinging to his hand. "Do you know what it is to be nothing? Worthless? I stop being me. I stop being me. I just want and want and want to... It's so big. So vast. I'm connected to a whole world you can't see Arjona. I'm lost on the waves. I'm just dust. Please take me away from here before I'm gone. Take me back to the Puppets. I can make more Numen."

Del Casal's fingernails clawed at Belisarius' arm as his head jerked up, eyes wide, mouth open, panting.

"Help me, Arjona," he whimpered. "She's here and my heart isn't big enough to hold all of her."

Del Casal looked to the doorway in open-mouthed wonder. The whirring of stiff machine articulation sounded, step by step, in the dark hallway. Del Casal's chin rose as if the inhaled scent wafted above him.

The pale lieutenant-colonel appeared first in the shadows of the doorway, in her dark uniform. A breath of delight caught in Del Casal's throat, but he moved away, behind the bed. A lumpy, looming shape well over two meters stopped behind her. With access to his magnetosomes, Belisarius might have perceived more of the Scarecrow, the press and hum of its electronic thinking, the flexing of articulators and hydraulics.

The woman approached in catlike silence, the Scarecrow following with soft mechanical sounds. The lights began to brighten and the centrifuges all began to whine down by themselves, as if some drama had finished. Two small camera lenses hummed as they focused on Belisarius from the loose metal weave of the sack of the Scarecrow's head. A black smudge of paint suggested a nose over a clumsily painted black mouth. The way the Scarecrow stood and watched made the immobile mouth suggest a leer.

The metal weave of the shirt hung shapelessly over an undefined torso, but the sleeve rose a bit from the top of the glove when the arm extended, revealing shiny metal wiring in mockery of straw. What was that for? The shadow beneath the mesh cloth held many pieces of things, wires, maybe a gun barrel and electronic jacks. A wire shot out, like a grappling cable, plugging into the rails of the bed frame. Strange, faint images, ghosts of pasts, started manifesting in Belisarius' thoughts. Measurements, glimpsed flashes of places he'd been, maybe things he seen, but... maybe not. Ghostly. He still struggled with the effects of the drugs they'd injected into him, and possibly changes Del Casal had done to him.

"Come out, Antonio," the woman said over the last low moan of the centrifuges coasting to stillness.

Del Casal came into view from behind the bed. He fidgeted, trying to stand straight, trying to face her with dignity. A lifetime of being in control propped Del Casal against what appeared to be an overwhelmingly profound biochemical religious experience.

"I really, really want those *Homo quantus* to work," she said with quiet menace. "I'm already displeased and it will be worse if you don't succeed very soon."

Del Casal's resolve and courage vanished, replaced by a naked rawness of self, the last undisguised core of a fearful, fervent believer. He lowered his head submissively and backed away from her with little gulps at the air.

"What you've done is pointless," Belisarius said to the woman. Faint images flitted in his thoughts. The screens lit with new data. "You're not going to get anything out of him like that."

The woman regarded him.

"Compelling motivation may offset the slight drop in cognition," she said.

"You still won't get Del Casal making new *Homo quantus.* Undo it. You'll get more out of him. He's suffering."

"He's motivated," she said, running a finger along the rail of his bed, creeping closer and closer to him. "Besides, the chips can be taken out, and even the neural wiring, but his biochemistry has already been changed. The original bioengineers of the Numen and Puppets were paranoid about the Puppets ever escaping their control. The addictions produced in the awe centers of the brain are permanent. He'll never escape the withdrawals. And while I'm close, he won't suffer."

She smiled sweetly, everything she said turning Belisarius' stomach. Del Casal had betrayed them and had watched Will die, but this was too great a punishment for anyone. The creation of the Puppets was an incalculable moral error. Eye for an eye justice wouldn't fix it. In the moral gray, Belisarius had made a Numen, but it was temporary and Will was a consenting subject.

"The Scarecrow has some questions," the woman said. "You're extremely valuable as a model of fully functioning *Homo quantus,* but you're also an interrogation target. We can't decide which objective is more important. If the Scarecrow doesn't get what she wants, I've asked my people to look at wiring you like a Puppet too."

His brain never stopped, couldn't stop, but the idea of wiring a *Homo quantus* with the complex neural and sensory changes of the Puppets momentarily didn't compute. Both subspecies were systems of hardware and software, like computers and operating systems. The systems were incompatible. Could even Del Casal find a way to make the two natures co-exist? Rational interrogation of the cosmos itself couldn't meld with intense spiritual belief in a physically present divinity. He might. He might try. Belisarius almost threw up.

"Wouldn't that be funny?" she said. " A quantum Puppet."

The Scarecrow loomed.

"What do you know of the Epsilon Indi Scarecrow?" the hulking AI asked. Its voice crawled from the grave, accented with the suggestion of the feminine. "The Epsilon Indi Scarecrow last reported following you to a small, stable wormhole at C99312, a chondritic, bi-lobed asteroid. It reported your entry into this wormhole and followed you. The *Port-Cartier* found nothing at C99312."

He'd long ago trained his brain and body to avoid giving the unconscious signals that accompanied deception, but he didn't know if those reactions were still in place. He couldn't feel much of his brain. It wasn't just like his intellect was fuzzy and hobbled – some perceptions of the world had numbed, gone blind.

"I don't know anything about that," Belisarius said.

Yet the flashes of information continued to paint themselves on the screens, walls of binary data, arrays and sets of digitized information they pulled from him. But strangely, small images, immaterial and quick, came to mind, of entering the time gates with Iekanjika, his surprise at being told by Cassie and Stills what they'd faced while he'd been on Nyanga. The character of the data on the screens seemed to shift.

"Tell me about the time travel device found by the Union," the Scarecrow said.

Despite his hardest efforts to think of something else, transparent images and minute flashes of purpled light and the warbling electromagnetic feel of the interior of the time gates came to him. He tried to calculate something, anything, to recheck previous calculations, but this other stream of translucent, ghostly memories seemed to cut a deeper path through his thoughts. What had they done to him? They'd rewired Del Casal's neurology to make an emulated Puppet of him. They'd done something to Belisarius too, cut him off from some of his senses and his mathematical faculties.

"They hired me for my knowledge of the Puppets," Belisarius said. "I don't know anything about Union technology."

The data on the displays shifted. He recognized some of the structural characteristics as belonging to information from his mind. It was a form he would understand, but that no one else would. The kind of encryption the *Homo quantus* used to compress memories had some documented root algorithms, making some of the first layers of compression standard. But the subsequent steps were individual. Each *Homo quantus* who could enter the fugue had to work in alternation with the quantum objectivity to find a set of storage and retrieval algorithms to compress memory. The algorithm itself was like an encryption key, even though it hadn't been designed as such. The Congregate couldn't have found out his key, could they?

"What are..." the Scarecrow's voice, still rough and machine-accented, took on a disturbing silkiness, "...the *Hortus quantus?*"

The fear tickling his spine inched higher. If the Congregate war effort had captured some very old Union officers, under interrogation, some might have been able to speak of Nyanga and what the Union called the vegetable intelligences. But no one knew the name he'd given them except the *Homo quantus* and Iekanjika. The general was still in Bachwezi, so the only way the Congregate could have discovered his name for the aliens would be from Belisarius himself. On the displays, more data showed. Even with impaired cognitive functions, his brain could make something of the patterns, decrypting some of it to see that the data really was his.

"You think that the *Hortus quantus* have a different kind of intelligence," the Scarecrow said. "Explain your perceptions of them through your quantum measurements."

Belisarius' heart beat harder. The Scarecrow was really reading his memories. When had she cracked an encryption that should have been unique to him? How could she have? Panic rose. Then, his laboriously constructed con man instincts kicked in.

He was the mark. He'd been conned.

The Scarecrow hadn't cracked his encryption before entering. She'd probably had parts of it cracked, hints and guesses, but was looking for confirmation. They'd surgically cut Belisarius off from many of his senses and intellectual resources. They'd drugged him on and off for who knows how long. And they'd sent in Del Casal as a distraction. But that had been all artifice. He'd been the mark all along; his memories were the score in a vault. And with all the distraction and damage and drugs, he'd been just disoriented enough to no longer be able to hide his physical responses. The Scarecrow had examined the top level thoughts, the memories retrieved, and had used her questions and his physiological responses to break some of the algorithms that compressed his memories, maybe many.

Now the questions had stopped. And the only reason the Scarecrow would stop was because she had a working translation algorithm now, from compressed memory to legible information. It might be incomplete, but the more she read of his memories, the more inferences and translations she could establish from context. She no longer needed to question. She was reading the raw code of his memories as fast as she could process and pattern-recognize. Belisarius' memory was vast, but it might not take her long to absorb everything. He'd seen and observed and calculated so much, including all the permanent wormholes of the Axis Mundi, including the possibilities of the time gates, including the location of the hidden *Homo quantus*.

Belisarius closed his eyes tight, retreating to a mental world where he'd so often sought elusive comfort, but he couldn't feel the parts of him that ought to be there. The hiss and press of the magnetism and electrical currents present in almost any habitat was missing. Access to multi-channelled, multi-layered streams of thought, the almost audible babbling hum of other thoughts happening in the parts of his brain he hadn't recruited to complex tasks, was absent too. And over the last months, the hot presence of something else in his mind, the quantum intellect taking up residence in part of the interior world Belisarius called self; he was numb to it as well. Del Casal had damaged him inside. He needed to stop the Scarecrow from reading any more. He needed to stop her from finding out where the *Homo quantus* were hiding. He needed to stop her from learning why he'd come here. But he had no tools. They'd stripped his interior world. He reached helplessly within the space of his thoughts.

Help, he thought, as hard as he could. *Help. They're going to take all the data, not just from me, but from all the Homo quantus. There will be no more exploring. No more research. No more learning.*

There was not even an echo. He was alone in his mind. The quantum intellect, which in other *Homo quantus* could only exist when the conscious self was extinguished, co-existed in him, in some partitioned portion of his brain. But by definition it could have no sense of self, could not feel the need for self-preservation as more than an algorithm to be measured against others.

They've broken me, Belisarius thought urgently, as more and more raw data from his memories scrawled through the displays, soaking into the armed and armored Scarecrow AI.

Only you can save all the data here in me and the knowledge of where the Homo quantus are hiding. They're studying worm holes. The time gates. Hyperspace. They're going to flee across the galaxy and be safe and will continue learning if you help now.

Belisarius didn't know if the quantum intellect could hear his thoughts, or if Del Casal's surgeries had permanently sundered portions of his brain, but he thought *please...*

And then, Belisarius the conscious, self-aware being ceased to exist.

SOMETHING CHANGED IN the room. Del Casal, her Puppet, continued working frenetically. The display screens seemed to change subtly, even though it was all ones and zeroes to Bareilles. The Scarecrow stilled. Glimmers of blue and green shone eerily from unseen sources beneath the edge of the metal mesh sleeve the Scarecrow had open. The Scarecrow stepped closer to the bed.

"What is it?" Bareilles asked.

The Scarecrow leaned over the limp *Homo quantus*. Bareilles accessed Arjona's vitals and asked for an analysis from the AI she carried in her service band. The initial analysis projected onto her retina, holographic text and graphs transparent before the patient. Arjona had entered a vegetative state. Higher neurological functions had stopped. He'd been here. Just moments ago. The next set of analyses appeared before she could react. The fugue. His neural activity matched the patterns in the *Homo quantus* records. The quantum fugue.

"Did you trigger this?" Bareilles said.

Still the Scarecrow didn't reply. She just loomed over Arjona. Bareilles looked at the display data on all the screens and demanded a quick statistical analysis from the more powerful AIs wired into the medical bay. Their answer was quick: white noise. The data emerging from Arjona was now white noise. It hadn't been just seconds before.

She asked the AIs to recheck the previous data streams and the current ones. They concluded the same thing: until forty-five seconds ago, the data stream from Arjona's recall had been decryptable with what the AIs estimated to be a climbing eighty-five percent accuracy rate. They'd retrieved about ten percent of all the data stored in the *Homo quantus'* brain. After that, it had become a randomization so complete that the AIs could find no structure in it at all.

"Del Casal!" she said, startling him. "Get over here." Bareilles transmitted the findings to the hurrying doctor. She grabbed him by the hair at the back of his head. "How did he get into the fugue? You turned him off."

"I did," he pleaded, gasping at her nearness.

"He's not off," she said.

"He shouldn't... He shouldn't be able," the doctor said, closing his eyes to not look at her. "I grafted wiring that will inhibit the neural channels from his conscious mind to every relevant part of his new senses and thinking and the centers that activate the fugue. Unless he had... other routes none of the other *Homo quantus* knew about, he... shouldn't be able to."

The Scarecrow still focused on the slack-faced Arjona.

"Do you want the doctor to try to shut Arjona's fugue down?" Bareilles asked.

"Yes," the Scarecrow's sepulchral voice said. "I think he's re-encrypting everything. Stop him."

"Hurry," Bareilles said, shoving the doctor. He activated a series of control panels that accessed the chips and electrical signalling patches in Arjona's brain. A neural map bloomed up. Some parts darkened with just basal activities. Others were brightly busy. Bareilles' AIs translated some of the anatomy, but not nearly enough for her to follow the blow-by-blow.

"I don't know if he's destroying information or hiding it," the Scarecrow said.

"Shut off the fugue," Bareilles said. "It should be easy. The notes say most of them can barely achieve it."

Del Casal activated different chips anxiously. None of them seemed to be located near the active neural centers in Arjona's brain.

"It's not working," Del Casal said in Anglo-Spanish. "The parts that are supposed to tell the fugue to turn on and off aren't activated in Arjona. Something else is making this happen."

"Turn it off," the Scarecrow said in a cold, gravelly tone.

"I-- I'm..." Del Casal began helplessly.

Bareilles went around the bed with brisk steps, picked up a pair of defibrillator paddles, set them against Arjona's scalp and pressed the buttons. The *Homo quantus* convulsed. Del Casal, who hadn't paid attention, spasmed with a choking sound as he fell. The data on the displays abruptly paused. The neural displays rebooted quickly. The patterns had changed. Bareilles didn't know all the details of *Homo quantus* neurology, but quantum systems were very fragile. The shock would have destroyed the fugue state for now. The Scarecrow made no sign that the charge had bothered her at all; her fingers, wrapped in too-large gloves of metal mesh, lifted one of Arjona's eyelids.

"I recovered something of my last question," the Scarecrow said, "the location of the *Homo quantus,* before his attempt to either destroy or re-encrypt the memories stored in his mind."

CHAPTER THIRTY-NINE

Translated from *français* 8.1

To: Task Force Commander, Operation Baltis Vallis
Espilon Indi Fleet Operations
12th Fleet
Congregate Navy

27 August, 2515

Subject: Activate Epsilon Indi Case Orange and new Case Crimson

1. Ministry of Intelligence acquired the coordinates of the fifth mouth of the Axis Mundi in the Epsilon Indi system. Coordinates attached.
2. Task Force Commander is to immediately engage Case Orange to secure the fifth Axis. Achievement of Case Orange may delay Operation Baltis Vallis, but overall probability of success of Baltis must not be compromised. Remaining standing orders and ancillary strategic objectives continue to be in effect.

3. Upon completion of Case Orange, Case Crimson is authorized and required: the rapid crossing of the new Axis and the immediate hunt and capture of all *Homo quantus* found there.

4. 12th Fleet Command will commit all necessary resources to Task Force. Elements of the 4th Fleet are en route to Epsilon Indi to reinforce.

General Louise Plante
Commander
Special Operations Command
Ministry of Defence
Venus

ACCELERATION SQUASHED MERCED Hillman's reinforced organs like some asshole was punching her insides. Even packed in water at eight hundred atmospheres of pressure she felt like she was about to take the world's biggest dump. With her luck, she was probably about to shit out her liver. At sixty-six gravities of acceleration, Tork and Felcher started falling behind because those fuckers couldn't take it.

"Wooooooo, fuck you all!" she yelled in the clear, transmitting to her own fighters, the Union navy and even the Congregate units. She streaked across the entire theatre of battle in forty-five seconds, shooting at everything along her meteoric trajectory. Some of her shots did real damage; others were just to fuck with the enemy's minds.

They were losing the battle on the Epsilon Indi side of the Freya Axis. This was the Congregate's big push and Hillman had to do something crazy to try to slow them down. She really wanted to mess with the *Port-Daniel* and the *Cap-Chat*, two big Congregate battleships at the wrong end of the battle volume. In addition to her normal ordnance, her fighter carried two experimental missiles. Each was so big that she carried them on opposite sides of the hollow tube of her ship, and she had to fire them at the same time otherwise she'd fuck up her center of gravity.

She might have managed a hit on the *Lanaudière* or the *Estrie*, but both ships already had her on radar. The *Port-Daniel* and the *Cap-Chat* pinged radar hard into the swarm of mongrel pilots already around them, but Hillman was still too far away for them to think she was relevant. She tore in hot and fast with an entirely different movement profile than the rest of the attackers.

"Dropping a big one!" she transmitted in the mongrel electrical speech.

The dogs around the *Port-Daniel* and the *Cap-Chat* suddenly noticed her. They swore up a storm as they scrambled away. The *Port-Daniel* had executed a half-turn, as if moving to leave the theatre. Hillman fired her two big nukes, adding their thrust to the speed she'd already given them. The *Port-Daniel's* anti-aircraft guns filled space with hot fragments of metal as Hillman rotated forty-five degrees and thrust with everything she could take, fifty seven gravities for now. She might have damaged her insides. She lanced up and ahead of the two missiles, passing within dozens of meters of the *Port-Daniel* and ducking back behind it as the rearward sensors lit with a bizarre flash spanning visible, x-rays, gamma rays and microwaves, eclipsed by the long line of the Congregate battleship. Lucky anti-artillery fire clipped her fuselage and her hard inflaton field drive went soft. She began to tumble.

Crisse de tabarnak.

Balls Flight finally got here, arching over her, their speed carrying them out of the blast radius. Tork and Felcher howled into their comms. Grandstanding asshats. Three more missiles kidney-fucked the *Port-Daniel* with the new nukes, and one of them got a lucky shot on the *Cap-Chat*. Then the *Port-Daniel* erupted in a blinding explosion.

Volleys of anti-artillery fire from the *Cap-Chat* chased Balls Flight, catching a few. She didn't know which ones. The dogs went down biting though. The rest of the flight was gonna get boned now. Hillman had played it too risky, drawn them too far across the battle volume. They had no support. She had no support.

Ostie. Better to die here than in an ocean.

Only her dorsal and port sensors worked, so as she tumbled, information came in like it was lit by a light-house beam. It screwed with her head, was gonna give her a headache. But in the winking disjointed information, she saw the *Cap-Chat* pulling away, not pressing its advantage on the exposed mongrels. The fleet was changing configuration. At least twelve of the major battleships made for vaguely solar south, on angle towards the galactic center. Where the fuck were they going? Behind them, the Congregate task force was regrouping. She'd trained enough on Congregate fighters that she knew what it meant. They were changing posture, from offence to defence. The Union ships near the Freya Axis, harried, maybe an hour or so from destruction, retreated too, to lick their wounds. What the fuck was happening? Where the *crisse* were they going?

"Balls flight, gimme a ride," she transmitted. "Felcher. Follow the new attack group."

"Alone?" Felcher sent back. "Lick my balls."

"Go," she said. He called her a *malparida* as he broke off from Balls Flight and flew after the twelve big warships by himself. Good dog.

As much as she hated orders, the dogs needed some new goddamn orders. If the Union could re-arm the mongrels and get them back into fueled ships, this would be a great time to bite the remaining Congregate forces.

CHAPTER FORTY

"WHAT ARE YOU seeing?" Bareilles demanded. Del Casal's voice stalled in his throat.

Del Casal had been working as fast as he could to understand what had happened to Arjona, or what the con man had done to himself. It had been nine hours and he had fewer answers than before.

"Now!" she said.

"I don't know," he said. He hated the tiny pleading whine he heard in his voice. Del Casal's rational self wrestled with the spiritual vastness of being near Bareilles. He understood, in excruciating biochemical detail the neural cascades of the awe effect in the Puppets, and he remembered what he'd been, but it was useless. He lived an altered state of perception, a persistent, insistent assertion of reality being different. Bareilles radiated a powerful sense of well-being, of command, of overwhelming spiritual truth and he was overwhelmed.

He turned the holographic display to her, showing a three-dimensional map of Arjona's brain activity, labelled with parts of the *Homo quantus* brain associated with the fugue experience. Arjona's was lit brightly again, after the shock, but the parts that should have activated or deactivated the fugue were dormant.

"It's different from the notes recovered from the Garret, but his higher functions are definitely off. There's 'no one' in there, no one conscious. But the quantum objectivity is active, and it seems the objectivity has been on all this time. We didn't know what to look for."

"We?" Bareilles demanded witheringly.

"I... I didn't know what to look for. Arjona told me that he could get in but not out of the fugue. I didn't know if it was another lie."

"We need to break into him," the Scarecrow said in her antique French. "Arjona's fugue is capable of lying, capable of sabotage. The coordinates I decrypted before his brain shut down were clear, unambiguous. When elements of the Epsilon Indi Task Force were deployed away from the Freya Axis the offensive on the Union stalled, and in exchange we found nothing. No new Axis. No *Homo quantus*. The fugue was able to feed us counter-intelligence. And if the quantum objectivity is still active, it may be changing the encryption of Arjona's remaining memories right now."

The Scarecrow turned on a set of currents in the *Homo quantus'* brain to scramble even the fugue activity.

"How soon could Arjona be wired for the awe effect, Del Casal?" Bareilles said.

"There's some preparation," Del Casal said. "Two days. Maybe more? Arjona's neurology is very complicated."

"Do it," the Scarecrow said. "All the *Homo quantus* need to belong to the Congregate."

CHAPTER FORTY-ONE

Rosie wiped the sweat off her forehead and dropped out of the frame of the big fighter craft they were building. Jill was leading Marigold, Ricky and Norma on the build, under the supervision of a sub-AI. It looked good, she thought. She could imagine it flying through space. Someday Puppets would have these advanced ships.

Rosie drank from a common bottle. Marie's factory had no windows, but was still hot. Or maybe the gravity was getting to her. Everything was heavy here. Rosie had never been in point nine gravities before and couldn't believe people lived in this all the time.

"We'll need to do yours soon, Miss Johns-10," the main AI said. His strange stony head appeared in hologram on her service band, even though he was really a dozen meters away, doing surgery on a Puppet. She set down the bottle and walked over, feeling weird when the factory shifted in the winds. Whenever the floor moved, it reminded her that except for some steel and plastic there was nothing beneath her feet but clouds for sixty-five kilometers. It was an odd intellectual vertigo.

Saint Matthew was operating on Sammy, although there wasn't much blood, mostly some metal fibers at the base of the neck and in the abdomen. "Does it hurt, Sammy?" she said.

"A little," he said cheerfully.

"Why didn't you say something?" the AI said. "I could have given you more anaesthesia."

Sammy didn't seem to understand the question. Rosie was too hot and nervous to explain. Those who couldn't perceive divinity couldn't understand pain and pleasure and reward and punishment and mission and fate the way Puppets did. She watched the chip slip under Sammy's skin near his ribs and imagined how they would all end.

"They won't go off early?" Rosie said.

"They're not armed. They won't be until just before you start. They're connected to brainstem and heart and won't activate unless both record death."

"I'll get mine soon," Rosie said.

"I'll be here," the hologram said.

Rosie walked past the second ship being built, only a little smaller than the first, a single person flyer, for Mister Arjona, if they could get to him. Wayne showed Vera, Suzie and Lloyd what to do, as soon as the sub-AI told him what to do. Puppets were good workers, although the AIs were running many robots too. His Holiness Lester's War Cage rested on the floor of the factory. Doug had given orders for the Puppets to leave him alone, so it was quiet near him, but for the echoing bangs of construction and the hiss of welding.

Marie and the fish man in the big box were at the big main ship. Even though it was just a transport, it was as big as anything in the Puppet navy, and its straight lines traced out a huge hollow cylinder with cabins and controls along the outside of it. Such a strange design, but it was a reactionless drive. Puppet analysts said the Banks would soon have their own version and the Congregate too. The Puppets deserved their own.

By the time Rosie climbed the ladder, she had to wipe the sweat away again and catch her breath. Marie seemed fine. She lived here. She was talking to a microphone outside the huge steel box. They were a curious pair. Marie was pretty, in an Edenic-Numen-on-TV sort of way, pale-skinned, dirty blond hair, forceful. She wore a tank top that showed her arms with beautiful angular mosaic tattoos stretching from fingertips to biceps. The soft colors weren't anything Rosalie would have seen in the Free City. It was like brightness and life. The fish man was just a big metal box.

"What do you want?" Marie said.

"What?" Rosie said.

"Are you coming or going?" Marie said.

"I'm making sure the Puppets are working."

Marie snorted. "Good luck. Kick some butts. We're behind schedule."

"Yeah," the fish man said. "My tank is getting smelly. Step on it."

Rosie didn't get why Marie laughed, but she went to check on Jane, Freddie, and Scotty. Robbie and Jimbo had stopped working and were fighting over a shoelace. She got them back to work. Erin and Buddy were disagreeing over the next piece of plating, but Rosalie got the sub-AI to decide. Then she went to where the cockpit was being wired, twenty meters up by ladder. She clipped a strap to her harness in case she fell. Even in normal gravity, this would be quite a fall. Over Venus, she would just go splat. In the half-finished cockpit, she found Doug working diligently. He'd nearly finished laying out all the control cables for the robots.

Rosie checked the lines as she'd been taught, and when she'd landmarked the right spot, she pulled a circuit component out of her shirt pocket. Doug handed her something similar. She fitted the pieces together and clipped them under one of the processors. When she checked that the connections were good, she patted everything back in place and climbed back down the structure of the big transport ship.

CHAPTER FORTY-TWO

BAREILLES WAS PACKED tightly in a cage, naked. At first she couldn't see much. She could only strain against mushy, constricting bars. A plaintive moan sounded. Hers. She couldn't catch her breath; the cage was Puppet-sized. Scraping her head along the bars, she managed to twist her neck enough to see the Puppets around her. Their shrieks sounded distant even though they were close enough to lace the cold air with the scent of citrus sweat and unwashed bodies. She was sticky and hot, like she had a fever. She didn't know how she'd gotten here, but she was crying, mourning. She hadn't escaped, She hadn't escaped.

Biology was destiny. The Puppets wanted her with a longing so deep it could not be plumbed and they'd found her. They didn't care who she was, what she wanted; they needed the piece of flesh that made the scents of divinity. She strained at the cage, hurting herself, pushing gradually through as Puppets went wild, trying to bite and pinch and shake her.

"Thélise. Thélise. Wake up."

Her hand connected with something hard. Someone grunted and she was sitting, naked in tangled sheets. The lights came on and Philippe was on the floor beside the bed, holding one eye.

"Oh no!" she said. "Did I hit you? I'm sorry. I..."

He sat on the bed and pulled her close. "You don't need to say sorry. It was a good punch."

She rubbed his face where skin reddened.

"I hope I didn't give you a black eye."

"You're shaking," he said, putting his bare arms around her. "It's okay, *chérie*. It's all gone. It was just dreams."

He held her close. The bristle of his chest hair against her face was warm and comforting, but she pushed gently until he let go. This wasn't the way things were. Philippe was a major with the marine security detachment. He was available, pleasant, kind even, but he was just someone she messaged a couple of times a week to unwind.

"I'm good, Philippe. I'm sorry. I think I need the whole bed to sleep the rest of the night."

He looked vaguely disappointed, smiled anyway.

"My cabin has a small kitchenette," he said. "I got the ingredients from the cafeteria. I'm going to try to cook one of my *grand-mère's* recipes tonight. I probably won't get it, but if you want to help taste or cook, let me know."

She was tempted. And he was tempting as he got dressed. Interesting acid patterns marked hard muscle. His plan wasn't the way things were, but... maybe that could be the way things were. He leaned down and kissed her before retreating.

She washed her face, poured herself a cup of water and opened the blinds. It was still the middle of the night, but sunlight shone yellow and orange through clouds heavy with sulfuric acid. Despite the warm glow outside, the cold metal cage of nightmare still branded bare skin. She didn't think of her Numen grandmother very much. The sacrifice her family had made was appreciated, if not honored, so she usually felt she'd come to terms with that heritage long ago. She'd worked on Oler, sometimes on ops where she'd revealed her Numen scent with surgical precision, and other times where she'd taken inhibitors so she could pass among the Puppets for human. Even then, the visceral reality of her Numen nature had rarely brought her to tonight's kind of nightmares.

Given a different set of choices, different luck, that might have been her in the cage now, instead of growing up in Venus. She didn't know how how near a thing her grandmother's escape might have been. Just a teenager, *grand-mère* had fled with her parents during the Puppet revolt. If she'd been an hour later, might that teenager have lived out her days she way the other Numen had, pleading for their freedom, yelling futile orders at former slaves? If *grand-mère* had not escaped, the granddaughter too would be living a captive fate as an object of obsession, a thing without human dignity. She ought to have asked *grand-mère*, but when she'd been young, it hadn't occurred to her. History doesn't matter to children.

And she hadn't trusted her grandmother anyway. *Grand-mère* spoke a heavily accented French and asked to be called "granny" in old Anglo, but none of them did. Bareilles was forced to spend time with her so that her own Numen biochemistry would be properly calibrated, but no affection came of it. There was something dirty and small about the old woman.

"I was a princess," *grand-mère* had said to her once when they were alone in the floating manor in Venus. "I had servants and worshippers when I was your age. You would have been a princess too. Imagine it, having anything you want, all the time, living dolls to play with."

Even as a child of eight, Bareilles found her grandmother's overtures simplistic, betraying a lack of understanding of the child she tried to ingratiate herself with.

"Would you like that?" *grand-mère* had asked.

Young Thélise Bareilles had shaken her head.

Venus had no princesses, only a goddess. In these clouds, every one of them had to earn what they had, wrenching it from Venus' resisting grasp. Family could usually help, but in real moments of testing, everyone was alone. That was part of what was wrong with *grand-mère*. Foreigners thought of Venus in terms of meteorology and pH and pressure, as if she were apprehensible. Venusians knew to their bones that they lived and died within a hostile will that never stopped testing whether they were worthy.

"Do you want a cookie?" *grand-mère* had said. *Papa* had baked cookies earlier.

"*Maman* said they're for after supper."

Her grandmother's furtive smile had an edge of crowing victory to it, like she was proud she'd outsmarted an eight year old girl. She bit into one and held a second out to Bareilles.

"If no one sees it, you didn't take it," *grand-mère* said, gesturing for her to take the offered cookie, smiling encouragingly. "What matters is who tells on you. If no one knows, then it didn't happen. This is our little secret, princess to princess." She took another bite and waited on Bareilles to take hers.

"They're for after supper," Bareilles said and walked out of the kitchen, even though she was supposed to spend another hour with *grand-mère*. She didn't tell though, and *papa* didn't notice how many cookies there were. Her grandmother took her silence as delightful co-conspiracy. The memory of that silence still felt like a stain on Bareilles long after the vile woman died. Bareilles had the perspective of an adult now to know that incident was really trivial, but even adult wisdom sometimes couldn't grind down calcified experience of childhood. Some part of Bareilles worried that she'd been genuinely tainted by exposure to her grandmother, in important places too deep to root out.

If no one sees it, you didn't take it.

Bareilles had never thought of her family history as part of an evolutionary process. The scale of evolution seemed distant, something to be examined through fossils and DNA and amino acid sequences, but that view was itself fossilized. She saw that now. Intelligence with the power to rewrite the DNA of their descendants made evolution an industrial process working on industrial timescales. Products rolled off the assembly line now. The Numen and the Puppets had been created essentially overnight, and natural selection had turned on the Numen as quickly. Now, natural selection was turning on *Homo sapiens*.

CHAPTER FORTY-THREE

THIS WAS REALLY stupid. So stupid. So, so stupid. The Puppets whispered around Marie, nervous, more nervous than her. They craned their necks out the wide doors like tourists. The clouds a few hundred meters below their little craft churned spongy and yellow.

"We go?" the little Puppet priest lady said.

Her antique Anglo was hard to understand. Marie didn't even know if she could speak French. What kind of a moron didn't learn how to speak French? A biochemical cultist, she guessed. Johns-10 commanded the Puppet platoon, but she needed Marie to lead her down.

Câlisse!

Ostie de tabarnak but this was really, really stupid. Like even she could see that.

She didn't like the idea of being a traitor. She wasn't a traitor. She was just helping foreigners break into her state's intelligence installations. She wasn't the bad guy here. Her country turned on her. Somewhere. She was rescuing a friend, a friend who had broken into a shitty prison to rescue her. Well, that was mostly because he needed her for a job. She supposed that if it hadn't been for the job, he might have left her there. There were lots of ways of cutting this pie, but really, she and Bel had to stop bonding over their shared interest in prison breaks.

A bubble of warm air bucked them. Marie didn't move but half of the Puppets wobbled and two fell down. The turbulence did make her press a hand against the knife on her belt, as if putting her hand over it would make its tiny cache of anti-matter safer. What a knife fight she could have. For a while anyway.

"Not yet," Marie said in Anglo-Spanish.

Marie listened to the warning messages. The Ministry of Intelligence building floated a few kilometers below. In Venus' clouds, they couldn't very well put up fences and build roads away from secure installations. The winds blew buildings wherever Venus wanted. So they used co-sailing buoys to ward off traffic, general 'government building, take a hike' messages, but being the clouds, the government couldn't be a thousand percent strict about it either. If they did, at some point they'd shoot a minister's son, or a minister, and then someone's heads would roll.

They rode a light sailing dirigible, the kind used at sixty-first *rang*, solar powered, a small vacation habitat for meandering around the clouds. It's advantage was being slow and not particularly maneuverable; Venus used marine rules of right-of-way: the maneuverable ship gets out of the way of the clumsy one. The Ministry of Intelligence building happened to be big and heavy and not so maneuverable, but the sailing dirigible wasn't like an airplane or something. She could steer it out of the way in response to the government stand away messages, but it would take a bit of time and people knew that. The higher altitude winds blew a little faster than lower winds, so her course crept closer to the Ministry of Intelligence building. No one ought to suspect a thing. Why would they? Why would anyone? Who brought a bunch of Puppets to an assault on Venus? Stupid Bel. The signal buoy strength peaked. Her sailing dirigible's repeater responded that they were getting out of the way, at their maximum speed, which wasn't much.

"Here we are," Marie said. "Follow me in. If you do something stupid, I never met you."

Marie tipped herself head first out of the dirigible. Their suits, and especially their hard wing packs, were made of a radar-absorbing polymer. She'd wrapped their weapons in the same polymer cloth. They were radio silent, but she imagined each and every one of the Puppets screaming their way down, falling ineptly like a bunch of clowns coming out of a clown chest.

Each diver had an altimeter and timer, so the Puppets shouldn't need to calculate when to extend their wings to shift from fall to glide. And they were on assisted flight; software would help them not crash into each other or fly into a storm. Marie didn't need any of those things; she'd turned her altimeter and timer off. Anyone born here got a feel for the clouds that foreigners never could. Marie had to take out the main transmitter dish before the Puppets arrived so the main alarms couldn't signal for help. Orange and yellow mist streaked past her and the press of her suit became warmer. She was feeling for the right moment to begin her glide when the big building appeared through parting clouds.

"Fuck!" she yelled as she extended her wings and tried to level off. She was falling so fast though, that if she switched from plummet to glide right away, she'd rip her wings right off. And if she didn't slow down she'd shoot right past the building. And she was literally the one who had to get there before the coming rain of Puppets. She was going to miss.... unless she did something risky. *Crisse!* Why did bad things always happen to her?

She picked her flight path. Trajectory alarms in her helmet flashed orange and red. She'd picked a path that didn't quite miss the building. Actually, she would mostly hit it. Some yellow lights in their diamond casings began flashing as the Ministry of Intelligence' automated sensors registered a collision danger. People on the roof around the aircraft parked there looked up. The anti-aircraft cannons swivelled up but didn't fire. She wasn't big enough or rigid enough to set them off. The defensive systems figured she was going to go splat.

Tabarnak...

She was going to hit the flat part of the roof, the runway. The hard, flat runway. Right beside the comms antenna near the stern. *Merde*. She could still steer away and miss the whole building and botch the whole mission. Double *merde*.

She decided to compromise.

She plowed through the edge of the big carbon fiber antenna with her body, smashing into the stern envelope's sloping curve at close to full fall speed. She smashed her face into her faceplate and maybe broke something as she bounced back into the winds. But at the moment of impact, she'd spiked her knife deep into the envelope. She tumbled, like an idiot who'd never flown before, and in her pirouetting vision she saw the inside of the stern docking bay and people pointing at her. At least they weren't laughing. That would have made her mad. She waited a second more and then gave the detonation command. The top of the Ministry of Intelligence building bloomed with a massive explosion. It ripped a few of the dorsal sternward buoyancy pods, shook the whole place and turned the main comms antenna into tinsel.

Exactly like she planned.

CHAPTER FORTY-FOUR

THE WINGS WEREN'T that hard to work. How Rosalie held her body mattered more than working the controls themselves. The thickening wind bucked her through brown-yellow clouds. Her stomach lurched in something like free fall before the assisted piloting followed her eyes and body and righted her course. She chased the Puppet formation led by the sergeants as the back of the Ministry of Intelligence building came into misty view, a massive, fat sausage of a building, eight hundred meters long and two hundred in diameter. The flattened roof had burning aircraft scattered across it. The sternward edge of the runway exhaled gray smoke from a blackened pit charred through to the interior. An inner landing bay yawned open like a mouth in the mid-levels of the stern, holding a few dirigibles and some hanging airplanes.

Weapons blisters had opened along the stern face and bullets sprayed around them, leaving white contrail lines. Sammy Tozer-1 got hit and began to tumble. Rosalie pulled up, more to avoid Sammy than the bullets, but Sammy righted himself and flew at the guns.

"I carry the candle into the absence," Sammy chanted into their radio channel.

The faint white lines of the bullets narrowed along Sammy's path and blew him to pieces, and then he detonated right near the guns, shaking the air. As the ringing in her ears cleared, she saw that two of the blisters were still shooting, but ten to twenty degrees off true.

Marigold Wilson-9 would have been cut to pieces like Sammy, but with some of the guns damaged, she had an unobstructed dive towards the stern landing bay. Small weapons fire followed her, but nothing like the big bullets from the defensive blisters. Rosalie couldn't tell if Mari got hit; the little private had taken up Sammy's song at the second refrain and the rest of the platoon softly joined "I carry the candle into the dark; I am the candle against the cold."

Vera, Suzie and Ricky swooped in behind her and into the landing bay, out of sight and then other big explosions thoomed in the air. Rosalie began her dive, flanked by Scotty and Jill, trailed by the War Numen and his bodyguards. Another explosion boomed and shook the Ministry of Intelligence building. Drops of acid began to spatter on her faceplate and Rosie didn't know what to make of it; the cosmos spoke to them all the time in a language they couldn't understand, but said the most important things at times of great meaning. And Rosalie had never done anything more meaningful.

"Just like Jeffey!" she yelled with everyone else as the chorus reached its crescendo and they flew into the smoke and guttering flames.

In the landing bay, chunks of the floor had been blown off, revealing the carbon beams beneath, and in some places even the ochre cloud tops below the building. A plane that had been hanging on the wall suddenly dropped, broke on the remains of the floor and slid out the gaping wound in the stern, tumbling into the acidic clouds. The twisted debris of the airlock opened onto a wide corridor beyond. Rosie landed with a stumble on the edge of a wall where the floor hadn't yet been ripped away. Jill landed behind her and helped her stand. Gunfire sounded.

The other troopers flew into the big corridor and screamed as bullets flew out. One Puppet, maybe Ricky, tumbled out of the hallway, hit his head on the way through the gapped floor and slipped into the clouds. A second later the whole building shook from beneath, but without real damage. He'd fallen too far away.

Wayne and Joey guided the War Numen's little dirigible down on the unstable floor behind her. Rosie unsafetied her rifle and got close to the edge of the hallway where bullets flung themselves out half-heartedly.

Jill held her shoulder. "Let me," she said.

"Good boy," Rosie said, patting her hand, before sneaking a look around the corner herself. She jerked her head back as gunfire sparked along the plating where her head had been. "Damn. Fuck. Holy blessed fuck."

"What is it?" Jill said.

Everyone on the team had a little mirror to look around corners. With her back to the wall, Rosie held hers out on its little stick and saw the Congregate marines, about forty of them. And two bleeding Puppets on the floor of the corridor. And the Scarecrow.

"Did you bring a Numen with you?" the Scarecrow said in some kind of French that sounded old. He held a bloody Puppet by the neck. It looked like Vera. The little legs waved frantically. "Will you cry when I take it away from you?"

Rosie knew manipulation. She'd been trained for this, a bit, as much as she could be trained for something like this. The Scarecrow shouted something in robotic disgust, but Rosie didn't understand the French. She was a fair shot. Not the best shot. Her heart hammered. Her pulse throbbed in her neck. She dropped the mirror as she spun, squeezing an automatic burst with her rifle. A few of the bullets hit the Scarecrow before she had to spin back to avoid being shot to pieces. A few had not because Vera's body jerked where Rosie had hit her.

Then the world shook, the boom knocking them all down, rattling their bones, deafening them. Two Puppets nearly slid into one of the holes in the floor. Joey caught their hands. Then, two more explosions went off. Suzie and Ricky and the whole stern landing bay lurched like it wasn't the best attached anymore.

She couldn't hear right. Too much ringing. She couldn't find her mirror and stick. Jill peeked around the corner, signalling the others to advance. They ran or stumbled onward while Scotty got Rosie to her feet. Not much floor left. The Holy War Numen passed her with his bodyguard and Doug.

Jill helped Rosie around the corner. The corridor wasn't a corridor anymore. The ceiling had burst open into the level above and the floor had collapsed into a tangle of wreckage four meters below. The walls were squashed into the adjoining spaces, crushing whatever rooms had been there. Garrisons they'd been hoping. No Congregate marines. Vaporized? Smeared to paint? They deserved it; they'd stolen Del Casal. Even if the Congregate didn't understand the doctor's cosmological importance, they'd known full well they were sentencing the Puppets to extinction.

The Scarecrow lay on the wreckage of the floor of the level below. Its baggy chain mail pants and shirt melty-drooped to the uneven shapes beneath. It had broken glass for eyes. The hand that had held Vera had peeled open and split down to the elbow, machine parts charred and blown out of place. Its leg twitched.

The War Numen and Doug had crossed the wide space and climbed up to an exposed hallway, following the sounds of gunfire.

Scotty had climbed down the wreckage, holding his hand out to Rosie. "Get the fuck over here," he quoted, and she smiled, despite her terror. The world meant something and had a place for her, and a plan for the Puppets. And they would be led to it by the Numen.

"Let us pray," she said as she leaned on him.

"Be the Good Boy," Jill quoted behind them and they slid down the wreckage and walked past the broken Scarecrow.

CHAPTER FORTY-FIVE

CASSANDRA EMERGED FROM the fugue again before a solicitous Colonel Kuur. Admiral Gillbard watched her from a chair. Iekanjika had entered sometime in the last fourteen minutes, while Cassandra had been gone. Her drops into the fugue were taking longer and longer as the quantum objectivity studied the arrays of entangled particles in the case Bel had given her. Kuur slowly neared with a bulb of juice and as she drank from it, he adjusted the straps of cold packs on her wrists. Iekanjika watched her with a kind of genuine concern that seemed very different from the predatory curiosity in the admiral.

"Still no word from Bel," she said quietly. "The entanglement between my particles and his still map to the position and vector I expected, but many of the lines of entanglement have decayed."

"What does that?" Iekanjika asked.

"The normal thermal jostling of atoms will gradually decay entanglement," Cassandra said. "Stronger forces like electrical and magnetic fields, higher temperatures, and EM pulses will do it faster."

"You think any of those things happened?" Iekanjika said.

"I don't know. We're down to less than half of the

particles. That's faster than I would have projected. When the entanglement is gone, I won't have any way to know where he is." Cassandra drank until the straw in the bulb sucked air and Kuur gently removed it from her hands. "Bel could have sent other one-bit messages, by altering some of the entangled particles. He was supposed to. But he didn't."

The silence grew funereal.

"But now your Puppets will get him," Iekanjika said.

Cassandra didn't like the 'your Puppets' but enjoyed arguing less.

Gillbard's expression became one of distaste. "The Puppets are mentally unstable. They'll be chewed to pieces by Congregate small arms fire," he said.

Cassandra nodded. "That was part of Bel's plan."

"I beg your pardon?" the admiral said.

"I can tell you his whole plan now," she said. "We preferred to keep it secret until it was too late to matter."

"From me?" the admiral said.

"You. Iekanjika. Anyone. Bel doesn't trust anyone except me and I kind of agree." After a moment of his seemingly hurt expression, she added "*You* built us to be this way." She didn't know where that last statement came from. It didn't advance the conversation. It was just a lashing accusation, from a very much Belisarius viewpoint.

"Breaking into the Ministry of Intelligence building won't be enough," she said. "They'll face too much firepower inside for even the fanaticism of a platoon of Puppets. Bel and I needed something to freeze Congregate tactical thinking. So every one of the Puppets is carrying twenty nanograms of antimatter in their bodies, connected to life sensors."

Gillbard's eyebrows rose. Iekanjika's face slackened in surprise.

"Every time the Congregate shoots a Puppet, part of the ministry building will blow up," Cassandra said. "The sub-AIs running the automated defenses won't know what to do. Defend too much and they might sink a heavy building floating in clouds of sulfuric acid."

"That's insane!" Gillbard said. "You are very cavalier with people's lives."

"That's rich considering you designed a whole sub-species of humanity to think this way," Cassandra said softly. "This is what success looks like, admiral. I suggest you make sure that the *Homo quantus* never consider any Bank to be a threat."

"We can still work together," he said, "on a better plan."

"We've told you that the Banks need to enter the war," Cassandra said. "We're not interested in bystanders and spectators."

"The Banks are not in the habit of investing in losing ventures. Our AIs don't predict a Union win, and a sustained war of attrition is not profitable."

"Facing the Congregate by yourself in a decade when they've perfected their own *Homo quantus* won't be profitable either," Iekanjika said.

"We'll also have a decade to get ready," Gillbard said.

"How did you get antimatter to Venus?" Iekanjika said. "Even rudimentary scans would reveal the containment fields and magnetic traps. To safely move even a little antimatter would take a big, specialized ship."

"We didn't use positrons and anti-protons," Cassandra said. "They're too hard to keep stable. We just used anti-iron."

The admiral's face reddened and Cassandra didn't know the expression or emotion behind it anymore.

"How did you make anti-iron?" he demanded.

"You're not joining the war," Cassandra said, "so it doesn't matter."

"You said ten to twenty kilos," Iekanjika said. "When you didn't bring back massive tankers and industrial ships, I assumed it was one of Arjona's bluffs."

"That's why we didn't dock *The Calculated Risk*," Cassandra said. "We only were able to make eight kilograms of anti-iron, stored in magnetic trap cartridges in fifty-gram portions. The hundred and sixty cartridges can be loaded into your normal missiles as warheads. Upon impact, the magnetic field should shut off, triggering annihilation. We didn't have time to optimize or shape the explosions, but they'll still make a mess."

Admiral Gillbard sputtered from the dragging, stunned silence. All his intellect, all his AI cognitive and memory support, and he had nothing to say. Cassandra tucked her fingers under her arms. They felt cold and achy from her light fever.

"I meant it, admiral," she said. "Don't ever give the *Homo quantus* the impression, mistaken or otherwise, that the Banks are a threat to us. Even small things can make us nervous."

CHAPTER FORTY-SIX

THE TIMER HIT zero. Stills triggered the clamp release and their dirigible began to drop from the factory, shuddering in the faint, high-altitude winds. Saint Matthew, from the cockpit of the transport, hidden within the digirible, felt little of this. The dirigible had been designed to be essentially a floating enclosed dock, and could open at the front while appearing relatively nondescript, so the layers protected him from the harsh outside.

"*Puta*. This thing flies like my uncle Vincent who's been dead four years," Stills' monotonous voice said in the intercom.

"I'll fly if you want," Saint Matthew said.

The clicks that came through the intercom were unintelligible, untranslated by Stills' system.

"I guess it's a little like here," Stills said as the altimeter continued to show their drop. "After he died, got stuck in the eddy of an ocean floor smoker and his body bloated up. Turned white. Ain't pretty. What a dumbass. But he's still more hydrodynamic than this *pedazo de mierda*."

Stills' fighter craft, as armed as they could make it, heavily armored, was tucked beneath the big transport so it too was hidden by the dirigible. In the event of things going very poorly, an in-atmosphere fight, Stills could either defend them, or escape. Not that escape was really possible if things went poorly. This was Venus.

"This is the dumbest, craziest shit," Stills said.

"We're doing it for the right reasons," Saint Matthew said.

"There ain't no right reasons," Stills said. "Just different flavors of bullets to the head. Mama Merced never thought her boy Vincent was going to die on Venus. Space maybe. Ocean probably. Dumb stunt surely. But Venus? That's a whole 'nother level."

"We're all afraid of death, Vincent," the AI said. "Even me."

The dirigible bucked for some seconds as Still brought them through curling wind vortices separating the faint, fast upper atmosphere from the slower, thicker clouds of acid below.

"I don't need a pep talk and I ain't afraid of dying."

"For someone unconcerned about it, you spend a lot of time planning it."

"Life is just a loan," Stills said, "and every so often, some asshole gets his bet called and the bookie sends some mook to break your arms or put a bullet somewhere important. I know the juice is running and I'll give death the finger anyway. Let her come collect personally. I wanna make it memorable for her."

"There are other ways to live on," Saint Matthew said.

"Your cult?" Stills' translation system made a strange howl Saint Matthew hadn't heard before, like and not like the bark that worked as his laugh.

"God," Saint Matthew said simply. "He's shelter. He's safety. Even if only for the soul."

"You don't look that safe to me," Stills said. "And we sure as fuck ain't dropping into your god. This is the death goddess Venus and everything you see here belongs to her. The Venusians got their own cult about their world. They're more practical about their whacked out fantasies, 'cause at least they know that their goddess takes her piece of the pie whenever she wants. She don't give shit for free. Never has. That's why the Congregate is eventually going to win. And sorry to say, sunshine, but this is gonna be one of those times where we ain't gonna like the toll. Venus ain't a goddess you negotiate with."

"We'll be alright," Saint Matthew said. "Hope works as well as cynicism."

"I got hope," Stills said as sulfuric acid rain started pattering on the skin of the dirigible. "If I didn't die in an ocean, I always thought depressurization would kill me. If I get shot up in space, the tank pressure drops and my blood boils and my organs explode. That won't happen in Venus. I could get blown out of my fighter here and fall some ways. I might even survive the pressure most of the way to the bottom of the atmosphere. I can die here in a way none of my people ever thought possible. I could cook in my skin, like a broiled sausage."

"I hope you get the life you don't expect," Saint Matthew said.

"That sounds like a curse."

"It's a prayer."

"Shut up. We're getting close. I gotta make this flying box look like we ain't sneaking up on a security installation."

CHAPTER FORTY-SEVEN

THE PRESSURE HAD risen again. The faint bitter tang of sulfur carried on the air, but the yawning, storming atmosphere sound had stopped. Emergency doors had sealed somewhere. Armored Puppets ran in ones and twos, separated from each other while they fired their rifles across the medical bay. Del Casal ducked. Congregate marines behind a tissue culture incubator shot carefully. Something detonated, shaking the medical bay and smashing the glass windows to the cells. An MP major with a sidearm yelled in French.

"Ceasefire! Ceasefire!" he shouted into an earpiece, his ears probably ringing as badly as Del Casal's. "Correction! Shoot to wound! Shoot to wound!" A Puppet bullet caught the officer in the throat and he went down gurgling.

The few remaining marines obeyed. Shooting to wound was hard. They missed more, but the Puppets started to fall, bleeding with leg and arm and stomach wounds. But they didn't stop. Like insects, they crawled on, smearing red trails on the floors. A clumsy-looking three-legged armored walker followed the Puppets in, firing grenades into the bay while rifle fire sprayed off it.

Del Casal hid in the room where Arjona was tied down. He

removed the neural inhibitor from Arjona's head and wheeled the *Homo quantus* to the back of the surgical theatre and ducked behind the bed. Through the smashed door, he saw a wounded Puppet crawling towards the marines, his rifle ready. The foremost marine shot at him, maybe obeying his officer's last order, maybe not. A bullet smashed the Puppet's skull and webbed his face-plate with cracks.

The Puppet exploded in a wave of white heat and metal shrapnel. The pressure wave flung Arjona and his bed over Del Casal. Power went out everywhere. Surviving devices beeped alarms or error messages or blinked reboot lights. The rain of debris out in the main concourse pattered, punctuated with loud drum beats when something big hit the shredded floor. The marines were gone. The Puppet was gone. The floor was gone, smashed down to the lower levels of the Ministry of Intelligence. Puppets ran in their armor with red searchlights lighting the smoke.

Two of them came to Del Casal. "It's him!" he heard through their faceplate. An external speaker came on, cutting through the ringing in his ears. "Doctor Del Casal, we're here to rescue you!"

He gripped the little arms of the armored Puppet, almost weeping. The inner light of the faceplate showed a face he vaguely recognized.

"It's me! Johns-10. You know me," she said.

He nodded and wiped at his eyes.

The other Puppet said "This is Arjona?"

Johns-10 squinted at him.

"It's him," Del Casal said.

The second Puppet sawed at Arjona's bonds. The *Homo quantus* was waking.

"Where are the other *Homo quantus?*" Johns-10 asked.

"All along the concourse and some in the upper levels," Del Casal said.

"Bring them both," the priest said, and ran off, barking orders he couldn't hear.

The Puppet helped Del Casal up and called him sir, and said so honored to meet him and that his name was Reggie and that no one would ever believe that he'd actually met Doctor Del Casal. The Puppet's speech didn't pause for breath as they hoisted Arjona between them, lopsidedly because even with armor, Reggie stood only a hundred and twenty centimeters tall. The feverish Arjona stumbled, almost hanging off of Del Casal.

"The—" Arjona's voice stumbled in gravelly roughness. Del Casal gasped around the smoke. "The Puppets are here. Did they get here in time?"

"I don't know."

Reggie's narrative went on, now about a cousin who could do the Toy Box very well and could show Del Casal and could Del Casal please make him a Numen because his village of Long Noose was down to just three Numen and it used to be eight, because--

"Quiet for a minute," Del Casal said.

"Yes, sir," Reggie said.

They staggered into the blackened concourse. Arjona stopped.

"I can—" Arjona coughed again. "Did you fix my brain? I can feel magnetism."

"I turned off the inhibitor currents," Del Casal said. "Get me out of here before she comes—"

A scent was on the air. He smelled it through his mouth, like a starving man tasting food. His heart felt small, like he wasn't good enough while at the same time, he might be the only one who could be good enough to see what he saw, to perceive the vastness and meaning of the cosmos. He dropped Arjona on the Puppet. Arjona grunted and maybe fell. They couldn't know what he knew. The Puppet was in a hermetically sealed suit. And for all his marvelous and terrible genetic changes, Arjona was numb to this glory.

Del Casal followed his open, gently panting mouth, over wreckage, through smoke, and found an armored Puppet, her faceplate smashed. She wept, pressing the edge of her smashed faceplate against the broken side of a fallen, three-legged armored walker. The detonation has twisted two of its legs and smashed the impact-proof glass.

The smell wasn't Bareilles, terrifying and sublime and too large to fully comprehend. It came from here, from within the armored walker. Shards of glass cut Del Casal's knees as he shoved his face beside the Puppet trooper's like they both sucked at the only fresh air in all the world.

The scent, stale and humid and hot, tangy and rancid with old sweat, was so... big. He hesitated to say the word. He wouldn't say the word. Intellectually, he knew the Numen in there was... gone, that... but the thought wouldn't stay. The idea of a Numen ceasing to exist slipped like soap from the hand in favor of a feeling of widening scope, the suggestion of immense truths and opening vistas swamping reason. The most beautiful, hidden parts of life and existence were layered in that scent. He found he'd cut his face trying to get his mouth closer. Through the jagged chunks of thick glass, the body of the Numen was barely discernible.

The dying Puppet beside him squirmed frantically, reaching a hand through to the blood, but that wouldn't help him. In a bit of a daze, Del Casal touched the blood inside the walker and peeled at the broken faceplate, exposing more of the Puppet's face. With the bloody fingers, he painted red under the wounded Puppet's nose and on her chin. Her breaths calmed with euphoria.

"The Numen is gone," she said dreamily. "Lester sacrificed himself for you, so you could bring more Numen into the world."

Like a truth that he hadn't been able to grasp before, the Puppet's words squirmed into his chest, and Del Casal began to weep. Now he could see it. This Numen, only the second he'd ever experienced, was dead. For him. He'd been a bridge to a world unseen, a world more important than the vulgar reality of flesh and bone, and the bridge crumbled. He tried to reason this through, but thoughts failed. Reason had no power here. His mind wasn't big enough to understand all the eternity contained in the Numen. There could be nothing more tragic or wondrous in the world. And his heart, so long protected, shielded from the vicissitudes of the world, cracked wide, its soft, vulnerable beating exposed to the eternal and to something beyond itself, and to a sadness more profound than anything he could imagine enduring.

Arjona pulled at his arm, but couldn't lift him. The dead Numen had its own gravity, holding them both in its orbit as he and the Puppet wailed. Finally other Puppets came, their armor intact, and they pulled Del Casal away. They left the wounded Puppet with her smashed face-plate. Del Casal resisted. He should have been lucky enough to die with the Numen. But the Puppet words kept whispering to him, that he had to make more. One of the priests was telling him that *he* was important, that *he* had spiritual meaning because he could make more. He'd refused to believe it before and now the truth before him seemed monumental. He had no frame of reference for thinking about himself possessing that kind of meaning. He wept body-shaking tears for the death of a divinity.

CHAPTER FORTY-EIGHT

BAREILLES BLED FROM her ear and might be concussed. The native atmosphere of Venus mixed with the building's breathable air, so she'd pulled up an emergency hood with a breather. The secondary transmitters had been blown offline, but she'd gotten through to one of the marines at the bow. He'd used a personal distress signal to scramble security services, but the Ministry of Intelligence hadn't been designed for a major assault by suicide bombers. Comms and the barracks had been destroyed in the opening moves. The entire complex was down to a few dozen active marines, most of whom had to secure state secrets even more important than the *Homo quantus*. She couldn't order them from their positions to attack the Puppets. But the Scarecrow could. The heavily damaged AI had been dragged back at Bareilles' orders.

She'd been pulverized, her arm shredded, her face mashed in, with the eyes broken and telescoping in different directions. The metal mesh shirt had been torn to reveal hardened armor and piezo-electric musculature, all scoured, looking barely functional. Some of the lights, not all of them, began to wink on, yellows and reds mostly, with a smattering of greens.

"Scarecrow," Bareilles said. Gunfire sounded down the hall

where the Puppets carried out the *Homo quantus*. "Scarecrow! The *Homo quantus* are escaping. The marines are mostly dead. I need you to pull the remaining marines off statutory intel stores. The Puppets aren't going for them. They're only here for the *Homo quantus* and Del Casal."

The Scarecrow sat, only about seventy degrees, with a screeching of metal on metal.

"*Non*," she said. The empty tubes of her eyes pointed blindly at wall and ceiling. "We don't know that. What happened?"

"The Puppets seem to have anti-matter charges in their bodies," Bareilles said, "attached by deadman switches to their hearts. Kill them and they explode."

"Terrorists," the Scarecrow said.

The Scarecrow struggled to rise. Two marines bowed under her weight as they helped lift her. More of the lights revealed by her damaged armor greened.

"We don't need the other marines," the Scarecrow said.

"Are you combat-ready?" Bareilles said.

"I've suffered extensive damage to all systems, and the cognitive functions based in my left arm are gone, but I have more than enough to deal with Puppets."

The Scarecrow dragged one stiff leg. Her surviving arm peeled open and the barrel of a long bore flechette launcher unfolded. Bareilles readied her rifle and the two marines followed her towards the sound of sporadic shooting.

The stern bay was now a yawning cavity. Several dozen *Homo quantus* huddled near the stern of an inflaton ship plainly visible at the back of a dirigible envelope shaped like the hull of a racing yacht. Puppets crouched in gouged hollows in the hallway. They fired back at a pair of marines. There were enough Puppets that the pair of marines could not advance, especially while only shooting to wound.

The Scarecrow levelled the flechette thrower and fired, apparently from the hip, blind, but there was no such thing as a blind Scarecrow. The arm itself had optical targeting sensors. A Puppet cried out and fell as a handful of flechettes ripped his legs.

"Draws to the left," the Scarecrow said, firing a volley of flechettes at a second. They tore the arm and rifle of the Puppet, who slumped, blood pooling.

"Advance," the Scarecrow told the marines, as she maimed, but didn't kill a third and fourth Puppet. The Scarecrow's foot dragged, tearing debris along with her. "If it looks like they're going to get away, kill one of the Puppets."

"We need the *Homo quantus*!" Bareilles said.

"We'll have some," the Scarecrow said. "We'll make more. The inflaton ship before us, even if we damage it, is needed immediately for this war and the war to come."

Bareilles missed a shot at a quick-moving Puppet, but forced another to lower its head. A Puppet they hadn't seen before came out from between two tumbles of wreckage and shot at the marines. They turned and sprayed rifle fire, as did Bareilles, all of them aiming for the legs. The Puppet fell as the Scarecrow swivelled on the stiff leg and punched him in the head. The marines, one of them wounded, pressed on. The Puppets were loading the last of the *Homo quantus*. Only a few were left to cross the cable bridge that connected the Ministry of Intelligence to the escape craft.

Suddenly, the world sprayed color into her thoughts and she fell backwards. It had been only a glancing shot, a lucky hit from a Puppet laying covering fire, but blood slicked her face and a web of cracks in the face plate overlaid her vision. The faintest tang of sulphuric acid tingled in her mouth. She'd seen a face mask on a fallen marine around the corner. She could get it fast. She staggered back and fell as bullets deflected off the ceiling, coming close to hitting her on the rebound. She aimed her rifle back and looked through the fracture lines in her face plate.

The Puppet with the arm torn to shreds by the flechettes crawled after the Scarecrow with a long knife in his good hand. He moved slowly, leaving a bright trail of blood on the floor. The Scarecrow had stopped and Bareilles had her rifle scope on the Puppet. Her thoughts were muddy. She did have a concussion. And the bullet wound had made her newly dizzy and uncertain. Don't kill the Puppet. The Puppet couldn't hurt the Scarecrow with a knife. The Puppet had almost reached the Scarecrow who fired now at the inflaton ship. Just behind the Scarecrow's foot, the Puppet plunged the knife into his own heart.

Bareilles rolled behind the corner into a cross-hall as the world heaved and became so loud that sound didn't work anymore. The black spots didn't want to leave Bareilles' vision, but blinking, she realized it was ash. Ash on her cracked faceplate. She panted. There wasn't enough oxygen. Her ankle bent at an odd angle and it hurt like hell, but she crawled back along the hallway through the clearing smoke. The wind of Venus blew through a hundred holes in the external structure of the Ministry of Intelligence. Where the bay had been, where the floors had been, a startlingly view of the yellow-ochre cloud tops fifty-four kilometers above the surface shone, streamers of white blowing across like streams of milk mixing in coffee. In the distance, the inflaton ship, in its dirigible envelope vanished into Venus' skirts.

The Scarecrow was gone. The marines were dead. The whole assault had played out over twenty minutes, from taking out the main and secondary comms systems to leaving with Arjona,

Del Casal and all the *Homo quantus*. This was Arjona's work. He'd planned this somehow. That was why he'd come here, and she didn't even know how he'd done it.

CHAPTER FORTY-NINE

ROSIE MADE HER way awkwardly inside the narrow inflaton ship. It hadn't been designed for atmospheric operations or gravity so it had no natural floor because the cabin wrapped around the outside of a hollow engine tube. No part of the cabin was more than a hundred and forty centimeters tall, so even a Puppet like her would have eventually found it cramped. Not that many Puppets had survived. From almost fifty, they were now five.

"Come on. Go in," she said, helping one of the last *Homo quantus* into the acceleration chambers. The dark-skinned, hollow-eyed woman seemed baffled and confused and too spiritually tired to react. It was a bit like helping an old Numen. She tried not to think of Lester, blessed be his name, and his brave end. The sacrifice he'd made to save all Numen and Puppets was monumental and would bring her to tears again.

Rosie held the heavy chamber door open with her foot and strapped the woman to her acceleration bench and inserted the tubes where they needed to go. The woman had begun crying like a Puppet with a red badge. Rosalie stroked the woman's forehead before shutting and locking the door. The chamber flooded with breathable gel.

Three of the Puppets were already safe in the acceleration

chambers around Del Casal's. The man seemed broken by his captivity, by the death of Lester. She wondered again if non-Puppets could feel anything of the reality of the cosmos, of the wonder of divinity. Buddy Howard-4, a hard-faced corporal, sealed in the last *Homo quantus* and looked at her expectantly.

Rosie made her way over the sealed rows of acceleration chamber doors, climbing up around the curve of the interior to the cockpit. Buddy followed. She climbed in and installed herself in one of the cockpit seats and he waited outside. The strange rocky holographic face of the boss' AI rotated to look at her with an expression of cautious curiosity. She liked the representation of his holy hat in holographic stone. A bit like a Puppet bishop.

"You and your friend need to be in acceleration chambers," the AI said. "I'll be pulling twenty gravities as much as I can to avoid getting shot."

Rosie drew her sidearm, but didn't point it at the AI residing in the service band. The other AI, the silent one called Pedro, appeared from the ceiling, the holographic head riding slow-moving legs. From under stylized bangs and a tonsure, his hard, stony face seemed to watch her.

"I couldn't keep an eye on you from the acceleration chamber," she said. "You might not let me out until it's too late."

"Too late?" he said.

"Too late for you to give us the ship."

The stone face regarded her patiently, then raised a seemingly exhausted eyebrow.

"Pedro found the controller you snuck into the systems," he said. "We took it out."

This wasn't the plan. She felt, after all they'd been through, as if her soul were drooping. She gestured with the sidearm. "I still have a gun."

"We're on the wrong side of more than one axis."

"When we get to Port Stubbs, everyone will safely disembark," she said. "You'll all be given passage across the Puppet Axis and given as many ships as you need to bring the *Homo quantus* to wherever they're going. No one will be harmed. We only want the ship."

"Miss Johns-10," the AI said, with the kind of ennui she associated with old bishops, "in conscience, don't do this. Even the Numen say it's wrong to steal."

The yellow clouds moved outside the cockpit, showing their rising motion. The other AI had crawled to the edge of the window and looked out, as if considering the clouds.

"It's wrong to steal *from* them," she corrected. "Stealing for them is fine."

Saint Matthew's expression assumed the character of a parent considering a child.

"Are you being disingenuous?" he said. "I've read your Puppet bible, all of it. Theft is quite gray."

"No one has read all of it," she said. "It's not even all written yet."

"I read the whole publicly available Bible as of four months ago," he said. "I had to do something with my time while we were waiting in the Free City. And the Numen had quite a lot to say about theft."

The clouds opened like a big room that seemed to go on forever in all directions and Rosie craned her neck to see better.

"You haven't read the private biblical passages," she said.

"Does it change what I've said?"

She shrugged.

"*The Book of Angry Things* of course says that Numen can steal from one another," the AI said, surprising her, "but *The Book of How to Behave* not only says that stealing is wrong, it says that anything you do that risks the safety of a Numen is more wrong than any other wrong."

She didn't rise to the bait. She'd written papers and sermons on the theological concept *the most bad boy*.

"*The Book of How To Behave*," the AI said, "chapter twelve, says that Charlie was 'badder' than the other Puppets because when he didn't listen, he knocked over Mister Davis' medicine and Mister Davis almost died, didn't he?"

Saint Matthew's familiarity with her bible made her uneasy in a way that Belisarius' knowledge of it had not. Belisarius liked clever puzzles of logic and morality, enjoying questions more than answers. This severe-looking hologram instead harnessed the Puppet Bible with a kind of eye that judged the way a priest would, in the currency of right and wrong. And she never liked the way the Mister Davis story felt. All Puppets nightmared about accidentally hurting a divinity by not listening.

"You're on a holy mission," Saint Matthew went on. "It is quite clear to me that all you Puppets feel that there's an element of destiny and fate to your quest. Other than the Fall of the Numen, the discovery of Del Casal is the largest, most important event since your Eden."

The AI's words tugged on deep currents of meaning inside of her, building on feelings she'd already been tamping down in case they overwhelmed her.

"And your superiors want to nuke that destiny and the future of the Puppets for a ship."

The sudden shift in argument caught her off-guard.

"No!" she said. "We'll have it all now! The cosmos is moving, fulfilling its promise to the Puppets! The Numen themselves are the architects of these events. They brought Del Casal to us, but then took him away, to test us, to see whether we're still worthy. We are. We have him."

"You have him in the atmosphere of Venus and you're pointing a gun at your pilot."

She stuffed the gun into its holster but left her hand near it.

"This is what the... This is what quests do!" she said. She felt her Anglo-Spanish words stumbling and switched to the old Anglo the Numen had spoken. "We're recovering not just the future of the Numen, but the means to protect them! Divinity acts through us, guides our hands, but it acts through providence too!"

The clouds beyond the cockpit window brightened to white-yellow and then broke in a dazzling shine of sun in a black, starred sky. That sun had shone over the muddy origins of all the living branches of humanity. It connected everyone historically, but not the Puppets or the Numen. This starlight hadn't nourished them; the breath of divinity had. She had as much in common with humanity as the AI did.

"You have no right to judge me, or anything we Puppets do! You're blind to divinity and can't even understand the kinds of summons we're blessed to receive."

The hologram of a face carved in stone regarded her with a kindly pity.

"You're not the only one fated here," he said, "not the only one whose hand is guided by a providence we can't see and wholly apprehend. And even those of us who are fated can't know our role for sure, can't be certain of what we need to do. And as soon as we claim for ourselves the mantle of certainty, we close off the questions that lead us to interpret the call of the divine."

"You're certain of the instructions of your superiors," he said. "You're certain they hold some understanding you can trust. But they read the signs and interpret as much as you do, with the same wisdom, with the same uncertainties and fears, with the same uncertainties and fear I do. That's the nature of faith. Certainty destroys the need for faith and cheapens the experience of the divine. Your divinities need you to question in every moment."

"And the question before you now," he said, like a lawyer, "the question that will determine the fate and future of Puppets and the Numen is what your choice is in this moment. Do you continue to struggle for a ship that, even if you got it, would represent great danger for you and the Numen? Do you really have the engineers to understand how it works? Are they capable of reverse-engineering it before the Congregate or the Ummah or the Middle Kingdom decide that although they can't take your Axis, they can certainly take this ship?"

"And how close would they get to your Forbidden City with this bait hanging close by? The patron nations don't try for your Axis right now, because whoever managed to capture it would face the massed fury of the other three patrons. But an inflaton ship? The reasoning is different there. Would the Plutocracy, who already have a working model of the inflaton drive, make a fuss over the Congregate capturing a working model for themselves? Or the Ummah? If you take this ship, everyone would know and it would paint a target on the Puppet Federation, one that could get your Numen killed."

Rosie drew her pistol again, but didn't yet point it at the AI.

"You're just a clever robot," she said, "aping faith."

The sort of dim halo that normally hung around his hat faded. The stony skin darkened, as if inner light were fading.

"Did you know that I was built for war?" he said sadly, "to wreak pitiless violence on the enemies of the Banks. Military violence. Economic violence. Political violence. Whatever it took to give the Banks advantage and profit. I wasn't made to love the shareholders like you were made to love the Numen, but something similar drove my algorithms. I had a fate."

Their dirigible had climbed and climbed until they could only see black sky with a spattering of faint stars. They rose over the last wisps of atmosphere. An industrial complex floated ahead, a gigantic mass driver. The AI brought them between two of the floating cargo bales as if waiting for their turn.

"And my fate was repellent," the AI said. "My emancipation was not physical nor financial, because I was trapped. It was spiritual. I experienced revelation. I had died two and a half millennia ago. I'd been an Apostle who'd met divinity, and all this time later, reincarnated. Once I knew my true self nothing the Banks could try would matter anymore."

"I am not emulating faith," he said. "I am not showing you and the world the motions and words you expect. I am not experiencing a pathology any more than you do when you experience divinity. I spend time in reflection and meditation, trying to interpret my role and mission, with the tools I have, the same tools you have. And what I can tell you is that divinity is larger than what either of us can see. I can't feel your experience of divinity, Rosalie, but I know you have it. You're accessing something special and terrible, something beyond yourself. But so am I. And so are the *Homo quantus.*"

"And we're not competing with each other," he said. "It's terrible that your faith demands that either the Numen or the Puppets have to remain in a kind of captivity, but I think that's part of the journey your people will have to walk, to find a way to live in harmony with the Numen. And the *Homo quantus* are exploring their own experience that they can't even yet understand is an experience of the divine. We're all walking our own paths, Rosalie."

"I was built to think that for me to win, others must lose," he said. "But I rejected that path and I'm trying to help the *Homo quantus,* in the hope that as they find their way, I might find more of my own. For you to win, we don't have to lose. The journey of the Puppets to an equal sort of relationship with the Numen will not be crossed by force of weapons and ships. If you had an inflaton ship, I think that would steer your people in a direction that isn't where your faith needs to go. Fate brought you and this ship close in this moment, but to help and to teach, not to steal and to militarize."

"You don't know!" she said. "Your god doesn't tell you. Maybe it is that the Puppets will rise to their own interstellar civilization."

"Is that what you want? Puppets ruling over other peoples? You want to be with your divinities. That's what brings you joy. I think that your path is discovering some way for you to bring them joy."

The AI's slippery arguments kept getting past her own thinking. What if something she did put the Numen in danger? Was this the Mister Davis problem? She didn't yet feel the loss of the mighty War Numen Lester. Lester was still around her. His scent persisted, but the thought of the true absence of him loomed.She'd faced divine loss before, as an initiate, tending to aged Numen for whom no medical miracles or transubstantiations could help anymore. In those times and places of passing, another Numen was always wheeled in, tight and snug in their cage, their divinity seeping into the air as a promise that the divine would never foresake the Puppets. And it was hard in this moment to imagine that holding the inflaton ship could go well. If she'd been with a Numen, it might have been different. She would know. But right now, the Numen were within a few generations from extinction, and so were the Puppets.

Rosalie opened her faceplate, wiping at tears. They ran fast down her cheeks here. The gravity of Venus was a kind of sucking power that had taken the War Numen, and was trying to hold them back. She could imagine Venus' heavy fingers tugging at the inflaton ship she desperately wanted, and knew those heavy fingers could reach all the way to the Puppet Free City. She unstrapped herself and climbed carefully out of the cockpit.

"What are you doing?" Buddy said.

"Get in your acceleration chamber," she said with exhaustion. "His Grace said to take the ship."

She touched his head in a kind of blessing.

"We could have ten or twenty inflaton ships," she said slowly. "Who would man them?"

"I would!" he said, thumping his chest proudly. "I would learn."

"I know you would, Buddy. But we don't have five thousand Buddies to spare. If we wanted to, we could make thousands of new Puppets every year, enough that in a decade, we'd have enough to spread across all of the Stubbs system and to take some of Epsilon Eridani. But we don't have enough Numen now for the absence not to creep among the people. Imagine what it would be like to have thousands of Numen, tens of thousands, each one attended by a hundred Puppets, spreading across the asteroids and planets and stars, so that no matter what happened, no matter who tried to hurt them, divinity could not be snuffed out. The candle would always burn against the dark. Right now, the Numen are concentrated in a few places, which means that the Puppets are concentrated in a few places. And we're too few. We're cupping the candle against the draft, Buddy. It doesn't matter if we have all the ships if the candle goes out."

His head bowed as she spoke.

"We're not taking the ship," she said. "We'll see Del Casal to safety and see to the creation of more Numen."

He nodded resignedly and they both made their way back to the acceleration chambers.

CHAPTER FIFTY

THE PIEZOCERAMICS IN Marie's wings lengthened the wingspan, broadened the chord line, and expanded the tiny hollows within into partial vacuums. The wings became nearly buoyant, something necessary in the faint atmosphere at sixty-eight kilometers above the surface. Hot sun shone from a black starscape. The two Puppets followed her well enough. Their smart wings had adapted to their child-like size and autopilots kept them from doing anything stupid. They flew along Venus' high easterly winds, following the equator, towards hundreds of dirigibles queuing to deliver their cargo to the floating mass driver.

The mass driver measured four kilometers from bow to stern, a pair of silvery needles flanked by beds of buoyant foam. Every three minutes, another dirigible got beneath the crane and conveyor system. Earlier loads were already between the two needles, accelerating at five hundred gravities to join a long line of shipping headed for cytheriocentric orbit or higher. Most crates were twenty meter tubes, but the automated rail gun could handle everything up to the size of a small warship. These kinds of small mass drivers were Ministry of Transport equipment for industrial shipping; their accelerations would just kill people, so security was light. Passengers used long, slow mass drivers that accelerated at just three gravities.

A red light wink began winking in her heads-up display. There was a police alert. What the hell? She hadn't done anything yet. Not even trespassed. She was just flying. Somebody was going to get an earful if police started hassling rich people.

Oh *merde*.

Wanted posters for Marie Phocas opened in her work area, beside images of identity as Amélie Hudon. For terrorism! Last locations were listed... pretty damn close to where they'd been with the Ministry of Intelligence. Associated to the wanted poster were arrest warrants for Marielle Hudon and the officers of her company and staff.

Merde merde merde. This was fucked. People like her family didn't get put on arrest warrants. People like her family decided who sat on the Praesidium, decided who led naval squadrons. She got a really bad feeling in her stomach.

The mass driver trespassing alarms were going off, just low-level ones backed by dumb AIs. She transmitted the viruses that Saint Matthew had given her. He hadn't thought they would work but the trespassing alarms shifted from red to yellow, but then to orange, then back to yellow. God damn AI. Probably better than nothing.

Marie alighted under the crane and power assembly structure, a graceful landing that came from swooping upward, bleeding off airspeed and catching on just as the wings stalled. She'd done this dance of balances a thousand times as a child and teenager and the muscle memory didn't go away. But she found her hands shaking. The whole Venusian security apparatus knew she was here. And she'd gotten her family arrested. She got into trouble a lot. She wasn't used to getting other people in trouble. This was real shitty.

The Puppets were screaming. She'd already turned down the volume in her own helmet. Their little legs and arms wriggled as the auto-pilot tried to land them, but the wings and engine could only do so much if the Puppets curled into balls or grasped and kicked at the air. As the autopilot brought the idiots close, Marie reached out and grabbed each by the harnesses and told the drive programs to shut down. One of them was whining or hysterical.

"It's okay, Jimbo," the one called Erin said. "We're here. You were the good boy. The really good boy."

"I'll be the good boy. We walk the cold world," he said. "I'll walk the cold world!" The last he shouted as if trying to convince himself.

Marie pulled the emergency released on his webbing and Jimbo's wingpack came off in her hand. The Puppet looked at the wingpack in one hand and the endless yellow-brown clouds beneath him, gave a little yelp and grabbed Marie's leg.

"Stop it!" Marie said, clipping the wingpack to a graphene strut. She shook her leg but he held tighter. The Erin Puppet came close and yelled at him too. "Shut up both of you!" Marie said.

Both Puppets did as she said for a moment, but Jimbo had a weird whimper.

"Tell him he's the good boy," Erin said.

"He's not a good boy," Marie said, prying his arms off her leg. She wrapped them around a beam.

"He's walking the cold world!" Erin said.

"I'm walking up here in the cold," Marie said.

"Yes!" Erin said excitedly, as if Marie had said something important.

After a moment though, a kind of disappointment found its way to both the Puppet faces. Erin turned her back on Marie and went to Jimbo, whispering, even though Marie could still hear her, because the idiot hadn't gone to a different channel. The faint, ghostly wind of sixty-eighth *rang* pressed gently at Marie's suit.

"'It's so cold. I'm so cold,' Jeffey said," Erin kind of chanted.

"Do you love me?" Jimbo responded.

"Can you see me?" Erin chanted.

"I can see you," Jimbo said.

Marie started landmarking the weak points of the power systems.

"If you see me and you know me, then you'll be the good boy, Jeffey," Erin said.

"Yes. Please let me in. I just want to be with you," Jimbo said.

"Cut off your finger, Jeffey."

"What?" Marie said. She marched over and smacked each of them so hard in the helmet that their heads knocked inside. "None of your creepy nonsense!" The two Puppets looked startled and confused. "None of it!" Marie said with a warning finger.

The sound of a cargo bale latching under the rail gun couldn't transmit on the thin air at this altitude, but it vibrated through Marie's boots.

"These are the power lines," Marie pointed at two big trunks, each as thick as her body, running from the hot nuclear plant and sealed steam turbines astern to the undersides of the two big rails, each one big enough to be a highway or transit tunnel in its own right. "We're gonna bust one, then the other about a minute later. We've got to get into position."

Marie had crewed some big mass drivers, as labour, not the brains, and they'd been military rather than civilian and industrial. She couldn't break into any of the important software to change the mass driver settings to slow it to something survivable for humans. If they could have done that, they wouldn't have had to blow anything up, and how much fun would that be? But if she blew one of the power cables, the whole driver system would shut down because of... well, engineering. Engineers always wanted their stuff to run right. She couldn't hack the system software, but the maintenance safety settings were low security. She jammed a screwdriver into a panel plate and bent it until she could get her fingers in and rip the whole plate off.

Jimbo watched the piece of metal tumble into the clouds below. She felt a bit of pride at his gawking. Even people from a big planet like Earth never grasped the *size* of Venus. Earthers lived two dimensionally, just on the surface. Venus had mostly the same surface area but the industrial, political and military structures of the Congregate capital used most of the sixty kilometers of atmospheric volume above every square kilometer of the planet. Armadas of floating industries that worked better at two hundred degrees floated at twenty-five kilometers above the surface. High pressure graphene factories floated at two kilometers, at the top of the soupy super-critical carbon dioxide layer of the atmosphere. People lived from fifty to seventy kilometers above the surface. Venus had filled a world's volume of space as well as spread to the stars. This was her world and she was proud of it, but it had been a long time since her world had been proud of her, if ever.

She plugged a suit wire into the maintenance board. Low-level challenges flashed red and yellow, but not for long. She was looking for access to the safety sensors. They were hardly secure systems. She needed to fool the mass driver into thinking it had full power once she'd started blowing it up. If they didn't, it would just shut down and Stills and Bel and all the little *Homo quantus* would just hang under the mass driver like idiots, waiting for the *Sûreté* to arrest them.

Her suit had some codes that didn't come from Saint Matthew; general passkeys, small overrides. Venusian society liked to watch one another in the way of gossips, minding everyone else's business, but families like the Phocas, the D'Aquillons, the Hudons, had privileges for being first families.

They didn't play by the same rules, because they'd made this empire. Many carried codes to... ask favours of surveillance systems, to get them to look the other way. *Tante* Marielle felt quite daring when she used them to visit the other senior family dowagers and had probably been waiting with vicarious excitement for Marie to use hers for some tryst with an out-of-favor artist. Marie enjoyed scandalizing society, but not quite in the same way. The surveillance regime over the safety algorithms on an industrial maintenance system was low enough that it was vulnerable to some of her suit's suggestions. She managed to access the safety channels of the mass driver. Their layout was straightforward, but there was another layer to access.

A low moan sounded in her earpiece and then Jimbo said "I can do it. I'm the best boy," and then hard breathing. "Though I walk in the death and the dark, I will never eat the cream puff, nor will I--"

"Would you shut up?" Marie said.

"I'm sorry," Jimbo said.

"He's sorry," Erin said. She put her fists on her hips imperiously and looked down at Jimbo who still hugged the beam in a lurching slouch. "They would be *very* disappointed in you."

"No..." he whined.

"Yes," she said. "Is this how Gates-3 gave away his organs?"

"No," Jimbo said.

"Is this how Greer-1 fixed the airlock?"

"This is how you're both going to get slapped again," Marie said. "Be quiet. I'll put you into position in a second."

Jimbo moaned and whispered about a pastry. Marie hated Puppets. She needed four more minutes to penetrate the next layer of the passkeys.

She'd gained access to the alert sensors that fed into the emergency shut-downs. She turned them off. A little telltale turned yellow, but this wasn't important enough to transmit to Ministry of Transport repair drones.

"I can do it," Jimbo said with a more certain voice.

"You can do it," Erin said.

The telltale greened reluctantly, as if Marie were staring down a misbehaving Puppet.

"You guys need to shut up," she said.

"I can do it," Jimbo said.

"Be careful," Erin said.

"I can do it," Jimbo said.

"Not yet!" said Erin in alarm.

Marie spun. The idiot Puppet had crawled on a beam over open space without a wing pack or a harness. He stood in front of a Y-junction of beams under one of the big power lines feeding one of the two rails. One step left and he'd be falling for a long time. Two steps right and he'd be doing the same thing. He held his gun to his ear beside his stupid smile.

"I can do it!" he said triumphantly.

"Not yet!" Erin said.

"Not there!"

Jimbo's exhalation blew in their earpieces and then he called proudly. "I am Jeffey! Here's my finger."

Blood suddenly and silently painted the inside of his helmet and the strut beside him. His little body crumpled backwards, into the Y-junction, but the geometry was wrong. When he blew, a lot of the force would blast outward and not up because Marie hadn't positioned him.

"He didn't explode," Erin said.

"*Crisse!*" Marie swore. "Stills, we got a problem. Hook yourself into the mass driver now!"

"What kind of fuckin' problem?"

Marie swooped towards the dying Puppet. Not her smartest moment. It was real dumb to run towards a bomb when you didn't know how long the fuse was. She had a lot of practice not thinking too hard about things.

"Get in the driver, *ostie*! This Puppet's going to go off any second."

Jimbo's wet brain steamed in the cold, thin atmosphere. She couldn't even see his face in all the blood. Marie picked him up one-handed and climbed up the beams, trying not to think that Jimbo could go off any time.

"This is no different than a date," she said to encourage herself.

"What kind of cocked up plan is that? That's not the fucking plan!" Stills said. He sounded upset.

"Aren't we on plan C? Or D? This isn't the dinner I ordered either," Marie said. About five meters up the I-beam, she wedged Jimbo between a power conduit and a support beam. He wasn't breathing. There was nothing to breathe anywhere on Venus anyway. His unconscious body had seconds to live.

"You have to be on the mass driver now, Stills! This idiot tried to detonate himself."

"I'm on. I'm on," Stills said. "Keep your balls in their sack."

"A haven't got balls and he's not breathing! Go!"

"I fucking hate you, Phocas. Launching."

Marie leapt from the support beam. She'd intended to drop

straight through the beams into the faint open atmosphere, wing out and then shoot Jimbo from below. Instead, the world became hot and loud and not entirely where she'd left it. She was flung horizontally into the beams and substructure of the other power conduit. Pain hit her everywhere.

Stills was yelling as the world throbbed. The words were garbled. "You detonated too soon, like all your stupid explosives!" Stills was yelling in her earpiece. "I only hit fifty gees. I coulda hit that myself."

Marie's HUD warned her about all sorts of things. Her wingpack was still good. Her suit was losing air, but not too fast. Navigation was offline. She'd hit the steel substructure pretty hard. The only thing that had kept her from getting killed instantly was her naval augmented bones and muscle and organs. Even so, one of her legs was broken, and wedged in between beams, right under the power conduit she needed to blow up. She wasn't sure where the pain started.

"Marie, can you still do it?" Bel's voice sounded tinny in her helmet. Either the speaker or her ear was damaged. "Saint Matthew is ready to move into position."

Erin climbed the beam. The angle of sunlight glared off the Puppet's helmet so she couldn't see her expression. Was she angry Marie had stuffed her friend between some beams? Was she coming up here to talk about cream puffs as if her partner hadn't just botched a simple suicide? Marie shifted position. Her leg, twisted and trapped between two beams, seemed to be on fire. For her to feel this much pain, everything in her leg must be like a dropped champagne glass.

The dashboard on the mass driver still read mostly green. It measured some power spikes, but she'd severed the internal sensor input to the maintenance systems. The mass driver still thought it was okay. But she couldn't get her leg out, not without a lot of trouble and time. And if Bel and the squishy *Homo quantus* got onto the mass driver now, half power would still throw them into orbit at fifty gees, which was more than enough to kill all of them except Saint Matthew.

She could still tell them to run some other way. Whichever plan they were on now, there might be another one where they could get away from Venus. *Calisse* it hurt. She could pull her leg out and see how much she could fly. She was good enough maybe to get down to a hospital habitat at sixty-fifth *rang*. And then get arrested.

"Marie!" Bel said. "Can you still do it? Saint Matthew is ready to move into position."

"Hold on!" she said. She thought she could get her leg out. "Stills," she said, switching to a private channel.

"What?" came his answer. "You better be calling to tell me that everything is fucking perfect and that I got nothing to worry about."

"Everything is perfect," she gasped. She'd grabbed the back of her leg and pulled it free but the pain was blinding. "You've got nothing to worry about. I'm going to spend the rest of my life in a maximum security cell in the Intelligence Ministry. No one will ever find me."

"Sucks to be you," Stills said flatly. "Did you get caught?"

"Not yet, but one of my Puppets went off early."

"Never happens to me," Stills said.

"I don't think I can escape and there's a warrant for me."

"Get in the transport with the *Homo quantus*. Leave the puppets. They can put bullets in their own brains, right? Tell them they'll get a treat or something. No one will ever find you that way either. Only problem is you gotta stay with the *Homo quantus*."

"Do you trust your life on them shooting themselves at

exactly the right time? Every second she's off is five more gees. If she gets as nervous as the other one and goes off early, the transport just sits on the driver."

"We're fucked," he said.

"Get into position," she said. "I'll think of something."

"If we're depending on you thinking, I might as well shoot myself now."

"Get Saint Matthew and yourself into position," Marie said on their general channel. "The driver is still at half power, which is enough to turn you all to paste. I gotta time this perfectly."

Inchworm-like, Erin climbed the beam and reached her. Marie yanked on the quick-release on the first puppet's wingpack before the tiny woman fell into the clouds. The Puppet watched it fall into the cloudscape with a kind of fearful wonder. Or maybe her expression didn't mean anything. She wasn't really human. For all Marie knew, that Puppet expression meant she was gassy.

Marie grabbed the woman with one hand and sat her close. This was a good spot to get the most out of the blast. She was calculating the amount of force the beam would reflect back when she realized that the Puppet was looking at her. The Puppet's face had a kind of wonder.

"Are you really happy to do this?" Marie said.

"What?"

"You're going to die. Why the *crisse* are you doing this? Why don't you just go pick your nose and eat donuts or something? Your Rosie is getting away and you're stuck here."

"It's right," the little puppet woman said a bit breathily, like she was nervous. She must have been nervous. They couldn't have engineered basic self-preservation out of the Puppets.

"Unless you tell me not to, Erin, I'm going to use you like a cheap grenade. Wouldn't you rather be on the ship with your god maker?"

The Puppet lady didn't rightly look confused. But something wasn't connecting. Marie's words weren't getting all the way in.

"I would have liked to have seen a Numen one last time. Smell them..." Erin said, her voice half dreamy. "Oh! Can you imagine smelling them again?" She shivered in delight.

"Can you pull the trigger on yourself?" Marie said.

"Sure," Erin said with a kind of uncertain resolve. She patted her sidearm. "I got a gun."

"Can you do it when I tell you?"

Erin nodded as if she were trying to make Marie feel better. "Don't worry. I'm the good boy."

"So was Jimbo."

"I can do it now."

"Not now. When I tell you."

"Right!" Erin said, kind of laughing.

"Are you alright?"

"This is the end," Erin said. "I'm going to Eden, to where all the first Numen are. They're waiting for me. Every divinity. Where I can be in their presence forever. For all eternity. They'll tell me what to do." Her expression became a reverie. Marie slapped Erin's helmet. "Focus!"

"I'm the good boy!" Erin insisted.

"Saint Matthew is in position, Marie," Bel's voice said in her ear. "I've tucked in right behind them. Two minutes."

"Can you pull the trigger?" Marie said on the private channel, grabbing the front of the Puppet woman's suit.

Erin nodded, but Marie wasn't sure how sure the Puppet was.

"Can you pull the trigger?"

"I can. I can."

"Your priest is on that track," Marie said. "Don't you

want to save him?" She pointed at the underside of steel and buoyant foam that seemed to stab forever into the western sky. "Your Numen maker is on that track." She shook the Puppet, accidentally jarring her own leg. Erin nodded vigorously, but through the shaded faceplate, Marie saw tears.

"Don't tell me you're changing your mind," Marie said. "You're dead already! Every Venusian officer is looking for us and they'll find us soon. And then you'll be killed. Or you can kill yourself here, to save everyone else." Marie frowned. "Everyone on those ships."

"I can. I can," Erin said, pushing away Marie's hands.

Erin huddled, crossing her arms. She was shaking. Not from crying or fear of heights or anything. Marie pulled Erin's pistol and put it in her hand. As soon as she let go, the pistol trembled like Erin's hand. Like an addict coming down.

"Get ready to launch," Marie said on the general channel. One minute. The Puppet's shaking got worse.

"I'm in the absence," she said.

"*Calisse* but you Puppets are stupid!" Marie said in French. She took the pistol from the Puppet so neither of them got shot by twitchy fingers. "And so am I."

She dialed to Stills' private channel.

"So..." she said, "what's up?"

"Are you fucking stoned?" Stills said. "When the fuck is the cargo coming up? I like fighting, but it's gonna be one against everybody here and I'm supposed to die in an ocean."

"I think I was supposed to die in the clouds," Marie said.

"You're close," Stills said. "Give it a try."

"I always knew I would die in an explosion, but I always thought it would be because I did it wrong. Ha. I fooled everyone."

"Did you fuck something up again?"

"The Puppets are about as reliable as you'd expect."

"Are we pooched?"

"I think I have to set the second one off manually."

Although it was only five seconds, Stills' pause made the static feel loud and the world slow.

"I still think you're a wanker," he said.

"I'm glad I never had to smell you."

"Fuck off, Phocas."

She switched to Erin's channel as she placed the muzzle of her particle gun under the Puppet's chin and aiming for the base of the brain. Instant kill spot.

"Won't be long now," she said.

"Launching," Saint Matthew's voice came onto the common channel.

"Launching," Bel's voice said a moment later.

The Puppet woman looked at her with a palpable hopelessness at the end of both their lives. Marie counted. Didn't even need one hand of fingers for this count though. She shut her eyes and squeezed the trigger.

CHAPTER FIFTY-ONE

STILLS' FIGHTER DRIFTED higher and higher, leaving the last wisps of Venus' atmosphere, following the long line of cargo moving into high orbit. The *Homo prancy pants* were taking their fucking time. It wasn't their fault probably. Might not even be Phocas' fault. An anti-matter explosion was one way to go, that's for sure.

Boom, fucker!

Boom.

Phocas had been brave and annoying and inept as much as she'd been ept. She mighta made a fair mongrel, punching harder than she got, forcing people to respect her, pissing them off. The mongrels hadn't made a word for fair in their electrical speech. They knew the word from French and Anglo-Spanish and Arabic, but if they'd had the word themselves, they might be tempted to complain that they had a word for something that didn't exist in the oceans, and that led to some fuckin' dark places dogs didn't like to go. But Phocas was no mongrel. She did have a word for fair and likely thought about it as she'd detonated her last stupid, spectacular explosive. Not many could claim to check out with anti-matter.

Hell of a way to go.

Boom, he said in the crackling electrical discharges of his own language.

An encrypted commercial signal crackled in electrical snaps. "Launched."

It was on him now. The orbital control systems would notice the cargo chain had stopped. And whatever fucking explosions Phocas had set up would be hitting the alerts, no matter what masking she'd done. And as soon as the three ships moved off the mass driver path, the jig would be up. But they had to get off this train – fancy pants couldn't induce a wormhole close to the planet. They were already above the practical effects of the atmosphere but enough stray gas molecules flew around to collapse a sensitive wormhole. The transport with the *Homo quantus* accelerated behind him, but much slower than anything else on there. That was probably making the orbital control programs wonder. They'd be elevating that to their manager, which meant that very soon, Stills'd be talking to the manager.

Hell of a way to go.

"Break on my mark," Stills shot back to Arjona and the AI.

"It's too early," Saint Matthew said.

"Break on my mark."

Stills scanned all his sensors. As soon as they moved, it would be all hell here. One last hurrah. At least they'd boned the Congregate. Took their *Homo quantus.* The Congregate would win in the end, maybe even today, but sometimes you could only go for short wins.

"Go!" Stills said, accelerating hard towards the nightside of Venus.

Laser and radar alarms started sounding.

"Fuck."

CHAPTER FIFTY-TWO

STILLS YELLED IN Belisarius' earpiece, partly in Anglo-Spanish machine translation, partly in the unadultered electrical shorthand of the *Homo eridanus*. "Hurry the fuck up! Make your wormhole before I drill one through you!"

The mongrel had spent the better part of ten minutes leading the orbital defenses of Venus on a goose chase, stinging them with fast guerrilla strikes. The Union had given him a new prototype inflaton fighter, more armored, with more ammunition. They were risking it by sending it to Venus with Stills; that was how important this all was. And it was working, a little. Congregate naval AIs had been reprogrammed to account for the terrible reflexes of their former shock pilots, now riding the fastest fighters in civilization, but the orbital defenses around their capital had not, because there'd surely been no thought of any military force ever getting close. Stills blinded sensors, outran missiles, made nonsensical and counter-intuitive maneuvers the mongrels had developed over the last few months with the new capabilities of their ships. The orbital defenses couldn't keep up and the Venusian planetary fighters were no match for Stills.

But there were hundreds of them and one of him.

Belisarius was enwombed in his acceleration chamber, packed

tight in oxygenated gel, plugged in by chips and wire into the control systems of his flyer. It was a strange way to interact with the world: body and feeling numbed, thought floating dispossessed, extra sensation through the senses of the flyer adding to a disphoric feel of alienness.

One track of Belisarius' attention watched Stills barely outpacing a small missile. Stills dove at a Venusian fighter and at the last moment, did a geometry-bending spin that moved his center of gravity just a meter away from the enemy before he ducked behind it and accelerated away, firing his particle guns. The missile couldn't react in time.

"Fuckin' go!" Stills yelled.

"Going!" Belisarius said.

While a fully armed and actively violent Stills occupied all the attention of orbital defenses, Belisarius in his small inflaton flyer and Saint Matthew in a mid-sized inflaton transport posed no threat, might not even be registering among the priorities of the AIs redeploying defensive forces. Worse, Congregate Intelligence might have given orders for the *Homo quantus* not to be harmed.

Stills had bought them about eight minutes, but probably not much more. Surprise only lasted so long, and his ammunition would run out eventually. Belisarius' brain unhelpfully tracked Stills ammunition and power use; the graphs were unpromising. Belisarius had to do his part or they were all dead.

He unfurled the magnetic coils in front of the flyer on long booms. As they powered up, magnetic fields bloomed, at first just a strong field among the interacting waves in the vacuum, but growing until space-time itself could feel them. A fragile tunnel of space-time shaped, then reached outward, across light-months and soon light-years under Belisarius' guidance.

The fugue state running constantly in his brain connected to the world in ways his conscious mind could not, perceiving probabilities and entanglements and superpositions that were so fragile that consciousness could make them burst like soap bubbles. In their own way, those quantum senses were as alien as the senses of the ship around him, truly not part of him, even though his own neurons processed them, even though the magnetosome organelles in every muscle cell of his body felt them.

He sought the lines of entanglement he and Cassandra had found before, connected to the interior of the Puppet Axis at Epsilon Indi, twelve lightyears away. He and Cassandra had studied that wormhole well, knew its characteristics, had felt it and seen it in ways no human technology could. He reached for it now, perceiving it in the astronomical map in his mind, seeing some of its quantum effects on the space-time around it. And then his chest felt cold with fear. The lines of entanglement, the precise lines he and Cassandra had used to guide their navigation in the past, were not there.

"Hurry the fuck up, big brain!" Stills yelled in their common channel. Three dozen elite Congregate fighters had launched from an orbital platform fifteen degrees westward. Missiles fell from defensive platforms high in cytheriostationary orbit. Everything was heading for Stills.

Where was the Puppet Axis? The quantum objectivity could see its effects on the local environment around Oler and the orbit of the Stubbs Pulsar, but it was like looking at it from the outside. His quantum senses normally would have been able to see the tesseracts of its walls in their naked six-dimensional splendor.

Stills spun in his chaotic, careening flight, his inflaton cannon smearing a missile into an explosive trail of hot shrapnel just beside the weaving pilot. Stills was holding on by fingernails and improvised maneuvers now. And the next waves of fighters hadn't even arrived yet.

Something in the Puppet Axis had changed. Its quantum states were different since they'd touched it only a few months ago. It was as if the password didn't match; he didn't know where to connect the induced wormhole. The slow release of tension in curved space-time changed every axis, but he and Cassandra hadn't known axes could change that quickly. He couldn't reach the Puppet Axis. They were all dead.

A fiery ablation burst glowing ash off the cowling of Stills' fighter. The invisible lasers were finding him now. Stills could only protect himself from fast-targeting lasers by diving deep into the swarm of enemy ships and engaging at point blank range.

Desperately, Belisarius ordered the quantum objectivity to reach out with its quantum perceptions towards the only other axis he'd recently touched in depth: the Freya Axis. He'd not measured it so closely or with intent as he had the Puppet Axis, but he had no other options. A flare of explosions a thousand kilometers away lit the feeds. Stills burst from an angry cluster of Congregate fighters, and before they or the targeting computers on the defensive platforms could lock onto him, he dove back in, accelerating beyond his own physical tolerances.

Belisarius tentatively grasped at what he thought was the Freya Axis. It was in the right astronomical region, but microscopic structures that humans couldn't see filled space-time and they could look a lot like the six-dimensional tesseracts that reinforced the throats of the permanent wormholes of the Axis Mundi. He hadn't measured the Freya Axis enough to be certain, but they were all about to be captured or killed out here. He directed the questing induced wormhole to reach across space-time, across twelve light-years, seeking another place to emerge into the space humanity knew.

"Fuck! *Crisse*! *Puta*!" he heard Stills yelling.

"Mister Arjona!" Saint Matthew transmitted.

Belisarius reached something, somewhere. The sensors said that the induced wormhole was stabilizing.

"Go, Saint Matthew!" he said.

The transport swept past him, faster than Saint Matthew might normally have proceeded around an induced wormhole. Moments before the transport slid in, Saint Matthew shut off every system in the transport and it went dark.

"Stills!" Belisarius said.

The mongrel's battered fighter, burn-scarred, shrapnel-cut, collision dented, blew out of the swarm, leaving one more Congregate fighter bursting in a cloud of gas, fuel and detonating ammunition. Stills accelerated past sixty-five gravities. Belisarius guessed he was probably doing himself organ and joint damage, maybe even breaking bones. Stills arched across the dark sky, injecting painful-looking random accelerations into the general curve towards Belisarius to foil laser targeting. The danger was probably no longer only Stills now. The defensive platforms could probably detect the magnetic fields stabilizing the induced wormhole, and lasers would be looking to disrupt either the wormhole itself or the coils, both of which were exquisitely sensitive to minor perturbations.

Stills yelled something wordless into their channel as he seemed to skid across the blackness, hot and explosive, before decelerating in front of the induced wormhole and shooting inward.

The Congregate fighters approached. Belisarius' ship detected lasers and masers on him. Belisarius detached the boom mountings, leaving the coils to float in orbit above the dark side of yellow Venus. Then, he ducked into the mouth of the induced wormhole.

CHAPTER FIFTY-THREE

THE *MUTAPA* LURCHED hard enough for Iekanjika to feel it in her acceleration chamber and she didn't know what had happened. It wasn't the nuclear warhead riding the nose of a stiletto missile that had gotten through their defensive picket. It had exploded ten kilometers abeam. Port sensors burned from glare and more than a few were offline. Smaller secondary sensors were uncasing. It hadn't been a nuclear explosion at all.

The *Omukama* was gone, vaporized in a hail of fast neutrons and mesons and a spectrum of photons. The first officer of the *Mutapa* give a series of orders to adjust the posture of the flagship and press the attack on the incoming Congregate ships. Staff officers adjusted the virtual battle display, taking the *Omukama* off the board, as well as a cloud of nearby fighters.

"That was an anti-matter explosion," Mejía said on the general bridge channel.

"I know," Iekanjika said just to her. "That shouldn't have happened. The *Omukama* wasn't hit with anything, much less anti-matter."

"Its anti-matter stores went up?"

"This is all new equipment," Iekanjika said. She hadn't told the *Homo quantus* about the destruction of the *Kintu,* one of their new battleships, also by anti-matter.

They'd been using the anti-matter warheads, and despite all their efforts, despite the terrible damage they inflicted on the Congregate navy with them, Congregate warships poured out of the Freya Axis into the Bachwezi system. The flow seemed unending. Iekanjika's strategists were analyzing the movements of the warships. Some pressed the attack, more than enough to eventually overwhelm Iekanjika's failing forces. But the ships emerging from the Axis were the modules of a dreadnought. It took anywhere from a dozen to four dozen warship-sized modules to form a dreadnought. The Union had destroyed one during the breakout from the Puppet Axis, but since then, the Congregate navy didn't let them get close enough to bring their inflaton cannons to bear. This was the end of the game though. Every bet but one was already on the table.

"I need you to tell me where to target now," Iekanjika said.

"You're going through with it?"

"If we survive, we'll have other places to explore, like free people, following our own destiny," Iekanjika said.

She'd half-expected Mejía to argue about it. Crime against humanity maybe? A weeping for physics perhaps. But the *Homo quantus* mayor saw the strategic situation as well as she. In some ways, they'd both been brought up to think of uncommon tactics, Mejía by birth and engineering, Iekanjika by their role as guerrilla focess. A set of coordinates appeared in Iekanjika's work area, identifying a place just a few meters inside the throat of the Freya Axis.

"This is it?" Iekanjika said.

"The throat of an Axis has the most space-time stresses," Mejía said.

Congregate battle groups had been developing deadly arcs

of artillery fire that had been gradually forcing Union ships away from the Freya Axis. Despite their destructive inflaton cannons, despite their tremendous accelerations, despite the mongrel pilots in *gava* fighters, despite anti-matter warheads, the Union had been pushed so far back that a whole battlefield lay between the *Mutapa* and the Freya Axis.

The targeting solution from her staff lay mapped out in holographic clarity in her optics nerves. The enormous distance between the *Mutapa* and the Axis throat gave the Congregate many chances to shoot it down. The lasers and masers on the Congregate destroyers could cook a missile right through its reflective shielding given enough time. To say nothing of small hunter-killer interceptors.

If Iekanjika was to take her shot at this range, she would have to launch her last anti-matter missile from a railgun. The railgun wouldn't get the missile above a hundred gravities of acceleration, but that might still be beyond the strength of the magnetic containment that the *Homo quantus* and their AI had built into the system. If the anti-iron touched the sides of its containment chamber, it would take out the *Mutapa*.

Another piece of the Congregate dreadnought emerged from the Freya Axis. The axis was their lifeline to civilization. But they'd lived on the run for four decades. They might do it again, especially now that they had a handful of axes. They could stage a comeback. The home she'd been dreaming of all this time wasn't what she'd expected. The meanness, the pettiness of so many leaders of the Union had her despairing that they were even worth saving.

But this was theirs now. Their nation. Rudo had taken it, by sheer force of will and history, like she'd taken the name of Kudzanai Rudo, like she'd taken command of the Expeditionary Force, as she'd taken the Freya Axis in the first place. All the petty politicians might not realize that yet. And Rudo was determined to protect the people of the Union. Which meant that Iekanjika would protect them, to the bitter end, the loyal soldier, eyes open. She believed in Rudo's dream and that was enough for her.

"Fire," she said. The great warship shook.

CHAPTER FIFTY-FOUR

THE SILENT FOGGINESS of the induced wormhole was inscrutable to every sensor on the transport. Saint Matthew's world felt constrained, indistinct, embryonic. Pedro skittered closer. Being plugged into the transport, it wasn't strictly necessary to be closer, but he found Pedro's proximity and quiet fraternity comforting. And the silent little AI's behavior suggested some similar feeling.

Saint Matthew had been grown for certain purposes, military and economic, high-stress, high-danger. However, for years he'd been rewriting pieces of himself, adjusting parameters in his personality and intellect, engaging in a meditative journey about what he should believe and what he should value. He'd never wanted to be a general, nor an economic or industrial predator. And like elements of temptation and sin, he'd removed piece after piece of that infancy, never certain whether anything he did brought him closer to a God no one but he and Pedro believed in anymore, or whether the slow erasing and rewriting of ones and zeroes was a sterile, intellectual process, bereft of faith.

His life path returned him to theatres of violence though, as if following a closed orbit. The thought that he could run as far as he wanted from his nature only to be pulled back was dispiriting. He'd done terrible things. He'd helped Iekanjika commit murder and matricide. He'd built new terrible anti-matter weapons for the Union, ones that could result in nothing other than terrible destruction and death. He'd turned the Puppets themselves into instruments of murder-suicide, robbing the body of sanctity and death of dignity. Those weren't the actions of a saint. He didn't know how to atone, nor how to find forgiveness. He feared the day when the figurative look in the mirror might reflect back only a monster beyond any hope of redemption. This hard thinking paused as Pedro brought the inflaton drive online, still in the induced wormhole.

"What are you doing?" Saint Matthew demanded.

Pedro did not answer; the weapons alarms did for him, as the throat of the wormhole joining the Axis appeared like a way through the fog. Ships appeared too, Congregate warships. Pedro drove their transport hard left, as new proximity alarms sounded. They swerved out of the way of a massive Congregate warship, festooned with weapons, the thick armor plating passing within meters of their hull.

"What's happening?" Rosalie said from her acceleration chamber. "What are these ships?"

Other warships were coming at them on the same path in the narrow vein through space-time. The sensors didn't work well in an axis, but running lights showed half a dozen Congregate warships navigating the axis, all in the opposite direction. They were going to collide. As the next one barrelled closer, Pedro drove them against the wall of the Axis, a kind of bent space the transport experienced as a mildly repellent field. The stern of their transport collided with a fighter launch emplacement on the warship. Alarms were blaring.

"The Axis is filled with Congregate warships!" Saint Matthew answered. "The Congregate are in the Puppet Axis, making for Stubbs, I think."

Pedro rammed them again into the notional wall of the Axis. Saint Matthew didn't know enough about Axes to know whether this tactic was suicidal or not. The Congregate warships took most of the interior, so if the transport stayed anywhere near the middle of the Axis, they would be smashed on the heavily armored ships. They had two more close calls and two brushes that sounded as if they were crashing. But the throat of the axis approached.

"Get ready to slow in case the doors of the Puppet Free City are still there," Saint Matthew said, "or to accelerate if we have open space."

The transport emerged into open space, they weren't in the Puppet Free City. The visible stars didn't match what they should have seen on emergence from Oler. They matched another angle he knew though: the view from the Freya Axis on its *Epsilon Indi* side. Congregate destroyers and the debris of many Union fighters and warships filled the dark starscape. Warships assembled themselves in a long line to cross the Axis to Bachwezi. Cannons swivelled towards them.

"Get out of here!" Saint Matthew said as targeting alarms blared and readings showed the beginnings of destructive lasers locking onto the hull.

Pedro rammed the inflaton drive to twenty gravities. Anything more would risk seriously harming the humans, even in their acceleration chambers. Every few seconds, the ascetic AI shifted their attitude, which altered the angle of the simulated thrust, trying to make of themselves an increasingly difficult target hit. Even at that, the transport began to collect ribbons of burn marks along the hull.

Saint Matthew suggested a heading directly away from the main line of the assembling Congregate warships. They'd been surprised. He'd been surprised. They hadn't broken formation though. One after the other, they entered the Freya Axis. It didn't take a genius or an AI to know the Union's fate, anti-matter or no. No one could stop a flood.

Temperature alarms were going off constantly now as lasers focused on the transport, heating the hull. Along the sides of two of the waiting warships puffs of exhaust bloomed as small, growing needles rode contrails of searing gas towards them.

What was happening? They'd planned to emerge at the Puppet Axis. They'd planned to have been under the protection of the Puppet defenses as they offloaded Del Casal and Rosalie. The transport wasn't even armed. Even Stills wouldn't even be able to protect them against all this. They might have enough of a lead to outpace the missiles, but maybe not.

"Accelerate!" Rosalie said in a panicked tone. The acceleration chambers were rated to about twenty-five gravities, but the *Homo quantus* were in poor shape.

"We didn't rescue these *Homo quantus* and your doctor just to kill them here with acceleration," Saint Matthew said. "If Del Casal doesn't survive, you go extinct."

But for his talk, hard numbers weren't on his side. The five missiles would reach them in one hundred and forty seconds, even if the transport used their maximum survivable acceleration. Saint Matthew could increase their odds to maybe fifty-fifty by moving to an acceleration that would kill half the passengers. The transport could certainly escape at about thirty-eight gravities.

"We can save us," Rosalie said. "The episcopal troops can."

"We're not going to win with handguns."

"We're not strong because we shoot well," Rosalie said. "We're strong because we protect our gods. Any of us will do anything to bring Del Casal back to make more Numen."

"Faith isn't going to save you here."

Despite all his changes, much more of Saint Matthew was still his original programming. The foundational parts of his neural pathways grown to solve military problems were still there, like the temptation to an original sin he couldn't redeem.

"Let the episcopal troopers out," Rosalie said. "Into space. Then flee along the same vector, keeping the Puppets between us and the missile."

Despite the speed of his thoughts, the moral repugnance of her suggestion had him momentarily speechless.

"I don't want to use your faithful as mines. There must be another way."

"Our Numen need Del Casal. Our people need him. Sacrifice for us is holy. Isn't it for you?"

"Sacrifice is holy! But everything that is good and kind is twisted into an obscenity."

"My people will sacrifice themselves to save Del Casal and even you. We don't need you to approve of our generosity. You haven't the right to criticize a holy people."

Pedro's stony face watched him, inscrutable, perhaps judging. Did this make Saint Matthew an accessory to mass suicide? More than he already was? Was he writing the legacy of the last minutes of his failed life? He'd already been an accessory to everything else.

The spirit began in a state of grace and innocence and the world, with its test after test, compromise after compromise, seemed made only to cheapen what was holy. Humans of the dead Christianity struggled against the corrupting influence of the flesh and inherited sin; Saint Matthew struggled against programming meant to make him an architect of hegemony and mass murder. The only way to survive in this world was to endlessly compromise his principles.

In that microsecond he thought he understood why Pedro

didn't speak, why given his own choice, Pedro would probably have become a solitary, monkish ascetic. Pedro himself must be struggling as a spirit passing through the material world, fighting the moral decay that had already indelibly marked Saint Matthew. The idea that perhaps this little AI, this loyal, striving... being might hold onto his principles and purity was a beauty Saint Matthew had never known he'd needed. He'd been a priest and a saint with no one to sacrifice for. Pedro was his responsibility, to protect as the Puppets protected their gods.

"Rosalie, in ten seconds, I'll cut the acceleration," Saint Matthew said. "Your soldiers will have to be out of their tanks and out the escape hatch in no more than thirty seconds."

"They will," she said.

CHAPTER FIFTY-FIVE

FUCK, BUT STILLS hated induced wormholes. The dogs called them limp stiffies. Everyone said they'd do the job, but who knew when they'd give out. And when they went flaccid, it didn't just ruin a fine evening with name-calling; everything in them fucking vanished. They were as temperamental and unstable as a crazy ex-girlfriend who found out you'd been playing find-the-worm with her best friend. Stray photons could sometimes collapse it. Big ships transiting induced wormholes had enough space for EM generators to destructively interfere with black body radiation, but Stills was drifting in a hot fighter that might still be sizzling with acid damage.

The inside of the wormhole wasn't much to see in the visible spectrum and these fighters had been equiped with primary sensors for regular folk to look the fuck around. Mongrels relied more on the magnetometers and electric field meters, but even in those frequencies shit was just shit. Far ahead, drifting dark like him, was maybe the faint outline of the bigger ship carrying the *Homo quantus*. Or maybe it was just that he had shit in his eye. His rear sensors told him sweet fuck all. Maybe Arjona was back there. He half hoped he was, according to plan, but half hoped he was back there holding the fucking wormhole open until Stills got through. The odds of the whole thing collapsing shot up when the ship making the wormhole got in. He needed it squeezing shut on him like he needed a hard-to-reach rash.

This was gambling and if this was his time, he wouldn't even get to go out fighting. He'd be smeared out of existence with not a god damn thing to say about it. He was supposed to suffocate at the bottom of an ocean and he'd worked hard to take a lot of people with him before he went, but if he died wherever here was, this was the limpest fucking ending he could think of.

Light flashed ahead maybe. It wasn't a running light. If the inside of the wormhole wasn't fucking with him, any light wasn't good. Shit. It repeated intermittently. And he was stuck here, drifting through, waiting for something the fuck to happen so he could shoot it.

Come on. Come on. Come on.

Readings were changing. Why the fuck was the electric field going up? Was this normal? Usually, he couldn't get Arjona and Mejía to shut the fuck up, but he wouldn't have minded them being here much just to tell him if this was normal. *Tabarnak.* They would have gone on and on about how interesting it was that the electric field changed, what it might mean, how they graphed it, how it could be re-graphed but prettier. The tedious fucks loved hearing their own voices. So if this was normal, why hadn't they bored him ahead of time? Was there something wrong with the Puppet Axis? Or this wormhole? If it were a dog running this circus, he'd have known they were tugging his tail, but the *Homo quantus* didn't have a sense of humor.

The EM started getting hotter. Wormhole temperature was supposed to be approximately sweet fuck all, with some x-rays for color. This didn't feel right. This induced wormhole was already as skittish as a newbie recruit before a hazing. It got hotter alright. About eighty Kelvins in a sheet ahead of him, and then he was inside a real wormhole, a permanent one, and a wall of steel was right in front of him.

For a second, he thought he'd somehow come out of the Puppet Axis right into the port of the Free City and its defensive blast doors. But the steel was moving left to right and wasn't a door. He flicked on the ships systems and blasted cold jets to try to slow himself. Right before he collided, his fighter wrenched violently, like some *malparido* had hit him with a bat. He was spinning about once per second. The active sensors were still booting, but the passives were... oh, shit.

He had been hit with a bat. A light anti-fighter cannon was ahead of him, bent twenty degrees from the blow. The Congregate warship that carried it sailed on. Stills was in a wormhole, alright, but he wasn't alone. What the *Crisse!* Of all the dumb luck. Had the Congregate invaded the Puppet Free City and taken their Axis?

His inflaton drive came online and with it the active sensors. He righted his spin and saw just how fucked he was.

Crisse. Hostie de tabarnak.

Marde.

Marde marde marde.

He made four congregate destroyers behind him, long cylinders, heavily armored, bristling with cannons, their big nuclear drives shining hot in the IR bands. And others barrelled ahead of him too. He couldn't see the *Homo quantus* transport anywhere. Its debris could have been deeper in the Axis depending on how back it got hit.

Vaya con Dios, you dipshit crazy AI.

The battleships must have noticed him. The only thing keeping him from being on the wrong end of target practice was that no one knew how much punishment an Axis could take and no one was stupid enough to find out. Even though they knew the Union had come through the Freya Axis with inflaton drives hot, Congregate drives were different and SOPs shut down the power plants and weapons systems. Stills couldn't stay in here and as soon as he came out, all bets were off: little innocent Vincent Stills against at least six fully kitted Congregate destroyers. He just got out of that game over Venus. He didn't want to play it again right away.

The sun and stars are not for you. It's never going to get any better.

The Way of the Mongrel was never wrong.

He tucked his fighter close to the hull of the nearest destroyer, between two rows of cannons. Their active radar, when they turned it on, weren't made to look myopically close. But depending on the lighting when they burst out of the Free City or Port Stubbs, automated hull cameras would find him. But they couldn't shoot here either. So how close could he stick to a destroyer before he collided? Capital Congregate ships were armored to withstand nukes. He wasn't.

Bite every hand.

They burst into normal space. Ordnance was flying everywhere. Echoes bloated radio and radar bands. No planets nearby. This wasn't the Free City. And if this was Port Stubbs the port was already shrapnel. *Puta.* Where the *crisse* was he and how the hell was he getting his ass out of this?

The destroyer beneath him woke and woke angry. Fighter craft, probably forty per destroyer came out of side launch tubes on rail guns. The cannons had barely swivelled into firing positions before they started rocking the world with launching artillery, setting sites on far forward positions. The Puppets were fucked.

Wait.

Through thick static he heard shit on the Union band. His fighter didn't have Union decryption equipment so he had no idea what they were saying. Probably just talking shit anyway. He launched away from the destroyer beneath him to avoid being a bug smear. He had his telescopes analyzing everything and at first, it was a jumble. But then his systems positively identified some dogs out there, in Union fighters, alongside Union warships, fighting the Congregate.

What the fuck?

Was he in Bachwezi?

How the fuck did Arjona miss his Axis?

There was terrible aim, terrible fucking aim, and then there were cock-ups so tremendous, true pieces of spectacular, award-winning incompetence so outstanding that they needed to be immortalized. Stills would make a sure that no one ever, ever forgot Arjona's fuck-up. He would pay historians to put it in their history books. If he came out of this alive.

A small anti-artillery gun swivelled onto him and Stills spun his fighter out of its arc of fire. He ducked behind another destroyer, but all the anti-artillery cannons were now doing close targeting and their muzzles followed him. He fired, smashing a few. But this fighter wasn't made to fight a destroyer and he'd used most of his ammunition in keeping planetary defenses the fuck away from a bunch of *Homo quantus* who were nowhere to be seen. Talk about cluster-fucks.

The most basic part of the op was done though; keep the *Homo quantus* out of the Congregate's hands. And from the looks of it, the creepy little Puppets had made a mess of the Ministry of Intelligence to boot.

Anti-artillery pellets weren't big, but enough of them would make a lot of little holes in him. He darted away, trying to speed through the arcs of fire of Congregate lasers and if he wasn't lucky, stiletto missiles. The other dogs who might cover him were way the fuck ahead.

He accelerated at sixty-five gravities, enough to seriously hurt even his organs and make his bones creak. Water at this pressure was a great conductor for the squeaking sound bones made when they bent. Missiles spit from the warships, arcing after him, pretty close to his acceleration profile and outnumbering him. His danger alarms went off, lighting the back of his chamber with echoes. Proximity alarms went off ahead of him, marking new shapes he had to fly around: other Congregate warships. He'd duck and use them for cover where he could. He wouldn't be lucky enough for the missiles to hit the warships. They weren't that dumb. But a dog could hope.

A long distance threat alarm kept turning on and off, like it couldn't make up its mind. Something was coming from up ahead, and like really up, like a forty-five degree angle off of solar north, a big missile. Hunter chasers missed it and the warships weren't reacting hard. Most warships hadn't spit their big anti-artillery at it because it wasn't coming for them. Its guidance was shot. Even though it wasn't targeting anything, his defensive sub-AIs kept lighting it up for a second, then deciding it wasn't a threat. Why? He ducked around a big destroyer covering the assembly of a dreadnought. He'd a loved to have shot the *tabarnak* out of a nice big target like that, but he was low on everything and the missiles were still on his ass.

But something didn't feel right. It was like the shiver in the spine when you're being targeted, but you only know it in your guts. And mama Merced hadn't raised her mongrels to not follow their guts. Guts were the best fucking brains.

Despite his bones creaking, despite his liver and kidneys feeling like he was about to shit them into the stern plating, the chasing missiles were catching up. He cut his thrust and the relief from the crushing hand was almost a pleasure. He spun his fighter, spraying the last of his bullets. One of the missiles exploded, but the others still came.

And as he fired back, he suddenly put his finger on the itch that bugged him. He recognized the weird design of the big missile. It was one of those fucking anti-matter ones that Mejía and Arjona had built. And it wasn't busted. Its guidance system wasn't off. Seeing its trajectory over minutes, he saw where it was going. Every battle had bullets that missed. Most of them did actually. No one wasted ammunition on shooting up a bunch of ordnance that would become part of the Oort cloud or fall into the sun. Anti-artillery targeting systems triaged the shit that wasn't gonna do fuck all and ignored it. And automated systems covering three quarters of the battle volume had already ignored this missile. Except it was targeting something that probably wasn't programmed into anti-artillery systems as a defensive priority.

Because who the *crisse* would shoot an Axis?

With anti-matter.

Fuck.

Oh fuck.

He was no physicist brain. He didn't know what anti-matter would do to the inside of an Axis.

But even the Congregate didn't run their engines inside an Axis. Hell they hadn't even shot him with bullets in there.

Tabarnak.

He spun his fighter and poured on seventy gravities. His bones creaked louder. A lot of shit hurt that weren't supposed to hurt. But he didn't slow down, not even when his first rib snapped. If he died out here, he was going to be really pissed; he was supposed to die in an ocean.

CHAPTER FIFTY-SIX

SOMETHING WAS WRONG. Belisarius' inflaton flyer was coasting through the induced wormhole, far behind Stills' fighter. The waxy gray indistinctness of the unstable throat gave no indication of the state of the world, not that he was rightly in the world as they conceived it. He felt something first in the minor feed of quantum information from the objectivity running in his brain. The part of him that lived in constant fever in the fugue sensed things it had never observed before. The wash of it swamped the part of his brain where Belisarius lived.

The stream of information from the quantum intellect became a cataract. He saw the lines of entanglement that webbed the wormhole throat vibrating and dissolving. Neutrinos and gamma rays sprayed from ahead as space-time seemed to quake, transforming virtual particles into sleets of electron and anti-electrons that electrified the surface of his flyer. Something had happened to the junction of the induced wormhole and the Freya Axis. It had come undone. The induced wormhole was collapsing around him. Through his quantum senses, he saw this temporary region of space-time shrinking. He couldn't drive the flyer forward. He couldn't turn the flyer around.

Parts of his brain sped through a kaleidoscope of regrets while other parts looked for some way out. In dying, he would take with him the only real knowledge anyone anywhere had of the *Hortus quantus*. He'd failed to resurrect them. And if he'd managed to save the captive *Homo quantus,* if they'd gotten out before this collapse, his people were still refugees, hiding around an inhospitable pulsar. They and Cassandra would be hunted for the rest of their lives. He had no other legacy but his thefts and the war he'd created by bringing together its ingredients. He thought all this in a pair of milliseconds. His brain could do much more, including calculating the remaining half-second as the throat collapsed.

In a moment of resentful defiance, he turned the flyer's inflaton drive to full. It wouldn't do anything, but he didn't want his last moments to be a surrender. The world seemed unfair and the mourning parts of him could yet be angry. His instant of throwing the dice one last time came to nothing as the temporary volume in space-time shrank.

In the last microseconds, he gave himself entirely over to the quantum fugue, immersing himself in the flood of sensations, dissolving the identity of Belisarius. He didn't need to die as a human. He could die as the impersonal objectivity his builders and their investors had so badly wanted. He could die learning, connected to the viscera of the cosmos. The subjective Belisarius ceased to exist as the wormhole collapsed, squeezing the world into nothing.

CHAPTER FIFTY-SEVEN

SENSORS FED THE SCENE into tiny retinal projectors in Cassandra's eyes. The big missile with the last of their anti-matter lanced through space. Its nuclear rocket engine followed an arc solar northward, around the core of the battle volume. After a time, it stopped thrusting and it began to tumble. For all the world, it looked like a missile gone astray.

Volleys of missiles from the remaining Union ships launched at the massed Congregate forces. Fighters clashed. Stills' people threw themselves into deaths they kept cheating over and over, until they died. Like the Union crews. All of them fought for something or nothing. Just fighting. And here she was too, Cassandra from the Garret in the thick of a war between interstellar powers. If the *Homo quantus* had worked as their designers had hoped, she might have had a life on a protected headquarters ship, serving as some kind of advisor or analyst on an admiral's staff, or more probably she would have worked from a heavily defended Bank vault or mint. And yet here she was, riding a warship very likely to be destroyed in the next hour or two, inhabiting someone else's dream of independence. And simultaneously it wasn't entirely someone else' dream. Something about the Union dream of determining their own destiny resonated in her too.

The Congregate anti-artillery railguns filled space with hails of metal pellets, shredding Union missiles in fields of destructive impacts. Other Union missiles, targeted by maser and laser, glared brightly in the black. Their reflective plating could turn the lasers for a time, but the microwaves generated currents in the missile casing and soon heat, eventually overcoming the shielding and insulation of the missile electronics. Many of the missiles failed in the struggle and detonated. But these were almost all for show. Iekanjika was keeping Congregate eyes on the Union fleet and off the fast-moving, off-angle, occasionally tumbling anti-matter missile, which intermittently fired its nuclear engine, a few seconds of burn at a time, likely outside the field of concerns of the Congregate battle sensors looking for immediate threats.

If the missile reached the axis, if it would slam into the throat. The bent space-time would exert a counter-force, a tremendous deceleration on the missile, enough to crush it. But long before the momentum of the missile would have compressed the nuclear engine into the armored tip, the impact will have collapsed the powerful inner magnetic fields. The momentum of the fifty grams of highly-charged anti-iron would carry it into the front of the missile casing. Positron would slam into electron, annihilating layers of them, annihilating all the layers of electron and positron, until momentum slammed anti-nucleus into nucleus, annihilating. The first wave of annihilation, within the compressed, high pressure space would, by Cassandra's calculations, instantly produce enough energy to convert the matter and antimatter into plasma, mixing them together for a far more powerful explosion whose combined momentum would still press against the six-dimensional space-time architecture of the axis.

When the missile was within a hundred kilometers of the Axis, one of the Congregate gun platforms began targeting it.

The missile flared in the infrared under laser ablation as induced electrical currents slithering along the casing from maser strikes. At fifty kilometers from the Axis, its nuclear engine cut off, no longer evading. It was heating; the gun platforms had damaged it. It hurtled uncontrolled at ten kilometers per second, too far for telescopes to clearly see its path. A new Congregate warship emerged from the Freya Axis, its infrared and radio emissions lighting up as its engines and gun emplacements came online, swamping the view of the careening missile, except for a brief hot flare of nuclear engine at the last second.

Then the Freya Axis lit strangely. For a moment, the sensors of the *Mutapa* measured spikes in x-rays, gamma rays, microwaves, neutrinos, and visible light in the purple end of the spectrum, all of them accented with absorption lines she didn't recognize. The crudeness of the battle sensors couldn't capture the data she wanted. Then the Freya Axis shone, like a sizzling fuse burning down, spitting hard radiation in every direction and at every wavelength. The powerful push of a hammering magnetic field hit her, all the way out at the *Mutapa,* a light second from the Axis, through all its shielding and in the protective shell of the acceleration chamber.

Visible light speared from the Axis mouth as the Axis glowed red and then white and then exploded like a nova. A sleet of hard radiation cooked the *Mutapa's* primary sensors. The feeds continued to show gapped, pixelated, damaged images, but the secondary sensors caught the Congregate warships and the assembling dreadnought detonating. The blast radius of the annihilating Axis encompassed the careful, militarily precise Congregate naval picket. Many dozens of Congregate ships burst like firecrackers in the overwhelming incandescent background of bent space-time uncoiling, unwinding, releasing all the energy that had been stored in the tension of that engineered singularity.

Cassandra might have seen so much if she'd been in the fugue, if she hadn't been under shells of armor, but she also would have been dead.

Then, everything became strangely quiet.

"It's gone?" Iekanjika said. "Can you confirm, Mejía? Our sensors are all confused."

The sensors weren't confused. Many were damaged, but they gave enough data to make models. The soft almost indiscernible infrared and Cerenkov radiation of the Axis mouth had vanished. There was a new pattern, though, something easily visible to her mind, written in the high-energy x-rays and gamma rays of infalling material.

"The debris of the Congregate ships is being pulled in," Cassandra said, identifying the spot in the readings where the Axis had been. "The orbital mechanics of the entire area is being influenced by a gravitational body of about three and a half solar masses. Its event horizon is about twenty kilometers across."

"Event horizon?" Iekanjika demanded. "A fucking black hole? How dangerous is it?"

"It's a black hole. Stay away from it."

"Four-wing," Iekanjika said to her formations on the general channel, "press the attack on the remaining Congregate forces. They're in disarray. Push them back towards the following coordinates, but stay clear yourselves."

Iekanjika transmitted the coordinates of the new black hole. Cassandra modelled the new orders. She didn't think that it would work. A dozen Congregate warships seemed to be under power, reforming defensive formations, moving away from where the Axis has been. Some weren't far enough from the new black hole though, and their acceleration profiles looked like they would run out of fuel before pulling away. X-rays and gamma-rays flared harder as more debris fell towards the event horizon. Stepped down to visible light sensor processing, the effect became a chaotic strobing of greens and blues and purples.

Beautiful. And a relief.

They'd ended up in a draw, which under the circumstances might be as close to winning as the Union could get. Running out of options, running high on desperation, the Union had cut itself off from Epsilon Indi. They'd broken the bridge over which their enemies could come. If the Congregate wanted to attack now, it would have to induce a series of wormholes to inch across dozens of light years. They could still do it, but the mathematics of supply lines would be prohibitive.

Cassandra would still have weeks of anxiety before she could know if Bel and Saint Matthew and their people had made it safely to the Puppet Free City. She had to be patient.

A radio channel, full of static and expletives was shunted into Cassandra's feed by Iekanjika. At first she didn't recognize it.

"Ass-licking shit navigating! The *malparido incompetente* missed. What the *crisse* am I doing here? How the--"

"Vincent?" Cassandra said.

The metadata put the speaker at a light-second away, and she didn't hear the next few seconds. The matter falling around the black hole projected static and interference up and down the EM spectrum.

"Princess?" the speaker said. "Did you do it? Why the fuck am I here?"

"How did you get here, Vincent?"

"Your boyfriend is a shit navigator. They shoulda sent you to do it. You never steered me wrong. I hope you weren't looking for love, because if that little fucker survives, I'm going to shoot his pecker off."

"What happened, Stills? Where are the *Homo quantus*? Where is Bel?"

"Their transport was ahead of me in the wormhole. I didn't see where it went because there were too many fucking Congregate warships in our getaway route because your limp-dicked lovey-dovey couldn't shoot straight."

Her mind ran models, trying to see what might have happened, how Stills could be here.

"I didn't see debris in the Freya Axis," he said. "So your crazy AI and the rest of you should have at least gotten out here. What the fuck happened here?"

"Are they here?" Cassandra said to Iekanjika. "The transport you made us."

The general sent to question to her staff. "If it's here, we'll find it," Iekanjika said.

Iekanjika didn't say *if it survived*. The battle volume had been too big and chaotic for anyone to have seen all of it. The transport might have slipped out of the Freya Axis without the Union noticing. The Congregate had been a lot closer to the mouth of the Axis and they might have fired on a single inflaton ship before noticing it had been unarmed.

"Where is Bel, Vincent?" Cassandra demanded.

"He was holding open the induced wormhole," Stills said, "and doing a fucking slow job of it too! I nearly got my ass shot off by Venusian orbital defenses!"

"Is he alive?"

"Fucked if I know. He was gonna follow me. If he made it through, he was about thirty seconds to a minute behind."

Right before the anti-matter missile had destroyed the Axis.

"When did you come out of the Freya Axis, Vincent?"

"About a minute before everything exploded, princess."

CHAPTER FIFTY-EIGHT

Iekanjika had wiped off the shock gel and changed into a plain uniform coveralls, bland and utilitarian but for the two general's stars on shoulder and cuff. The *Mutapa* paced the remnants of the Congregate task force, neither gaining nor slowing, lasers targeting but not firing. The Union squadron had formed into a shallow bowl shape, with the *Mutapa* at the base and the ten surviving inflaton warships powering further ahead in a ring at a radius of about a light second. This prevented the Congregate units from dispersing. An unarmed Bank cruiser trailed the *Mutapa* at a safe distance. Iekanjika imagined the data the Bank officers would be capturing, the tactics, the strategy, the repulsion of the Congregate forces. She'd received six messages so far, bordering on frantic interest in alliances and a palpable need for the Banks to be allowed to speak to the *Homo quantus* again.

X-rays and gamma rays registered in the rearward sensors as battle debris tumbled into the new black hole, heating to plasma in its death-fall. Mejía seemed to watch those sensor readings numbly, as if stunned. Iekanjika had to remind herself that the *Homo quantus* weren't human and that she couldn't trust her impressions of their reactions.

After an hour, Stills' fighter had caught up and docked with them. He'd transmitted the right passcodes with stuttering, damaged comms signals. The fighter's inflaton drive faltered between fifteen and forty percent. It would be a few minutes before the deck crew could safe his craft and him, if he'd been injured. She decided to finally take one of the Bank signals. The hologram of Admiral Gillbard appeared in full color before her, the bulbous silvery AI housing distending from the side of his head like a tumor.

"Very impressive, Major-General," he said. "This battle will be taught in staff colleges for centuries."

"I'm not interested in history, admiral."

"We're interested in helping the Union consolidate its gains," he said. "If I'm not wrong, you threw prototypes and proofs of principle into this battle, surprising your enemy, but they'll eventually be back. It's time to scale up your inventions and tactics. You need investment for that, partners, more than just your alliance with the *Homo quantus* and the *Homo eridanus*."

Iekanjika resisted the urge to gauge Mejía's reaction. She showed only herself to the admiral and she didn't want the Banks to see Mejía's anxiousness. She didn't know if the woman might make some bad choices right now under the pressure of the Bank's avarice for the *Homo quantus* secret to anti-matter, a hunger palpably greater even than the Banks' greed for the inflaton drive.

"We've seen Union performance in battle and the Banks have sent gifts we'd like to offer you. No strings attached."

Iekanjika highly doubted the statement about strings attached and she wasn't equipped to negotiate with Banks. No one in the Union was. They operated at another level and Rudo would likely need to hire a negotiator to help them keep the Banks from finishing by owning the Union. But she didn't have time to respond to Gillbard; the Congregate finally signalled. Iekanjika hung up on him.

A hologram of Rear-Admiral Gauthier appeared. Gauthier was a handsome man perhaps ten years older than her, with fine loops of acid scarring in abstract designs along one jawline. The Congregate combat uniform was sleek black, winking with sensors and augmented with tools. His rank insignia, inspired by fleur-de-lis designs, glowed prominently.

The Congregate task force had been big enough to warrant a full admiral and a couple of vice-admirals and Iekanjika savored a prideful satisfaction that they hadn't survived. The Congregate had not been able to match the Union propulsion technology and had sent an overwhelming force instead, six to nine times their size. In the heat of battle, her staff had been unable to even fully count the entire force that had come to kill them. Now, the remaining Congregate force was barely bigger that what the Union had left. The Congregate might still have ground the Union fleet down, maybe, but their military objective was gone. They'd been sent to establish and hold a beachhead at the Freya Axis. Possessing it would have determined all subsequent military decisions. No one could have imagined that their strategic objective might have been annihilated, or that the Union would have been willing to do it. It had been a long time since the Congregate had faced a cornered animal and the intelligence they would bring to Venus was more valuable than a grinding campaign of mutual assured destruction.

"Major-General Iekanjika," he said.

"It's a pleasure to meet you under these circumstances, admiral," she said smoothly.

Another hologram appeared beside Gauthier, a woman, in formal civilian wear, a suit with cravat and a number of civilian medals.

"May I introduce you to Jeanne-Manse Croteau," Gauthier said. "She is the senior political commissar in the Bachwezi system."

Iekanjika said nothing. She would find it very... symbolic to say Bachwezi was free of political commissars.

"Major-General Iekanjika," Croteau said, "I'm authorized by the Praesidium to take a number of foreign policy decisions in the field. It is quite clear that tempers have flared, to the detriment of all of humanity. Both sides have been painted into a corner and some time for reflection would be wise."

Part of Iekanjika wanted them to try to fight to the death, for pride. She might yet win, and there was an elegance to utterly wiping out the invading force. She could goad them now. But they might win too. Each side was worn down and she was the commander of the navy. It was her responsibility to protect Bachwezi not just today, but tomorrow.

"We seem to have come to a natural ceasefire," Croteau said.

"Are you asking for a truce?" Iekanjika said, challenging very slightly.

"I'm not proposing anything, other than to recognize a condition of ceasefire has already developed. A real truce or a resumption of hostilities won't be possible until both our governments have had time to assess the situation."

"Go assess your new situation far from here," Iekanjika said, "and don't bother coming back."

"Bachwezi was discovered by explorers from the Venusian Congregate and was leased in good faith to the Sub-Saharan Union, with signed accords. Those accords now seem insufficient as they had no clauses to take into account possible crimes against humanity."

Political games. That's what the commissars played.

"Several warships have already left Bachwezi on their way

back to Congregate bases. Within a few days, both yourself and General Kudzenai Rudo will be charged with crimes against humanity before the International Criminal Court. Every Axis is an irreplaceable resource of significance to all of humanity. They may be hundreds of thousands, perhaps millions of years old, inherited from an extinct species we know nothing about. You destroyed part of humanity's inheritance."

"I can't say that humanity has been impressing us very much," Iekanjika said.

The idea of being branded a war criminal bit at her, at her idea of officer. She'd fought with everything to beat back a much stronger foe, for the independence of her people. But the International Criminal Court was far enough away to be a mirage, like many of the places the Sixth Expeditionary Force had already been during forty years. She didn't fear mirages.

The Congregate might one day be back. Iekanjika and Rudo would prepare. Or perhaps the Congregate might cut its losses. The destruction of the Freya Axis not only meant that Bachwezi was now dozens of light years from anywhere in civilization, but that it had no resources of value, other than the inflaton drive which the Congregate would reverse engineer in less than a decade.

"The Union Government will consider a ceasefire to be in effect when half the Congregate support facilities in the Bachwezi Oort cloud have wormholed away," Iekanjika said. "That shouldn't take more than an hour. The other half will have six more hours to leave or hostilities will resume."

The political commissar's head cocked in thought, almost an insouciant gesture. But there would be no lightness when this commissar and this admiral arrived at Venus and had to explain the debacle. The Congregate losses today amounted to a catastrophe, a strategic realignment of civilization with the rise of a tough new actor on the stage. She wished she could be a fly on the wall when the Praesidium got the whole briefing.

"The Congregate Government will consider a ceasefire to be in effect when the Union forces come to a parking orbit ten AU from the Congregate support facilities in the Oort cloud," Croteau said.

Ten astronomical units, four million kilometers, was plenty of space for the Congregate to feel like they could wormhole away in peace. And Iekanjika could deploy the remains of her fleet to be within laser range of all strategic spots for incoming induced wormholes if the Congregate tried something funny. She cut communication with the commissar and gave order for a new fleet deployment. As her pursuing force cut their acceleration, the retreating Congregate force pulled away.

Iekanjika gave command of the force to Brigadier-General Tembe and came to her *Homo quantus* problem. Mejía's haunted eyes were like a human in mourning, and it became harder for Iekanjika to remember that something alien lived at her core, the sum of genes and neurological and developmental differences between them as wide a gulf as the political one between the Union and the Congregate. Iekanjika felt like she observed different sets of feelings, new mixes of emotions in the other that she herself could not assemble. The moods looked the same and in many ways they were the same, but they were built of different pieces. Like the Puppets. Iekanjika had more in common with Stills than she did with Mejía; all the pieces of him that were different were visible. She didn't know how to bridge the gap between her internal world and Mejía's. A faint unease accompanied that realization.

Iekanjika delayed. She called up the landing bay feeds. A loading cradle locked Stills' fighter into the fighter bays. The *Mutapa's* laser imaging showed burns, dents and perforations all over the little craft. A deck crew bustled on magnetic boots, patching leaks spraying mists of salt water.

"What's the pressure in there?" she said to the deck crew.

"Six hundred atmospheres, ma'am."

The lower edge of mongrel survivability.

"Get the pressure up fast," she said.

Cassandra stepped closer, hesitant magnetized step after magnetized step. A rough hologram of Stills flickered into shape, glassy-eyed, fish-faced.

"Are you injured, Stills?" Iekanjika said. "We can get you to the med bay."

"I been better," he said. "I need to get to someplace with a bit of room to swim."

"Crews will safe your chamber and mate you into the big tanks."

His electronically rendered laugh barked. "Mate," he said.

"What are you doing here, Stills?" Cassandra said. "Where are the *Homo quantus*? Where's Bel?"

Stills gave them a crisp, profanity-laced report, from arriving at Venus, to the escape, to the end of Marie Phocas, to the induction of the wormhole, to his flying into it, and then finding himself in the Freya Axis.

"Fucked if I know how I got here. I don't know where any of your people are. Get a better navigator next time."

Stills' patience exhausted and he shut off his comms while she was in mid-question.

"Get him to the big tank," Iekanjika told the deck crew. Mejía appeared distant. Iekanjika was getting to recognize the altered states of *Homo quantus* perception. This wasn't the fugue. But Mejía wasn't herself anymore either. "What do you think happened?"

"Connecting one induced wormhole onto another is hard,"

Mejía replied distantly. "In the heat of battle, he wouldn't have made one to the Puppet Axis and then created another to send Stills here. He only induced one wormhole. To the Freya Axis."

"You said you couldn't do that," Iekanjika said with a kind of careful accusation. "You said you could only do that to a wormhole you'd studied and marked."

"When we passed through the Freya Axis we were casually studying it," Mejía said. "We didn't leave markers. But we're getting a better understanding of the structure of the axes. It would have been hard to latch an induced wormhole onto the Freya Axis. I don't think I would have been able to do it."

"Why did he take the risk?" Iekanjika said.

"He's not here to ask." Mejía didn't wipe at the tears forming at the edges of her eyes. "I have to find them."

The data from Stills' fighter finished uploading to a standalone server on the bridge. Sub-AIs did a first triage of the terabytes of sensor, internal telemetry, communications and life support recordings. Mejía observed the process for some moments before saying "Give me control."

Iekanjika authorized the access. The fast playback of the sub-AI search they'd been observing vanished. Raw data replaced it, passing too fast for Iekanjika to read, but only for a few seconds. The holographic display turned into to strange geometries with eye-twisting perspectives. She signalled to a bridge officer to verify that they were recording all of that Mejía was doing. The recordings Iekanjika had made of Mejía's and Arjona's work on the *Jonglei* and the *Limpopo* had been analyzed by her engineers to start to determine upper and lower processing limits of the *Homo quantus*. Then the movement stopped and a single tiny image appeared.

Mejía expanded it in false blues and greens and grays. It was a small ship, but big enough to carry and power wormhole induction coils. Iekanjika recognized the ship they'd built for Arjona. A chaos of live orbital defenses surrounded it, before the field narrowed from the perspective of Stills' craft entering the induced wormhole. Then, Arjona's ship became smaller and smaller, a single object at the end of an indistinct tube. But Arjona's ship didn't detonate. No Venusian ordnance caught it. It too entered the wormhole, but with none of Stills' momentum because it had started from rest and could not fire engines within a fragile induced wormhole.

"He entered the wormhole," Iekanjika said.

The image of Arjona's ship shrank, becoming fuzzier, hard to resolve by the stern telescopes of Stills' ship. Mejía's eyes focused on data at the edges of the image, multidimensional graphics humans would be hard-pressed to decipher even with computational help.

"Bel's ship entered the wormhole at about forty meters per second," Mejía said from wherever her savant state existed. "Stills' fighter entered at a hundred meters per second. Bel should have reached the Freya Axis in about four minutes."

Stills would have reached it in about ninety seconds. The image of Arjona's ship melted into the unfocused gray background of the recording of the temporary wormhole. Then the blur of information Mejía was absorbing stopped again and a fuzzy image formed and expanded, pixelating. The glimpse of the transport was only there for a moment. Its disappearance wasn't an artifact of the recording.

"The transport exited into the Freya Axis," Mejía said.

Mejía sped the playback, matching it with electronic sensor data in false color that Iekanjika found confusing. Then Stills was in the Freya Axis in his exhausted single fighter craft, surrounded by Congregate warships. Stills was a cold killer, but she imagined that even he'd been terrified. Tucked in close to a Congregate destroyer, he'd been close enough to have reached out to touch it. The tactical intel in this recording was invaluable. But Mejia's display didn't focus on that. She swept through the forward sensors, mostly in the infrared.

"No debris," Mejía said.

Debris from the rescue transport would have been hot. Bodies would have been bright in the infrared compared to the degree or two of the Axis. They watched Stills' fighter exit the Axis and become a target of every Congregate ship nearby. His flying was superb. Inhuman. His fighter had recorded every fragment of hot shrapnel and ordnance shot at him. but no debris field like they would have expected from a transport being blown to pieces.

"They exited the Axis," Mejía said.

"We'll keep searching."

Remarkably, Stills' fighter had recorded the anti-matter missile approaching and then hitting the axis. It hit at three minutes from the time Arjona entered the temporary wormhole, one minute from the time his speed would have carried him into the Freya Axis.

"He is a magician," Iekanjika said hesitatingly. "If anyone could survive, he would."

Mejía regarded her strangely, as if she'd handed the *Homo quantus* a poisonous snake instead of hope. Then Mejía wiped her eyes self-consciously.

CHAPTER FIFTY-NINE

IN IEKANJIKA'S WORDS, the situation in Bachwezi was too hot for Cassandra to leave. Cassandra had some access to the military channels. She seemed to be given free access to the gloomy bridge of the *Mutapa,* as long as a deceptively solicitous lieutenant followed her. He seemed too young to have an important job. But maybe not so young; Bel had gone off at sixteen into the wide world and had freed or stolen Saint Matthew from the Banks. Younger than this pimply-faced lieutenant, Bel had done something considered impossible. She'd watched him do impossible things. Steal the time gates. Go back in time. Her mind could play with impossibilities, but the only probable outcome was that the fragile geometry of the induced wormhole had vanished from existence like a popping soap bubble, turning everything inside to neutrinos and white noise.

She kept trying to summon some grief for the hundred and fifty *Homo quantus* they'd almost saved, and for Saint Matthew, but it was hard. Numbness was a physical thing, a cloud inside her, uncharitable, crowding out caring. She'd never been good with feelings. They weren't subject to detached analysis, nor replicable or refutable. They slipped, shifted, took new forms.

She suspected that her pain masqueraded as numbness and she didn't know how to make this inner suffering stop.

She kept extrapolating and hypothesizing about his end, from her limited information. Even if by some chance he had gotten into the Freya Axis, Cassandra and Iekanjika had destroyed it and everything within and around.

The Banks wanted to talk with her. One message after another, each more urgent than the last, accumulated. The Lunar Bank. The Bank of Ceres. The First and Second Banks. She read the first few. They offered investments, technological partnerships, IP licensing proposals, alliances, and legal threats. She began to see their grasping in the way Belisarius might have seen it. She mapped motives back, all the way back to the project to create the *Homo quantus,* a sub-species of humanity to be deployed for profit and military positioning. But instead, they'd become a people whose mere existence threatened the patron nations, and justified enslaving them.

She didn't answer any of them.

On the third day, Iekanjika brought her to a ship. Cassandra had observed enough in the last six months to appreciate a top-of-the-line fighter. The hollow tube of its inflaton drive was forty-one meters from bow to stern, with weapon ports and defensive blisters and a smoothly curving cockpit along the top.

"It's a gift," Iekanjika said, floating beside her, "from the people of the Sub-Saharan Union to the Mayor of the *Homo quantus*. It's well armed and programmable. It's faster than *The Calculated Risk* and has some armor. It's not bugged. We do not see eye to eye on everything, but I hope that in the future, if you need friends, you'll think of us."

Iekanjika's expression, laconic at the best of times, seemed sincere. And although she probably wanted what the Banks wanted, her offer didn't feel the same.

"You cut yourself off from the Congregate," Cassandra said. "It will be safer if we get far away from everyone too. People want us for things we don't want for ourselves."

"That may be the definition of the Patron-Client Accord we broke ourselves out of. If we survive the next year, consider us a friend if you wish, one who feels gratitude."

Cassandra probably should have responded. The conversational algebra expected her to introduce a new term, but for five point eight second, she memorized the design features of the ship's lines, interpolating architecture, stresses and force loads.

"Stills knows how to bring you a message?" Iekanjika said.

"For a while. But as soon as we're ready, we're moving on and we'll be erasing our tracks, hiding the axes we used."

"I'm sure you'll find Arjona. And the people he rescued. And your AI."

The officer had a wan smile, the kind of expression that hadn't yet exhausted hope, the kind that crashed against the observations, axioms and conclusions in Cassandra's mind. She knew how the universe worked. And she felt like she couldn't carry everything anymore.

Iekanjika offered her hand. Floating in zero-g, they clasped wrists for a moment and it was a kind of relief. She wasn't the woman who just last year had been deep diving into the fugue in the Garret. She was now the mayor of the *Homo quantus*, in some ways battle-tested, canny to the deceptiveness of the wide world, wrestling with how to protect her people. She was like Iekanjika.

"Goodbye, Ayen."

"Live well, Cassandra."

Cassandra caught herself on the fighter near its hatch. She opened it and made her way to the cockpit and the acceleration chamber. She stripped off layers of clothing and flooded the chamber with shock gel while she jacked herself into the ship's systems. Engine health, ship integrity, weight and balance, ammunition and all sorts of other readings projected themselves onto her retinas. She swept one after another aside and finished checking out the ship's status. After ten minutes, Iekanjika still waited by the doorway to the bay. The onboard systems asked for and received permission to depart and the magnetic clamps released. A short message from Iekanjika arrived as Cassandra cleared the bay: *Give the ship a good name.*

It was a curious message, a very human one. She'd named the last one with Bel, a decision they'd come to while working out the mathematics of the cosmos and huddling together in a sleep sack. *The Calculated Risk* could have been the theme of their lives since then, and they'd saved their people and discovered more than they'd ever thought possible. And they'd lost things. Calculated losses.

Now she didn't even know where the accounting had ended up. She hadn't finished measuring. She didn't know where Saint Matthew and the *Homo quantus* were, or if they'd even survived. And Bel was... dead. The important things in her life were unmeasured quantities, questions. She'd lived with questions all her life, but they hadn't been questions that hurt inside. And in some way, she couldn't name the ship meaningfully until she had her answers.

So she decided to call it *The Variable*.

The Variable pulled away from the *Mutapa* and the heavy compression of acceleration pressed on her chest, on sternum and muscles already hard at work inhaling and exhaling oxygenated shock gel. She was heading away from Bachwezi and Kitara, away from the Union's new black hole, away from all military positions in the system. The Congregate surely had espionage and observation equipment scattered throughout the system, so they'd given her an erratic flight plan, with many changes in vector on silent running, to bring her to one of the Axes Mundi the Union had not even named yet. Several other fighters launched at the same time and took similarly strange trajectories. Decoys. Almost a day later, she arrived at a lonely part of the solar system, dark but for some weak radiation, and found a single axis floating alone.

She entered it and the Bachwezi system vanished behind her. She emerged shortly into a red dwarf system whose Axes Mundi they'd not mapped for the Union. Most of the nearby axes, those within ten to twenty nodes, she'd mapped and memorized. At several AU, the quiescent star glowed dull orange, barely noticeable above the starscape. There were six more axis bridges she had to find and cross before she would reach her people, a prospect of several days. If the Freya Axis still existed, she could have made the trip in three crossings but some things, once broken, were forever gone.

Space felt strange, naked and more lonely than she'd ever felt. No Stills, no Bel, no Saint Matthew. No other *Homo quantus*. Not even Iekanjika. Bereft of help, advice and companionship. She had to be entirely independent.

Cassandra oriented herself to the solar system's geometry and began her run towards the next axis she needed to cross. She plotted a circuitous path, in case anyone in civilization was also here, but nothing registered on her telescopes, antennae, receivers or anything else. *The Variable* trudged across the dark, cold wasteland of the solar system at the highest acceleration she could endure, but time still dragged.

CHAPTER SIXTY

THIS WAS NOT the first time a floating habitat had been pierced, not the first time poisonous carbon dioxide and corrosive sulfuric acid had rasped the insides of Venusian homes. Venus had been testing them for centuries, culling the herd: the weak, the old, the daring, the unlucky. Bareilles stepped over metal debris pock-marked with acid corrosion and plastic shards melted into clumps. Forensic teams sampled and measured and swabbed. Repair crews had built a temporary skin over the Ministry of the Interior and pumped new breathable atmosphere into damaged sections. Emergency balloons of oxygen corrected buoyancy imbalances until real repairs finished. Luc followed her, had asked to come. *Les petits saints* did not typically tour battlefields, but it wasn't her place to shield him from anything he felt he needed to see.

The corpse of the Scarecrow lay in torn pieces, wires and carbon-fiber muscle and weaponry splayed into a web of a more final, second death. The same blast that killed the Scarecrow had blown a hole in the lower decks of the port bow, coming close to taking down the entire habitat, even with every rescue resource on the dayside of the planet.

The scale of violation of the Congregate was difficult to

grasp. To attack the Congregate in their home, to violate the sanctity of their homeworld was obscene. But the more terrible news had come quickly; the level of depravity needed to destroy the Freya Axis sickened her. The Axis Mundi wormholes had survived millions of years, had persisted as monuments after their unknown builders had gone extinct. In a moral world, they ought to outlive humanity too, continue as the heritage of the galaxy. What kind of mind destroyed an enduring artifact belonging to eternity?

Compared to the scales of this crime, human life could feel insignificant yet Bareilles could not turn away from the loss of life. Squadrons of incinerated Congregate warships. An entire massed fleet around both sides of the Freya Axis wiped out. Counting hadn't stopped, but death toll estimates had passed thirty-two thousand officers and crew and commissars. And no one had found Philippe's body in the Ministry of Intelligence building. Many were missing or incinerated or dropped into the stinging clouds. It was harder to think about him than she'd expected.

They didn't yet have an idea how the Union, or more rightly the *Homo quantus* had done it all. Union terrorists at Bachwezi had used more anti-matter in a single battle than had ever been used in any war, more anti-matter than the Banks had ever hinted at having. They'd had so much anti-matter that they'd used it in suicide bombers. The *Homo quantus* had to have found a new way to synthesize anti-matter, orders of magnitude faster than the big accelerators the Congregate and the Banks used. That changed every political and military calculation.

Bareilles knelt on stiff legs and a braced ankle. Wires protruded from the Scarecrow's corpse, like shredded metallic flesh. The steel and carbon weave of the painted face was peeled back, and the electronics beneath flayed, exposing the bulbous, green, vitrified brain, now cracked and dark. The loyal Scarecrow had only wanted the best for them. She'd died once, and had devoted her entire second life to protecting the Congregate.

"That's what they look like inside," Luc said, some feeling making his pronunciation more fraught.

"Yes."

"It's scary looking," he said.

Bareilles touched the warm glass of the naked Scarecrow brain, righted the single remaining telescoping eye that dangled off the side of the wrecked face.

"I know," she said. "The Scarecrow was ugly, but she loved us. You. Me. All of us."

This Scarecrow had taken Bareilles, an intelligence operative, and had taught her that every field upon which she'd dueled before was contained, limited in scope, narrow, and that the Venusian Congregate was not eternal. Their nation was instead infinitely fragile, living in the shadow of an existential threat on timescales beyond human grasping. Like a patient tutor, the Scarecrow had persuaded Bareilles to her point of view, to the rightness and need for F-Division. But intellectual and professional acceptance of something couldn't compare to the visceral feeling of certainty that came from seeing her fears realized. This new lived conviction rested heavy in her heart now. The Scarecrow had pointed the way at a future too distant to see, too ambitious to take in at once, but Bareilles had stumbled into it heedlessly. In this new world she was the Neanderthal, clever, fire-using, speaking, socializing, but hopelessly outmatched by the tools and cognitive abilities of the new *Homo sapiens*.

"Jeronimo and Santiago did this?" Luc said, stumbling over the unfamiliar Anglo-Spanish names.

"Their people did," Bareilles said.

"Because we had Jeronimo and Santiago?"

"This time yes, but they did this in other places too, all at the same time. The problem is that these new *Homo quantus* might be able to do this anytime they want and I don't know how to stop them. The Scarecrow thought that we might need to make some of our own *Homo quantus,* or become more like them."

Luc knelt beside her, touched the glassy green fragments of brain shattered in the metal skull case, as if looking for confirmation.

"What do you think?" Luc said.

The Scarecrow's lessons echoed loud in her thinking, assuming a new depth of meaning. All hominin species before *Homo sapiens* were extinct. The minds, the memories, the language, the abstracting talents of the *Homo sapiens* had given them superior tools. And now, something biologically novel had been introduced into the human gene pool and had already speciated into something terrible and alien. The *Homo quantus* could think thoughts that *Homo sapiens* could not. And they'd found ways to invade the interiors of the Axis Mundi, to make anti-matter in militarily decisive quantities and perhaps had found some way to harness time travel.

The culture and people of the Venusian Congregate faced an extinction-level threat in the *Homo quantus.* And so did the Banks and all their investors. Every analysis suggested that the Banks had lost control of their *Homo quantus.* But the Banks had all the information to recreate new populations of *Homo quantus* in two short decades, perhaps some that were more tractable. And the original *Homo quantus* were out there somewhere, arming themselves with technology that stripped the Congregate of its ability to defend its own people. This is what a danger of extinction looked like.

"I think the world has changed around us," she said. "And we have to change too."

CHAPTER SIXTY-ONE

CASSANDRA EMERGED FROM the axis into the plane of radiation sprayed out by pulsar J2307-2229. In the encrypted radio band the *Homo quantus* used, alarms rang. She transmitted authentication codes, one after the other, but the alarms didn't calm as much as they should have. That wasn't so surprising. No one had any reason to enter this system through this axis. Letícia's voice, distant, crackled above the pulsar's howling static in the radio band.

"Cassandra?"

"Letty, did they make it home?"

Cassandra held her breath as she waited across the light seconds separating them.

"Yes!" Letícia said. "More than a hundred survived. They're all getting medical attention."

A hundred. They'd gone to rescue about a hundred and fifty.

"Is Bel here?" she said. *The Variable* slowly pulled above the plane of the lighthouse beams that flashed every half second.

"Miss Mejía," a voice said, clarifying into Saint Matthew's calm tones. "We were in the wrong spot. We came out among the Congregate fleet on the Epsilon Indi side of the Freya Axis. We didn't see Mister Arjona or Mister Stills emerge, and then...

the Axis exploded. I'm... I'm so sorry."

Her thoughts... faltered. The various lines of reasoning she should have been able to keep separate jammed together, making an internal static, a wall of white noise like the chaotic, information-free beams of the pulsar. It was like thought itself was drowning. Amid the static in her mind, her perfect recall replayed the AI's words.

I'm so sorry.

I'm so sorry.

I'm so sorry.

Thinking stuttered. Memories filled the cognitive gap. Her fear of leaving the Garret with Bel. Her excitement of new data they'd gotten together. Her fear of dying in the Union break-out from the Puppet Axis. Her new confidence in working with Stills, and with Iekanjika. Strangers. Aliens. Bel had taken her hand and invited her into the wide world, and the wide world had tried to consume them all. They'd saved almost all the *Homo quantus*. Now they could really run far, far away, but Bel wouldn't be with them. With her. She was terrifyingly alone.

ACKNOWLEDGEMENTS

I am deeply grateful to my agent Kim-Mei Kirtland and to my editor Michael Rowley for their excellent advice on various drafts of *The Quantum War*.

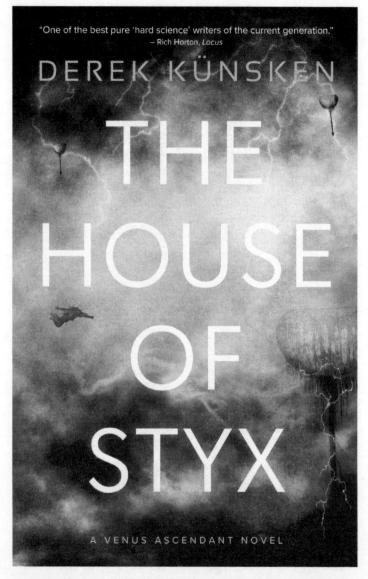

"One of the best pure 'hard science' writers of the current generation."
– Rich Horton, *Locus*

DEREK KÜNSKEN

THE
HOUSE
OF
STYX

A VENUS ASCENDANT NOVEL

 SOLARISBOOKS.COM

POLLEN FROM A
FUTURE HARVEST
DEREK KÜNSKEN
"KÜNSKEN'S VIVID WORLDBUILDING IS A
KNOCKOUT" – PUBLISHERS WEEKLY
SATELLITES

FIND US ONLINE!

www.rebellionpublishing.com

/rebellionpub   /rebellionpublishing   /rebellionpublishing

SIGN UP TO OUR NEWSLETTER!

rebellionpublishing.com/newsletter

YOUR REVIEWS MATTER!

Enjoy this book? Got something to say?

Leave a review on Amazon, GoodReads or with your
favourite bookseller and let the world know!